Praise for Tara Johnson

"Bringing facets of Civil War history to life, *Where Dandelions Bloom* is an engaging journey of hidden identity and of discovering what's most important in life—and in love. A story certain to delight fans of historical romance!"

TAMERA ALEXANDER, *USA TODAY* BESTSELLING AUTHOR OF *CHRISTMAS AT CARNTON* AND *A NOTE YET UNSUNG*

"In her sparkling debut . . . Johnson crafts an inspirational tale of love, fortitude, and what it means to do the right thing when the very concept of 'right' is challenged."

PUBLISHERS WEEKLY, STARRED REVIEW

"A timeless and timely theme of helping persecuted people blooms into an unusual Civil War romance that explores Keziah's search for a purpose, the intersection of faith and practice, and how single acts have far-reaching effects."

FOREWORD REVIEWS

"Debut novelist Johnson does not shy away from the horrors of slavery and the important role of the Underground Railroad, but the tone of this historical romance is much lighter than expected. . . . Fans of the genre will be pleased."

LIBRARY JOURNAL

"Keziah and Micah brave danger and death to help slaves journey to freedom, reminding readers that choosing right often involves great sacrifice."

CBA *CHRISTIAN MARKET*

"A truly lovely debut novel. [Told] through the eyes of an unlikely heroine awakening to the injustices of slavery, *Engraved on the Heart* brings Savannah, Georgia, during the Civil War to life. Tara Johnson writes with honesty and compassion, undergirded with solid research. The characters are lovingly drawn, and Keziah's growth from sheltered weakness to faithful courage is simply radiant. A book to savor and an author to watch!"

SARAH SUNDIN, AWARD-WINNING AUTHOR OF *THE SEA BEFORE US* AND THE WAVES OF FREEDOM SERIES

"Set amid the beauty of Savannah, Georgia, at the onset of the Civil War, *Engraved on the Heart* is a story that is as spiritually profound as it is romantic, its heroine as memorable and unique as her lovely name. Johnson weaves a tale of secrets, selflessness, and service where love and truth triumph. A remarkable, memorable debut!"

LAURA FRANTZ, AUTHOR OF *THE LACEMAKER*

"Through the eyes of pop-off-the-page characters, readers are whisked into turbulent Confederate Savannah, from charming balls to the intrigue and danger of the Underground Railroad. Woven throughout this vibrant tale are strong spiritual threads sure to inspire. Lovers of Civil War fiction will rejoice to add *Engraved on the Heart* to their collections. I'll be looking for more from Tara Johnson!"

JOCELYN GREEN, AWARD-WINNING AUTHOR OF THE HEROINES BEHIND THE LINES CIVIL WAR SERIES

"Blending realistic, relatable characters and the heartrending issue of slavery against a beautifully painted backdrop, Tara Johnson presents a debut novel that will leave you satisfied and yet still wanting more. Both major issues—living with an uncontrollable health issue and being trapped in servitude—could become oppressive or maudlin, but Johnson expertly handles both and weaves them so intricately into the story's fabric that a beautiful tapestry of overcoming hardship and experiencing freedom emerges. I highly recommend this engaging and intriguing historical novel."

KIM VOGEL SAWYER, BESTSELLING AUTHOR OF *BRINGING MAGGIE HOME*

"Tara Johnson delivers a stirring tale of danger and hope in *Engraved on the Heart*. I was invested in Micah and Kizzie's love story from the very first chapter—and fell more than a little in love with Micah myself."

ROBIN LEE HATCHER, RITA AND CHRISTY AWARD–WINNING AUTHOR OF *YOU'LL THINK OF ME* AND *YOU'RE GONNA LOVE ME*

Where Dandelions Bloom

WHERE
Dandelions
BLOOM

TARA JOHNSON

Tyndale House Publishers, Inc.
Carol Stream, Illinois

Visit Tyndale online at www.tyndale.com.

Visit Tara Johnson's website at www.tarajohnsonstories.com.

TYNDALE and Tyndale's quill logo are registered trademarks of Tyndale House Publishers, Inc.

Where Dandelions Bloom

Designed by Eva M. Winters

Edited by Danika King

Published in association with the literary agency of Books & Such Literary Management, 52 Mission Circle, Suite 122, PMB 170, Santa Rosa, CA 95409.

Unless otherwise indicated, all Scripture quotations are taken from the *Holy Bible*, King James Version.

Scripture quotations marked NLT are taken from the *Holy Bible*, New Living Translation, copyright © 1996, 2004, 2015 by Tyndale House Foundation. Used by permission of Tyndale House Publishers, Inc., Carol Stream, Illinois 60188. All rights reserved.

For information about special discounts for bulk purchases, please contact Tyndale House Publishers at csresponse@tyndale.com or call 1-800-323-9400.

Library of Congress Cataloging-in-Publication Data
Names: Johnson, Tara, date- author.
Title: Where dandelions bloom / Tara Johnson.
Description: Carol Stream, Illinois : Tyndale House Publishers, Inc., [2019]
Identifiers: LCCN 2018038406 | ISBN 9781496428356 (sc)
Subjects: | GSAFD: Christian fiction. | Love stories.
Classification: LCC PS3610.O383395 W48 2019 | DDC 813/.6—dc23 LC record available
   at https://lccn.loc.gov/2018038406

Printed in the United States of America

25   24   23   22   21   20   19
7   6   5   4   3   2   1

For those who have been hurt, broken, and discarded . . .
There is a God who sees you. He causes beauty to bloom in the
hardest places. You are treasured and held in his heart.

"He will give a crown of beauty for ashes . . ."

ISAIAH 61:3, NLT

Prologue

Gabriel Avery hit the unforgiving pavement with a grunt. Above him, the thin, dirty faces of his foes looked down on him with sneers.

"Give it up, Avery."

A kick to his middle caused him to fold his body inward as he clutched his burning stomach. "I've not a penny to give you."

A few more blows to his back and legs before the oldest of the boys heaved an impatient sigh. "Come on. He ain't got nothin'."

Their shuffling scrapes faded from the bottle-littered alley. Gabe sat up with a groan but couldn't suppress a smile of victory. Hiding the nickel inside his shoe had worked. They'd always discovered the coinage in his pockets, but he'd finally found a spot safe from their eager hands.

Rising, he swiped at the dirt clinging to his trousers. Mither would scold him hard if he were to put another tear in them.

Clothing came dear, and Da was working long enough hours as it was. They could ill afford to buy new clothes. It was difficult enough for Scottish immigrants in New York without adding clumsiness and neighborhood bullies to the list of living expenses.

Gabe sighed. The slums gobbled up more and more of the city. With their encroaching darkness came more trouble-makers. More boys wanting to scrap, and fewer places he could go to be left in peace.

The odor of rotting cabbage, urine, and musty newspapers thickened the air. A door in the alley creaked open just before the contents of a chamber pot were thrown onto the uneven stones with a splatter. Gabe winced and took a step backward.

Mr. Giuseppe scowled. "I don't want any street rats hanging around."

"I'll not trouble you. I'm passing by."

The barrel-chested Italian narrowed his dark eyes to slits. "See you do, or my aim will be better next time."

Mr. Giuseppe meant it too. The hot-tempered man had done more than bluff in the past. Gabe wasted no time scampering from the alley. Cramming his hands into his pockets, he burst onto the crowded sidewalk, thankful for the sunshine despite the sweat trickling down his back. He shuffled through the teeming mass of people scurrying to their various destinations—work, appointments, restaurants—when a shop window captured his attention.

A new business inhabited the old abandoned bakery. The formerly empty glass front that had boasted nothing more than spiderwebs was now filled with pictures of every size. Black-and-white faces stared back at him. Mothers and children, proud military leaders, a boy with his dog, an elderly couple leaning against the porch of their farmhouse . . . every framed portrait was more captivating than the last. Curling his fingers against the glass, Gabe pressed in for a better view as the crowds around him melted away.

"Do you like what you see, lad?"

Gabe startled and looked up to find a man with a handlebar mustache smiling at him. His blue eyes danced.

"I've never seen such wonderful pictures before. Each one is like a story."

"Well said." The lean fellow knelt until they were eye level and studied the images.

"How are they created?"

"It's called daguerreotype. You've heard of cameras before?"

"Yes, sir."

The man nodded. "Good. Well, a daguerreotypist takes a sheet of silver-plated copper, exposes it to the light of a camera lens, and uses mercury vapor on it. After that, other chemicals are applied before it's sealed behind glass. Whatever image was captured by the camera lens remains forever."

"It's . . . wonderful." Gabe drank in the sight of the little boy with his arm slung around his dog as they stood watch on a rough-hewn log porch. Surely that boy didn't have to fight off hordes of pickpockets and greedy tormentors each day. He must not deal with the stench of a cramped city constantly swelling ever larger, or watch his mother and father scrimp and save for the smallest pittance of comfort. Did his ceiling leak when it rained? Was his da too exhausted each evening to play with him?

This daguerreotype must be a sort of magic in its own way. Still moments of perfection in happy lives. Something yawned wide in Gabe's chest. "I want to learn."

The man rose and placed a hand on his shoulder. "My name is Franklin Adams, and this is my shop. Come inside. I'll show you how it's done."

Chapter 1

TEN YEARS LATER
APRIL 12, 1861
HOWELL, MICHIGAN

"Cassandra Kendrick! What have you done?"

Cassie cringed at the slurred, booming voice hovering just beyond the barn door. She crouched, pressing her back against the prickly wood wall, and breathed through her mouth lest the sweet motes of hay floating around her cause a sneeze. She could not let Father know her whereabouts. Not until his temper cooled or his alcohol-sodden brain plunged him once again into a sleeping stupor. For him to find her in his current condition would not bode well.

In her eighteen years, history had taught her that much in abundance.

"Come out, come out, wherever you are."

The ominous timbre slithered down her spine. She squeezed her eyes shut.

Thud, thud, thud.

Her pulse pounded dully in her ears, the rhythm far too rapid. Could he hear?

His sluggish footsteps faded, as did his familiar curses. She allowed her back to relax a fraction and dropped her head against the barn wall, wincing when strands of her hair stuck and pulled against the splinters of wood.

Breathe in; breathe out.

She waited for several long moments. He had deceived her before. She had crept from her hiding spot only to have his meaty fingers clamp around her throat.

The barn door squeaked open on rusty hinges. Her breath snagged, but it was Mother's careworn face that appeared. Sunlight streamed around her silhouette.

"He's gone."

Uttering a sigh of relief, Cassie pushed away from the wall and brushed poking shafts of straw from her skirt. "He found out, then?"

Mother nodded. "Came from town and went straight to the crock."

Cassie grimaced, imagining his reaction when his calloused fingers scraped the inside of the empty container. "He didn't accuse you, did he?"

Mother waved her hand in dismissal, though the tight lines around her eyes remained. "It doesn't matter. He laid not a hand on me. In truth, it's unlikely he'll remember come tomorrow."

Cassie stepped over tackle and crates, squinting against the bright sunlight. She straightened. "I'm not sorry. You know I'm not."

"I know." With a sad smile, Mother turned to leave, murmuring instructions over her shoulder. "Time to hang the wash."

That was all? No reprimand? Cassie said not a word. Avoiding Father was the part she had fretted over most, but fearing her actions had disappointed Mother . . .

Perhaps Mother wasn't sorry either. The thought gave her pause.

Cassie trudged through the grass-splotched yard as chickens squawked and flapped around her skirts. The worn garment tangled around her ankles.

At least she'd bought them time. Yes, she'd taken the only money to be had from the crock, but the tax man's demands were sated. If Mother had agreed with her actions, why did she not say so? Why could she never stand up to Father?

Before they had rounded the corner of the cabin, a wagon careened down the dirt road in front of the house, churning up splatters of mud and jostling with enough clatter to wake the dead. Cassie frowned. The driver was recognizable enough. Peter, her sister Eloise's husband, jumped from the bouncing wagon a hairsbreadth after he'd set the brake. His blond hair was windblown as if tossed by a dervish. His eyes were bright, sparkling with an excitement she'd rarely, if ever, witnessed from the sulky man.

Mother's face filled with sudden angst. "What's wrong? Is it Eloise?"

"Of course not." His Irish brogue lilted high as his chest puffed out with a billow. He hooked his thumbs around his suspenders. "You've not heard the news, then?"

Cassie stepped next to Mother's side. A cold stone sank in her stomach. "What news?"

His lips curved into a smile, revealing crooked yellow teeth. "Why, war, sister. War has been declared."

Chapter 2

April 15, 1861
New York City

Gabe Avery snaked his way through the swarm of people clogging Broadway, suppressing the urge to vent his frustration at the slow progress. After growing up in the city, he was rarely bothered by the crowds anymore, but this was different. Urgency bade him hurry. He must know if the rumors were true.

As he tipped his hat to an older matron coming toward him, he almost collided with a wayward boy of no more than six. The dirty moppet scurried past him without a pause, reminding him of a rat slinking between broken crates in an alley. He shook his head. The lad was likely to cause an accident.

The odor of horse dung mingled with the sharp sting of axle grease as people and carriages clattered past. Only a little farther . . .

There. The Brady Gallery was within view. A pulse of euphoria traveled his veins.

Please, God, let him say yes. . . .

He slowed as he approached the prestigious gallery and stopped to catch his breath. He'd been here dozens of times before, but never had he been so anxious. So unnerved. Tugging his vest into submission, he inhaled a thick pull of air, grasped the doorknob, and tugged.

He stepped into the gallery, his senses heightening despite the calming effects of green strategically gracing the papered room. Faces met him at every turn, each photographed form boxed within a gilt frame. Some somber, some cheery. Some lithe of form and some frumpy.

All of them were fascinating.

The faintest traces of iodine wafted toward him. Someone must be readying glass plates for exposure in the back.

His boots sank into the plush carpeting as he stepped into the main salon. A solitary couple perused the displays, murmuring softly to each other as they commented over the Imperials. The painting-size photographs were so lifelike, he felt if he reached out and touched the glass, the images would jump in response. Gabe stood off to the side and fisted his hands behind his back, willing his frayed nerves to cease their buzzing.

A man stepped through the dark-green velvet curtains concealing the workrooms from the gallery. Gabe's breath strangled as every coherent thought scattered from his head.

The man was of medium height but exuded quiet confidence with his slow, smooth gait. His dark hair was peppered with gray, though most of the hair of his goatee was still black, and he wore a cream-colored duster. The spectacles perched on his aquiline nose framed dark eyes that were sharp, missing nothing.

It was him. Mathew Brady.

Gabe wiped sweaty palms against his trousers and cleared his throat. "Mr. Brady, I presume?"

The man smiled faintly, causing slight lines to crinkle around his eyes. "One and the same."

Gabe offered his hand, and Brady shook it with a firm clasp. "Mr. Brady, sir, I have long been an admirer of your work. Your advances in daguerreotype and imprint images have inspired me."

Brady's dark brows rose, his scholarly features lightening. "You have studied the science of photography?"

Gabe paused, trying not to babble like an overwrought child. "Indeed. Your brilliant portraits fueled my interest in profound ways."

"And have you a camera?"

His tongue almost tripped over the stem of words bubbling to burst forth. "Yes, sir. I've worked and saved diligently over the past several years and recently acquired my first."

"What model?"

"An Anthony camera, sir."

Brady raised his brows higher. "Impressive. There are none better. I employ Anthony cameras exclusively in my own studio."

Gabe released a tight breath. Yes, he knew. He knew every detail about the renowned portrait gallery and the methodology of its master.

"What's your name, son?"

He'd never introduced himself? "Forgive me. My name is Gabriel Avery."

"And what brings you to my studio today, Mr. Avery?"

His mouth was cotton. "I heard a rumor you are considering undertaking a remarkable endeavor. Is it true that you are planning to photograph views from the war?"

Brady's goatee twitched in response. "News of my fanciful daydreams has spread already?"

Fearing he'd overstepped propriety, Gabe could do little more than nod. "Word travels fast, sir."

"Indeed." Plucking the wire-rimmed spectacles from his nose, Brady drew a square of dark cloth from his coat pocket and began to polish the lenses, a frown pulling his mouth into a grim line. "It's become an ambition of mine, I confess. The magnitude of such a historic event calls for an accurate record, wouldn't you say?"

"I agree entirely. Is it true that you have considered hiring photographers to complete it?"

Brady gave a nod. "I have weighed the merits of it, yes."

Gabe's heart leapt. "If I may be so bold, I'd like to apply for the job."

"I figured as much. Do you have examples of your work?"

Gabe's fingers nearly knotted. So much so, he fumbled over the clasps of his satchel. Removing the samples he'd so carefully selected, he handed them to the photographer.

Brady hooked his spectacles back over his ears and onto his nose before perusing the photographs, his face void of expression. Gabe's heart raced as he waited, each second drawn longer than the last.

Finally Brady spoke. "These are quite good. You certainly are adept at using the chemicals for the wet-plate process, although you still have some to learn about the proper use of light to acquire sharper, crisper images."

"Yes, sir." Gabe held his breath.

Brady pursed his lips. "Unfortunately, none of my plans are definite as of yet. And you can imagine the staggering expense of mounting such a venture. Equipment, traveling darkrooms, horses and their feed, chemicals, plates, tripods . . . to say nothing of the government's cooperation with such a venture."

Gabe's heart sank like an iron anchor. The disappointment tasted far more bitter than he'd imagined.

Brady rubbed his chin, his face thoughtful. "However, I see nothing wrong with striking a tenuous arrangement."

His breath hitched.

"Check back with me in one month. By that time, I hope to have permission from President Lincoln himself. If I can figure out a way to embark on such a campaign, I would like to hire you as one of my photographers."

Gabe's pulse pounded in a heady rush. His tongue cleaved to the roof of his mouth. Before he could utter a sound, Brady held up a warning hand.

"On one condition, however. You must agree to use your own Anthony camera and must purchase your own tripod and Harrison lens if you do not have one. I would provide any stereoscopic cameras needed."

Gabe tried to calculate the sum in his head. The lens would come dear. He'd had no use for a tripod as yet, choosing to perch his delicate camera on boxes or tables for the time being. There would be no such luxury in the middle of war.

He spoke slowly. "Such an investment is beyond my current means. What if I were somehow to obtain the proper funds and arrangements for photographing the war fell through?"

Brady's lips twisted into a dry smile. "That is precisely my own conundrum."

It was a risk. A big one. Where would he ever find the money for such equipment?

Brady continued, "In addition, all photographers would be required to spend several weeks working in one of my studios before travel. If I'm to fund such an extravagant and elaborate ordeal, I must be assured that my photographers are properly trained. As such, you would be representing me and the reputation I've spent years striving to attain."

Learn from Mathew Brady himself? The thought left Gabe

light-headed. Such an opportunity was beyond belief. It was a priceless gift that would never come again.

As suddenly as the elation rose, it deflated. The opportunity was contingent on money . . . money he did not have. One month. Was it possible to purchase a costly Harrison lens and tripod in such a short time?

Please, Lord. I'll never ask for another blessed thing. . . .

"What say you, Mr. Avery? Do we strike a pledge?"

Gabe stared at Brady, his mind spinning like a top. How could he decline? If it was the Almighty's will, he would make a way.

Before he could hesitate any longer, Gabe clasped Brady's slim hand. Despite the excitement coursing through him, a niggling unease remained. Where could he possibly procure those kinds of funds?

Brady's brows rose. "One month?"

Gabe swallowed. "One month."

What had he done?

———— ◆ ————

HOWELL, MICHIGAN

"Well, Cassandra, say something."

She could form no response. Hysteria . . . panic . . . what words could possibly suffice for the tumult raging inside?

Father glowered, his dark brows lowering in a look that brooked no argument. "Erastus Leeds has been our closest neighbor for nigh unto fifteen years. I've had nary a complaint with him."

Father might not have any complaints about the surly man who watched her with far too much frequency, but she had a long litany of grievances. His glances were too leering to be gentlemanly. Every time she caught his intense stare, Cassie felt the urge to cover herself and hide. From across the table, her gaze sought Mother with a beseeching look.

But instead of coming to her aid, Mother lowered her eyes to the stew cooling in the bowl before her, her thin shoulders drooping.

And Cassie knew then that she was alone.

"The wedding will take place in a fortnight."

She dropped her spoon against the chipped bowl with a clatter. "So soon?"

Father shoveled in another mouthful of potatoes and carrots. "I see no need to wait."

The meager contents of her stomach soured. Her heart hardened. "How much is he paying you?"

His dark head jerked up, his eyes glinting a warning. "What did you say?"

The small flicker of hot indignation in her middle fanned into flames. "How much did he consent to give you as my bridal price? Enough to keep you deep in your cups for quite some time, I imagine."

As soon as the words escaped, she knew she'd overstepped.

Mother sucked in a dry gasp as Father dropped the stained napkin to the table and stood, pushing the chair back with a thick scrape.

She didn't even see the hand that slammed into her face with a stinging crack. Pain exploded as her head snapped to the side. Tears burned, but she would not give him the satisfaction of seeing her cry. She would not.

She turned her eyes slowly back to meet his stormy face. Licking her lips, she tasted blood. But she forced herself not to look away.

"You are dissatisfied with my choice of husband for you?"

She swallowed but refused to speak.

Father stepped close, and the sour stench of his whiskey fanned across her skin. "I chose all four of your sisters' husbands. They have offered no complaints, nor have they shown a shadow of the rebelliousness or ingratitude you've displayed tonight."

Of course her sisters hadn't complained. They were terrified of him. Everyone was. But Cassie knew too well the heartbreak of her sisters' marriages. Two of their husbands loved the bottle more than their families, while another had roving eyes for anything in a skirt. The fourth was lazy and expected Nellie to do all the planting and harvesting. All four husbands treated her sisters as nothing more than servants, objects to cook their food and sate their lust.

She would not blindly embrace the same fate.

Her gaze flickered back to Mother's downcast face. Her lined features were pleading, silently begging Cassie to agree, not to cause any more turmoil or fray the tenuous thread of Father's explosive temper.

For Mother's sake, she would hold her peace. For now.

Taking her silence as submission, Father plunked back down into his chair. "In a fortnight you will be wed to Erastus Leeds."

The stew settled like mortar in her belly and she excused herself from dinner. She was trapped like a bird in a cage. She could see the freedom beyond the wire enclosure, but her wings could not beat with enough strength to break the bars. Her lungs felt strangely bereft of air, as if she were slowly smothering. She burst from the house with one destination in mind. The only person she wanted to see, to pour out her misery to, was the only woman who had ever understood and cared for her heart. Granny Ardie.

Running from the farm felt good. She hadn't meant to, but what started off as a quick walk slipped into a sprint. Wind slapped her face. Her lungs and legs burned. She ignored the homespun tangling around her legs, the rocks piercing the thin soles of her worn shoes. She sucked in cleansing gulps, and for a moment, she was unleashed. Free.

If only outrunning her problems were as easy.

Following the crooked fence jutting up from the ground, she plunged into the woods that led to the cabin. It was not much farther.

Several minutes later, she turned a corner of the dirt path and stopped, heaving deeply. Granny's tiny cabin stood the same as ever. Constant and welcoming.

Forcing herself into slow, measured steps, she walked up the creaking porch stairs, noting their slight sag. She must repair them soon. For certain Father would never do it. He had never given his mother-in-law a moment of attention.

She pushed open the wooden door, wincing at the raspy creak of old hinges. "Granny?"

"Is that you, Cassie, love?"

"It's me." She shut the door behind her and blinked, letting her eyes adjust to the shadowed cabin. Following the scent of cooking, she slipped past the front room and walked into the warm kitchen tucked away in the back. As she approached, she heard the crackle of meat popping in an iron skillet. The aroma of frying onions and fresh-baked johnnycakes wafted around her.

Granny turned, a smile wreathing her face in wrinkled lines. Her blue eyes twinkled. "Here I was, asking the good Lord to send me some company, and he brought my favorite person."

Cassie's eyes stung. She never cried. *Never.* Yet Granny always knew what her bruised heart needed. Keeping the tears at bay, she pasted on a brave face. "And you are *my* favorite person on this whole big earth."

Granny shuffled slowly to the table and plopped into the scarred chair with a groan. "My old bones can't do what they used to. Care for some supper? Nothing fancy, but I've just enough for the two of us."

The two bites of stew she'd choked down could hold no candle to a meal made with love. "Of course. You rest and I'll serve."

Cassie turned to fill the tin plates with steaming johnnycakes, crispy salt pork, and succotash of fried squash and onions. She blinked away the stinging sensation. Her infernal eyes. What was wrong with her that she suddenly couldn't squelch the urge to bawl like a newborn calf?

Setting the plates before them, Cassie grasped Granny's knobby fingers as the elderly woman's voice cracked out grace. Cassie did not feel the peace that usually followed the prayer.

She had just plopped a dollop of butter atop her johnnycake when Granny's soft voice probed.

"What's wrong?"

Cassie blinked, her throat clogging shut as she rasped out a strangled laugh. "Nothing."

Sighing, the older woman laid aside her utensil and squinted, staring at Cassie with far too much discernment. She resisted the urge to squirm.

"I've known you all your life, Cassie, love. Out with it."

Her breath hitched for only an instant before the dismal news burst from her lips. "Father demands I marry Erastus Leeds within a fortnight." Everyone in the area knew the odious man. If anyone would understand, Granny certainly would.

Granny only picked up her fork once more, chewing slowly. Her eyes were thoughtful. After a lengthy pause, she said, "I see. But you must have known you would have to marry eventually."

Panic squeezed her heart when Granny did not immediately

dismiss the preposterous notion. "Of course, but Erastus Leeds?" She shivered, feeling the revulsion to her bones. "The man is slick as fish. I don't trust him. And his name . . . makes me think of leeches."

The older woman chuckled.

Cassie frowned. "Surely you don't agree with Father."

Granny sighed deeply. "No, I don't. Truly, I didn't agree with any of the matches he arranged for your sisters, either. But understand, love, war changes things."

"War." She glowered. "Not likely. Father has been squandering more money down at the gaming hall. He's short of coinage for his whiskey. He keeps throwing away what little Mother manages to save. She scrimps and scrapes and he loses it in hand after hand of faro."

"I know, lamb. I know. And more's the pity. We need to be more diligent in our prayers for him."

The likelihood of her father turning over a new leaf within a fortnight was slim to none. No, Cassie couldn't wait for that kind of miracle. Something must be done and soon.

Lifting her chin, she firmed her lips. "I refuse to marry the man."

Granny shook her gray head and frowned. "I don't see how you're going to avoid it. Unless you're planning to marry another before the appointed time or join up to fight." She ended the sentence on a guffaw.

Cassie straightened, her heart pricking with a sudden idea. Her mind whirled. Could she be so bold?

"Promise me something, Cassie."

The soft plea scattered her churning thoughts. "Yes'm?"

"Promise me you won't decide on anything—whether to submit to your father's wishes or refuse him—until you've prayed long and hard."

"But I—"

Granny's lips formed a thin line. "Promise me."

The thought rankled, though why, Cassie didn't want to examine.

"I promise."

Still, the shimmer of possible escape refused to leave her be.

Less than an hour later, she trudged home and slipped inside unnoticed. Easing into her room, she lowered herself to the floor, sitting in front of the hope chest nestled at the foot of her bed.

As a little girl, she had dreamed of the day when she would marry and finally use the treasures inside. Year after year, she and Mother had tucked in special items—a delicate yard of lace, a blanket, a floral-patterned teacup, a goose-down pillow—things a new, dewy-eyed bride would need to set up house.

As she ran her fingers over the items, a tiny porcelain hand peeked out from between the folds of linen. Cassie pulled out the treasure. She had almost forgotten the china doll Granny Ardie had given her Christmas morning when she was six. She had named her Elizabeth. The doll had gone with her everywhere.

Fingering the lace of Elizabeth's faded pink frock, Cassie lifted her eyes to study the mangled features and ran her fingers over the jagged hole marring half of the doll's face. The bitter memory from years ago rushed back.

She had been sitting on the kitchen floor, pretending to give Elizabeth a cup of tea while Mother looked on, smiling as she made preserves.

The serene moment had been shattered when Father burst in. He staggered and slurred, enraged over some imaginary infraction. Mother cowered under his drunken heat.

"Where did you get this?" He snatched up the precious doll and waved her through the air.

Cassie had gasped. "No! Please! Granny gave her to me."

"Bah! A waste of money." With a sneer, he threw Elizabeth into the wall.

Cassie had cried bitter tears when she turned over her little friend to discover one eye and half of her sweet, smiling face were gone.

Cassie was no longer a child, yet the memory wrapped around her heart with cold tentacles, hardening into an unforgiving knot. Clutching the doll to her chest, she heaved a deep sigh, knowing she could not, would not marry Erastus Leeds.

The decision left few options, but one possibility kept gnawing at her, refusing to budge. Could she do it?

Granny's admonition tugged. *"Promise me you won't decide on anything . . . until you've prayed long and hard."*

Oh, she would pray, all right. Pray she wasn't preparing to make the worst mistake of her life.

Chapter 3

May 15, 1861
New York City

"Mr. Avery, I'm happy to report that I have received the proper permission from our Union commanders, as well as President Lincoln himself. The adventure to document war pictures will go forward."

Gabe stood before Mathew Brady, feeling as if he ought to pinch himself. It was truly happening.

Brady plucked his spectacles off his nose, his face thoughtful. "As I previously mentioned, each photographer will be required to complete a month's training with either myself or my esteemed assistant Mr. Gardner." He gestured to the bushy-bearded Scot in the corner of the studio.

Gabe offered a polite nod, which Gardner returned.

Brady smiled. "I trust you were able to acquire the proper lens and tripod?"

"Yes, sir. I have the necessary equipment and am ready to begin my training anytime."

Gabe squelched the guilt gnawing his middle. His elderly neighbor Jacob had insisted on the loan when he heard about Gabe's lack of funds. Since the deaths of Gabe's parents, he and Jacob had shared many evenings together in their crowded tenement building—playing checkers, drinking coffee, and sharing lighthearted conversation. Jacob was the grandfather he'd always longed for, which was why, when the elderly man had thrust a wad of bills at him with his blue-veined fingers, Gabe had initially refused.

"I couldn't possibly. This must be your whole life savings!"

"Ach!" Jacob waved an impatient hand. "You're like my own boy. Right proud of you I am. You have a talent with your magic box. You'll not see an opportunity like this come again. Take it."

He shook his head. "I'll not take your money. You need it."

"If you won't take it because of your stubborn pride, then consider it a loan."

"I'm not sure how long I'll be gone. It could be a few months. Maybe longer if the fight drags out. I wouldn't be able to check on you, see how you're faring."

Jacob had cackled. "I got a whole building full of nosy neighbors to check on me. You'll write, I'm sure."

Still Gabe had balked. "What if I fail? What if nobody buys my photographs? You will have lost all that money because of my inadequacy. And my job. It's taken me years to work my way up from unloading ship cargo and being a dock rat. Sullivan has me keeping inventory of the freight and managing the new workers." He cupped the back of his neck. "Tossing away that opportunity after all those years of work might be the most foolish thing I've ever done." He stood and paced the length of the room. "That job won't be waiting if I mess up this chance. With all the Irish and German immigrants roaming the docks, Sullivan will replace me like that." He snapped his fingers with a frown.

Jacob arched a white brow. "Planning to fail, then, are you?"

"No, of course not. But—"

"You'll succeed. I have no doubt. If it makes you feel better, you can pay me back with interest. If you fail, it's only money. I can't take it to glory with me anyway."

Gabe pushed back the memory and focused on Mr. Brady, his head flooded with dizzying excitement. "I'm ready, sir."

Brady nodded. "Let's get started, then."

Following the photographer into the preparation room lined with chemicals and glass plates, he inhaled a shaky breath.

I'll not fail you, Jacob. I promise I will not.

———◆———

DETROIT, MICHIGAN

Cassie's heart thumped like a thousand trampling feet.

She stood in line at Fort Wayne, awaiting her turn with the medical evaluator.

Thus far, escape from the farm had been easy. She'd snuck away in the early morning hours while the night was still black as tar. Binding her chest and donning Father's trousers and shirt had been strange, but at least the baggy clothes were comfortable. She had to wear her own boots since none her size were to be had, but the worn shoes were roughened from farmwork. No one would think they were ladies' boots.

The hard part had been cutting off her mane of brown hair. Before she could back out of the plan, she'd grabbed a razor and shorn off the thick tresses.

Cassie's fingers instinctively rose to feel the sudden lack of sleek weight. Below the brim of her cap, only a few inches of her hair emerged, not even long enough to brush her shoulders.

What did it matter? Mourning the locks would be less misery than life bound to Erastus Leeds.

She'd left on foot and, hungry and exhausted, had arrived at Fort Wayne several days later and dutifully enlisted to fight for the Union. The commanders told her that until enough soldiers were mustered to fill her military company, the newly arrived soldiers were free to become acquainted with the fort while they waited. So she'd lingered, feeling lost among the swarm of new faces, curt words, and cold buildings.

Until now, no one had questioned her disguise, but when one stern-faced commander told her the US War Department dictated all recruits must undergo a thorough physical examination, she had nearly retched.

Would she be required to undress? The thought almost made her bolt from the line of chattering men. Surely the physician would know she was a woman, even without disrobing. Doctors could tell such things just by looking, couldn't they?

Please, God, don't let him find out.

Her heart pounded until she grew dizzy.

"Next!"

The bark made her jump. Realizing it was her turn, she walked into the small medical building on quivering legs. The structure was nothing more than a shed. She shut the door behind her and fought the urge to cast up her accounts. Running her clammy hands down her trousers, she took a deep breath of the stale air. The physician was scribbling something in a ledger.

"Name?"

She cleared her throat, afraid her nerves would emit nothing more than a tiny squeak. "Thomas Turner."

The physician scribbled some more. "Height?"

"Five feet, six inches."

"You're thin."

She lifted her chin. "I'm only eighteen. I reckon I'll fill out."

The man lifted her wrist and turned it over, examining it. She held her breath. Could he tell?

"A few calluses. What sort of living has this hand earned?"

She resisted the urge to yank her hand away. "Until recently, I've been chiefly engaged in receiving an education and working a farm."

The physician shrugged and dropped her wrist, scribbling some more, the scratching sound scraping her nerves raw.

"I don't suppose your size matters much as long as you have a trigger finger, can carry a gun, and have enough teeth to tear open powder cartridges. At least three, to be precise." The doctor frowned and narrowed his eyes at her. "You do have your teeth, correct?"

"Yes, sir." She opened her mouth to prove it.

He grunted. "Are you in good health?"

"Yes, sir."

The doctor nodded and waved her away in dismissal. "You're fit to serve." He scrawled something on a clean sheet of paper, thrust it into Cassie's hands, and yelled for the next recruit.

As she stumbled out of the medical building, Cassie found herself trembling, a surge of giddiness pouring through her. She'd passed.

Glancing down at the stiff paper clutched in her hand, she read the doctor's hasty note.

Thomas Turner: fit to serve as private for Company F, 2nd Michigan Infantry.

Cassie relished her moment of triumph. Finally the tide was turning in her favor. All that remained was to take her oath of allegiance to the United States and she could disappear into the mass of soldiers streaming into the heart of the conflict.

A niggling guilt gnawed at the edges of her heart. Mother. Granny. Surely they must think she'd abandoned them.

She pushed the black thought away. No, not any more than the thousands of other soldiers had abandoned their families upon enlisting. Like them, she could defend the Union while she was here. The abolitionists who'd flooded Michigan had imparted the cruelties of slavery to her at a young age, and she planned to do her part for the cause.

Or was she hiding behind it? Unease crept over her like a humid mist.

She sobered. The coming months would determine her fortitude in nearly every way, but surely nothing could be as horrid as marriage to Erastus Leeds . . . or her father's foul temper.

Chapter 4

JUNE 9, 1861
NEAR WASHINGTON, DC

Cassie slogged through the thick mud turning the road into a quagmire of glue. Sweat stung her eyes and ran in rivulets down her back, pasting her grimy shirt to her skin. She squinted through the rain and grimaced against the fifty-pound pack strapped to her back. As far as the eye could see, there was nothing but mud and a snaking trail of exhausted, blue-backed soldiers weaving through the woods.

The June day was sweltering. Unbearably so. Shifting the soggy pack on her aching back, she stomped through the mire, her belly cramping with hunger. How long had they been marching? Hours? Days? One day seemed to bleed into another as they moved toward their destination, a place only the general knew.

She could show no weakness. None. As of yet, no one had guessed she was a female. She was quiet and mostly kept to herself. The men assumed Thomas Turner was an aloof fellow.

Proficient in his duties but quiet. Caked as she was in sweat and dirt day after day, she'd certainly lost whatever female softness she'd had before enlisting . . . if she'd ever possessed any at all. Her sisters had always teased her about her lack of interest in the feminine graces.

Father had always wanted a boy. His vocal disappointment and irritation with four girls was continual until his wife grew round with her fifth child . . . the long-awaited male he'd bitterly grieved over not having.

A boy he'd finally had, but the child had not lived. Father's grief had been all-consuming. Cassie came along not long after, but she could not replace the boy he'd lost.

She wiped away beads of sweat and rain from her eyes with the back of her grimy hand. If Father could only see her now, even he might mistake her for a boy.

"Halt!"

The command stopped the soldiers like a braking train. The shout filtered through the weary ranks . . . a short rest that would be followed by a push to build fortifications. This was the spot, then. The land where they would likely face the full force of the fiery rebellion.

Since enlisting, the skirmishes she'd engaged in had been few. Nothing more than short-lived fights by small companies unwilling to face the full arsenal of the Union without a large contingent of soldiers backing them up.

This would be different. Even through the drizzling rain, the air was charged with some kind of intangible spark. An anticipation as if the world were holding its breath.

It made the monotonous weeks of drilling for endless hours seem a luxury. Early morning reveille, marching in columns, dressing the line . . . all of it sounded blessedly restful now, despite its tedium.

Too much excitement was hard on the body.

"Turner! You mind giving me a hand?"

Cassie whirled to see George Hanover looking at her with desperate need. The cannon he had been pulling for miles was stuck, sinking into the muck of the road.

Dropping her own pack, she slogged toward him and grasped the filthy rope encircling the cannon's bearings.

She counted, "One, two, three . . ."

The two of them yanked and pulled in the incessant drizzle, muscles taut and screaming as they tugged it free, inch by inch. George's neck was mottled red with the effort as they slowly made headway.

Cassie hadn't had much trouble adjusting to the rigors of military life. Born and raised on a farm, she had already earned her muscles. Upon joining the regiment, she was shocked so many of the city boys who had enlisted did not even know how to load their cartridges. When she had taught a handful of them how to load and care for their guns, the irony was not lost on her.

A female teaching males how to fight. What a strange turn of events.

Maintaining her disguise hadn't been as difficult as she'd feared, especially since the soldiers went weeks without bathing and slept in the same grimy clothes they marched in day after day. If she was careful with her speech and mannerisms, perhaps no one would ever know.

They lugged the cumbersome load to a drier spot and stopped, panting against their burning lungs. George looked up, narrowing his gaze to something at the rear of the snaking line of soldiers.

"What is *that*?"

Cassie followed his line of vision and frowned at the sight

of an odd wagon ambling along behind the regiment. Its shape was peculiar. Much more boxlike than the average covered wagon. Smaller as well.

She squinted. Though far away, she could tell the man perched atop the driver's seat was not wearing a blue uniform, nor was he dressed in the garish red trousers of the Zouaves. The senators and congressmen who occasionally visited to boost morale would never have stooped to hauling a contraption like that through miles of slimy mud.

"You think he's one of those journalists from Washington?"

Cassie frowned. "In that odd wagon? Seems like a fool's errand if he is. Report on the war by trailing troops into battle and risk getting his head blown off?"

George shrugged. "We're risking the same."

The thought slammed hard. "True enough." Sometimes she couldn't help wondering if there was another way to escape marriage to that no-account snake.

Squeezing her eyes shut, she almost shook her head. No. She was no longer Cassie Kendrick. She was Thomas Turner. If she had any hope of surviving the charade, she must erase, irrevocably and completely, all memories of the person she was before.

George turned away from the approaching wagon and lifted the brim of his kepi, wiping a streak of mud across his forehead. "Come on. Let's finish getting this Rebel chaser into place. Besides, I'm hungry." The freckled fellow grinned. "A chunk of hardtack is calling my name."

Cassie chuckled under her breath. "Just remember you need enough teeth to tear open your powder cartridges. Hardtack does its best to make you lose the teeth you've got."

Thumping her on the back, George laughed. "I only need three. Two on top and one on bottom. I've still got plenty to spare."

———— ◆ ————

Gabe scanned the soggy land stretched before him and attempted to squelch his frustration. The infernal drizzle was dampening his excitement.

He could not risk damaging his camera in the rain, nor would the light prove sufficient for exposing the plates.

"Patience, Gabriel. The Almighty has a hard time using those who keep running ahead o' him. . . ."

He smiled to himself. He could still hear his mother's soft admonition murmured so many times when he'd been a squirmy, bursting, impatient mess of a child. In some ways, he still was.

Surveying the scene, he could scarcely believe the tract of land had been transformed so thoroughly in the span of a day. The thick woods bordering the green pasture had been thinned. Felled oaks, maples, and pines had been turned into a fence of sorts, bracing cannons in place for the fight. A long, snaking trench had been dug, perfect for reloading cartridges while under fire. The entire place smelled of churned earth and loam.

Where should he set up his camera on the morrow? He eyed the swell of a hill to his left that would provide an ideal view of the Union camp.

He longed for a crisp photograph of the encampment . . . especially considering it would likely look much different after battle.

The thought saddened him more than he'd anticipated.

"Care for another cup?"

Gabe smiled at the jovial man across the campfire. "Nah, any more and I'll not be able to sleep a wink."

The other soldiers chuckled as they stared at the crackling flames dancing in the night's stillness. Their chatter was light, but the sober reality of what lay in wait tomorrow smothered their spirits like a blanket. No one had dared utter their dark thoughts out loud.

A bearded soldier named Briggs nodded toward Gabe. "I'm glad to know your purpose here. When I saw that contraption you were driving, I confess I was a bit worried."

Gabe fingered the rim of his empty tin cup. "What did you think my purpose was?"

Briggs shrugged. "Don't know. Anything I'm uneasy about, I tend to shoot first and ask questions later."

The men laughed and Gabe's nervousness faded. This troop was a friendly sort.

"Nothing but photographic equipment, I assure you."

Weeks grinned and scratched his thatch of straw-colored hair. "Me and some of the others have taken to calling your wagon the Whatsit—'cause not a blamed one of us knew what it was!"

Gabe threw back his head and laughed at the good-natured ribbing. "The traveling darkroom is an oddity, to be sure. Despite its boxy shape, Mr. Brady spared no expense. The shelves even have locks to keep the chemicals from spilling."

Weeks leaned forward. "So you can take photographs of us?"

"Certainly. Mr. Brady's idea is to get a thorough and complete rendering of all aspects of the war."

The taste of coffee soured on Gabe's tongue as he remembered Mr. Brady's admonition before he'd left New York. *Capture the truth, Mr. Avery, in all its stark nakedness. The truth is often shocking, but its honesty is needed if we are to ensure a fracture in our glorious Union is never repeated.*

The order seemed confining. Truth was important, naturally, but so was heroism and beauty. Why could he not also capture the gallant acts of the soldiers? Images that might blot out the ugliness of war?

The men's excited voices yanked him away from the turbulent thought.

Weeks's eyes brightened. "Could you take a small photo of me? For my sweetheart back home?"

The others sitting close to him snickered and elbowed him in the ribs. His cheeks reddened. "At least I got myself a sweetheart, unlike some of you poor sods."

Gabe grinned. "I don't mind doing that at all."

Soft crackles of the fire soothed the air as the men quieted.

"Say, could I get one of those photographs too?"

"Me too?"

Gabe stretched his legs out before him. "Of course. Mr. Brady allowed some extra supplies for such things. The photos will be small, but I'll be happy to take them. Perhaps the weather will permit it tomorrow morning."

The men smiled, light gleaming in their expressions as they sipped their bitter coffee. Some chattered about what their sweethearts would say to receiving their likenesses.

Weeks motioned to another soldier sitting farther back than the rest. "What about you, Turner? You want your likeness made for anyone?"

The slim, quiet fellow continued cleaning his gun with a rag, barely looking up. "Nah. Ain't got no sweetheart."

Briggs guffawed. "You should meet O'Keefe's sister then. Homely little thing, but she sure can cook."

O'Keefe glared at Briggs, his eyes narrowed into slits. "Don't say my sister is homely."

"Why not?"

"Because she looks just like me!"

Gabe studied the quiet fellow ignoring the group of unruly men. Turner, was it? "You have a family member who would treasure your photograph? Your mother, perhaps?"

Turner lifted his head, his face shadowed by the brim of his navy kepi, and studied Gabe for a long moment before dropping his eyes back to his gun. "Nope."

George laughed. "Trying to get Turner to talk is like trying to get blood from a turnip. He's a man of few words."

Briggs grunted. "True enough. And the best sharpshooter in our troop."

Gabe glanced back to the somber Turner. "Is that so? I want to be on your good side, then."

The ghost of a smile curved the soldier's mouth.

"How did you get so good at shooting?"

Turner's eyes twinkled. "I don't spend all my time jawin'."

At the men's howls, Gabe joined in. Warmth filled his chest. For the first time in years, he felt as if he belonged.

What a strange, amiable sensation.

———•———

Cassie threw the remains of the bitter chicory coffee into the grass and wiped out her cup with the cuff of her coat sleeve while watching the stranger with a wary eye. He moved among the men with ease, sticking out like a sore thumb in his brown trousers and white shirt. No kepi, either.

What were the generals thinking allowing some untrained novice to follow them straight into battle? And a photographer at that? War was no place for sweet pictures of lovesick soldiers. He was going to slow them down . . . or get them all killed.

Irked, she turned away as his low baritone drifted through the air. Briggs, Weeks, Meade, even George had cottoned to him as if they were long-lost friends.

Squelching the irritation blooming in her chest, she stood and, grabbing her rifle, walked to her tent, determined to get a few hours of sleep. The Rebels might engage them tomorrow and she needed to rest up.

Especially if her job entailed protecting not only her comrades, but a talkative photographer as well.

Chapter 5

"I'm going to expose the plate. Remain completely still."

Giving the soldier a final glance through the enormous lens, Gabe hovered under the black canvas. "One, two, three."

He pulled the shutter free, letting light strike the sticky glass plate inside, and mentally counted off the seconds required for exposure. It wouldn't be long. The sun was bright today, having chased off the rain and thick clouds. He grimaced when Weeks started to squirm. "Don't move!"

The restless soldier stilled and, upon hearing Gabe call, "Finished," blew out a thick exhale of air.

"It's mighty hard holding still for so long, Avery."

"I imagine it's a bit easier if the subject doesn't pose his body like a banty rooster."

Weeks shot him a mock glare as the soldiers gathered around them snorted. "Priscilla won't be complaining. Not when she can see my handsome face every day."

Gabe smiled at their antics, knowing the playfulness was

only a masquerade to calm their frayed nerves as they waited another day for the Rebels' attack.

He wasn't blind. He had witnessed the hushed whispers between the commanders. He had seen messengers delivering letters reported to have come from Washington. The men would be facing the fury in mere hours. If his camera provided them some kind of meager distraction from the severity of their task, he would gladly oblige. Tension hung over the trench-marked camp like pulled taffy.

"I'll head into the darkroom and get these developed."

Across the camp, Turner stared at his camera and tripod, his expression unreadable.

Raising his voice, Gabe shouted, "What say you, Turner? A photo?"

Turner shook his head and looked away as if embarrassed to be caught gawking.

Shrugging, Gabe lifted the cumbersome equipment, tugging it to the Whatsit while the soldiers returned to work, preparing their guns and cannons.

He smiled to himself. Priscilla was patiently waiting for Weeks's handsome face. He'd best get to work.

———— ◆ ————

Cassie ducked low as the scream of cannons split the air, her breath tight as the impact rumbled the ground like an earthquake. She squinted through the haze of gunpowder. To her right, Weeks was hunkered within the trench. The skin around his mouth was black from gunpowder. Sweat and dirt streaked his face.

Cassie tasted the grit between her own teeth. Taking a deep breath, she lifted herself above the trench, aimed at a Rebel locked in combat with one of her own, and pulled the trigger.

The explosion burst in her ears but the man's shriek of pain seemed far louder. Her heart brittled.

A bullet whizzed past her ear and she ducked low again. Dirt pelted her face. She blinked against the flecks burning her eyes.

The assault had come at daybreak. Golden streaks of butter had barely painted the sky when the scouts had sounded the alarms. An ungodly noise followed not long after . . . screeches like a horde of demons unleashed from their chains. The hair on the back of her neck had prickled. The terrifying shrieks intensified as the gray backs topped the hill and opened fire.

It had been chaos ever since.

A scream sounded to her left. George?

She whirled. No, not George. A soldier farther down had been clipped in the shoulder. His cries of pain pierced the air just before another cannon howled overhead.

Bedlam pressed in on all sides. Smoke and blood filled every pocket of air, every corner of earth. Each time cannon fire fell into silence, the screams of wounded and dying men crowded in, their wails intensifying into a roar.

Hands shaking, Cassie fumbled for another powder cartridge and ripped it open. Spitting the residue of black powder from her mouth, she finished loading and turned when Briggs yelled from farther down the trench.

"Turner, cover me!"

She nodded. The big man stood and fired. She pointed her own gun and took out a Rebel approaching from his right.

Briggs ducked back into the trench and grinned, his teeth stained black. "We got 'em both. I owe you one!"

Cassie yelled back over the whizzing bullets and crash of cannon thunder. "You sure do!"

Briggs laughed, his eyes bright. He was in the thick of it and had never seemed more alive.

"Turner!"

Cassie whirled to see Captain Johnston yelling from behind the fortifications. Crouched low, she eased from the trench, half-running to his side as he shouted commands.

"Yes, sir?"

His face was sweaty as he turned to her, his jaw tight. "Turner, we got some Rebs in a sniper position from the rocky terrain above. I need a man willing to climb through that mess of trees behind us and pick them off."

Throwing her gun over her shoulder, she nodded. "Yes, sir."

Captain Johnston clapped her on the shoulder. "Good man. Take them out!"

Another boom of cannon fire. A shrill whistle. An explosion to her left. She stumbled to regain her footing as the impact tilted the ground beneath her. Captain Johnston shouted more commands, his barks drowned out by another roaring cannon.

Using the smoke for cover, she ran hard and fast to the thick copse of trees behind their trenches. Breath burned her lungs as she hastily scanned the best option. It must be high enough to see, easy to climb yet within range.

Spying the desired spot, she hoisted herself up, climbing limb over limb. Her muscles strained. The rifle swinging from its strap on her shoulder pounded her back with every jostling step.

The screams of pain ripping through her regiment hastened her steps until she sat perched high in a majestic maple. Thankful for the leaves hiding her position from the enemy, she tore open another powder cartridge and prepared her gun. This was no different than all those times on the farm when she'd clipped pesky critters that crept around the chicken house.

Father had been so proud the first time she'd shot a raccoon lurking near the coop. The gun had seemed heavy in her nine-year-old hands as she sighted down the barrel. Father's voice had been unusually steady that day, his eyes clear and focused.

"There now, Cass. Breathe, aim, and squeeze the trigger."

The deafening noise had paled in comparison to the feel of the gun ramming into her shoulder, but Father's shout of delight chased away the trembling in her middle.

"Perfect shot! Better than any boy, I'd say."

Father's eyes had twinkled and Cassie had beamed at his praise. If only he were always so carefree and kind. But then he would pick up the bottle again and the father she knew vanished, swallowed by a monster.

Boom, boom, boom . . .

The cannons whistled with eerie foreboding before blowing dirt, rocks, and men into the air as if they were nothing more than rag dolls. The trees not more than thirty feet away were splintered and riddled with shot, their limbs snapped and twisted.

She wiped away a thick trickle of sweat from her eyes and scanned for the Rebel snipers. Blasted smoke made it difficult to see.

Was that movement from a rocky outcropping across the way? Lifting her gun, she watched the shadow shift. It was definitely a sniper . . . and he was targeting her regiment.

Breathe in; breathe out. Her heart hammered as her vision narrowed to a point. She squeezed the trigger. The limb she sat on swayed with the kick of the gun. The dark form crumpled from his rocky stronghold. A surge of relief and something altogether indefinable flooded her veins.

She scanned again, reloaded, and narrowed her eyes when a burst of gunpowder came from the trees opposite her own position. Another sniper.

This one would be tricky, tucked as he was in the refuge of

tree limbs. Just like herself. If she took a shot and missed, it wouldn't take him long to ascertain her position and cut her down like a scythe through grass.

The pillar of air in her lungs burned as she remained entirely still, waiting . . .

A screech shivered the air. She watched in disbelief as a Union cannonball slammed into the tree holding her prey, snapping off the top half like it was nothing more than a twig. The sniper fell to his death in a whoosh of cracking limbs.

Exhaling heavily, she forced down the panic clawing her throat. She was safe. For the moment.

An ominous chuckle sounded below the tree. She sucked in a breath at the sight of a gray-clad soldier waving a deadly-looking knife at someone, circling him as a bobcat would his prey. How did a Confederate get so far into their camp? And whom was he taunting with that infernal knife?

Squinting, she bit her tongue until she tasted blood. The Rebel was threatening the photographer.

Gabriel stood still, never letting his eyes leave the soldier murmuring his vile threats, yet his whole body was tensed.

With a shout, the Confederate knifed the air, attempting to slice open Gabriel's belly, but he lunged away from the dagger with a speed that stole her breath. The enraged soldier advanced again but missed, and Gabe never stumbled.

Realizing she could help, she lifted her gun to her shoulder and took aim. With a sizzle of powder and a deadly boom, the Rebel dropped dead. His blood pooled at the base of the tree. Gabriel panted and looked up.

A flash of more gray-clad soldiers from deeper in the woods snagged her attention.

Jaw tight, she reloaded and fired three times, watching in relief as the targets fell.

Knowing she had given her position away, she scrambled to descend before a bullet found her.

Before her feet had touched the ground, Gabriel muttered, "Boy, am I glad you were there."

Heat burst from her lips. "What fool notion led you to think you could waltz up to the battlefield?"

He patted the smaller camera in his hands and blinked as if she were daft. "To get an impression, of course. That's why I came."

Turning from him with a growl, she ground out, "Get back to the Whatsit and stay there. Like we don't have enough to do without saving your hide."

Instead of obeying, he trailed behind her like a curious puppy. "I thank you. You saved my life. That was some mighty fancy shooting."

"That was some mighty fancy dancing."

His chuckle dissolved into a cringe when shells shrieked overhead. She ducked and clamped down the irritation as the photographer shadowed her every move. Crouching low to the ground, she sprinted as fast as she dared back to the trenches, dodging spraying chunks of wood, dirt, and rocks as more gunfire splintered the trees.

The Rebels were clipping them down like hail beating wheat into straw.

"Where are we going?"

Gabriel's shout behind her only increased the crawling sensation mounting in her belly. She ignored him and ducked lower as a shell exploded nearby, almost splitting open the ground beneath her feet. Her teeth rattled.

Finally spying Captain Johnston up ahead, she saluted. "Snipers are dead, sir."

Captain Johnston nodded curtly, the lines around his eyes and mouth pulled tight. "Good work, Private Turner."

"Sir, I've got some bad news. While searching for more snipers, I discovered four more Rebels coming in from the east. One of them was preparing to slaughter Brady's photographer here." She hooked a thumb over her shoulder to remind the captain of Gabriel's pesky existence.

Captain Johnston's dark eyes flickered from her face to the photographer's and back again.

"Sir, the Confederates appeared to be moving in formation. The Rebels might well be flanking our side."

The captain's face grew pensive. He didn't even wince when a soldier's dying screams rent the air. After a long moment, he spoke. "We cannot hold our position if they have another contingent approaching from the east. I'll call for retreat." He scrubbed his face with blackened fingers. "Turner, I'm assigning you and Private Warner to sniper posts. Get high and take out any Rebs you see. Give us a fighting chance to retreat without more loss of life."

"Yes, sir."

Captain Johnston turned to the photographer with unrepressed annoyance. "And you! Get back to your contraption of a wagon and stay there!"

———— • ————

Gabe rubbed a hand over his bleary eyes and mentally shook away the fatigue settling around him like a shroud.

Two days of nonstop marching and the whole regiment of soldiers was now momentarily safe . . . safe and exhausted.

When the armies had ceased firing and the final cannons had been rolled away, he'd set up his camera and begun to work. The once-serene stretch of green, virgin pasture was now porous—a scarred, splintered, bloodied mess of mud and sticks. And the dead—mangled, twisted corpses already bloating—had haunted his every waking thought since.

Such waste. Such devastation. When the army ambulances rolled in to check for the wounded, he'd nearly wept at the somber fog that hung thick over the massacre. Few spoke. Those who did murmured in whispers, soft as the brush of angels' wings. Even that felt sacrilegious somehow.

When he was satisfied he had properly captured what needed to be seen, he'd hidden himself in the dark comfort of the Whatsit and developed each plate, reliving the horrid, ugly images all over again. For the first time, he wished the chemicals used to expose the images were strong enough to make him pass out and forget. He'd not eaten or slept since.

Trailing the retreating army into safety was even more taxing. There was no rest and nothing for him to do but sit atop the wagon, lead the horses, and think. There had been far too much time to think.

It might have been different if he hadn't known some of the men beforehand . . . if he hadn't heard of their homes and parents, their hobbies and dreams and sweethearts and quirks and habits. But he had.

Soldiers like Benjamin Hunter, whose likeness he had captured only three days ago. Benjamin, with his easy smile and silly quips.

"Say, Avery, do you know why I can't waltz? It makes me dizzy. But I suppose I must get used to it since it's the way of the whirled."

Gabe had even known Benjamin preferred milk in his coffee to sugar, and that his youngest sister had just finished her first nine-patch quilt. How was Benjamin to know Gabe would capture his likeness again, only this time his features would be bloody and mangled, his eyes staring vacantly at the sky?

Gabe slammed his eyes shut. He couldn't scrub the image from his mind. Would that he could. How would Benjamin's parents, his sister be able to bear the grief?

And now, with the night blanketing all of them and the camp quiet in exhausted slumber, he could not rest. Instead he stared at the dancing fire and sipped bitter coffee from a dented tin cup. Low murmurs of soldiers standing guard drifted toward him from time to time, but most of the camp was torturously silent.

"Can't sleep?"

The low voice startled him. Private Turner was watching, a chunk of hardtack in his hand.

"No. Too much on my mind, perhaps. You?"

"The same."

The quiet man settled opposite the fire and slowly chewed the unforgiving meal clenched between his fingers as he watched the flames flicker and sway. A single curl of acrid smoke rose high into the sky. Gabe blinked when the smoke twisted and changed. It was no longer gray tufts but souls leaving the earth behind and rising into heaven.

"You okay?"

Turner's voice snapped him back to his senses with a start.

"I suppose. That was my first battle to photograph. It's much to take in."

Turner said nothing. Only chewed and stared into the fire.

Feeling ill at ease over his foolishness in the battle, Gabe cleared his throat. "I believe I should thank you again for saving my life."

Turner offered a shadowed smile. "You're welcome."

Leaning forward, Gabe studied the sniper, suddenly curious about the fellow's story. "Where did you learn to shoot like that?"

The small man took so long to answer, Gabe feared he was being ignored.

Finally he murmured, "I grew up on a farm."

"Ah. Shooting at foxes near the henhouse, crows in the corn . . . that kind of thing?"

"Something like that."

They fell silent again until Turner spoke up softly. "I admit, you held up against that Rebel pretty well, especially being unarmed."

Gabe chuckled softly. "That's not the first time I've had a knife pulled on me." Turner raised a brow and Gabe grinned. "I grew up in New York City."

"Not in the upper-class neighborhood, I assume."

He cradled his tin cup. "Far from it. My family lived just outside of Five Points slum."

"I take it that's an undesirable place."

"Quite." He took another pull of the bitter brew. "My parents were Scottish and we migrated to America when I was just a boy of six. Being an immigrant in New York is difficult. Overcrowding, the deceptive preying upon the ignorance of new people in a strange land . . . You learn to live by your wits or not at all."

Turner stared at the flickering fire and smoking wood but said not a word. So Gabe filled the silence with memories.

"It wasn't uncommon for someone to pick your pocket or for some depraved individual to accost you if you happened to be out after dark." He laughed. "I remember one time a fellow tried to steal Mither's reticule."

"Mither?"

"Sorry. I meant Mother." He took another sip and let his thoughts drift back to that muggy summer afternoon.

"Da and Mither had a pittance of money. More than some, but not much to rub together, so when she realized the thief was trying to steal, Mither's temper lit like a strike of lightning." He chuckled. "Before the weasel could escape with her reticule, she yanked it from his clutch and began beating him over the head with it, raining down Scottish epithets and well-placed blows to his poor skull."

He glanced across the fire to see Turner smiling below the brim of his kepi.

"The thief sped away like the devil himself was on his tail. Don't ever anger a Scottish mother. She's worse than a whole pack of mama bears. Of course, my da had a temper of his own. One time—"

"Do you ever hush?"

Gabe startled at the outburst. When he saw Turner lower his head to hide his embarrassment at the hasty utterance, Gabe couldn't suppress the twitching of his lips. He threw back his head and laughed.

Turner's shoulders visibly shed their weight and a grin bloomed on his shadowed face. "Forgive me." He looked down into his tin cup. "That was rude."

"Nay. Not rude. It's true. I've always been a talker. It nearly drove my da to run for the hills."

"It sounds like you had a good relationship with your father and mother."

"Aye. I did." But the sudden image of Da lunging at him assaulted the sweet memories and snuffed them out. The flash of a blade slicing . . .

No, that hadn't been his da. Not really.

Pushing down the black memory, he blinked and focused on the soldier across from him. "What about you? Are you close with your parents?"

Turner didn't speak for a long moment but finally cleared his throat and replied in a soft, clipped tone. "With my mother, yes."

"And your father?"

"No." Turner snipped off the conversation like thread between scissors. "I just wanted to apologize for being short with you in battle. When bullets are flying past my head, well, it makes a man punchy."

Gabe rubbed the back of his neck. "I deserved it. I shouldn't have gotten that close to the battle lines, but—" he shrugged— "I wanted to see. No, I *needed* to see if capturing a picture of the fighting was even possible."

"And?"

He shook his head. "Too many issues with light and exposure speed." He offered a lopsided smirk. "Not to mention the bullets and cannonballs screaming toward my camera."

Turner chuckled low and Gabe felt a pang of satisfaction. The serious fellow had actually laughed. Imagine that.

Perhaps it was Turner's youth or the way he seemed so aloof, but something about the soldier reminded Gabe of himself not so many years ago. Turner had erected a barricade around himself and didn't welcome any intrusions.

Growing pensive once again, Turner slowly lifted his gaze. The shadows from his kepi fell away, revealing bright-blue eyes. "Why did you come? I mean, what does Brady hope to accomplish in all this?"

Sighing, Gabe threw the meager remnants of the cool coffee into the grass. "Brady wants to document the conflict, for as long as it lasts, as a historical record. Nothing more. Before sending me out, he kept saying, 'We learn who we were to decide who we want to be.'"

Turner grunted.

"Speaking for myself, I initially decided to come out of pure excitement. The opportunity to learn from the greatest photographer of our time, better my skills, and embark on a grand adventure seemed too good an opportunity to pass up. But now—" he swallowed as his throat constricted—"after seeing the carnage, I don't know." He frowned. "This conflict, the hate is so ugly. So hideously vile. I don't want to dwell on the cruelty. I'd rather capture beauty, as meager as it might be."

"Beauty amid all this?"

"Beauty can always be found if we train our eyes to see it."

Turner was silent as he shook the remaining drops from his cup into the grass. He stood slowly and leveled his gaze at Gabe. "I wish you the best."

"Thank you. Obviously I need someone to keep me out of mischief." He sobered. "And I definitely need a friend."

"Consider yourself to have both."

They shook hands, and as Turner departed for his tent, Gabe smiled.

A friend. A quirky, mysterious puzzle of a fellow, but a friend nonetheless.

Chapter 6

Cassie winced, shifting the fifty-pound pack across her back, wishing she could simply drop the cumbersome load and forge ahead with only her rifle. The relief from the oppressive weight would be a luxury. She dragged in a breath of muggy air, longing for one cool breeze to stir. Instead the heat hung heavy and thick.

Their regiment had marched through Virginia, melting into the thousands of Union troops preparing to make a stand against the Rebels just outside the capital. Cassie blinked against the sweat stinging her eyes as she stopped to catch her breath. Wave after wave of shimmering Union blue marched onward, resembling lapping waves of the ocean.

At her side, George groaned, rubbing his flat stomach with dirt-crusted fingers. "Ach, my stomach. Cursed dysentery."

Offering him a sympathetic glance, she shuffled along in the laborious march. "I heard a surgeon tell a nurse dysentery might be killing more soldiers than bullets or minié balls."

"I believe it. Hard to march when your stomach feels like it's going to fall out."

She nodded toward the trees and bramble lining the road. "Look for some blackberries. They will help."

With a renewed burst of energy, George broke formation to seek the treasured fruit.

"What is the poor boy going to do come winter when there is nary a blackberry to be found?"

Turning, she shrugged at Weeks as he clomped behind her, stirring up a cloud of dust. The statement was true enough. Little could be found to sate their already-shriveled stomachs. Coffee, beans, and hardtack only went so far. Meat was scarce and sometimes blue. Not fit for consumption, though some of the boys tried and regretted it with a vengeance later.

"I guess Providence will provide us the answer when we come to it."

Weeks wiped at the sweat trickling down his temple. "Either that, or we'll all be dead."

Briggs released a hearty laugh. "Not me! If I go down, I'm taking the whole blamed army of Johnny Rebs with me!"

The boisterous declaration brought cheers from those around him, but Cassie could not join their confident shouts. Unease niggled the pit of her stomach. Nerves? Perhaps. Fear? Most assuredly. Only a fool would go into battle unafraid. No, it was something more.

The clattering wheels of a barouche approached from the east, drawing their attention to the bouncing conveyance. The small forms of a man and woman perched atop the covered seat grew larger as they drew alongside the shuffling soldiers. The sleek Morgans tossed their glossy manes and pranced as if dancing through a parade. The driver, a portly man with a tall black hat and side-whiskers, waved at the soldiers. His voice boomed over the throng. "Well done, lads! Show Jeff Davis what the Union is made of!"

Cheers rose thick as dust. The woman wearing a dress resplendent with rows of lace and frills lifted her gaze from below her pert parasol. Upon seeing Thomas Turner, she blew a kiss from her gloved hand. Heat swept into Cassie's cheeks. If the debutante only knew . . .

Briggs's laughter cracked like cannon fire. "Turner! You've an admirer, you do!"

Cassie dropped her gaze to the churning dust of the road and ignored the jests.

Weeks dug his elbow into her side. "What'sa matter, Turner? It's not like you got a gal back home."

Cassie frowned. "It just seems like poor taste for the city dandies to parade around the troops and act so flippant."

Jackson, a soldier with dark hair and an easy smile, shrugged. "Maybe they're trying to lift our spirits."

"War is no garden party. It's life and death. I don't want any distractions."

The others fell silent at her muttered sentiment. She felt like a wet blanket but would not take back the thought. She had no desire to attract any attention, nor be distracted. By males or females alike.

Still, if the audacious debutante realized Private Thomas Turner was not a male at all . . .

The thought made her snicker.

The men gathered in small clumps, relishing the rest, however short it might be. Despite the urgency to get to the Confederate capital and capture Richmond, the colonel had found it difficult to move the large number of troops in a hasty manner. They had walked only twenty miles in the past two days. Heat shimmered from the earth in scorching waves.

Sitting on a fallen log by the road, Cassie rubbed her ankles, silently cursing the woolen socks that had chafed her skin raw.

Glancing across the weary bunch, she found little comfort in knowing she was not alone. Briggs's bluster had cooled into quiet exhaustion. Weeks looked ready to drop. George, having found no blackberries, held his cramping stomach, emitting occasional moans of misery. Cooper grimaced, yanking his swollen feet from his shoes. He rubbed his aching toes with a glower. Poor fellow—his boots had been nearly falling off when he enlisted, so the regiment gave him a pair. The problem was both boots were for left feet. No more matching pairs were to be had. Cooper had marched for days trying to convince a left boot it should fit his right foot.

The boot appeared to be winning.

Everyone looked done in. She glanced toward the annoying debutante and her pompous father, who refused to leave them be. Now the girl had her fluttering sights set on Gabriel Avery. Her high-pitched laughter drifted through the air, scraping at Cassie's nerves. Gabe was smiling, leaning in, and saying something that brought the girl's eyelashes into a fanning frenzy.

Something hot tightened Cassie's chest.

Briggs chuckled, snapping her attention to where it belonged . . . away from the nauseating pair. "Jealous, Turner?"

Cassie nearly sputtered. Jealous of Gabe talking with that dunderheaded slip of a—?

"Looks like your admirer has taken a shine to the photographer."

Cassie forced her muscles to relax. Why had she assumed Briggs was asking if she was jealous of the attention Gabe was lavishing on the pampered princess? "Nah. Ain't got time for females anyhow. Got a job to do."

"Hear, hear!" The men sitting nearby lifted fists in camaraderie, yet their careworn faces and shoulders drooped.

A fly buzzed near Cassie's ear and she swatted it away, frowning when Gabe finally tore himself from the simpering female hanging off his arm and approached the weary regiment sagging beside the road. He dropped into the dust beside their group, wiping his sweaty forehead with the sleeve of his shirt. "Canteens refilled and ready?"

Weeks lifted his own canteen and took a noisy slurp of water from it with a grin.

Briggs squinted against the sun beating down on their sweat-soaked kepis. "Looks like you could use a drink yourself, Avery. Or perhaps it was the charming company you've been keeping that's made your face all red. Quite a good show we've been watching."

Weeks chortled and Gabe smiled. Cassie dropped her gaze and refocused on her chafed ankles.

"The lady took an interest in Turner here, but he wouldn't give her the time of day."

Gabe lifted his brows high. Cassie ignored the teasing. Blasted woolen socks.

Weeks leaned forward. "Pretty thing, don't you think, Avery?"

He shrugged, and Cassie felt the twinge in her middle slowly evaporate.

"Pretty enough, I suppose. Seems a bit young, truth be told."

Cooper smirked. "Wouldn't matter to me none."

Gabe plucked at a straggly weed at his feet, tossing it away. "You don't have a girl, Cooper?"

Weeks snorted. "You smelled his feet lately? No lady in her right mind would sign up for that."

Cooper glared. "I suppose your feet smell like lilacs?"

Weeks smiled smugly. "My girl hasn't any complaints about the way I smell."

"If she were here, she would."

Cassie felt her mouth tugging upward at their silly jests.

Gabe nodded toward Briggs. "What about you, Briggs? Got yourself a woman?"

The man's wide, bearded face softened. "Sure do. My Moira's the prettiest thing you ever did see. Full of sass and pluck, too. Gave me a strapping son and two girls as beautiful as their ma."

Cassie paused and studied the faraway look in her friend's eyes. Big, exuberant, larger-than-life Briggs was smitten. That was plain to see. What would it be like to love and be loved with such devotion?

"How old are your children?" Gabe asked.

His eyes twinkled, chest puffed out in pride. "Seth will be twelve next week, and the girls are eight and six."

"And here I thought you were a crusty old bachelor. Haven't heard you mention them until now."

Smiling gently, Briggs patted his chest with a meaty paw. "I don't say much, but I carry them all in here."

Weeks frowned at a cluster of soldiers congregated on the far side of the road, milling around a couple of women, their faces all but obscured by the clutch of admirers. "Speaking of the fairer sex . . ."

Gabriel frowned. "Who are the men talking to?"

Weeks arched a brow. "Don't you know? Amid that throng are two females. Soiled doves, to be precise." Weeks lifted the brim of his kepi, revealing matted hair. "If you're looking for more, shall we say, *mature* female companionship, you might want to say hello."

Heat scorched Cassie's neck. She longed to flee. Her companions suddenly seemed dangerously, irrevocably male.

Gabe frowned. "I'll not be introducing myself." His face darkened.

"Not lonely, I take it."

Gabe stood, his jaw rigid. "Doesn't matter if I am or not. Women weren't meant to be treated in such a way. I couldn't stand before God if I did . . . nor could I live with myself." He offered a tight smile. "They'll be calling to move soon. I better get back to the darkroom."

He departed, leaving silence in his wake.

Cassie stared at his receding form and blinked. She'd never heard a man speak of women in such a way. As if they were meant to be cherished, not used. She'd certainly never seen it demonstrated in her own life.

Who was Gabriel Avery anyway?

The sun had not yet risen when it began.

Chaos. Screams. Torn flesh. Exploding earth. Sizzling bursts of gunpowder. Shaking so severe she feared her teeth would be rattled from their sockets. Acrid smoke. The gritty taste of sand and dirt. Ears buzzing into a numbing hum. Clapping booms of cannons and the shrill screech of shells. And blood. So much blood.

Death was everywhere.

Had the sun been snuffed out completely? It seemed so. Perhaps it was only the thick fog of smoke. Perhaps it was from the screams of agony that choked out all other sensations. Whatever the reason, light and all that was good in the world vanished.

Her own regiment had only just crossed the creek in Manassas when they were greeted with a volley of gunfire. Somehow, amid the din of exploding rifles and bone-jarring cannons, the colonel's sharp yell of "Left flank, march!" could still be heard.

After getting into position, she and her fellow soldiers hunkered down, ready to fight, when bullets began ripping through their ranks, picking off men like ducks on water. The shouts filtered down through the line: minié balls. The Rebels were hitting them with the cruelest weaponry known to human flesh. A bullet that flattened when it struck bodies, ripping apart both muscle and tendon while shattering bone.

The whistling shriek of cannons sliced overhead, and Cassie crouched lower, tearing open another powder cartridge with her teeth and spitting the acrid taste into the dirt. A cannonball hit nearby, plowing through the ground. The world tilted on its axis.

Somewhere in the distance, drums rat-tat-tatted the signal to engage. All she could muster was one primal desire. *Survive.* Nothing more.

A large tree crashed to her left, and screaming soldiers attempted to flee as its splintered top careened to earth. Gun ready, she licked her lips and aimed for anything foolish enough to be wearing gray. Farther down the line, she could hear Briggs yelling, "I got a bullet for you Johnny Rebs, sent straight from Lincoln himself!"

Soldiers paired up and carried stretchers between them, ducking and weaving through the melee to rescue wounded men. Not more than twenty feet from her, the runners spirited away a wounded soldier whose face had been nearly ripped off. On her left, a fellow soldier saw it and vomited.

Don't look. Load and fire. Load and fire.

She had just hunkered back down to reload when George screamed to her right. His body was propelled backward as if he were nothing more than a shirt on a clothesline, flapping helplessly against a blast of wind.

"George!"

She heard the scream, only faintly realizing it was her own. The earth trembled beneath her as she scrambled to his side.

He coughed and moaned, "Chest . . ."

Not even bothering to look, she hooked his arm around her neck and dragged him toward the surgical tent. Dirt and rock exploded around her. Her muscles burned like fire as she slunk across the battered, torn earth, heaving his deadweight with her.

Silence suddenly eclipsed the tumult and she knew there was little time.

Throwing herself over George's limp form, she felt the ground fall away beneath her. Her body exploded in pain as she was dropped back to the ground.

A piercing whistle whined in her ears and she blinked. She could see bursts of gunfire from muskets and rifles, saw trees bend and snap. She could see the shouts forming on mouths and lips, but no sound issued forth. Everything seemed to have slowed, like her body was trapped in molasses.

The cannonball had landed far too close.

Shaking off the numb, dizzying sensations, she hooked George's arm around her neck once more and trudged forward, every muscle in her body screaming for relief. Sound, shouts slowly filtered back into her consciousness.

The dirt-sprayed canvas tent soon flapped before her eyes. With a cry of relief, she lugged George inside and collapsed, thankful for the strong hands that lifted her burden onto a waiting cot.

She could hear the surgeon issuing commands to a nurse, his voice faint. *"Bullet to the chest . . ."*

"Lucky to be alive."

"I've never seen anything like it."

Fearing her friend was close to the end, she finally found her footing despite her quivering legs and pulled herself upright.

She moved to his side, but instead of the blood-soaked chest she expected to see, George was actually awake. Pale but . . . smiling?

Blinking, she looked at his exposed chest. A giant red mark covered his heart. Dark bruises were already forming.

A voice near her ear startled her. "You the man who brought him here?"

Nodding dumbly, she stared at the surgeon, wondering at the odd smile that ghosted his mouth. "I don't understand. I thought George took a bullet to the chest."

"He most assuredly did. Providence, however, was looking out for him." The doctor fumbled through George's discarded shirt and pulled out a small book. A pocket Bible—with a bullet lodged squarely in its middle.

Gasping, she looked back at George's sweaty, powder-streaked face. He offered a weak grin. "I promised Ma I'd keep my Bible in my shirt pocket at all times."

Cassie's breath was light with amazement. "Trust you to take Proverbs 3 literally."

"What does it say?" His voice was raspy.

She felt herself smile. "Verses 1 and 2 say, 'My son, forget not my law; but let thine heart keep my commandments: For length of days, and long life, and peace, shall they add to thee.'"

He laughed and then moaned, curling his legs up to his torso.

George would live.

Before she could think past that fact, stretcher poles were thrust into her hands and she was ordered to retrieve the wounded.

The task suited her fine because, after today, she didn't know if she could ever again point a gun and pull the trigger. Such a feat might be forever beyond her.

Chapter 7

GABE'S THROAT CONSTRICTED AS HE STOOD STILL, trying to comprehend the magnitude of the carnage laid out before him.

It was as if God's hand had reached down and fisted earth, trees, and people and uprooted all, yanking them from the solid earth with a rip and then dropping them with a sudden fury.

Bloody bodies lay in mangled heaps. Limbs were twisted; bones jutted at odd angles. Cannonballs, bullets, minié balls, fire—all of it had plowed through the earth, leaving only shattered, charred remains behind.

A thin haze of smoke still hovered over the gruesome landscape, filling his nose with its acrid stench. Weak cries drifted from those yet defying the clawing arms of death.

Gabe ducked below the black curtain and peered through the lens before snapping the plate into place for exposure. He repositioned the cumbersome camera and tripod, lugging them over stone and scarred soil, between blood and limbs, exposing plate after plate as fast as he dared.

Don't think. Look, frame, drop in the plate, remove the lens cover, count. . . . One, two, three, four, five, six, seven . . .

Over and over he repeated the motions, and with every plate he exposed, the nauseating sights before him embedded deeper into his soul, wedging like splinters in his mind.

When his plate box was full, he wiped the sweat from his temple and kneaded his eyes with the balls of his palms. For a moment the horror disappeared. From his eyes at least. Not his heart.

Heaving a shallow breath, he scanned the scarred ground a final time, looking for anything he might have missed. A few ambulance soldiers remained, weaving through the carnage for the last of the living.

He walked slowly toward the closest one and lifted a hand in greeting when the soldier looked up. Private Turner. The weary man's face was streaked with grime, but his eyes revealed gratefulness for a moment to catch his breath.

"Need any help?"

Turner rubbed his eyes with slim fingers and shook his head. "Thank you, no. I think we got them all, but I keep coming back. Looking. Hoping . . ."

Gabe nodded, his throat thick. "I'll help you."

Abandoning the stretcher in the middle of the field, they walked. Checking necks for pulses. The rise of a chest. A muted moan. But all was still and silent.

As he rose from the form of a fallen soldier whose right arm was completely missing, Gabe sighed, but his gaze latched on to something he'd missed. A scrap of yellow in the midst of the field of death.

Moving toward the sight, he felt a warmth unfurl in his chest that eased the heaviness. "Well, I'll be."

Turner came to his side. "What is it?"

He pointed, a faint smile lifting his lips. "Look."

There in the bloody, trampled field cradling mangled bodies, a lone dandelion stood, its bit of yellow a single ray of sunshine amid misery and decay.

Kneeling down, he lightly ran his fingertips over its feathery top. The leaves were wilted but the flower was mostly unscathed. A memory of his mother pierced the shadowed fog of his mind.

"I was only a boy of seven or eight, walking with Mither down the street in New York." He could yet hear the way her boots had clicked sharply against the cracked pavement. Could still smell the smoke from fireplaces, the spicy sausage hanging in the butcher shop, the scent of baking bread mingled with the stink of refuse and urine as they passed alley after alley. Her brown skirt swished against his side when she'd halted.

"I remember her stopping to point at a flower. She said, 'Look there, Gabriel. What do you see?' I squinted and saw a dandelion popping through the cracked concrete of an insurance building. 'It's a flower.'" He smiled softly at the memory. "'Aye,' Mither said. 'A dandelion. Do you know what that means?' I had no idea. She pulled me closer and said, 'Wherever dandelions bloom in mortar, it reminds us hope is still alive.'"

Turner sucked in a breath and knelt beside him. "How did it survive all this?"

"I don't know. But where dandelions bloom, hope remains."

———— • ————

Cassie tugged a bleeding soldier onto a torn litter. Balls of fire exploded overhead. Soldiers were flung backward as gunfire pelted their bodies. And then she heard it.

Her father. Laughing. Not the sweet, pleasant sound she vaguely remembered and had clung to from her early youth, before the bottle had completely snuffed out the remnants of gentleness from his soul. No, this was a dark, deranged laughter . . . a mirthless sound that dripped poison.

Through the hail of flying bullets, smoke, and plunging bayonets, she could see him. He stood in the midst of the screaming Rebels, his eyes glittering with something that caused her courage to scatter like dust.

She dropped the dying soldier's weight at her feet and turned to flee, her steps slow and thick. He was chasing her, his laughter growing louder, shriller. Why wouldn't her feet move faster?

Her boot snagged on something. A gnarled tree root? A rock? Her body pitched forward. The loamy earth rose up to meet her. She was falling, falling . . .

She gasped, her senses roaring to life in the darkness.

Thump. Thump. Thump. Thump.

Her heart beat a staccato rhythm as she gulped for air. Or was it the dull thump of deadly cannon fire? She couldn't tell reality from her nightmares anymore.

It was only a dream. Only a dream . . .

Cold sweat clung to the binding around her chest, and she lay still in the tent listening to the snores and steady breathing of the other soldiers. Usually she volunteered for cleanup duty or some such chore when the others retired, allowing her to slip in unnoticed well after the men were deep in slumber. A simple safeguard to keep her identity from being discovered.

After the past harrowing days, however, her body could take no more. As soon as the call to sleep had sounded, she'd crawled into the tent and collapsed on her bedroll. She'd snagged several hours of rest, but the screams of dying men, the hellish screech of the Rebels, and the dull pounding of cannons filtered into nightmares.

Yet despite the horrors now firmly ensconced in her heart and mind, it was not the piercing thrust from a Confederate bayonet that had awakened her, nor was it the terror of dragging man after man away from the fields of death, watching their mangled bodies and hearing their cries for mercy. No, the horror that had awakened her was the thought of her father—mocking, hurting. Maiming her battered heart all over again.

She rolled onto her side and curled into a ball as a thick knot lodged itself in her throat. The bedroll was scratchy against her cheek.

She had traded one hell for another.

Clutching a fistful of the blanket, she thought of her tattered quilt at home and for the first time missed it to the point of aching.

She had abandoned Mother to her husband's cruel, slicing temper. And Granny Ardie—who was watching over her? Certainly not her son-in-law, who was only interested in gambling and his cursed bottle.

What had Granny endured when they'd discovered Cassie was gone? Shock? Betrayal?

A broken shard of Father's belligerent laugh sliced through her tumbling emotions, resurrecting the nightmare once more.

Cassie pinched her eyes shut, but a new thought invaded. Had he had taken out his fury on Mother or Granny? Surely he had been enraged. She had rarely seen him calm or rational. If he'd hurt them because of her own foolish decision . . .

She swallowed and tucked her face against her bent arm. Growing up, she'd always thought her family was normal. How wrong she'd been. How different from Gabriel's. When his mother saw dandelions, she told him of hope. When Cassie had made a crown of dandelions as a child, Father had yanked it from her head with a growl, snagging threads of her hair in the process, and flung it to the ground. Remnants of the yellow petals remained crushed between his fingers as he waved his fist through the air.

"Weeds, Cassandra. You're not a princess, and you never will be. Get those fool notions out of your head. You're playing dress up with a crown of weeds."

Her throat thickened. He was right. Look at her now.

The memory of Granny's cracking voice whispered in her ear, as clear as if she were present. Amid the soft snores of exhausted soldiers, Cassie could picture her opening the pages of her worn Bible and reading the passage aloud. *"And be ye kind one to another, tenderhearted, forgiving one another, even as God for Christ's sake hath forgiven you. . . ."*

Forgive her father? The thought rankled, rubbing her raw heart until it felt shredded.

Forgive her father. Forgive herself. Both thoughts stung. Both felt impossible.

How to rid herself of the hurt? The guilt and anger? She was weary of dragging the heaviness with her. Tired of the nightmares, yet she had no idea how to grasp freedom from the pain.

God, how do I forgive such a man? How do I forgive my father?

Chapter 8

The banjo plinked a meandering tune as the regiment sprawled throughout the camp. Some wrote letters home. Others scattered into the meadow beyond, enjoying a leisurely game of baseball during the late-afternoon lull. A few had begun preparations for the evening meal while another group stood on picket duty, wilting under July's oppressive heat.

Gabe studied the pasteboards in his hand and yawned, the heat rendering him drowsy and limp.

Selby grinned triumphantly and threw down his hand. "Flush, boys. Pay up."

The men let out a chorus of groans and dropped their own cards in disgust.

"How many does that make for you, Selby? Three wins?"

"Four." The swarthy soldier smiled, his eyes twinkling. "But who's counting?"

Chuckling, Gabe opened his knapsack and tossed Selby the required payment . . . a square of hardtack.

Selby caught the unforgiving portions being tossed toward him with a laugh. "Weeks, your hardtack ain't full of maggots, is it?"

Weeks stretched lazily and scratched his head. "Not last I checked. I wouldn't know—not since we've been camped out here for a few days enjoying salt pork and beans."

Though the sandy-haired soldier appeared as relaxed as a cat in sunshine, Gabe knew many Union soldiers had defected completely or spent their free hours drinking rotgut in the local saloons. It was as if the entire Union army had the starch taken out of its resolve and flailed miserably as a result.

The quiet time had allowed him to develop the photographs of Bull Run in haste and deliver them by hand to Brady's Washington gallery, a luxury that might not be afforded in the future. Brady had seemed pleased with the prints until he saw the one of the poor soldier whose legs had been broken and pulverized into bone flecks and blood as he lay in the middle of the combat field.

Shrouded by a somber cloud, Brady pulled the spectacles from his nose, the lines deepening around his eyes. "Such things no man should ever behold . . . or suffer."

Gabe blinked away the memory. He'd sought something noble to capture, some remnant of life, but there had been nothing in that wasteland of scarred earth save for the lone dandelion.

Swallowing the knot in his throat, he forced a smile when Cooper asked if he was in for another round. He nodded toward Turner, who sat propped against the trunk of a wide tree. "Only if Turner will join us."

Briggs guffawed as he shuffled the wrinkled pasteboards.

"Turner ain't nothing but a young pup. He ain't joined us in a game yet." His dark beard tugged upward as he smiled. "Smart lad. He knows we would strip him down to his drawers given half a chance."

As the others laughed, Turner took his thumb and lifted the brim of his kepi. Those bright-blue eyes of his sparked. "If you're playing for hardtack and end up losing your drawers, you got bigger problems than being whipped by a pup."

Gabe grinned at the uncharacteristic barb from the normally quiet fellow. The others elbowed Briggs, who tossed Turner a challenge.

"Want me to deal you in or are you too busy napping?"

Straightening his hat, Turner slid him a lopsided smirk. "Deal me in. Losing hardtack won't make me lose a wink of sleep."

The *slip, slip, slip* of pasteboards from Briggs's fingers was a comforting sound among the chirp of birds and buzzing bees. As each of them studied their cards, Weeks's voice was soft. "How many do you think have deserted?"

Jackson grunted. "Too many."

Turner lifted his eyes to the group. "Hopefully not for long."

Pasteboards forgotten, Cooper leaned forward. "Why? What did you hear?"

Turner studied his cards. "I hear President Lincoln may have a new general for us."

Selby's eyes rounded. "Any word on who?"

Turner shrugged. "There's a rumor going around that it might be George McClellan."

Briggs whistled low. "Is it wrong to pray such a thing comes true?"

"Nothing wrong with wanting to see our troops drilling and fighting again instead of seeking out loose women and whiskey."

Cooper snorted. "Both are good company, but whiskey hasn't won a war, and certainly women never did."

Gabe startled when Turner flipped down his cards with a smug flourish. "Can anyone beat a full house? No, of course not. I can tell since you've all been displaying your pasteboards while I shared the latest piece of news."

Gabe glanced down at his hand. Sure enough, his normally guarded cards were tilted forward, forgotten in his fingers. Looking around the group, he saw the other men's necks redden as they realized they'd made the same mistake.

With a sly grin, Turner stood. "Keep your hardtack, gentlemen." He turned on his heel to leave but looked back over his shoulder. "Whether it be whiskey, women, or young pups, if I were you, I wouldn't underestimate any of the three."

He left with a confident swagger as the men burst into laughter.

Gabe leaned over the creek running south of the camp and splashed cool water over his heated face, relishing the respite from summer's sticky warmth. Water dripped from his chin. He ran his fingers over his prickly jaw. The stubble was long enough to warrant calling it a beard. He should shave soon or pick up arms with the scruffy soldiers he trailed.

The thought was amusing. He could aim a lens but not much else. He admired the pluck and courage of the men who had remained steadfast despite the tumultuous upheaval after the blistering defeat at Bull Run. Scooping up another handful of water, he doused his neck, allowing the rivulets to run under the collar of his shirt.

They were heroes all. And it was his privilege to capture their stalwart courage through glass plates, lenses, light, and chemicals. A testament to their bravery for generations ahead to laud.

Brady's praise of his latest images brushed through his mind. "With your permission, I may submit several of these to newspapers that have been clamoring for photographs from the battlefield." Brady had patted his back and smiled behind his spectacles. "You may be famous when it's all said and done, Gabriel."

"You may be famous when it's all said and done . . ."

Gabe couldn't deny his pleasure at the thought. Could he really? The son of Scottish immigrants who'd lived on the edge of the Five Points slum—could someone like him really make his mark on the world?

The thought was invigorating.

Fame would lead to more opportunities. More privileges. More money.

The temptations that could result filtered through his mind like sand through a sieve. He glanced back through the thick cover of trees to study the boxy outline of the Whatsit squatting in the cool shade. His photography studio. A swaying box on wheels, filled with glass plates, silver nitrate, clattering equipment, and brown vials brimming with sharp-smelling liquids. He'd been so proud of it weeks ago, though he knew its odd shape and presence was a matter of curiosity for many of the soldiers, an object of ridicule from others.

Discontent rose in his chest, warring with the possibility of future fame and grandeur. Someday his establishment wouldn't be on wheels and dragged from post to post by barn-sour mares. No, he would have a studio. A grand one. Maybe almost as grand as Brady's.

Da's rumbly voice from long ago invaded, scattering the puffed thoughts like a hard breath through curls of smoke. *"Contentment, Gabriel."*

He'd watched his da's large, calloused hands as he whittled

and carved, slicing his blade through the soft wood, dropping curls of pine onto the pile at his feet.

"But Collin Spence has the best aggie I've ever laid eyes on. He always has the best jacks and even has a store-bought baseball. I want one too, Da."

Da's eyes were stern, though the whisper of a smile curved his mouth. "Aye, young Collin has been blessed. But then again, so have you. You have all you need, plus some."

"But an aggie like that . . ."

The quiet scrape of knife into pine never stopped. "Gabriel, 'godliness with contentment is great gain. . . .'"

The memory brought tenderness. And a sting. Sighing, Gabe scooped up another handful of water and drank, his thoughts tumbling.

A footfall sounded through the bramble, snapping twigs and shifting rocks.

Looking up, Gabe spied Turner approaching the creek, though the fellow hadn't yet seen him. Here was a man whose story needed to be told, but the quirky fellow kept it locked away, sealed and impenetrable.

Gabe watched him yank off his kepi and kneel at the water's edge. Dark hair spilled out, brushing his shoulders. Gabe studied him, wondering why Turner was so blasted quiet. For though the soldier spoke little, his intelligence and courage were keen. And at times, Turner seemed lonely, palpably so.

"Cooling off?"

Turner suddenly stood and yanked the kepi down over his head fast as a musket flash, whirling toward Gabe. Gabe puzzled at the reaction. Turner was acting as if he'd been caught in a transgression. But the man had a right to drink and be refreshed, didn't he?

Maybe he was snappish, fearing an enemy had snuck up behind him. War made a man jumpy.

Raising his hands with a small smile, Gabe chuckled. "It's only me. No need for alarm."

Turner's shoulders relaxed, though his face retained traces of suspicion. "What are you doing down here?"

Gabe shrugged and eased back into the grasses lining the muddy creek bank. "Same as you. Getting a drink. Enjoying the quiet."

Turner grimaced and sat down, tucking his knees to his chest as he surveyed the gentle gurgle of the water washing over boulders. Plucking a nearby pebble between his fingers, he flung it across the creek, watching as it skimmed the water one, two, three times before sinking below with a faint plop. "Who could have imagined the entire Union army so demoralized in just a few short months?"

Gabe grunted, feeling Turner's frustration. "How do you account for it?"

Tossing another pebble, the young man murmured, "Fear, trauma, lack of leadership . . . probably all three." He shook his head. "We need McClellan before the whole army disintegrates."

"I agree."

They fell silent and Gabe studied the man's profile. No, not a man. A boy. Turner couldn't be more than eighteen at best. His skin was still smooth, his voice light, yet his demeanor made him appear older. Wiser.

"That was quite a masterful turn of the cards earlier."

"Wasn't too hard. All that group needs is a good distraction and they forget what they're doing." Straight white teeth flashed in his face. "Like keeping their cards from prying eyes."

Gabe watched a hawk dip and float across the creek bank.

"Still, you've gotten to know your fellow soldiers pretty well in a short time."

Turner looked away with a shrug. "It's not hard. Not really. Especially when you make a habit to watch much and speak little."

"Watching a person reveals their character, eh?"

"Something like that."

They fell silent. What made this young man who he was? What were his dreams? Did he have family?

"Penny for your thoughts."

Turner frowned and stared at a pebble he held, rubbing its smooth surface in circles with the pad of his thumb but stayed silent, his eyes fixed on something Gabe could not see.

"What are you pondering?"

Sighing, Turner dropped the pebble. "Forgiveness."

The answer surprised him. No fluff or polite niceties for this fellow. He showed his soul or nothing at all.

Gabe flicked away an ant that was attempting to crawl up his trouser leg. "Hard thing to do sometimes."

"Very."

A small word, but it held so much meaning.

"You needing to forgive yourself or someone else?"

Turner's voice was so soft, Gabe almost missed his answer. "Both."

"What's holding you back?"

Turner dropped his head and mumbled, his shoulders sagging. "I don't know how."

Gabe fell silent. He doubted the soldier had ever been so vulnerable with another in his regiment, and he had no intention of rubbing salt in a wound with an ill-timed comment. So he'd just listen.

The steady trickle of the lazy water's flow, the hum of bees and flies, the chatter of birds and squirrels mellowed the warm air until sleepiness crept over him like a shadow. Perhaps that was the reason Turner's direct gaze and question startled him.

"Have you ever had to forgive someone?"

He offered a lopsided smile. "Yes. My father. God, too."

Turner's brows rose in an unspoken question.

Gabe yanked down the edge of his left shirt collar, revealing the white scar that lined the base of his neck. It was not as thick as it had once been, but it was still present. A reminder of what had happened. "My da was a great man. A wise and a kind one. Me being the only babe, well—" Gabe shrugged—"he doted on me. Took good care of Mither too."

Turner's face was a mask, his expression unreadable.

"I was only a young man when he started slipping. No more than sixteen or so, I'd say. Da started acting strangely. He confused easily. Couldn't remember simple things. But when he started forgetting memories from long ago, things that had been locked in his heart for decades—" Gabe paused, reliving the pain—"that's when we knew. Something was wrong."

"What happened?"

"He began losing his mind. Mania, the doctor said." His heart scraped raw as old emotions resurfaced, throbbing with a hollow ache.

"How did you get that scar?"

Gabe released the fabric of his shirt collar and let it settle back into place, almost as if he could hide Da's violence. Such a thought was foolish. His father couldn't help it.

He plucked a long blade of grass and folded it edge over edge between his fingers. "I was attempting to give him his medicine and he snapped." He swallowed. "Maybe I moved too quickly. I don't know. Somehow Da had managed to hide a knife in his trousers. Before I knew what was happening, he lunged at me, screaming like the devil himself."

Turner winced.

"I must have blacked out because when I awoke, the sanitarium was hauling Da away and Mither was crying, trying to attend to both of us at once." His throat cramped. "It's a moment I never want to relive. I try to think of it as little as possible." He released a thick sigh. "The point is, that moment made me angry with Da for a time. I couldn't understand him. Couldn't understand why my hero had failed me. To make matters worse, with Da so sick, Mither was forced to get a job in a factory. I did as well. But the long hours, the exhaustion—" he shook his head—"the strain of it, along with the heartbreak of losing Da not long after he'd been sent to the sanitarium, did her in. She died only two years after my father." Pitching the rumpled grass to the ground, he looked directly at Turner. "To be honest, I was angry with God for allowing it to happen."

Turner frowned and looked away. "What changed?"

Watching the gliding arc of a sparrow, he lifted a shoulder. "Got tired of fighting God. What I realized, what I tell myself still, is that Da was sick. He didn't know what he was doing."

Turner laughed dryly, his face darkening. "Our situations aren't the same. The one who hurt me knew what he was doing. Made choice after choice to do so. He destroyed the lives of everyone around him and caused misery everywhere he went." He scowled. "He doesn't deserve forgiveness. I can't."

Silence stretched loud and thick.

Gabe stood slowly. "All I know is that forgiving gave me peace. It was like cutting myself free from a hundred-pound burden." He brightened, trying to chase away the dark clouds hovering between them. "Say, would you like a tour of the Whatsit? No one else has asked to see it and I'm eager to show it off."

Turner smiled. "Lead the way."

———— ◆ ————

Cassie smiled as Gabe showed her every single compartment of his traveling darkroom. His excitement and chatter had lightened her dark mood considerably.

As she stood in the small space, listening to him explain what each chemical was used for, she realized just how green his eyes were. They gleamed like gemstones when he was animated. His shoulders were wide—muscular but not bulky. The golden highlights in his sandy hair gleamed when the lamplight hit them just so . . . and his smile. Heavens, his smile could melt a heart . . . if the heart were so inclined. Golden stubble glinted in the lamplight. His jaw was strong.

With a start, she realized he was staring at her with raised brows, his face expectant. Heat rushed up her neck. He had asked her something and she was standing mute. Acting like . . .

Shaking the ridiculous thought away, she cleared her throat. "Pardon? I was so busy trying to take everything in, I missed your question."

He smiled again and her stomach lurched unexpectedly. Odd sensation.

"I asked if the smells bother you."

"No." She wrinkled her nose. "Not any more than Cook's beans."

Faint lines crinkled around his eyes as he laughed. Her pulse kicked.

"Mixing up collodion is foul-smelling business. Ethyl alcohol and sulfuric acid stink like death to begin with." He winked. "If I ever disappear, check the Whatsit. It's likely I have passed out from the odor."

She laughed lightly and caught herself, praying it didn't sound feminine. She must maintain her identity. She was Thomas Turner. Thomas. Thomas . . .

Swallowing down her nervousness, she pointed at another chemical vial. "And what is in that?"

"That, Private Turner, is silver nitrate."

"Isn't that used as a cauterizing agent?"

"It can be, but not for the wet-plate process."

Her interest piqued, she leaned forward, studying the odd array of vials, bottles, glass plates, varnishes, and papers scattered across the small table. "How does it work?"

"I hand-mix the ether with ethyl alcohol to make a solution called collodion and coat a glass plate with it. It sensitizes the plate to light. Then I immerse the plate in silver nitrate and place it in that large plate box over there." He pointed to a container enforced with brass corners. "Just don't get the silver nitrate on your skin. It will turn it brown or black. All the chemicals have to be mixed in here with as little light as possible or the photograph will be ruined before it's ever exposed."

"Hard to do in the darkness."

Gabriel chuckled. "Even harder to do with cannons shaking the whole blasted wagon apart."

She hadn't thought of that. "So you put the plates inside the camera?"

"Yes. Under the black curtain connected to the camera, I pull out a wet plate, drop it into the camera, and when I've decided the time is right, I remove the lens cap to expose the plate to light."

"For how long?"

He shrugged. "It depends on the light. Not usually more than three to five seconds, but it can take longer. Then I put the plates back in the box to protect them until I can bring them back here, where I develop them. I wash and dry each plate with water, then coat it with varnish to protect it."

Incredible. "So much work for one photograph."

"Ah, but that's the beauty of it. Once the glass plate negative is finished, the image can be printed on paper over and over again."

She blinked. "Amazing."

He leaned against the wall and crossed his arms. "Thanks to Mr. Brady, we can capture moments of eternal importance. We can offer comfort to families and sweethearts missing their men. We can help newspapers accurately report the truth."

"I had no idea it involved so much."

"So, my friend—" Gabe arched a sandy brow—"I know I tried your patience terribly that first battle, what with you having to save me." He smirked. "Was it worth it?"

Chuckling, Cassie picked up a bottle of silver nitrate and studied it carefully before placing it back on the table. "I had my doubts about you at first, but I think you've won me over."

She couldn't help but return his smile when the corners of his eyes crinkled once more.

"Well, that's one. Now for the rest of the regiment."

Cassie's paralyzed tongue couldn't say what she was thinking. Gabriel Avery had already won over everyone he'd met. And now he'd wormed his way into a reluctant friendship with her as well.

For some strange reason, the thought terrified her.

Chapter 9

JULY 31, 1861

Cassie tried not to devour the salt pork, corn bread, and beans on her tin plate, but her resolve weakened as her stomach greedily cramped for more. Judging by the slurps and belches from her fellow soldiers, all of them suffered from the same hunger.

Since General McClellan had taken over, order had been restored. Blessed routine and drills. Regimented time and rules. Precision. She welcomed the change. The chaos after Bull Run had almost been the Union's undoing.

Yet endless hours of drilling had worked them all to their breaking point. They were exhausted, falling into their tents each night, asleep before their heads hit the bedrolls. And they were all ravenous. It seemed as if their appetites could never be sated. Some of the men complained of loose teeth, a sure sign of scurvy. She'd not felt the signs and prayed the cursed malady would not be another cross to carry. War was difficult enough.

Sponging droplets of bean juice off her plate with the final chunk of corn bread, she popped the bite in her mouth and eased back with a contented sigh. She scanned the wide expanse of ground and found her own regiment easy to locate. Briggs's booming laugh marked their location. But the never-ending hum of conversation reminded her they were no longer a small band of soldiers. No, they had been siphoned into a massive army . . . an army of blue.

During drills, she was surrounded by new faces. At meals, the stern-faced men were always different. So many soldiers. She felt swallowed up, lost in a sea of anonymity. She rose and walked toward her familiar friends. They were her sole anchors amid the crush of soldiers.

At least the Second Michigan regiment mostly stayed together. They had built a camaraderie over the past couple months. It would be a shame to see them severed and scattered.

As she approached, Weeks hiccuped and picked his teeth with a blackened fingernail.

Briggs shoved a knife Weeks's direction. "Fancy an Arkansas toothpick? It's a mite easier to use than your fingers."

Weeks nodded his thanks. "Any word from your missus?"

Briggs scowled as he held his uniform coat over the snapping fire. The *pop*, *pop*, *pop* sound confirmed the lice crawling through the fabric were meeting a swift death from the blast of heat. "I have, not that it's any of your concern, what with you being wet behind the ears and all."

Weeks leaned back and tucked his hands behind his head, using a chopped log as a back support. "I ain't a pup, you know. Me and my girl might as well be engaged."

Jackson chuckled and scoured his tin plate with sand, buffing it with a stream of his spit for good measure. "Might-as-well-be and engaged are two different things. You too yellow to ask her?"

Weeks sniffed. "Don't wanna ask her in a letter. I want to be there in person. Besides," he snorted, "Little Mac's been keeping us so busy there's not much time left to woo our women, even by letter. I ain't never been so tired in my life."

George grunted. "Don't I know it. Just healed up from Bull Run and the captain has me felling logs and drilling like I'm fresh meat."

Briggs lit a pipe and flicked the match into the grass, stomping out the curl of smoke with the toe of his boot. Tiny wisps of white escaped through his nostrils as he puffed a white cloud with a soft *bop*. "Little Mac's tough, but we're better soldiers for him. Maybe when we face Johnny Reb again, we'll show 'em what we're made of."

Jackson nodded toward an approaching figure illuminated by the glow of sparks spiraling upward from nearby fires. Dusk had turned the sky to coal, yet the feeble light shone against a silhouette growing larger as he neared. "Looks like the photographer is coming this way."

Cassie looked down, hating the pleasure that filled her chest. Since Gabe had shown her his traveling darkroom, they'd talked continually. He was always seeking her out, asking for Thomas's opinion on interesting photographic possibilities and the best weapon to use in combat, as well as sharing all manner of interesting, humorous stories. Cassie had realized she didn't mind his chatter and chumming in the least. In fact, she was quite fond of his banter and lighthearted tales and found herself looking forward to their chats more than she ought. She needed to melt into the obscurity of nameless men fighting in the great conflict, not become buddies with an observant fellow who loved to talk.

Letting him get close, even while trying to keep him at arm's length, was too risky. If she were discovered . . .

Sand coated her throat, congealing into a lump so hard, it was like she'd swallowed one of Weeks's playing dice. She could not go back home.

Briggs's deep voice intruded. "You two have been thick as thieves lately, Turner. You finally warmed up to him, eh?"

She picked at the shredding sole of her tattered boot. "He's a good friend. And he does most of the talking, which suits me fine."

Briggs yanked off his kepi and ran his thick fingers through his shock of black hair. "That's the truth. He loves to talk. I ain't never seen a man who attracts folks to him more than Gabriel Avery. He's a good sort."

Before she could comment, her gaze snagged on the solitary figure of a young boy two fires over. He was alone, poking at his popping fire with a long stick. His back was hunched over as he sat on his haunches. No figure ever seemed so lonely.

She nodded in the boy's direction. "Any of you know that fellow over there?"

The group turned to look but collectively shook their heads. Weeks frowned. "There's thousands camped out here and you're asking about a mite like that?"

For some reason, Cassie was unable to take her eyes off the spindly lad. "Just seems on the young side, is all."

Something tightened in her chest as she watched him list-lessly stir the fire. Sparks shot up into the night. She rose and headed in his direction.

Briggs called, "Hey! Where you going? We're gonna teach Gabe chuck-a-luck."

She forged ahead, shouting over her shoulder, "You go ahead. I'll be back."

Leaving their grumbling behind, she picked her way over the dark terrain, mumbling in irritation when her boot turned in a snake hole. At her approach, the boy scowled. She'd thought he was perhaps thirteen when she'd seen him across the way. But this lad couldn't be more than nine or ten. She eased down next to him in the damp grass but stayed silent as he prodded the fire.

"You need something, mister?"

Smiling at the huffy tone, Cassie shrugged. "Just a bit lonely for some company, is all. That is, if you're agreeable."

With a sniff, the little soldier replied, "I reckon that would be all right. Just don't go jawing all night."

She managed a serious nod. "My name's Thomas Turner." She stuck out her hand, and after a moment's hesitation, the scruffy boy offered his own sunburned paw.

"Jonah Phifer."

"Nice to meet you, Jonah."

Grunt.

"Where you from?"

"Missouri." He wiped his nose with the back of his hand. "You?"

"Michigan."

Silence.

The gruff tone melted away as Jonah blinked at her in the light of the dancing fire. "Does it get cold up there?"

"Very."

Blond hair peeked out from underneath the brim of his kepi. "We get some snow, but I've always wanted to see a great big bully snow. Snow so deep you can build a house out of it and live like them Eskimos I've heard about."

"We get snow deep enough to do that."

His chest puffed out. "Of course, I'm used to the heat and humidity too. Our summers are tough. They'll make a man out of ya." Shooting her a haughty glance, he lifted a brow. "Something Michigan types don't know much about."

So much pride packed into such a tiny body. She kept her face serious. "You're right. I'm not used to this heat. I feel sticky all the time."

Jonah barked a sudden laugh. "My buddy Wes says stepping outside in the air during July is like getting licked in the face by a slobbering cow."

Cassie's chest bloomed with pleasure as she laughed along with him. What a funny little boy.

"How old are you, Jonah?"

"I'm ten." He raised his chin as if daring her to refute him.

Cassie grunted. "Hmm. I would have guessed thirteen or fourteen." A wispy expression of pleasure hovered over Jonah's mouth. "What's your job, soldier?"

"Errand boy." He frowned. "I was wanting to be a powder monkey for the navy. Trained for it and everything, but I couldn't get my sea legs." He sighed melodramatically. "I sure was looking forward to blowing stuff up."

She suppressed the mirth bubbling for release. "Sounds like an interesting job . . . if you take away the queasy stomach."

Jonah tossed a rock into the fire and smiled with satisfaction when it made the logs shift, causing the wood to snap and whistle. "I like that sound. What makes burning wood whistle like that?"

"Don't know."

"Me neither."

Silence.

"How did you manage to enlist? Being underage and all?"

Jonah's face turned dark. "Schoolmaster Howe encouraged the recruitment officers to give me a try. They take on drummer boys, so why not?" His little jaw tightened. "I'm an orphan." He turned to her with a scowl. "That don't make me lonely or sad or anything like that, you know."

"Of course not."

Straightening his spindly shoulders, Jonah scratched the straw-colored hair crammed under his kepi. "No, Howe thought he was getting rid of me, but what he didn't know was that I hoped to join up. I *wanted* to join up." Jonah glowered. "I was thrilled to get away from that old man."

"I take it you two didn't see eye to eye."

"No, sir." Jonah shook his head. "He hated me and I hated him."

"Why?"

He shrugged. "Don't know. He called me a poor little orphan boy a lot, and that made me fighting mad. Also called me the devil's son from time to time." Jonah turned to Cassie with an incredulous glare. "Now how could I be an orphan and the devil's son at the same time?"

She somehow managed to keep a straight face. "Doesn't make much sense."

"'Xactly. He sure could get mad. Like the last day, he took a switch to me. I asked him a question and called him 'Teacher.' He didn't like that none. He wanted us to call him Schoolmaster Howe." Jonah snorted. "He stopped in his tracks and said, 'Mr. Phifer, can you be so kind as to call me by my respectful name?' So I says, 'Of course, Schoolmaster Howe'd-he-get-so-ugly-and-mean.'"

It took all of Cassie's willpower not to burst into gales of laughter.

"Old Man Howe like to have whipped me raw that day. So, you see, when he was happy to recommend me as fit to serve, I was more than happy to oblige him. The captains here drill us until I'm bored out of my mind, but at least they don't whip me or call me the devil's son."

Keeping herself in check, Cassie nodded. "Well, I'm glad

you're here. Say, I've got a group of friends I'd like to introduce you to. We're gonna play some games before bed. You want to join in?"

Jonah's slow manner spoke of reluctance, but there was no hiding the excited pleasure that filled his eyes. "I reckon that'd be okay."

"I appreciate it."

They stood and walked side by side.

"I like you, Private Turner. You don't jaw too much at all and that's nice."

Cassie winked. "Happy to oblige, Private Phifer."

Chapter 10

August 2, 1861
Washington, DC

Left, right, left, right, left, right.

Cassie's heart mimicked the sharp snap of the snare drums as her regiment marched as one down Pennsylvania Avenue in front of thousands of hopeful eyes. Thunderous applause and shrill whistles lifted into a riotous tumult.

The blood of Bull Run had not yet been avenged, and all of Washington fixed its eyes on them, praying, begging Providence that the next skirmish would be met with victory.

Their military flags were hoisted high, flapping in the warm breeze. Cassie kept herself stiff as she held her rifle on her shoulder, unwilling to look anywhere but straight ahead. Her face she schooled into stern focus despite the shouts of excitement pummeling the air.

A sudden roar rippled down Pennsylvania Avenue and she knew *he* had arrived. Their general. Sure enough, a sleek black stallion proudly trotted by, carrying their commander on his glossy haunches. When the crowds saw him, handkerchiefs were waved like military banners. Boys whistled between their fingers, and men raised clenched fists into the air, nearly drowning out the booms and cracks of the drums.

As she marched, Cassie caught the visage of General McClellan astride his powerful horse as he turned to the crowd, his expression fierce.

"I give you the Army of the Potomac!"

More cheers and shouts arose. The soldiers kept pounding their march forward in thundering rhythm.

It seemed the entire North had fallen under the spell of their general as quickly as the troops had embraced him.

Yet despite her burgeoning hope that the tide would turn, she could not escape the dread pooling in her stomach. She did not want to go into battle again. She couldn't.

The rifle hoisted on her shoulder seemed to suddenly weigh twenty pounds more than it had mere moments ago. Dread tasted an awful lot like despair.

Left, right, left, right, left, right.

———◆———

"Did you see the president, Mr. Avery? Did you?"

Jonah jumped up and down as he pestered Gabe. Since returning to camp, Jonah had been a flurry of energy.

Laughing, Gabe ruffled his hair. "I saw him." He winked. "I even took a photograph."

"Fancy that!" Jonah stopped squirming and eyed him sharply. "You took a picture of President Lincoln with that box of yours?"

"I did indeed."

"Could I trouble you for a copy?"

He leaned down and propped his hands on his knees. "Tell you what, if you let me capture your likeness, I'll let you have a copy of both."

"I think I could oblige." Jonah's wide grin revealed crooked teeth. "I'm going to tell the others. Say, I might even end up in the papers. I'll be famous!"

As he raced away, Gabe chuckled. Jonah certainly brought vitality to the camp. Since Turner had befriended him, the little fellow seemed to blossom and grow under the attention of the men, who included him in their meals, conversation, and games.

"If anyone has the energy to be drilled for eight hours each day, it's that scamp."

Turner's dry tone caused Gabe to whirl toward his friend with a grin. "I've never seen him so excited. He's talked of nothing but getting a glimpse of Lincoln and his wife through their carriage window."

"The way I hear it, they were looking right at him as if, and I quote, 'no other soldier existed.'"

"Pretty soon, he'll be declaring the parade was in his honor."

Turner shook his head and dropped to the ground, pulling a bag from his haversack. Gabe glanced around the camp. The occasional man walked across the grassy meadow, no doubt assigned to some kind of menial task. The rest of the soldiers rested in clumps of blue. Some wrote letters home; others napped or occupied their free time by whittling some new treasure from whatever they had found. A group of boys—buglers, drummers, and errand runners—gathered to play a rousing game of aggies. Their childish laughter drifted over the hills, blanketing the camp in soothing melodies.

Dropping to the ground, Gabe sat back and watched, pretending to view the scene through the eye of his camera.

"Mighty quiet this afternoon," Turner said.

Gabe rubbed the back of his neck, kneading the tight muscles. "I must say I'm glad. The grand review parade sapped me of my gumption."

"Did you manage a photograph of President Lincoln?"

"Indeed I did. I filled up a whole plate box full of images. Took them right to Brady's studio, seeing as how it was only a few blocks away. Gardner was there, and thankfully, we were able to get them all developed. Without his help I'd still be there, up to my elbows in chemicals."

Turner tossed him a square of hardtack. He caught it midair and looked for a rock to break it open. Cursed things were like chewing on dried mortar.

Smashing his own hardtack against a sharp rock, Turner examined the remaining crumbles in his hand and groaned.

"What's wrong?"

He jutted out his hand to reveal the white crumbles inside. "Look. Weevils got into this teeth duller." Wrinkling his nose, he tossed the destroyed hardtack into the grass.

Deciding against busting his own snack open, Gabe grimaced. "I've suddenly lost my appetite."

Turner offered a lopsided grin. "I suppose if I was starving, I wouldn't mind so much. But seeing as how I'm not—not yet, anyway—I'll pass on the weevil meal for today." He snapped his fingers. "Say, I almost forgot to tell you. The big Swede in our regiment is wanting you to take a photograph of him. Asked me to make the request."

"Might as well. It's quiet. Soon we'll be moving out, and there will be no time. I'm trying to develop all the photographs I can now, being so close to Brady's studio and all. Soon I'll have to send everything to him by post. What's his name?"

"Private Sven Frenken."

Gabe nodded and stretched out against the cool grass, relishing the soft tickle of it against his skin. A warm breeze mellowed his muscles. "Swedish, eh?" He thought back on his parents and their vibrant European ways. "I've always wanted to see Sweden. Switzerland and Austria, too. If I could accomplish it by jumping aboard a steamboat, I'd do it in two blinks."

Turner was silent, as he often was, and pulled out a small knife and a stick, quietly slicing the bark away in long strokes.

Gabe prattled on, knowing his friend was listening. "Yes, Europe and then Africa. I'd take photographs of lions and elephants. Of Bushmen and grasslands. Did you know Africa has a creature called a giraffe?"

Turner kept working, although a small smile played around his mouth. "Can't say that I did."

"Tall animal with a neck longer than some houses. Spotted brown and black against yellow-and-orange bodies. I want to see it all someday." He let his imagination drift, let himself fall into the cracks of nearly forgotten dreams. "I would take images and sell them all over the world."

"And then what?"

Gabe smiled as he looked up at the blue patches of sky. "Why, then I would become a world-famous photographer, of course."

Turner grunted.

Angling his head to see his friend's profile, Gabe asked, "What about you? Where would you go if you could?"

"Don't know."

"Come on, Thomas." He rolled to his side and propped himself up on one elbow. "Anywhere in the world with no restrictions. Where would you go?"

Turner paused and looked into nothingness, his mouth twitching. "West. I'd go west."

"West?" Gabe frowned. "Is there much there other than sagebrush and dehydrated cattle?"

"Of course. Indians from countless tribes, cattle ranchers and farmers. Miners and wild animals. Outlaws and squatters. Gamblers and missionaries. More variety in landscape than all of Europe combined." As if suddenly aware he'd spoken much, he dropped his gaze back to his task. "Or so I hear."

"Where do you hear all that?"

"School. Our schoolteacher traveled out to Oregon Territory as a small boy. He told us about the things he saw."

Gabe watched him, sensing a sudden shift in his mood. "Nowhere else other than the West? A different country, perhaps?"

Turner shrugged. "If I did what I wanted, I would run."

"Run where?"

"Away. Far away. I would run so fast it would feel like I was flying. And I could leave everything behind. I—" He stopped suddenly and frowned before falling silent.

"Where would you go?"

Turner's shoulders appeared weighted down by some invisible stone. "Doesn't matter. As long as I'm running away."

Gabe eased back into the prickly grasses, mulling over Turner's words as bees and insects hummed near his ear.

Just what was Thomas Turner running from?

AUGUST 4, 1861

Dear Jacob,

I pray you are well, enjoying robust health and the Almighty's blessings. Despite the oppressive humidity and heat of Virginia, if I close my eyes long enough, I can picture you in your flat, reading the Atlantic Monthly or the *Times*, alternating between rubbing Sophocles's glossy coat and fussing at him for toppling your stack of newsprint.

How is everyone in our acquaintance? Did Antonio find a job? I have petitioned the Almighty on behalf of him and his family. I miss the Swedish family down the hallway who always greeted me with a hearty "God morgon, ja?" at the start of each day. Does the building still smell of colcannon and corned beef? I am not often the homesick type, as you know well enough, but I confess, when I grow weary of the smell of dirt and blood, of fear and gunpowder, I lay my head upon my cot in the traveling darkroom and try to remember every scent and sight of our neighborhood. It does my heart good.

Has Miss Esther been looking after you? She promised me she would. Who would have thought attending the Relief for Youth Charity Club would have led to so much attention from the female persuasion on your behalf? Despite your protests that you find Miss Esther's attention to be an invasive trouble, I suspect you harbor a fondness for the dear woman. Upon seeing her, your eyes twinkle in a way they never did when I came to play cards with you, or when old Gustav dropped in for a rollicking game of dominoes. Perhaps you are not so dedicated to your years of bachelorhood as you imagine yourself to be.

Despite your grousing, Relief for Youth has done much good for the young people crowding the streets of New York, giving them mentors and hope, just as you gave me. I encourage you to keep on with the noble task, even if it means fighting off the amorous attention of the fairer sex from time to time. Miss Esther has a heart of gold. Of that, I have no doubt.

Amid the business of my tasks—preparing plates and chemicals, waiting expectantly for the proper shot ordained with providential light, ducking bullets and cannon fire while developing a slew of war-story images—I have managed to find some leisure time on occasion and have made several friends. The men from Ohio have been kind, and I've grown especially fond of the soldiers making up the Michigan 2nd infantry. I've even had the opportunity to visit some with the Zouaves. They dress in the brightest colors imaginable—snowy-white shirts and bloodred trousers. How I wish I could capture the vibrancy of their colors with my lens! Perhaps their vivacity will shine through the stilted world of black-and-white.

I thank you again for your generous funding of the equipment needed for this venture. You and Mathew Brady have laid a world of opportunity at my feet. I shall not fail to repay you for your kindness. Perhaps if I am blessed with divine favor to be a world-renowned photographer, I shall claim it all began with the benevolent heart of my dear neighbor who is like my own grandfather. I am learning much . . . all things of photography, war, and the catching of stubborn fish.

With kindest regards,
Gabriel

A stream of muttered words caused Gabe to look up from the letter he'd penned. He stretched lazily along the bank of the swollen river and grinned at the scowl marring George's face as he attempted to bend a fork tine into a fishhook.

"Trouble, George?"

The soldier glared. "Your fishing pole doesn't look much better, Avery."

"True." He cast a glance at his own pitiful attempt lying in the grass near his feet. The pole was crooked, the twine tangled, and the hook looked better suited for a battle than a fishing expedition. He shrugged. "There are some skills a city boy has trouble acquiring."

"No kidding." George groused. "This was Turner's idea. He's the one wanting to fish. We should make him fashion all the poles."

Weeks laughed. "You're just mad because you're no good at it. On the other hand—" he held his own pole aloft—"take a look at this. Not bad, if I do say so myself."

George picked up a rock and chucked it at the gloating man. "The proof is in the fishing. You can boast when you catch something."

Turner smirked and adjusted his kepi. "You gonna jaw all day or catch some dinner? I'm tired of beans."

Weeks wrinkled his nose. "The meat they served yesterday was so spoiled, the flies wouldn't touch it."

The four of them settled along the bank with their poles and waited as nature lulled them into drowsy repose. Time slipped away like water dripping through a sieve.

The sun had sunk deep into Gabe's bones, tugging him into a sluggish haze, when Turner sprang to his feet. The line of his pole jerked and grew taut.

"I got one!"

Gabe snapped alert and stood as Turner fought to wrestle in the catch. "Looks like a big one."

"That's . . . putting it . . . mildly," Turner grunted through gritted teeth.

Weeks and George cheered as if watching a boxing match.

Turner's face was mottled crimson. "Blasted thing is fighting me tooth and nail! Here!" He shoved the pole into Gabe's hand and stepped into the river. "Hold it steady."

The pole strained in Gabe's clutch. "This monster is going to break the line!"

"Not if I have any say."

Turner thrust his hands into the shallows, where the fish writhed in a flurry of splashes. Gabe ground his jaw as he tightened his hold on the pole. Turner howled but snagged the belligerent fish and tugged him to the riverbank. His right hand bled as he held up his prize.

"Bully catch! The hook caught my hand, but see here. Must be close to ten pounds."

George stared at the unfortunate creature, his expression aghast. "What is that thing?"

Turner grinned. "Catfish. Not the prettiest creature but cooks into a fine meal."

"He has whiskers." Weeks's dry observation caused the lot of them to burst into laughter.

Rubbing his jaw, Gabe studied the fish with a smirk. "We should give him a name. With that sour face, and considering how much of a fight he gave, how about Jeff Davis?"

Turner shook off a patch of mud from his arm with a laugh. "Jeff Davis it is. A Confederate fish never could match a determined Yankee fisherman."

Chapter 11

AUGUST 9, 1861

The quiet of camp was disrupted when muffled shouting drifted through the trees.

Briggs looked up from cleaning his rifle, his dark beard tugging downward into a wary scowl. "What's that about, do you suppose?"

Cassie listened. More muted curses, then all fell silent. No shots.

She went back to scrubbing her plate clean. "Sounds like the pickets to me. The Confederates must be holding their lines close to ours."

Sven, the big Swede, lowered his thick blond brows. "I pray not. Makes me *nervös*."

Briggs grimaced. "Worst job in the infantry, if you ask me. All those hours of monotony with nary a thing to do but watch the flies, yet the first to take a bullet if the enemy approaches." He swung his swarthy gaze to Cassie. "You've watched them some, yes?"

She shrugged. "When I have the chance. Their job—" she shook her head—"there's something about it." She struggled to find the right words. "It's exhilarating and puzzling at the same time. Having to know all the signs and countersigns, listening for every footfall and snapped twig. Knowing any moment a Rebel might attack you . . ." She swallowed and continued scrubbing. "Takes a lot of courage, I'd say."

Sven nodded. "*Ja. Mod.* You take me to watch sometime, *ja?*"

"I'll take you the next opportunity we have." She turned toward Weeks. "You want to come?"

The lanky soldier shook his head with a wry smile. "Not a chance. I want to increase the distance between a Rebel bullet and myself, not decrease it."

George's eyes lit up. "I'll come! I've wanted to see what all the fuss is about. Heard the doc wants to see the same. I bet Gabe will be up for an adventure too."

"Sounds like we have a picket-watching party then."

They crept through the woods two days later, having taken advantage of a rare quiet hour after a particularly scalding round of drilling. The general had tightened down on their drills even more than before. They would be advancing soon. Cassie could sense it in her bones.

Doc had been too preoccupied treating ill soldiers to traipse through the thick bramble and George had not been released from courier duty, so it was only her, Sven, and Gabe who crept toward the Union picket lines. Cassie crouched low and listened for footfalls.

A flash of blue snagged her attention, and she motioned the men to move as quietly as possible. They snuck as close as they dared and settled on the ground, watching the navy-clad soldiers walk back and forth across the boundary line.

Sven's soft bass murmured, "Rebel pickets are just beyond the meadow, *ja*?"

"That's what the captain says."

They watched for a moment in silence.

"Nothing is happening," Gabe muttered.

"Not yet, but wait."

Long minutes went by as they watched the picket soldiers scrutinize the woods bordering the meadow. They made no sound save for the splat of spittle that hissed between their teeth before it hit grass.

A faraway voice shouted, "We're watching you, yellow Yanks!"

Cassie's breath caught as she nudged Gabe to attention. The picket soldiers stiffened, their faces tightening into iron as they clutched their guns with white knuckles.

Sven frowned. "Why aren't they answering back?"

"Since the cowbell dodge took out several of our pickets, the general says they are not allowed to talk to the enemy. The order hasn't deterred them much. On occasion—" she smiled—"they dole out a dose of the same medicine."

Gabe whispered. "What's the cowbell dodge?"

Cassie hunkered lower, keeping her voice as breathy as possible. "That's when the Rebs ring a cowbell and trick our soldiers into thinking a milk cow is nearby. No one will turn down fresh cream for their coffee. Just last month a picket wandered off to find the cow and found himself surrounded by six Confederates." She shook her head. "Nasty trick."

Distant shouts rolled across the meadow. "You tell old Abe Lincoln we said hello. I imagine he's still licking his wounds after Manassas!"

One of the pickets muttered a curse under his breath and motioned to his fellow soldiers. Another man brought him a bottle filled with amber liquid.

Raising it high, he shouted, "Here's to Jeff Davis! A toast for the devil!" He took a hearty swig and spit the contents into the grass, then wiped the back of his hand across his mouth and grinned. The other Union pickets burst into laughter.

Beside her, Cassie felt rather than saw Gabe smile. "So they make a habit of swapping insults?"

"Some days. On others, I've actually seen them lay down arms and trade newspapers with the enemy. Even tobacco or buttons."

Gabe blinked, his face slack. "And the captain is okay with this?"

"Seems to be. It's like an unspoken rule of some sort. No trouble will come to either side unless provoked." Leaning back on her posterior, she wrapped her arms around her legs. "I suppose that's why I enjoy watching them. It's a strangely vulnerable situation. Yet . . ." She watched the picket soldiers scatter from their huddle and whispered, "It gives me a strange kind of hope that light has not totally disappeared in the world."

The pickets fell back into silence and she noted the shifting sun. "Come. We need to get back."

The other two stood and Sven, forgetting the delicacy of the situation, released a booming sneeze. Cassie froze.

Muttered curses. Shouts from across the meadow. Bullets whizzed past, exploding wood chips and bark from the trees.

The Union pickets would have no reason to think some of their own were watching. But they might think a contingent of Rebels had crept up behind them.

The blood leached from Cassie's face. There was no time to explain. All they could do was run.

They dropped to their knees and began crawling like the devil was on their tail. More bullets zinged past, their metal heads lodging into trees with thunks, raining twigs and dirt down on their heads.

They scrambled on all fours until the whizzing bullets disappeared, then ran for their mounts. In minutes, they found their horses and rode hard through the thicket of trees. Cassie braved a glance toward the panting Swede. Sven's eyes were as large and round as saucers.

"I know one thing." He swallowed hard. "I don't like being at picket!"

Despite the seriousness of the moment, Cassie couldn't stop a laugh from bubbling out.

"Private Turner, the surgeon needs your help when you have a moment."

Cassie nodded at the severe nurse who approached her with exhausted eyes and pinched lips. The matronly woman looked as spent as Cassie felt. At least helping at the Alexandria hospital relieved her from the infinite boredom of mindless hours filled with drills, drills, and more drills.

Camp life had taken on a nauseating tedium as McClellan waited to attack. Why he delayed, no one seemed to know. Word had filtered through the ranks that Lincoln's detective Allan Pinkerton had told McClellan 150,000 Rebel soldiers were perched around the city, waiting to launch their assault. So the Union soldiers stayed, ready to defend the capital. Only the attack never came.

When a group of scouts returned and reported the giant barreled cannons the Confederates had aimed toward them were actually huge logs painted black, and that the Rebels had already fled, public opinion against McClellan had been scorching. One newspaper reported Little Mac had planted the Union's finest soldiers to stand guard against "Quaker guns."

Despite the humiliation, the general staunchly kept his forces outside Washington, where they did little but drill and complain.

It was a blessed relief when the field surgeon had requested soldiers to volunteer at the Alexandria hospital. Cassie was happy to oblige, even when the hospital work was a grueling affair.

Picking her way between the orderly rows of blanketed beds lining the room, she approached Dr. Goodwin. "You called for me, sir?"

The surgeon's frizzy gray hair stuck out around his head like puffs of cotton, evidence of how often he rubbed his fingers through it. Dark shadows and thick wrinkles lined his face, but his pale-blue eyes were still sharp and focused. "Thank you, Turner. A number of the men are suffering from lymphogranuloma venerum, and I need you to administer their medicine."

Cassie frowned. "I've never heard you speak of this illness before."

"It's not a disease most of the men want announced, since it is contracted by frequenting the brothels."

She kept her face impassive, though her stomach curdled in disgust. "I see."

"I've compiled a list of the men who need treatment. Can you read?"

"Yes, sir."

"Good." He nodded in satisfaction and handed her a penned list of names. "I need you to administer the treatments. Each of them need a dose of this." He held up a single capsule. "It contains balsam of copaiba, powdered cubebs, and magnesia. Make sure they take it with a fair amount of water."

Grasping the bowl of prepared medicines, she asked, "What can be done if these treatments fail?"

Dr. Goodwin frowned. "The next step would be applying black wash, composed of calomel and limewater, to the affected areas. Or urethral injections of nitrate of silver and sugar of lead."

Cassie winced. "I shall pray these pills will suffice then."

A grim smile tilted the doctor's lips. "Prayer would be in order."

She turned to seek out the men requiring the medicines. On her way to the first man's bedside, a burst of spirited conversation drifted through the buzzing room. Looking over, she watched Gabe pat a patient on the shoulder. A man whose head was heavily bandaged, his other arm in a sling. She blinked.

Private Sanders? The crankiest man at the Alexandria hospital was . . . smiling?

Gabe murmured something low, and the normally cantankerous Sanders laughed, his voice booming through the room.

Turning away, she pondered the happy-go-lucky photographer. How did he do it? How did he manage to befriend even the most unlovable people?

If I only had that gift, perhaps my father would have loved me . . .

She shook away the thought and trudged to Private Watkins's bedside. The young man was attempting to nap with his arm flung across his eyes. His groanings, however, let her know he was not actually slumbering.

"Private Watkins? Doc Goodwin has your medicine ready."

Another low groan. The arm rose as the clammy-faced man scowled. "I'd feel better if you just shot me and put me out of my misery."

"Come now. It's not as bad as all that. Perk up, soldier. Take your medicine and maybe the photographer will capture your image with his fancy camera. You may end up in the papers. Famous. You don't want to look like you've been sitting in a pickle barrel, do you?"

Watkins's mouth twitched at the corners, though pain still shuttered his eyes. "I suppose not." He frowned and tossed a cautious glance across the room at Gabe. "You don't suppose that fancy box of his can put curses on folks, do you?"

"No more than you've already done to yourself."

He reddened and looked away. She pushed the large capsule toward him. "Here. Take this. I'll fetch you some water."

Cassie served medicines and encouragement until her back ached from bending over the low cots. She assisted the able to their feet so they could have their image imprinted on Gabe's glass plates. Those with missing limbs chose to sit up in bed, the scratchy blankets discreetly covering the bandaged stumps that remained. Some were too ill to even lift their heads. The sharp sting of chloroform, the sour odor of whiskey, of unwashed bodies and fecal waste, seemed to cling to her like paste. Her stomach soured as the day wore on. Bile rose in her throat every time the doctor asked her to assist him in holding down a thrashing patient suffering from gangrene. The stench crawled like a living thing into her skin and coated her tongue.

Don't think; just do.

The afternoon sun was slipping away as she stepped outside the hospital and stretched her back, breathing in the warm air blessedly free of illness and death. Soldiers wandered on the outskirts of the property, sprinkling lime over the pit where chamber pots were relieved of their contents.

"How do you do it?" Gabe's low voice intruded near her right ear.

She turned with a start. "What do you mean?"

He crossed his arms and let his gaze rove over the hospital grounds as if studying the scene for another one of his war images. "How do you manage doing such gruesome tasks— treating syphilis and similar diseases, emptying chamber pots, assisting in amputations—and still keep your composure?"

She sighed. "It's not easy. Sometimes I think I can't bear

another minute. That's when I ask God for strength. And I try to execute the task in front of me without thinking."

He grunted. "I suppose I was doing much the same. Chatting with the men, trying to bring a smile to their faces while ignoring the rest."

She was silent as his jaw clenched.

"I admire those here who are suffering from acts of heroism. But others—" he grimaced—"can't keep out of the brothels." His face darkened. "Using and abusing the women there, forcing them to do vile things. They debase themselves and then wonder why they suffer in agony afterward." He cut her a sideways glance. "That's why I respect you, Thomas. You're not like the other men."

A rush of heat crept up Cassie's neck and warmed her cheeks. He thought Thomas to be honorable enough to walk the straight and narrow. If he only knew . . .

"And I've seen you reading your Bible at night when the others have retired." He turned to her with a smile. "It encourages me."

Guilt gnawed at her middle. *Liar.*

"I'm not an inspiration." If he knew she was just a girl, lying and pretending to be something she was not, their friendship would dissolve and evaporate like a flash from the end of a musket.

The taut muscles flexed beneath his shirtsleeves. "What really bothers me are the female nurses inside. Having to bathe the men, forced to wash out their excrement-ridden clothes . . ." He shook his head. "No woman should have to endure such indignities."

She blinked. Before she could stop them, the words slipped past her lips. "You really believe women should be pampered and spoiled, put on a pedestal. Don't you?"

"Providence ordained men to protect and care for their women." Something flickered in his eyes. Pain? Hurt? He dropped his gaze, his voice tight. "I didn't do that as I should have when it came time to care for my mother."

"I'm sorry."

"Wasn't your fault." He offered a lopsided smile, but it couldn't chase away the sudden gloom that had descended. "I failed her. If I had nurtured her as a woman ought to be, she might still be living." A muscle ticked in his jaw. "That is a guilt I must live with, but one I intend to learn from. If Providence ever blesses me with a wife, I'll meet her every need. She won't have to work like my mother did, nor will she desire to embroil herself in the fight for suffrage and independence."

Something about his comment stung.

"But what of women like Elizabeth Stanton or Lucretia Mott?"

His expression darkened. "Clearly they don't know the Good Book. Trying to confuse the God-given roles of the genders. I'm not sure what drives them. Perhaps power? Or pride?" He shrugged. "Whatever the reason, they should let their men protect them and stop with their silly prattle of trying to be something they're not."

Memories of Father looming over her with his fists clenched, his drunken blows slamming into her, knifed her like shards of glass. Even now, she could hear Mother's muffled cries of despair through the thin walls.

All the tumbling images, memories, and emotions slashed Gabe's argument to ribbons.

Her throat constricted. "Not every man treats his woman right."

He ground out slowly, "That's true, but . . ."

"The newspapers are saying Stanton and Mott declare women's rights are no different than the rights of the Negro. A cause—" she raised a brow—"for which we are currently fighting, are we not?"

Gabe said nothing. Whether he was contemplating her words or perturbed by them, she couldn't say.

Sighing, she turned away. "If you've finished getting all your photographs, you'll need to develop them. I'll leave you be." She walked away from the hospital, waiting for him to fall into step behind her. But no footfalls followed.

The loneliness screamed louder than it ever had before.

Chapter 12

SEPTEMBER 1, 1861

Dear Jacob,

Summer is ending, melting into autumn, and here we stay in Alexandria. Despite reports the Confederates have given up the notion of attacking the capital, General McClellan continues to keep his feet firmly planted in Virginia soil. Some of our troops are grumbling, hinting they fear their beloved general has turned yellow. Others contend he is privy to information the rest of us can only presume to guess. I'm not sure which it is, but I confess to growing weary.

I ought not complain since our close proximity to Washington has made it easy to transport the war images to Brady and Gardner in an expedient manner, but I long for a fresh perspective. New landscapes, new faces, new adventures. I have photographed everything around me twice.

Mr. Brady met me with hearty congratulations upon my last visit. Two Eastern newspapers have asked to publish a small collection of my photographs. They want to buy them and have their wood engravers print the images in their publications. Brady assures me payment will be forthcoming. When I receive it, I will forward the funds to you. Despite your arguments that recompense for the equipment you purchased is not necessary, I humbly request you to accept this gift. None of this would be possible without your generosity. All my needs are being taken care of here. The time is opportune to bless you as you have blessed me.

Amid the unremarkable routine of drills and conventional military life, we have had opportunities for festive distractions. Wrestling is a favorite among the soldiers, some of them even playing for coinage, though they delight most in boasting of their brawn when defeating a particularly challenging opponent. Before you inquire, no, I shall not even attempt to best one of these intimidating men. I'm content to capture the moments on glass.

Despite the occasional game of pasteboards or cheering for wrestling matches or baseball games, I find most of my free time in the company of my friend Thomas. He has shown me how to fish, snare rabbits and other small game. I always wanted siblings growing up and feel as if the Almighty has finally blessed me with a brother.

Give everyone in the tenement my regards. Write when your rheumatism allows.

Covering you in my prayers,
Gabriel

———◆———

Cassie smiled as a snore erupted from Gabe's slack mouth. The poor man had fallen asleep on the bank of the river, waiting for a bite on his fishing line.

If he continued snoring, she'd get nary a nibble.

The rest of the soldiers, who had slipped away for a bit of merriment, were peppered farther down the snaking river, although judging from the commotion drifting through the woods, they weren't having much luck catching anything to accompany their bland supper.

Something warm unfurled in her chest as she watched Gabe sprawled in the soft grasses lining the bank, his strong chest rising and falling in slumber.

He was tall, well over six feet. Trim and muscled. His hands continually bore the marks of working with chemicals. His fingertips were cracked and discolored. She took a moment to study the handsome planes and contours of his face—chiseled cheekbones, lashes that shielded emerald eyes. The hint of stubble shadowed a strong jaw. His hair fell across his brow, catching strands of sunlight and winking like shimmering silk. His perfect nose that trailed down to full lips. Lips that smiled often. Lips that teased yet spoke with thoughtful intelligence of God, of memories and dandelions.

What would it be like to press her lips against his? To have his arms wrapped around her? Heat poured through every portion of her body. Swallowing, she looked away.

The sensation was unwanted. Yet her imagination refused to be tamed. To have those lips whisper in her ear . . .

She sucked in a breath and turned aside, shamed by her wayward emotions. Gabe was her friend. Nothing more.

Yet why had these nagging feelings become so consuming?

Disgusted with herself, she stood and stomped the sensation

back into her legs. She had two goals. Only two. To do her part in the glorious cause of freedom and to keep her identity a secret. Gabe didn't fall into either one.

Liar. The taunt rose up like a specter once more, just as it had repeatedly since the day she'd confronted Gabe at the Alexandria hospital over his scalding opinion of independent women. She'd denounced the inconsistency of siding with the cause of abolition but opposing rights for women. Yet who was she to cast stones when she played the part of a valiant soldier, only to use it as a refuge to hide from her father's schemes and wrath?

Gabe groaned and blinked, stretching his long limbs as a sleepy cat would in a patch of warm sunshine. "Why are you stomping around? You're going to scare away the fish."

She offered a thin smile. "No, your snoring did that instead."

"So you're stomping mad?"

"Nah, just trying to get the feeling back into my legs."

A sudden splash and a roar of laughter sounded through the woods.

Gabe whistled low. "By the sound of that splash, they must have managed to throw Briggs into the river."

Chuckling, she pulled her line in, studying the empty hook. Sneaky fish. They had absconded with the cricket.

"Sounds like a good idea," he said.

"What does?"

"Taking a swim. Summer is nearly over. Perfect time."

A cold wave of terror snaked down her spine. "You go ahead."

Jumping to his feet, he began unbuttoning his shirt. She glanced down.

"Come on, Turner. Didn't you ever play in the swimming hole when you were a kid?"

"Of course, but I—"

Shedding the fabric from his shoulders, he smiled. "This

may be the last time for a bath in quite a spell, and—" he wrinkled his nose—"no offense, but you need one."

Panic clawed up her throat as he stepped close and pulled her uniform coat away. She folded her arms across her torso, praying he couldn't see the shape she'd hidden under the wool garment now thrown like a rag into the grass.

"I don't like swimming." She could not step a foot into that water. He would know.

"Too bad."

Before she could brace herself to fight, he picked her up, stepped into the river, and threw her in too. Flapping wildly, she sputtered as she broke to the surface, only to hear his deep laughter.

Coughing, she came to her feet, forgetting the water rose just to her waist. Liquid ran off her clothes and hair in streams.

His laughter ceased.

———◆———

Gabe's pulse galloped as he stood there staring. The cold water swirled around his legs, the mud at the bottom of the river squished between his toes, yet his body rapidly numbed to the sensations. All he could see was . . .

He swallowed.

Thomas stood in the middle of the river, water dripping off the ends of his shoulder-length hair, his fingers, his clothes. Clothes that were plastered to his body. A body that boasted feminine curves at every angle.

Gabe lifted his gaze to Thomas's and saw the fear lodged there. The shame. The guilt.

Water dripped off his lips and chin . . . lips that were far more delicate than he'd noticed before. His chest heaved and he knew.

Thomas, his friend—his *brother*—was a woman.

Anger heated his insides and he turned away, biting his cheek until he tasted blood. Sloshing out of the river, he stomped toward the bank and snatched up his shirt. He pulled it over his head and buttoned it with silent fury.

"Gabe, wait! I can explain."

He, she, whoever this person was, ran sluggishly through the river, panting breathlessly, grabbed his arm, and whirled him around.

"Listen, please—"

Gabe shook off her hand, and the woman took a step back, her eyes wide. Droplets of water threatened to fall from her lashes.

"How could you?" His voice was little more than a whisper, but the accusation lashed out like a whip. The woman winced. "You lied to me. Pretended to be my friend." A pain struck his chest. "I told you things I've never told a living soul. About my dreams, my family. I—" He choked on the words, the hurt too deep to verbalize. "I told Jacob you were like the brother I never had."

"I'm so sorry."

Running his fingers through his water-splattered hair, he longed to pull out a fistful of it. If this stranger across from him was a man, they might have come to blows. But Thomas was a woman. A *woman*. Instead he clenched and unclenched his fists, fighting for control. "Why?"

She sighed, her eyes flooding with something raw. "Please sit down and let me explain."

———◆———

Cassie sat in the grass, shivering despite the warm sun beating down on her shoulders. She grabbed her discarded uniform coat and tugged it around her torso, praying it would conceal her shape.

Not that it mattered now.

Gabe sat mulishly five feet away, but it felt more like five hundred. He looked across the river, a muscle ticking in his jaw. She could feel the heat of his anger warming the air between them.

No matter what she said, what she did, no matter how she justified it, she had lost him. The moment she'd watched understanding dawn on his face, the cord of their friendship had severed. Still, she must try to make him understand.

"My father is a hard man. Some would say cruel."

Gabe turned to her slowly, impassive.

"His vice is demon drink, which makes his temper even worse. Everyone who knows him is terrified of him. To defy him in anything is impossible without reaping painful consequences." She hugged the coat tighter to her body. "A lesson I learned many times.

"I have four sisters, and he arranged each of their marriages to hateful, selfish, greedy men. His only concern was their dowry and how long the sum could keep him in his cups. All of my sisters are miserable, as are their children." She shivered, remembering the lust in Erastus Leeds's eyes as he watched her from his property line. "When Father announced I would be forced to marry a man known for his insatiable desires and a fondness for spurning God and faith, I ran."

Gabe grunted. "And enlisted."

"Yes. It's the only place I knew to go where Father could not find me."

He looked across the river, his mouth pursed. "But to deceive in order to do it—to take on the appearance of a man, to work like one, to sleep in tents next to them—" He swallowed. "It goes against everything God intended."

Her cheeks flushed and she looked down at her soggy pants. "God also never intended cruelty to mark a marriage."

"That's true enough." He looked over, his green eyes piercing. Sad. "Why not apply to be a nurse? Or some other task? Why not simply start over fresh somewhere without deception?"

She blinked. "I had no money. No resources. And you know as well as I do that no one would accept a young, unmarried woman as a nurse. They must be older. Preferably widows." She shook her head. "Please try to understand. Every other door was slammed shut to me."

He was silent so long, she feared he would never speak. Finally, slowly, he ground out, "I do understand why you chose the path you did." He sighed deeply. "I might even have done the same."

Her heart fluttered.

"But—" he frowned—"acting the part of a man . . . I just—" He dropped his gaze. "You lied to me. I don't know when I've ever felt so betrayed."

Her hopes plummeted like a stone in water. She offered no rebuttal. What could she possibly say? His accusations were true.

She lifted her head slowly, stiffening under the disapproval darkening his countenance.

"What is your real name?"

It had been so long since she'd spoken it, it felt almost foreign in her mouth. "Cassie. Cassie Kendrick."

He said nothing.

"Can't we at least be friends of some sort?" She heard the plea rasping her voice. "Maybe not as we once were, but—"

He held up his hand. "Please, don't. I can't . . ." He clenched his jaw, appearing to fight for control. "I can't pretend to condone this."

Hurt pinched her heart. The pain was worse than she could have imagined. Lowering her head, she whispered, "Will you tell the captain?"

His shoulders slumped. "I don't know. I just don't know."

Then he stood and left, ripping out the threads holding her heart together with every step he took.

For the first time in years, Cassie cried.

Chapter 13

October 3, 1861
Alexandria, Virginia

"There now."

Cassie mopped the feverish soldier's head with a damp rag as he coughed into a stained handkerchief. The veins in his neck stood out as he strained to expel the irritation filling his lungs.

Gasping, he fell back against the lumpy cot. "Gotta get better."

Cassie lifted her brows. "And do what?"

"Fight, of course," he rasped through cracked lips.

She shook her head. "You would be the only one." She slipped the edge of a tin cup against his mouth and let the water dribble past his lips. "General McClellan has yet to give us marching orders." She struggled to keep the disgust from her voice. The entire army had squatted outside the capital for months, doing nothing but drill. Drill for what? No skirmishes, no battles—not even the hint of a change. He'd plunked his army down and refused to move, refused to engage the enemy. And refused to explain why.

She had ceased meeting each day with the expectation of change. Life had become a stagnating disappointment. If only they would move or do something. Anything. Anything to keep Gabe and his somber scowls away from her.

He'd barely spoken a word to her since that terrible day a month ago. Only talking when necessary and maintaining polite greetings in the company of the other soldiers. She'd caught him watching her as she went about her work, but every time their gazes collided, he looked away with a tight jaw. And her heart ached.

The others in her regiment had noticed, and at their pointed questions, she'd told them she and Gabe had a disagreement but wouldn't elaborate further. She was known for keeping to herself. Apparently Gabriel hadn't said a word to anyone either, as she was still Private Thomas Turner. At least he'd been merciful in not exposing her charade.

The ill man grimaced against his cot. "I don't understand the general. Why hasn't he given orders to move? The Rebs are long gone."

"I don't know." She blew out a heavy breath, trying to ignore the thick odor of sweat and sickness that hung in the hospital room. The air was more than stale and stuffy. It was turning putrid.

Some days she wondered what had possessed her to volunteer to feed cranky men, empty bedpans, or dig graves. Yet she knew what drove her. She longed to put distance between Gabriel and herself. The pain was keen. She missed his friendship too much to see him day after day and not feel the slice of hurt wedging deeper into her soul.

Work kept her busy, her mind numb and her body too exhausted to think.

With a scowl, Private Dillinger nodded toward the paper folded by the bed and closed his eyes, the strain visible on his pale face. "Will you read me the latest war news?"

Grabbing the oily pages, she muttered, "Isn't much to tell, but I'll look." She scanned the bold headlines of the *Tribune* and winced. "Not much to read on battle lines and troop movement, but there's plenty written about our leaders."

Dillinger groaned. "What does it say?"

"Apparently—" she grimaced—"Walt Whitman is quoted as saying they feel 'a mixture of awful consternation, uncertainty, rage, shame, helplessness, and stupefying disappointment.'" She skimmed further down the page. "Some senators are hinting that perhaps McClellan wants the Union to fail because he has Southern sympathies."

Dillinger coughed and frowned. "I don't believe that."

"Neither do I."

Still, for the sake of the cause—and Cassie's own sanity—she needed Little Mac to make a decisive strike. Anything to keep her thoughts from the photographer would be a welcome change.

———◆———

OCTOBER 21, 1861
LEESBURG, VIRGINIA

Gabe tapped impatient fingers against his leg, waiting. Waiting, waiting, waiting . . .

The sun was rising far too slowly for his preference this morning.

It was nearly cool enough for his breath to fog in the morning air, though the pale light would hardly illuminate the frosty cloud. Orange streaked the horizon, yet he needed more light. More time.

Since Captain Philbrick had hurried to report the Rebels were perched on the other side of the Potomac in an unguarded camp, General McClellan and General Stone wasted no time in preparing a contingent to advance. Gabe had overheard the captain telling his men they might be able to overtake Colonel Evans's men if they made haste.

Even knowing the regiment of soldiers crossing the Potomac was fairly small, and that Thomas—no, Cassie—was among them, Gabe had grabbed his camera, lens, and box of glass plates and trailed them as they rowed across the river in the dead of night. It had taken hours to find the perfect spot, hours of climbing around on rocky outcroppings while juggling his precious equipment, but he'd finally located an opportune place atop a small bluff to capture the battle.

Now to pray the light would prove sufficient.

He was determined to get a photograph of the actual fighting. It would likely be blurry and poorly exposed, but he couldn't resist the challenge. He was weary of the sameness of everyday life. Weary of the anger churning in his gut. Weary of *her*.

Gabe couldn't help watching Cassie anytime she was nearby. He searched for telltale signs of femininity, some clue he'd missed before, yet the illusion was flawless.

The memory of her curves as she stood in the river that early autumn day flickered through his mind again and he steeled himself against the flush of heat creeping up his neck. Her performance was not flawless enough to erase the images scorched into his memory.

She had seemed so sad in the past weeks, so distant and quiet, yet he kept his heart hard and dwelt on her betrayal. It stoked the anger that was dying inside. It was safer to be angry than to think.

He'd seen her gathering up her pack, ready to march forward with the rest of the soldiers, but he turned away from the sight. She shouldn't be here. Shouldn't be subjecting herself to the rigors of a man's world. Shouldn't be deceiving.

She'd already seen far too much, heard too much, and blended in far too well for his comfort. He should have reported her. Yet something held him back. What?

Shifting his weight from foot to foot, he clenched his jaw and looked through the lens, desperate for some kind of distraction.

Still too dark, but not for much longer . . .

He lifted the black curtain away and scanned the valley sloping below. A figure scurried up the bluff. He squinted. A scout, perhaps?

His movements were far too harried, his stride too fleet. Something was wrong.

He heaved his way to the top of the bluff, and Gabe saw the strain and dread on his face the larger he loomed. When he'd crested the top, he placed his hands on his knees and panted.

Gabe eased away from the rocky outcropping he'd positioned himself in front of and offered a canteen of water to the winded scout. "What's wrong?"

Water dribbled down the man's thick beard as he gulped the refreshment. Handing it over, he wiped the trickles away from his mouth with the back of his hand. "Captain Philbrick . . . made . . . a mistake."

Gabe frowned. "What do you mean?"

The scout shook his head and heaved thick breaths. "No Rebel tents. Only trees. He scouted it at night. Made a mistake."

Gabe groaned. All their work. The wasted hours. The anticipation. All of it destroyed. Kicking a rock near his feet, he raked his hand across the back of his neck. "So now what?"

The scout sighed. "I tell the captain. And we leave."

With a growl of frustration, Gabe grabbed his plate box and prepared to hoist the cumbersome camera and tripod back down the bluff.

This day was not going as he'd anticipated.

The sun finally appeared. Taking a moment in the arduous hike, Gabe hastily positioned the camera and tripod, determined his effort would not be completely wasted. The soldiers had yet to brave the waters of the Potomac to cross back into friendly territory. He might as well imprint an image of their return in the midst of the debacle. His job was not to judge the captain or his decisions . . . only to capture the moments as they unfolded.

He squinted into the sky. At least the sunshine was finally alive, glinting sharply against the river like sparkling, fiery diamonds. The soldiers scurried down the pass below him, ready to pull themselves into their boats and row against the swirling currents of the Potomac.

Ducking under the black curtain, he dropped in a wet plate and removed the cover of the lens. *One, two, three, four—*

Rocks sprayed around him. Explosions. A sharp whizzing sound. Flying twigs and pebbles.

What was happening?

He crouched low, swinging away from the black cover, shielding his head when dirt sprayed again, assaulting his eyes and striking his skin. He stumbled away from his camera. The world tilted.

A sharp sting followed by an odd burning sensation clamped his calf muscle like an iron vise. The numbing crept up to his knee, and he knew . . .

Shot.

His legs slipped out from under him. He was falling, flailing, grasping . . .

Pain.

Black nothingness.

Chapter 14

IT HAD HAPPENED SO QUICKLY. One moment, she and her fellow soldiers were trudging toward the river to catch the boats preparing to cross. The next, chaos erupted.

And she knew who was to blame.

Her traitorous eyes had turned to glance behind her for the twentieth time to ensure Gabe was managing his cumbersome equipment as he crept down the bluff behind the exhausted regiment. She shouldn't care. He had spurned her completely, making it clear that he found her transgressions unpardonable.

Yet she did care all the same.

It seemed he was lagging behind. Was he attempting to capture an image, or was he struggling to bear his load and traverse the rocky terrain? She wanted to fall back, longed for some small assurance that he would make it without mishap.

When she realized he was setting up his tripod for a war image, she sighed, frustrated at herself for noticing. He'd taken the cap off the lens, and she blinked, squinting as the sun reflected off the glass like a lighthouse between the rocky crevices.

The thought had just crossed her mind that if the enemy were lurking about, the light would be a flag to mark their location.

Then the Rebel bullets started flying.

Her heart hammered to a stop. Gabe had inadvertently given their position away.

Men shouted. She'd ducked, covering her own head as a man to her left screamed when a bullet whittled into his arm.

Feet scrambling. Rocks and twigs snapping. Rifles gripped in white knuckles.

At the captain's shrill cry, "Engage the enemy!" she should have obeyed, but her feet would not move. She whirled around, her heart pounding in her throat when she realized Gabe's tall silhouette no longer stood on the rocky ledge. Instead, he lay in a motionless heap at the feet of his tripod.

A wave of soldiers pressed against her, slamming her shoulders, propelling her body into battle, but she fought the crush attempting to distance her from the ledge. From the camera. From Gabe.

Pushing, shoving, clawing her way through, she stumbled as she panted to climb the steep bluff. Hand over hand. *Pull. Heave.* Sweat stung her eyes. Her lungs burned with need.

At last she reached his sprawled, motionless body and dropped to his side, slinging the rifle against her back as she allowed her hands to inspect his limp form.

A nasty bullet to the leg, just below his knee. A few cuts. No other wounds that she could see. Crimson blood pooled in the sand below his leg. She must get him help before the blood loss was irreparable.

Licking her lips and tasting salt, she sucked in deep, tight breaths and surveyed the area around her. She could not take the camera and his equipment. It would have to be retrieved later or counted as a loss. She could do little more than manage him down the steep hill. If that.

With a quick prayer for help, she hooked her forearms under his shoulders and started dragging him backward with strained grunts. Moving his deadweight to the river would be close to impossible without Providence's blessing.

His head lolled to the side and she gritted her teeth, her muscles burning as she moved him a few more feet. Grunt, drag, strain, drag.

"Gabe . . . it's a mighty good thing . . . you're . . . already out," she panted. "Because this trip . . . is going to be . . . no picnic."

Sounds invaded. Far away at first. Muffled and watery. Murmuring voices. Sloshing water in a basin. Groans. The clink of metal against metal. The sharp sting of medicine snagged his senses, pulling him out of the darkness.

Yet he was helpless to find light. His tongue felt thick. A burning agony pulsed from his left leg.

His throat was dry. Swallowing, he groaned when the pain scorched sharper. As he turned his head to the side, a matronly voice that sounded like gravelly pebbles came from somewhere up above.

"There now. Come back. You're safe."

Summoning all his strength, he opened his eyes. White canvas loomed overhead. His gaze roamed over the strange space. How did he get here?

Last thing he remembered was positioning his camera over the valley. A valley filled with tired, blue-clad soldiers. An army contingent retreating. And then . . .

Shot!

He gasped, his muscles tensing as the memories came roaring back. A calloused hand pushed against his chest, forcing him to lie still. Pain radiated up his leg in waves. Sweat beaded on his upper lip.

A stout woman with a mop of springy gray curls appeared overhead, her face lined in a scowl. "You try to get up again and I'll put a bullet in your other leg." She tsked under her breath, but despite her harsh threat, her eyes were warm.

Before he could rasp out a word, she saw his need and placed a tin cup to his mouth. Blessed water trickled into his parched throat.

"Not too much at once, dearie."

When he'd had enough, she whisked the cup away and studied him sharply. "Do you remember what happened?"

He lifted trembling fingers to his temple, kneading the skin. It was hard to think above the pain in his leg.

"A little. I was on a bluff somewhere above Leesburg when a scout told me Captain Philbrick had been mistaken. There was no Confederate camp. I was heading down the slope, and I remember stopping to take a view with my camera." He paused. "Bullets started flying all around." He glanced up at the gruff woman. "Was the scout wrong?"

She shook her head, jowls swaying slightly and gray curls bobbing like corks on a pond. "No, from what I hear, the captain indeed made an error. But it appears you and the soldiers you were with somehow alerted a different Rebel contingent to your whereabouts."

He sank back into the lumpy cot with a groan. "How? Where did they come from?"

"Don't know. Word is spreading it was a Confederate troop from Mississippi and Virginia. Not sure. They must have seen something that made them aware you were nearby." She swirled a cloth through a basin of water, squeezing the excess water free before pressing it to his brow. He let his eyes slide shut in pleasure at the cool contact. "It's an awful mess, though. I know that much."

He sighed, attempting to glue the hazy pieces together. "So I was shot in the leg. How did I get here?"

A small smile creased her cheeks. "A scrappy soldier somehow managed to save your neck. Pulled you down the bluff and rowed you across the river before finding a litter to carry you here." Her brows furrowed. "Poor fellow looked like a beat dog when he showed up lugging you behind him. Took more pluck than most men have, I'd wager."

Gabe's heart thumped slowly. Who on earth would have done that for him? He'd made many friends, but this? Willing to get shot to pieces to save him? His throat tightened. He wasn't worth it. He had done nothing to aid the cause. Nothing.

"Did you speak with the man who saved me? Get his name?"

His nurse frowned. "Can't say that I did."

"I must find out. Thank him. Repay him if at all possible."

She snorted. "Good luck to you, then. I've never seen such chaos in all my days."

He braced himself, dread coiling within. "Why? What happened?"

The nurse glanced over her shoulder and dropped her voice. "It seems quite a melee ensued. Most of the men were dodging bullets. A small group tried to row like the devil across the river, but it took too long. Them only having four boats didn't help a whit either. By the time Colonel Devens got word sent that reinforcements were needed, it was too late."

His stomach tightened, cold fear seizing his breath. "Too late? Were they all killed?" *Please, God, no . . .*

"Not all. But most of those who didn't make it back across the river were captured by the Rebs." She grimaced, her eyes softening as she broke the news. "Some of the men drowned trying to make it across the Potomac without boats."

The breath in his chest dissolved. What of his friends? Weeks, George, Selby, Briggs, Sven? A sudden crush of fear washed over him. *Cassie?*

A cool gust of wind rippled the walls of the surgical tent, tugging the fat curls framing the nurse's face. He turned away from her probing stare and slammed his eyes closed. The pain in his leg refused to cease its scalding throb.

But the ache in his chest at the thought of Cassie's death cast a far more painful blow.

"I hear tell you're a photographer."

He nodded dumbly.

"Should have had your camera in here hours ago. It was a sight to behold."

A niggling unease clawed at him. "What of my personal possessions? My camera and equipment?"

She frowned. "I've not seen anything delivered here. I'm sorry."

Gone. His livelihood. Jacob's sacrifice. His dreams. Shot down in an instant.

Yet it was Cassie's face that kept stabbing him with fresh waves of misery. He moaned.

"Here. Take some medicine. It will help with the pain."

A spoon slipped between his lips. Something sticky and bitter coated his tongue before he succumbed to merciful nothingness.

Chapter 15

"DID YOU HEAR Colonel Baker was killed in the skirmish? . . . How many drowned, do you think? . . . Where did they take our men?"

Jonah's rapid, never-ending questions frayed the edges of Cassie's already-taut nerves. After pulling Gabe to safety, she had stumbled into camp, spent beyond measure, and had promptly collapsed onto her bedroll. Sleep had been fretful and jarring. Her mind wouldn't rest.

She'd risen and waited for news with the soldiers who had escaped the doomed excursion across the Potomac. They passed the afternoon in quiet. The silence in camp had turned thick and oppressive.

Save for Jonah's nonstop chatter.

"I wonder if the captain will let me visit Gabe," he said now.

Cassie dropped another wedge of firewood into the back of the supply wagon with a clunk. She'd been filling it under orders that a regiment on the other side of the camp needed a bigger supply of wood for their fires. Yet she suspected the commanders had given the majority of them tasks to keep their minds occupied.

It wasn't working.

"I don't know. I suppose it will depend on the captain's mood and how much he needs you at camp."

Jonah shoved his chapped hands in his uniform pockets. "Ain't like there's much to do around here. We haven't moved since summer. One of the soldiers from Ohio told me he heard Little Mac is going to have us stay put through the winter." He wrinkled his freckled nose. "If you ask me, he's turning yella."

Heaving another wedge of wood into the groaning wagon bed, Cassie gave him a stern look. "You shouldn't say such things."

Jonah shrugged. "I'm only saying what other folks are thinking."

"But they have the sense not to gripe out loud where others can hear."

Huffing, Jonah kicked a rock at his feet as she bent to retrieve another stout log. "So do you think they'll let me see him?"

She chucked the last wedge in the wagon with a hot puff of breath. "I told you I don't know."

"Maybe they'll let me go if you come with me."

Cassie looked away. She wanted to see Gabe more than anything. Wanted to be assured with her own eyes he was well. That he would recover. See his smile and hear his voice again.

But he had no desire to see her.

Clearing her throat, she frowned, trying to look gruff. "You won't be seeing him now when you've got a load of wood to deliver across camp. Get going."

Jonah swiped at his nose with a grubby hand, muttering under his breath as he scurried up to the driver's seat and snapped the reins, lurching the sleepy horse into motion.

Cassie sighed. She wasn't good company for the little fellow today. She wasn't even good company for herself. Not until she knew how her friends fared. Briggs was safe, having been told to stay behind, but George, Selby, and Weeks were still missing, along with a handful of others.

And she missed Gabe terribly.

A sharp longing bloomed under her ribs as she found herself moving to her tent. She ducked inside, letting her eyes adjust to the darkness. Briggs was gone, called away by the captain. George's bedroll remained painfully empty.

Her heart pinched as she knelt to run her fingertips over the contraption at her feet. One of the other soldiers had gone back and retrieved Gabe's camera with its long, cumbersome lens. The tripod and plate box had been destroyed.

When the soldier had recognized her, he put it in her possession for safekeeping. Gabe would be pleased to have it back.

Letting her fingers dance over the cool metal edges, she thought back to the wink of sun that had flashed against the end of the exposed lens. Only moments later the Confederate guns had begun blasting. What would Gabe do if he knew his innocent task had caused the skirmish?

Because surely the brilliant flash had been the alert that snagged the Rebels' attention. There was no other explanation. From her vantage point, it had resembled the quick flare of sparking gunpowder. The Confederates must have thought the same.

Gabe would be crushed with guilt. He was a good-hearted man who hated to inflict hurt on anyone. She'd seen that in him quickly enough. He still carried the self-imposed burden of his mother's decline and death. Would he hold himself responsible for the soldiers' deaths as well?

She gingerly lifted the heavy camera and held it to her chest. The delicate instrument in her possession was the closest thing to having Gabe with her. Jonah's plea to go to the hospital with him tugged at her with both temptation and dread.

Would Gabe welcome her visit if she carried the hope of his livelihood and future with her?

She doubted it would matter if she brought him a whole wagon full of photographic paraphernalia. She had broken their friendship with her deception. He might never forgive her.

And it was no one's fault but her own.

———•—

Gabe leaned heavily on his crutch and scowled at Martha as she reproved him.

"Don't slump, Avery. Take some pride in yourself, for pity's sake."

Huffing a tight breath, he attempted to straighten his back with little success. "This crutch is too short for me."

"Good." She lifted her plump chin. "You'll heal faster if you learn to do without it."

Gabe was sick to death of this blasted hospital. It had been a week since he was brought in, and the room seemed to shrink with every passing day. The moans of men thrashing in misery grew louder. The doctors scurrying to and fro, more frenzied. And his nurse, Martha, only grew more churlish.

The familiar burn of pain in his leg reminded him more time was needed for a full recovery, but each day he was growing stronger. He let the crutch fall to the floor as he hobbled across the room in an unsteady limp. Searing stabs of pain radiated up his leg, but he would not fall. He would not. Not in front of Martha's withering glare. He gritted his teeth as sweat beaded on his brow.

He moved slowly around the crowded hospital room, trying not to breathe through his nose as he encountered the sour odors of illness seeping from dying men, unwashed bodies, full chamber pots, and sweat-soaked linens.

He rounded the room, pushing back against the pain, and eased down to his cot with a grunt of satisfaction. He'd done it. It was the longest walk yet without his crutch. And the pain that had taken away his breath only a week ago was duller, bearable.

Martha cackled. "Make a man mad enough and he'll fight every time. Good work, Avery. You'll be discharged anytime now. Doc Goodwin believes you're ready."

He could leave. As quickly as the elation washed over him, sharp disappointment knifed through his chest.

Leave? And do what? His camera, his tripod, his plates and plate box . . . all of them were gone. Likely shattered to pieces by bullets. A sudden empty despondency seeped through him like rainwater dripping into a trough. He'd failed. Failed Jacob. Failed Mathew Brady. Failed himself.

Martha prattled on with her gravelly voice as he brooded, her words nothing more than a scratchy hum in his ears. He needed to write Brady. Tell him what had happened. As soon as the thought came, he pushed it away. Scribbling it on paper would make it reality, and that was something he didn't want to embrace. Not yet.

As his nurse ambled off, intent on scolding another unfortunate patient, he rubbed his aching calf.

"Boy, am I glad you're not dead."

The high voice snapped his senses alert. Turning to the right, he couldn't stop the smile from spreading across his face at the sight of Jonah Phifer—always grubby, always mouthy.

"Jonah!" He laughed, and the mirth sounded strange. Had it only been a week since the battle? Perhaps, but levity had ceased long before that. He hadn't laughed much since the day Cassie's lie had stung him like a whip.

Gabe shook away the thought and patted the empty space on the cot next to him. "I'm glad I'm not dead too. Come sit a spell and visit with me. I'm anxious to hear about the others." Was he? He'd had no word. He wasn't sure what was worse—truth or ignorance.

Jonah plopped on the cot, making it squeak and shift beneath him. "Camp is dull as crackers since Ball's Bluff. Ain't much news to tell." Swiping under his nose, Jonah sighed, then suddenly brightened. "Well, maybe a little news. General McClellan decided to keep us put for the winter."

Gabe groaned. "I was hoping we would get to move on. We've been hunkered down since July."

Jonah swung his spindly legs as he studied the room of sick men, missing nothing. "It don't bother me so much. At least putting up winter cabins is giving us something to do. Briggs has been heading up a lot of the building, chopping down trees all day. He says he doesn't mind the work, though. Keeps his mind busy."

"Still, I was hoping for something new to photograph." Then he remembered all over again. "Not that it matters. My camera and equipment are destroyed."

Jonah offered a sly smile. "You sure about that?"

Gabe blinked, trying to comprehend the odd look on the lad's face. "I assumed so."

With a wide grin, Jonah jumped up. "Stay put. I've got something to show you."

Before Gabe could reply, he raced through the hospital room, nearly knocking down a nurse carrying a tray of bandages. *Land of Goshen* . . .

A moment later, he returned, lugging the most beautiful thing Gabe had ever seen. Unshed tears stung the backs of his eyes.

Jonah stood before him and offered it with outstretched hands. "I believe this belongs to you."

His camera.

Gabe took the delicate piece of equipment and tugged it to his lap, running his fingers over the edges, checking for nicks, cracks, warped metal, broken transition pieces . . .

It was unscathed.

Gratitude swelled up in him like an ocean wave. *Thank you, Lord.*

Inhaling a shaky breath, he smiled. "It's perfect. But what did you—? How—?"

Jonah shrugged. "One of the soldiers went back to retrieve it. He thought you'd be mighty pleased to have it."

He swallowed. "Indeed I am."

"The feller that brought it back said your tripod was bent and the plate box were destroyed, but the camera looks good."

He ran his fingers once more over the cool metal. "I can't believe it."

Jonah scratched the mop of hair under his kepi. "Folks keep saying only Providence could have spared it. Especially after all that happened that day." Jonah frowned. "I'm still mad I missed the excitement."

Gabe scowled. "*Excitement* isn't the word I would choose. But then again, I have no idea what happened, other than the scant details my nurse shared with me."

Jonah eased back down to the cot. "Ain't good. Briggs was told to stay back, you know, so he's fine but bully mad he wasn't there for the others."

Dread spiraled through his chest. "What others?"

Jonah looked afraid he'd said too much. "Weeks and George were taken prisoner. So were Walker, O'Sullivan, and Miller."

He cringed, pity for his friends consuming him. George,

who'd defied incredible odds at Bull Run. Weeks, who was consumed with love for his girl back home. "What of Selby? Johnson?"

Jonah looked away and mumbled, "Drowned."

A hollow ache gnawed. Too young. His throat constricted.

There was one more he must know about, but he was hesitant to even say the name. "And, uh, what of Turner?"

Jonah turned back. "He's fine. Looked like something the cat dragged in when he returned to camp, but he made it without much damage. He might be the bravest man I know."

"Brave? I suppose." If bravery equaled foolishness, "Thomas Turner" had that in spades.

Jonah jumped up from the cot. His hands were fisted at his sides. "I thought better of you than that."

Surprised at the boy's fervor, Gabe straightened. "What do you mean?"

"I mean I figured you'd show a bit more gratitude for the fellow who saved your hide."

The air thinned in his lungs. "What?"

Jonah's expression went blank just before awareness filtered across his freckled face. "You don't know, do you?" The boy stared at him. "Thomas Turner was the one who dragged you down that mountain to safety. He's the one that kept you from bleeding to death. He saved your life."

Chapter 16

November 14, 1861
Alexandria, Virginia

Among the fading reds, oranges, and golds of autumn's trees, Cassie knelt and scraped her fingers against the forest floor, snagging a thick stick and dropping it into the heap of kindling in the middle of the litter. She straightened her aching back.

Her load was only half-full and she was in no hurry to return to camp. The anticipation that permeated long weeks of waiting outside Washington for General McClellan to give marching orders had melted into disappointed apathy. Why didn't they move? The passing days were growing into a blur.

At least the nip in the November air was invigorating, as was the earthy scent of loam and cedar. In this stretch of woods, she was finally alone. Blissfully alone with no prying eyes watching to see if she was something other than Thomas Turner, man of war.

The deception was wearing thin. Not that she wasn't good

at it. On the contrary, she spoke like a man, could walk like a man, and could easily keep up with the tasks assigned to the soldiers . . . something she accredited to God's grace and being raised on a farm. Everything on the outside declared her to be solidly male.

But she was a woman. A woman exceedingly weary of pretending to be something she wasn't. A girl desperate for an embrace from her grandmother. A girl who longed to don her simple homespun dress and wander through the woods barefoot. She was tired of lying, of the perpetual strain, of the crude crush of men always around her.

When Captain Johnston had pulled her aside three days ago, informing her she had been granted a fortnight of respite before winter set in, Cassie had stumbled and stuttered her way through the conversation.

"Private Turner, you should take your fortnight of leave. I have no idea when I can grant you permission to visit your family in the future. War is uncertain."

Take her leave? And go . . . where?

There was only one place she wanted to go and one person she wanted to see. Both were forbidden to her if she wanted to avoid her father.

"But I have no family, sir."

Captain Johnston had frowned. "You don't have to retain family to take a furlough, you know. And there are at least a dozen others I'm sending away to gain rest. I insist you take advantage of this opportunity. You're a valuable asset to the Union, and we need you ready for whatever comes in the spring."

She picked up the ends of the litter and dragged it behind her across the forest floor, relishing its soft hiss as it slid over fallen leaves and cushioned beds of moss. She didn't want to dwell on anything other than the snatched moments of solitude when she could be Cassie Kendrick.

With a smile, she unslung the rifle from her shoulder and set it on the ground, then tugged off her kepi and tossed it on the litter, running her fingers through her silky hair. She really should cut it again, but something held her back. The other soldiers' hair looked like hers, longer than normal, and no one thought them feminine. Still, she should not take the risk. As soon as she found blade or razor sharp enough, the thick tendrils would be shorn again.

She sighed in contentment as she massaged her scalp, allowing the cool air to settle into the silky threads. She should enjoy it while it was still somewhat clean. The last time she'd attempted to bathe was three days ago and the water had been bitterly cold. Her teeth had chattered for an hour afterward. The chance of bathing again was remote until after winter's thaw.

Crunch, crunch . . .

She froze. Footfalls through the woods. She was not alone.

Heart hammering against her ribs, she lowered herself to the ground and reached for her gun. Her fingertips scraped the cold metal of her rifle. She rose slowly, gripping the weapon, and listened.

Crunch, step, crunch, step . . .

The gait was uneven. Breath thinning, she'd raised the rifle when a person appeared from behind a stand of pines.

Sandy-blond hair, strong build, piercing green eyes . . .

Her heart thudded to a stop as she set aside the rifle with limp hands. He stopped and stared at her with a small smile.

Gabe.

Her breathing felt sharp and much too rapid. He walked steadily toward her, a hitch evident in his stride. It had been weeks since Ball's Bluff and she'd seen no sign of him since.

Jonah assured her he'd delivered the camera, but all other traces of Gabe's existence had been wiped from the camp, save for the Whatsit that sat lonely and unused on the outskirts of the cabins under construction.

"Hi, Thomas."

She startled and then looked down as heat crept up her neck and into her cheeks. The kindness in his voice did little to settle her turbulent emotions.

"I—I thought you'd left," she stammered.

He said nothing. Only studied her with an odd expression. Partly amused and partly . . . she didn't know what.

"I mean, your traveling darkroom is still at camp, but I figured Brady hadn't had time to send someone for it, and—"

Gabe interrupted with a chuckle. "I've never heard you speak so quickly, Thomas Turner."

A soft giggle escaped. "Your jabbering must have rubbed off on me somehow."

He laughed, and something deep inside her, something she feared was dead and locked away, began to open and warm.

His eyes darkened as he stepped closer, a shadow flickering across his face. "I haven't left. I'm here, and it's because of you."

He knew? Her chest tightened and she looked away. "Who told you?"

"Jonah."

She frowned. "I didn't want you to know."

He released a huff, rife with exasperation. "Why not?"

She snapped back to meet his gaze, tasting the fear on her tongue. "Because I didn't want you to think I did it as some sort of pitiful plea to change your mind about me. To make you feel guilty or some other attempt to manipulate."

He stepped closer and the air between them grew charged. "Why did you save me, then?"

She looked into the sculpted planes of his face, into his intense eyes with their faint lines at the corners. Her tongue refused to work. She couldn't say what suddenly struck her with astounding force, like a hammer against an anvil.

She loved him.

How could she have been so foolish? So undisciplined? She hadn't wanted to, yet her heart had crumbled like ash just the same.

Fisting her hands, she expelled a tight, shaking breath and looked away. "I couldn't leave you there to suffer. You needed help."

He said nothing, only watched her. The silence between them grew uncomfortable.

Clearing her throat, she nodded toward his injured leg. "How are you feeling?"

He smiled gently. "I'm not dead, thanks to you."

Heat warmed her insides and tinged her skin.

"I'm still a little sore but well otherwise." His eyes crinkled. "Thankfully it doesn't take strength like Briggs's to capture images on glass."

Glimmers of their past friendship resurfaced. It might not be as it was before, but anything was better than the agonizing past few months of thick silence covering loud anger.

"Jonah told me he returned your camera. I'm just sorry the soldier who retrieved it couldn't salvage the rest."

Leaning against the trunk of a pine, Gabe shrugged. "The camera and lens were the most costly. I traveled to the capital for the past several weeks and met with Brady. He said things like this were bound to happen during war. He's pleased with my work and will replace the tripod and plate box himself."

"I'm glad."

Gabe looked off into the autumn woods surrounding them.

"Not that it will matter overly much in the coming months. I heard General McClellan is keeping the men here for winter. Not much to capture when it's so quiet."

"That's true." She bent and retrieved another thick branch and added it to the litter of kindling. "Captain Johnston is insisting I take furlough while we're hunkered down."

His green eyes sharpened. "Where will you go?"

Scooping up her discarded kepi, she jammed it back on her head. "Don't know. The only person I want to see is my grandmother, but it's too dangerous. If Father discovers I'm there . . ."

Gabe frowned. "Surely he wouldn't hold you against your will."

"He most certainly would."

They fell silent. A bird chirped nearby, reminding her how very alone they were in this long stretch of woods. With a sigh, she knelt and picked up the ends of the litter, ready to drag it back to camp.

"Wait." Gabe's face was alight with something almost child-like in its mischief. "I have an idea."

She stopped, brows furrowed.

"Let me go with you."

"What?"

"Let me go with you. Captain Johnston said you must take a furlough. You want to see your grandmother. Where does she live again?"

"Howell, Michigan."

"Right. I'll go with you."

Dropping the litter to the ground, she took a step back and licked her lips. "But how? Why?"

"It's the perfect solution. I'm still recovering, so Brady won't think a thing of my leave. You can travel in your uniform. After we arrive, if we do happen to run into your father—" he grinned—"I'll tell him I'm your new husband."

Her heart hammered in staccato beats. "Have you lost your mind?"

Chuckling, he shook his head. "Not at all. It's the perfect solution."

"But to lie? To deceive like that—?"

He rolled his eyes. "Would you be crossing some moral line, *Thomas Turner*?"

The absurdity of her protest halted her like a crashing train. At the dry look on his face, she couldn't keep a laugh from escaping. "A valid argument. But I couldn't ask you to make the sacrifice. You're still healing. The journey alone would prove trying."

He stepped closer, suddenly serious. "Please let me do this. You saved my life. I owe you an enormous debt, especially after the way I've treated you." His expression shadowed like clouds drifting over a summer sky. "I've been thinking. Although I still don't agree women should be mingled with men, especially in battle—" he inhaled deeply—"I was wrong to break apart our friendship the way I did."

Cassie crossed her arms over her chest, remembering the pain of his complete rejection. "You were hurt. And I *did* deceive you."

"For self-preservation."

She looked away, trying to avoid his probing gaze. "You don't have to do this."

"I want to . . . Cassie."

Something about the way he said her name sent shivers of awareness skittering down her spine. She shook the thought away. *Don't think. Don't feel.*

"Besides, I've always wanted to see Michigan." He shoved his hands in his pockets and winked. "What better way to try out my new equipment than with a fresh canvas and a good friend?"

A good friend. Though she feared the trip would prove a mistake, she couldn't resist the urge to spend time with him.

She slowly nodded, unable to squelch the sassy remark spilling from her lips. "All right. You can come, Avery. Just promise you won't jabber the whole time."

Laughing, Gabe picked up the other end of the litter, ready to help her haul it back. "I'll try my best, Turner."

Chapter 17

The shriek of the whistle fought against the soothing lull of the swaying train car as they chugged along the winding stretch of northbound tracks. The compartment was stuffy, filled with stale air and grim, weary passengers. Older men wearing black coats and expensive vests were scattered throughout the train, mingled among stout matrons and exhausted mothers attempting to keep their young children quiet through the never-ending trip.

Gabe smiled dryly to himself. Every time he grew sleepy enough to nod off, a bloodcurdling scream from a cantankerous child snapped his drowsy senses back to life. Apparently he wasn't the only one bothered by the whining boy. The entire carful of people spent long moments searching their belongings and pockets for candy, trinkets, or anything to soothe the fussy little tyke. After sucking on a peppermint stick, the cranky toddler finally drifted off to sleep on his mother's shoulder.

Unfortunately, the cross child had already awakened him one too many times. Sleep eluded him.

Looking across the seat, he noticed Cassie had nodded off as well, her dark head resting against the rumbling wall of the car. Dressed in her uniform and kepi, no one had realized she was anything other than a war-weary soldier on furlough.

He took a moment to study her as he'd wished to do since she'd revealed her identity. She had perfected the stance and walk of a man, wearing the identity like a second skin. The large uniform coat hid her feminine curves. But watching her now—the pucker of her full lips, her delicate bone structure, her smooth skin and thick lashes—he wondered how he had never seen through her disguise. She had become adept at hiding her face in the shadow of her kepi, but he knew from experience the wide brim shrouded eyes so brilliantly blue, they would be stunning if she dressed as herself . . . a young woman far too independent for her own good.

He looked away, still muddled and confused over the whole situation. Since he'd apologized, they had struck up a tentative friendship—one more delicate than before. They chatted and laughed over trivial things but had avoided deeper conversations. It was as if they were tiptoeing around each other, afraid the thin strand of camaraderie would fray with one misspoken word or look.

He didn't like it.

Glancing out the grimy, soot-streaked window, he watched the countryside pass by in a mud-colored blur. He longed for the amiability they had shared before. The ease, the laughter and soul-stirring conversations. Everything had changed, and yet nothing had changed. He was still Gabe. She was still the same friend he'd admired since they met. Why the odd feelings?

He turned to his left, noting the portly fellow across the aisle was also slumbering, his head bobbing forward against his massive belly. The buttons of his vest strained with the girth. His jowls were slack, aquiver with the motion of the train. A low snore burst from the back of his throat.

A petite woman with delicate wrinkles around her eyes was knitting furiously, working the soft-pink tangle of yarn through her clacking needles with a speed that matched the chugging train. Noticing Gabe's perusal, she shot him a sideways smile but never ceased the fluttering of her fingers. "Louis is through with the newspaper if you'd like to read it."

Gabe nodded his appreciation. "Thank you. I can't rest for some reason. Reading the paper would be a welcome diversion."

She paused only long enough to pass it over, her mouth twitching into a smile. "If my husband keeps snoring, no one else in this car will be able to rest either."

He chuckled and grabbed the oily paper, quietly snapping it open to scour the headlines. The task was difficult because of the seat's continual sway beneath him. Back and forth, back and forth.

War on every page. Troop movements. Casualties. Strategic cities and conjectures on what each general might do next. Orders from Washington. Orders from Richmond. Gabe pursed his lips. The war was smothering . . . snuffing out life and hope in every direction, leaving abysmal shadows in its wake.

He had almost discarded the bleak news when a headline caught his eye.

Congress to Establish Congressional Joint Committee on the Conduct of the War after Disaster at Ball's Bluff

A flicker of curiosity flared to life.

The skirmish at Ball's Bluff near Leesburg, Virginia, is another black mark on the Union's already-marred record. Between General McClellan's hesitancy to move the largest mass of troops away from the capital and his inability to crush the Confederacy as Congress had hoped, the spirits of our blessed Union are flailing, though not in despair. President Lincoln has pleaded for patience, even in the face of many Republicans' outspoken criticism of McClellan's tactics. These critics claim he has done nothing more than stage his grand reviews and parades of our valiant men up and down Pennsylvania Avenue, though we note the latest parade of 65,000 men was a brilliant spectacle.

Patience may indeed be a virtue, but after the humiliating fiasco at Ball's Bluff, the long-suffering of our great nation is growing thin.

The skirmish, which ended with the deaths and drownings of over two hundred soldiers, as well as the death of United States Senator and Colonel Edward Baker, has caused Congress to take note of ineffectiveness within the ranks and among their leadership.

Reports of how the clash began are varied. Early information declared the burden of guilt lay with deficient scouts who informed General Stone that moving a small contingent across the river would catch a band of Confederates unawares. Other reports lay the blame at the feet of Captain Chase Philbrick, who, it is said, mistook a line of trees for a cluster of Confederate tents in the dark of night. As information is sorted through the perplexed hands of Congress, however, it is clear that the majority of the blame lies with General McClellan, who initially ordered the scouting party to gauge the position of Confederate General Evans's soldiers across the Potomac,

as well as an unknown photographer who inadvertently
announced the Union's position to an isolated band
of Rebels.

Gabe's breath thinned. An unknown photographer? His pulse hammered as he gripped the wrinkled pages tighter and scanned the condemning words that cut into his soul like shards of glass.

One soldier recuperating from the disaster insists he saw a
flash from a photographer's camera just before Rebel guns
began firing. Private Jonathan Ayers declared the sun
was quite brilliant by midmorning and the camera lens
reflected beams that alarmed the enemy.

He couldn't breathe. The tremors from his hands rattled the paper in his grip. The only photographer he knew who had traversed the impossible terrain was him. *Please, God, no. . . .*

Whatever the reason for the debacle, Congress is
establishing the Congressional Joint Committee on
the Conduct of the War. The minds of Washington are
concerned McClellan is ineffective and believe the inner
workings of the Union forces must be examined more
thoroughly.

Nausea curdled his stomach as he slowly lowered the paper. He racked his brain, trying to remember what exactly had happened. Setting up his equipment on the hill overlooking the river valley. The sunlight was finally sufficient. He'd removed the lens cover, and then bullets began whistling all around him. His heart gave an odd lurch. It was him. He was the one who had caused George and Weeks to be captured and dragged to a Confederate prison. It was his fault the Rebels had fired. And it was his fault Selby and Johnson had drowned trying to escape enemy fire.

Dear God, no.

He glanced at Cassie sleeping against the unforgiving wall of the train car. What would she think if she learned the truth?

Swallowing, he resisted the urge to cast up his accounts. He had endangered her life as well. She'd fought the tide of retreating soldiers to go back . . . for him. She'd dragged his lifeless body down the mountain and had saved him. He didn't deserve it.

He dropped his head in his hands and bunched fistfuls of his hair, watching the floor beneath him shift as the train sped onward.

God, forgive me. It was all my fault.

———————

Something was wrong with Gabe.

Ever since Cassie had awakened, he'd seemed distracted. Pale. She'd caught him several times studying her as if he wanted to say something, but then he clamped his lips shut and looked away. And he was so quiet.

Gabe was never quiet.

He hadn't said a word when they disembarked from the train, nor when she had plunked down coinage to rent a horse and small wagon from the town livery. Here they were, bobbing up and down in a rickety wagon dragged by a decrepit mare, and the only sound was the plodding of hooves through wet leaves and mud.

Had she done something wrong?

Their renewed friendship was tenuous, she knew, yet he

wasn't acting upset with her. More like he had turned inward on himself, wallowing in some dark place she could not see or hear.

A frigid gust of wind rattled the wagon, causing her to burrow deeper into her woolen coat. She'd forgotten how much colder it was in Michigan than in Virginia. Had she really been gone only six months? It seemed a lifetime ago.

Clenching the reins in his red-tipped fingers, Gabe angled his head. "So tell me about this. About your home."

She cleared her throat, shivering. The metallic scent of snow filled the air, although the pewter sky was dry. "What do you want to know?"

The whisper of a smile tugged his mouth. "For starters, what is your grandmother like?"

"Wise. Kind. Funny. And probably the only person on this earth who has truly loved me for who I am."

He gave her a long look before swinging his gaze back to the road. The gray horse noisily clomped ahead, flinging up flecks of mud. "You two are close, then?"

"Yes. Extremely. She taught me about God, about life, and everything in between."

"Is she expecting you?"

She shook her head. "No. She has no idea what happened to me. I ran away many months ago."

He frowned, his brows pulling low. "You just up and left without a word?"

Guilt pricked her conscience, and she turned away from the faint accusation lacing his tone. "I had to."

Silence, aside from the creaking wagon and the squelch of mud and rocks under the nag's hooves.

"So are you going to tell me about the man who was so terrible you'd rather run than marry him?"

"Someday."

Emitting a soft chuckle, he shook his head and offered the first real smile she'd seen on his face since leaving the train.

"And you?" She pursed her lips. "Are you going to tell me what has put you in such a solemn, dark mood?"

His smile siphoned away into a straight line. "Someday."

Chapter 18

GABE CUT A SIDEWAYS GLANCE AT CASSIE, hunkered down in her uniform, her face partially shadowed by the brim of her kepi.

The farther into the woods the mare took them, the more tightly wound she seemed. She'd pulled out her battered Bible, reading it quietly for the first part of the trip, but as the wide road was swallowed by trees, their limbs reaching up like clawing fingers, she'd shoved the Bible into her haversack. Her eyes darted warily back and forth across the narrowing trail. When he'd attempted to swing right onto a thinly marked road, she grabbed his hands, forcing him to halt the droopy mare.

"Not this way." Her complexion was pale.

"Why?"

Licking her stiff lips, she whispered, "This road cuts through the woods and leads to my parents' farm."

"All right. I'll go straight. Is the trail wide enough to manage the wagon?"

"Yes. I'll tell you where to go."

They meandered for at least an hour, dodging hanging limbs, sharp turns, and bone-rattling bumps from naked rocks jutting out of the dirt, but he didn't mind. The thick, loamy scent of wet earth rose up around them, cloaking him in a serenity he had rarely experienced. The metallic cold couldn't dampen the beauty of the surrounding forest, the last crimson and orange leaves drifting from the trees like fluttering paper. He wanted to stop and capture the landscape on wet plate, but seeing how rigid Cassie had become on the bobbing bench, he held his tongue. There would be time later.

"I envy you."

She turned to face him, her eyes questioning. "Why?"

He gestured to the scene before him with his free hand. "Growing up with all of this. It's breathtaking."

She glanced around them, trying to see the land as he saw it. Her lips curved. "It *is* beautiful. Why do you suppose we don't appreciate the beauty around us when we have it?"

"I suppose that means you rarely saw it as beautiful."

Shrugging, she wrapped her arms around her middle. "I've always thought this land lovely, but shadows have a way of snuffing out beauty."

Unable to stop himself, Gabe reached across the seat and squeezed her cold fingers with his own. She inhaled sharply but didn't break away. After a long moment, she even relaxed, keeping her hand tucked in his. Something unfurled in his chest.

They rounded a stand of maples and she freed her hand, sitting taller in her seat before stopping him with a hand on his arm. "We're here."

He pulled the horse to a stop and took in the sight. Towering trees gave way to a small clearing that boasted a weathered log cabin. The porch held a low roof and a solitary rocking chair.

The steps sagged. A stone chimney crept up one side, and the scraggly remnants of a garden could be seen behind the house. To the right was a small barn that looked ready to topple over, yet he knew it was inhabited from the low moo of a cow inside. He squinted, able to make out a smaller building tucked behind the cabin. A storage shed perhaps. The scent of woodsmoke hung in the cold air.

It was a simple home, but the way Cassie's face lit up, a person might think it was inhabited by Abe Lincoln himself.

Her breath rapid, she whispered, "Tie the nag to this tree for a minute. We can get her unhitched and settled in the barn in a bit."

Before she could jump from the wagon, he gripped her elbow, making sure to keep his voice low. "What if your grandmother has visitors?"

"I'm in uniform, remember? And I don't see any other wagons. She's likely alone."

He nodded and longed to squeeze her hand again as a flicker of trepidation skittered across her delicate features.

They walked side by side across the yard. The ground was spongy, evidence of a recent rain. The porch groaned beneath his weight as they approached the front door. With her eyes fixed ahead, Cassie wiped her hands down her trousers, inhaled a deep breath, and knocked. Silence. No footfalls. She grasped the handle and pushed the door open.

They stepped inside and he blinked, trying to adjust his eyes to the darkness. Most of the windows had been shuttered, but one glass window let in soothing, pale light. A hissing fire popped in the stone fireplace. A small woman with a head full of gray curls dozed in a rocker next to the fireplace, her lap covered with a rag quilt.

Cassie said nothing, but the trembling of her chin spoke

volumes. She knelt down in front of the aged lady and placed a gentle hand on her covered knee. "Granny? Granny, it's me."

The old woman stirred and shifted, blinking slowly. Her gaze suddenly sharpened as she realized two strangers were in her home. "What are you—?" She trembled. "How did—?"

Cassie pulled the kepi from her head, and Gabe watched as silky strands of mahogany slipped down to her shoulders. Cupping the woman's cheek, she leaned in and forced her grandmother to look her in the eyes. "It's me, Granny. It's Cassie."

Recognition dawned just before the old woman's face crumpled. She choked on a sob and wrapped Cassie in a white-knuckled hug. "Oh, my child! My beautiful Cassie! I was so afraid . . ."

Gabe watched in wonder as the sharpshooter of the Second Michigan Infantry, the courageous hero of war, laid her head on her grandmother's shoulder and wept.

———◆———

She was home.

With a smile she couldn't stifle, Cassie carried the steaming bowl of creamed potatoes and platter of fried chicken to the table, adding more to the small feast she and Granny had prepared.

Chicken, potatoes, thick squares of corn bread with sweet, creamy butter, fried apples, and tea . . . all of them luxuries.

Gabe inhaled with appreciation. "A sight better than hard-tack, beans, and coffee, I'd say."

Cassie grabbed three cups from the shelf as he rose to assist Granny into her kitchen chair.

Granny smiled at him and pinched his cheek. "Can't say I mind a looker helping me to my chair for a change."

"Granny!" Despite her embarrassment, she couldn't repress

the giggle that burst forth at the woman's forward behavior. She'd never seen her so smitten with a man before.

Gabe winked, easily guiding her so she could settle into her seat with grace. "It's my pleasure when the company is so lovely."

Pink tinged Granny's cheeks. Cassie shook her head and eased into her own chair. Granny Ardie. Blushing. Playing the coquette. And Gabe certainly didn't seem to mind the adoration.

Granny extended her blue-veined hands, indicating she expected each of them to grasp on. "Shall we say grace?"

She slipped her hand into her grandmother's but could not squelch the odd flip in her stomach when Gabe's warm fingers wrapped around her own. Her hand suddenly seemed strangely small.

Closing her eyes, she bowed her head as Granny's gravelly voice lifted a soft, sweet petition.

"I thank thee, dear Lord, for this food, the abundance of provision, and especially for—" her voice caught before she cleared her throat—"bringing my precious Cassie back home, even if only for a short time. And I thank thee for her handsome friend gracing this humble table. May we always be thankful to thee. Amen."

Cassie added her own *amen* that blended with Gabe's as Granny released her. Gabe, however, hung on for a moment or two longer than necessary. Warmth crept up her neck.

She had just dipped her spoon into the potatoes when she felt Granny's gaze on her. She looked up and drank in the utter love and wonder in her pale eyes.

"I can't believe you're here. How I've missed you. And a Union soldier? I—" Emotion overcame her, cutting off the soft words.

Cassie took her knobby hands and squeezed. "Not exactly what you pictured in my future, eh?"

She shook her graying head and patted Cassie's hand before taking up her tine. "Not in the slightest. Though I worry for your safety, it's a sight better than Erastus Leeds, is it not?"

Cassie chuckled and speared a chunk of fried chicken, popping it in her mouth with a sigh of pleasure. Delectable.

"Who is Erastus Leeds?" Gabe was studying her in confusion.

"The man Father was insistent I marry." She turned to Granny. "Did he marry another? Please say it's so."

"No, child. He's still alone on his farm. Well, nearly." Granny suddenly clamped her mouth shut, her wise eyes flickering with something tumultuous.

"What is it?"

Brow furrowed, she shook her head. "It's not for me to say."

Cassie pushed her plate back and fixed Granny with a look she prayed would make her cave. "You've already aroused my suspicion. What do you mean he is 'nearly' alone?"

Granny took a deep breath.

"Constance Slattery visits him at least twice a week and always stays through the night."

Heat crept up Cassie's neck at the indelicate topic. She couldn't repress the sarcasm from slipping through. "I take it he's not missing me overly much, then."

Granny sent her a reproving look. "We ought not take pleasure in his vice."

"Sounds like you're well rid of the man."

Gabe's soft observation caused her to glance over. His eyes were alight with a fierceness she had rarely witnessed in his jovial countenance.

"Indeed." She poked at the fried apples and finally braved the question that she'd dreaded. "Was Father upset?"

"*Upset* is an understatement. He bellowed and stomped

about like a penned bull for three weeks. I've never heard such yelling and cursing in all my days."

Cassie cringed, her stomach in knots. Dropping her fork to her plate with a clatter, she sat back in her chair and toyed with the napkin on her lap. "Does he suspect where I went?"

"Not a clue. After he and Erastus came to blows over your absence—" Granny's lips twisted in amusement—"he lit out to find you and drag you back home. He was gone a week but eventually gave up. Your sisters thought you had a beau and ran off to elope."

"Sisters?" Gabe shot her a smile. "I'd forgotten you mentioned having sisters. How many?"

Granny answered. "Four." She gazed for a long moment at Cassie. "One of them pops in to check on me each week. Imagine them catching you here. And dressed as a Union soldier." The lines deepened around her eyes. "Are you planning to wear your uniform the entire time?"

Cassie sighed and worried the edge of her fraying blue cuff between her fingers. "I was hoping to be rid of this while we were here. It's filthy and needs a good scrubbing." She managed to stem the tears pricking her eyes. "And for a week, I'd like to be Cassie Kendrick . . . not Thomas Turner."

Granny reached over and cupped her cheek. "Of course, love. You can bathe and wear one of your old dresses you kept here for overnight visits. We'll wash this dandy uniform tomorrow and put it out of sight for a week."

"What if one of my sisters calls?"

Granny cackled. "Then I suppose you and Gabe will have to hide in the cellar."

Gabe put down his cup and winked in a manner that caused Cassie's toes to curl in her tattered boots. "And if we see her sisters or Mr. Kendrick, we've already concocted a plan." He swung his gaze to Cassie, his expression communicating more than the words he uttered. Or was it only Cassie's imagination? "If her father appears, I will claim the role of new husband to your granddaughter."

Granny giggled like a little girl and resumed eating. "I doubt you'll have to worry about John stopping in anytime soon. He hasn't come since—" All at once, Granny paled and grew silent.

Dread pooled in Cassie's middle. "Since what?"

Granny dropped her fork and wove her fingers together, her face drawn. "Not since your mother passed away."

Something cold and dark squeezed around Cassie's heart. She couldn't breathe. "How?" Had she done this to her? Had the shock of her departure sparked a fire of problems that consumed her poor, weary mother? Or perhaps Father, in his rage—

"She died of pneumonia, child." Granny wiped away a stray tear. "It happened suddenly. There wasn't anything you could have done."

Her throat burned. She stood on shaking legs and mumbled an apology. "Pardon me for a moment."

Tears blurred her vision as she fled, bursting through the back door and into the bleak cold of night.

Chapter 19

GABE SLIPPED OUTSIDE AND DONNED HIS COAT, searching for signs of Cassie. As he turned the corner of the cabin, he heard soft sniffling in the darkness.

"Cassie?"

The sniffling ceased, and he could picture her hastily wiping away the tears. Always so desperate to keep herself and her thoughts hidden.

He walked toward the edge of the dying garden. Honeyed light spilled from the cabin windows and illuminated a square of churned earth. Cassie stood just beyond the patch of light, leaning against a gnarled tree. He came close but did not touch her. She merely needed to know he was there. That he cared.

Long moments ticked by.

"I'm sorry about your mother."

Silence. Then another strangled sob. He stepped forward and pulled her to him, wrapping his arms around her. She burrowed against his chest and clung to him as she wept.

"Shh." He laid his head on hers and rubbed her back as she cried. Had he ever seen her this vulnerable? This undone? Not even her confession at the creek had unleashed this kind of unchecked emotion in her. She kept everything inside . . . until now.

Somehow, just holding her while she cried made him feel as if she trusted him more than anyone else in the world.

"I know. It hurts."

She shuddered against his chest, her voice muffled. "What if my absence contributed to her death? Father is always gone, leaving us the brunt of the farmwork. Until I ran, I was the one who shouldered the majority of it. What if she couldn't bear up under the load? What if it weakened her?"

He sighed and kept stroking her slim back. "You're borrowing trouble, Cass. You don't know anything like that happened. She contracted pneumonia. It wasn't your fault."

Her sobs trailed off into silence, broken only by the slightest hitch of breath and the occasional shudder racking her body. She pulled away, wiped her eyes, and stepped from his embrace. He felt the loss of her warmth as cold air rushed in to replace her.

"Forgive me for bawling all over you so."

Why did she continually act like she didn't feel? Like she had no emotions? Perhaps she had been hurt so many times, it was easier to bury them than express them.

"No need to apologize."

With a deep breath, she lifted her face to the sky to take in the countless stars strewn across the darkness. She looked as if she wanted to say something more but dropped her head and walked away, murmuring over her shoulder. "I should get back to help Granny clean up."

She had nearly rounded the corner before he called out,

unable to squelch the thought that formed. "It's not weakness to cry, you know."

She stopped and turned, lifting her gaze to meet his with painful slowness. Her chest heaved ever so slightly. "It is in my father's eyes."

And then she was gone.

———•·•———

Light invaded her senses, jabbing mercilessly at her eyes. She blinked and nearly jolted at the sight of the chinked log wall. She eased up on one elbow, squinting against the bright sunlight that streamed through the glass window. With a sigh of pleasure, she snuggled deeper underneath the patchwork quilt and wiggled against the straw-tick mattress. Surely heaven couldn't be any better.

She stretched, relishing the delicious warmth and softness that molded to her curves. A floral fragrance drifted through the air, a reminder that she had enjoyed a hot, steaming bath in the big copper tub the night before. Her hair still carried the scent of the lavender soap Granny had shaved into the water. The cotton nightdress was blessedly light as it curled around her legs. The thought of donning trousers again nearly made her weep.

She ran her fingers through her hair, enjoying the feel of it hanging loose against her shoulders. Sighing, she sat up and gazed out the window at the sunlit autumn morning. She would cut it before they left, but there was no harm in enjoying it a bit longer for the next few days, was there?

The small joy evaporated as last night's revelation drifted in like a cloud and snuffed out her cheerful mood.

Mother was dead, and Cassie was to blame.

Swinging her legs over the side of the bed, she nearly yelped when her bare feet slapped the cold wooden floor. The shock almost made her crawl back under the covers. She pushed away the heaviness shrouding her heart and forced herself to rise. She didn't want to miss a moment with Granny. The time would pass too quickly as it was. Moving to the old wardrobe against the wall, she opened the door with a soft squeak, eyeing the simple frocks hanging inside.

At least she could be Cassie Kendrick for today.

———◆———

Gabe shoved the last chunk of wood into the kitchen stove, his skin tingling with the warmth shimmering from the oven.

"What smells so wonderful?"

Granny Ardie wiped her gnarled hands against her apron. "Cinnamon twists."

He placed his hand over his heart with a melodramatic flourish. "I do believe you've won my heart, dear lady."

Granny swatted the air between them with a cheesecloth. "Behave yourself, Mr. Avery. You can't go on teasing an old lady like that."

Laughing, he walked to the washbasin and splashed water over his dirty hands. Granny Ardie was a gem. No wonder Cassie adored her so.

Granny peered into the oven and shook her head. "Not done yet." She closed the oven door, wincing as she straightened. "My back doesn't cooperate like it once did." She shuffled to the table and sat down with a groan, gesturing to the coffee in waiting cups. "Please, visit with an old woman while we wait for Cassie and our breakfast."

"Happy to oblige." He eased into his chair and inhaled the aroma of the black brew curling in wisps from the cup. Taking a sip, he sighed in pleasure. Coffee. Real coffee. No chicory to be found.

A sweet smile wreathed her face as she looked at him over the rim of her cup. Her eyes were so blue . . . so much like Cassie's. Ardie must have been a beauty when she was younger. Even now with her aged lines, she exuded a sweet spirit. A gentle grace that was subtle yet striking all the same. Like a daisy in a field of prairie grass.

"I am so delighted you've accompanied my Cassie, but I'm afraid we never got to visit properly last evening. Are you a soldier as well?"

"No, ma'am. I'm not as brave as your granddaughter. I'm a photographer."

"Fancy that! I've read daguerreotype is complicated."

"It can be. The new photographic processes are even more so, especially when cannonballs are flying overhead."

Cringing, she sipped. "No doubt." A small smile played around her lips. "Which would make you just as brave as our soldiers, to my way of thinking."

He shook his head, uneasy with the comparison. "My own feeble attempts at courage have more to do with trying to please my employer than any noble cause, I'm afraid. The soldiers are heroes of the highest degree."

"And who is your employer?"

"Mathew Brady."

Her white brows rose. "I've heard of him. Impressive."

"I still can't believe he was willing to give me a chance. My own images could never compare with his."

"He must have seen something in you. Some untapped potential." She leaned forward. "As do I."

Before he could question her further, the sound of rustling skirts caught his attention. He whirled around to greet Cassie as she entered the kitchen, but his words caught in his throat.

She stood on the threshold of the kitchen, wearing a

pale-lavender gown patterned with tiny sprigs of flowers. Though the style was simple, the bodice conformed perfectly to her small waist and feminine curves.

Her dark hair had been washed clean, hanging in glossy waves to her slender shoulders. She had found two simple hairpins and tucked the sides away from her face, leaving the rest of her thick locks hanging free. A soft blush tinged the apples of her cheeks, even as those brilliant-blue eyes shimmered with an unspoken melancholy.

She was breathtaking.

His pulse galloped wildly, though he didn't know why. This was Cassie. Thomas Turner. His friend. But somehow . . . not.

She stooped to plant a kiss on Granny's upturned cheek. "Good morning!"

Her voice was soothing, like the gentle cadence of a creek, but he could do little more than mumble in response. He felt odd. Strangely aware of her presence. What was wrong with him?

Granny stroked her cheek. "Good morning, Cassie, love. Did you rest well?"

"Even with the news of Mother—" she hesitated a moment, face flickering with a shard of pain before she locked it away—"I slept better than I have in ages. Truth be told, I wish I were still tucked into my bed."

An image of her lying across a bed, her dark hair curling against the pillow, slammed into Gabe so hard, he choked on his coffee. Coughing, he winced when she pounded him on the back like he was little Jonah when he crammed too much jerky in his mouth.

"Easy. There's plenty more. No need to gulp it down like it's disappearing."

The humor in her voice was just as vexing as the harsh

spasms racking his throat. After regaining control, he looked up to see Cassie had flitted to the oven to retrieve breakfast, but Granny was staring at him with an odd kind of scrutiny, a smile ghosting her face.

He averted his gaze and toyed with the rim of his cup until his traitorous gaze returned to watch as Cassie lifted a pan of cinnamon twists from the oven. Heat rose from the yeasty bread, filling the room with the scent of sugar and cinnamon. A tendril of mahogany hair sprang free from its pin, and she pushed it back with a slender hand, her skin flushed from the warmth of the oven.

"Now there is an image worth capturing."

Granny's amused observation barely filtered through his senses. He tried to speak, but it came out more as a croak. "Indeed."

Chapter 20

SWINGING THE AX OVER HIS SHOULDER, Gabe slammed it into the wedge of wood with a grunt of exertion. *Thwack!* The wedge split wide and fell apart in perfect division, landing with two clunks on the ground.

Despite the cold afternoon air, Gabe wiped away sweat collecting on the back of his neck and grabbed another large chunk of wood.

He couldn't get the blasted image of Cassie in that dress from his mind. He thought stacking a supply of winter wood for Ardie would help erase the unnerving memory.

It wasn't working.

He brought the ax down once more, scowling when the blade dug deep into the wood and remained stubbornly steadfast. Placing his foot against the wedge, he yanked the ax from its middle, a grumble lurking in the back of his throat.

"Ax getting dull?"

A soft voice invaded, and his head snapped up to see Cassie standing ten feet away, holding a cup in her outstretched arm.

Was there nowhere he could go to escape her? At least until he sorted out these odd sensations and emotions ricocheting through him? Perhaps he was ill.

"Yes, I think it's a bit dull." He reached for the outstretched cup, nearly wincing when his fingers brushed hers. This new awareness wasn't welcome. He gulped the water and relished the way the cold liquid swept down his parched throat. "Thank you. I was thirsty."

Her husky laughter filled the air as she studied the mound of wood. "Small wonder. Did you chop down half the forest?"

Irritation swarmed the back of his neck. With her? More likely with himself.

He set down the cup, picked up the ax, and lifted another wedge of wood onto the chopping block. "While we're here, I might as well as make sure your grandmother is taken care of for the winter."

"That's kind of you."

"It's nothing." He brought down the ax again but misjudged the trajectory. The blade slipped, barely clipping the edge. Slivers of wood went flying. With a growl, he threw the ax to the ground.

Her giggle brought his eyes to hers. "Something amusing, Turner?"

She grinned. "I've just never seen you this way."

"What way?"

"Irritated. You're always so cheerful." She shrugged. "It's amusing to see you so flummoxed."

His frustration siphoned away. It wasn't her fault he was upended. Actually, it was her fault, but he'd rather be shot than admit such.

"Sorry. I must have awakened in a mood."

"No matter. Having a sharp ax would help, I'd imagine. Let me see if Granny has a whetstone in the toolshed."

As she sauntered away, he couldn't help but notice the sway of her hips, the gentle grace of her movements. All the masculine traits of Thomas Turner had been wiped away, leaving only feminine beauty in their place.

Stop it! He tunneled his fingers through his damp hair. He couldn't be attracted to Cassie. He couldn't. She was his friend and nothing more. He could never be with someone like her. She was too independent . . . only a hairsbreadth away from being one of those cursed suffragettes who rankled him so.

And what if he couldn't tamp down the attraction he felt in her presence? Others would notice, and her careful disguise would disintegrate into smoke.

Scraping his fingers over his face, he sighed but found no relief from the tension. He was only feeling this way because of the shock of seeing her in a dress. Yes, that must be it. After being in a camp full of sweaty, smelly men for months on end, it would be odd if he weren't drawn to her in some way. And there would be no escaping her presence for the next few days. Wherever he turned, she had been—and would be—there. He was only thinking about her because she was all there was to think about.

He stretched his aching back, groaning. Photography. That's what he needed. He would escape this afternoon for an hour or two and capture images of the charming cabin and its surroundings. Perhaps Granny would even let him photograph her with her dignified bearing and sweet countenance.

Yes, diversion. Diversion would work. It had to work.

Please, Lord, let it work.

———◆———

Cassie pushed back a wayward lock of hair falling over her brow and resumed scrubbing the pot. In the corner of the kitchen,

Granny sat in her rocker, knitting socks she declared would accompany Cassie back to camp. The creak of the rocker, the soft clicking of her knitting needles soothed Cassie's torn heart.

"You ought not be washing that potato pot."

"I don't mind. I rather enjoy it. The simplicity of it, the normalcy of household chores, is a welcome change."

"I imagine so." Granny heaved a thick sigh. "Are you sure you must return?"

Cassie cringed but did not hedge her answer. They had always been honest with each other. "Yes. It's my duty."

"I know your father's temper left you little choice. It's just that I miss you so." Her lips trembled. "I wonder if enough time has passed to cool his anger."

Cassie shook her head. "You know as well as I do that when he's been in his cups, he has no conscience. No memory. Only rage."

Granny brooded. "Any chance Gabe would stick around? Put a ring on your finger and settle into wedded bliss?"

She scrubbed the pot with renewed vigor. "Don't be absurd. He has no feelings for me of that sort." Something about the admission stung.

Granny harrumphed and mumbled under her breath. Cassie ignored her. Entertaining such a fancy was futile.

"I would never ask him to do such a thing anyway. And even if he wanted to, he couldn't. He's duty bound to finish the work Mr. Brady has begun."

Granny frowned. "But I—"

They both stopped as the rattle and jingle of an approaching wagon drifted through the air. Cassie abandoned the pot, hastening to the window. She gasped as the wagon emerged from the trees.

It was her sister.

"Eliza," she breathed. "She's here."

Granny's eyes widened as she bolted upright in her rocker. "Go outside and into the cellar."

With a nod, she slipped out the back door, picking her way across the dead grass. She shivered. Why hadn't she stopped to grab a shawl?

As she rounded the corner, Gabe stepped from the woods, a smile lighting his face. "You'll never believe what I saw. The most brilliant-crimson cardinal God ever made! It was—"

"Hush!" She grabbed his hand and pulled, dragging him to the cellar door.

His brows rose high. "Where are we going?"

"Into the cellar." She stooped, clutched the grubby latch, and yanked it open. The cool, damp scent of earth swirled around her as she stepped into the dark hole, thankful for the stairs to guide them as they descended.

"Why?"

With a huff of exasperation, she grabbed his shirt and yanked him in behind her, nearly toppling his muscular weight into her own. His warm breath fanned across her neck as they fumbled down the rickety steps.

She looked up to see the yawning expanse of gray sky overhead. "Botheration. I forgot to close the door."

His voice was low and far too close to her ear in the near darkness. "I'll get it."

He crept back up the stairs and pulled the door shut, plunging them into utter darkness. Scraping sounds and footfalls against the stairs. Fingers brushed earth. She could hear his steady breathing but could not see anything but inky black.

"Tell me again why we're down here?" The amused sound of his voice only a foot or two away startled her.

"My sister Eliza arrived. Quite unexpectedly."

"I see."

She rubbed her arms. "Eliza was always the one who could never keep a secret." Old barbs and betrayals rose afresh in her heart. "Took delight in sharing them."

Gabe was quiet as she furiously tried to warm herself. How long would Eliza stay? An hour? Two? The thought of hunkering in the damp, cold space all night nearly made her groan.

Gabe's soft voice intruded. "Well, I would attempt to see what food treasures your grandmother has stored down here, but I'm afraid I would only discover a rodent or cobweb instead."

"Wise decision," she said dryly.

He leaned against the earthen wall, but when his shoulder brushed hers, he stepped away as if stung. He cleared his throat. "I like your grandmother. She's a dear old soul. Vibrant and understanding."

"She is that." She couldn't hold back the smile that formed. "And a terrible flirt, I'm afraid. At least when it comes to you."

His low chuckle at her side caused shivers to travel down her arms. "She just knows it's easier to catch flies with honey than with vinegar."

"And why would she need to catch you?"

He shifted his weight in the darkness. "She's merely judging my character. Wanting to know if I'm trustworthy where her granddaughter is concerned." She heard rather than saw the grin curving his lips. "She adores you."

"She and I have always had a special bond."

She felt him shift to cross his arms. "I can see why. You're both lively, both spiritually minded, both intelligent, and," he teased, "both full of surprises." He rubbed his own arms absently. "Do you think she'll let me capture her image?"

An irrepressible giggle bubbled over. "You flash that handsome smile she's so fond of, and she'll agree to anything you say."

His voice took on a teasing tone as he leaned in. "Why, Cassie Kendrick, do you think I have a handsome smile?"

Never was she so thankful for a lack of light. Her tongue turned to cotton. She opened her mouth to offer a peevish retort, but her brain stalled, unable to conjure up a rebuttal.

A long beat and she hissed, "Oh, hush up."

His infectious laughter chased away her embarrassment, and they both fell silent.

Ten minutes passed. Twenty. She squirmed, eager to generate whatever heat she could muster in the earthen tomb. At least, it was beginning to feel like a tomb. She lost feeling in her toes, her fingers. Even her nose. A slow ache of cold started in her stomach and radiated out in tremors. Her teeth chattered.

"Cold?"

She blew a warm breath of air onto her stiff fingers. "V-v-very."

"No sense suffering alone. Here. I'll wrap my arms around you so we can share some heat."

Her throat suddenly grew dry as his fingers groped for her, capturing her arms with a hesitant touch before slipping around her torso. He rubbed his hands up and down her back to impart his warmth into her trembling form.

Against his chest, she couldn't help but notice the tight pull of muscles through his torso. The strength. She resisted the urge to bury her face in his shirt. He smelled of fresh air and woodsmoke.

He sucked in a gasp. "What was I thinking? Here." He released her and wiggled out of his coat, then draped it across her shoulders, tucking her back into his arms before she could protest.

"No, I don't want you to lose your coat. You—"

With a clang and a squeak the cellar door overhead swung open. Light flooded the space, making Cassie wince against the onslaught.

A feminine gasp sounded as Eliza's face appeared overhead, her features slack in shock.

"Cassandra! What do you think you're doing?"

———◆———

Gabe sat next to Cassie in her grandmother's cabin, feeling as if he were being inspected on the auction block.

He met Eliza's amber eyes from across the room. He would not flinch, though she studied him with a calculating gleam. Ardie sat in the rocker, watching the visit with amusement. Cassie squirmed next to him on the couch.

"Believe me, Eliza, I didn't mean to give you such a fright."

Eliza offered a small smirk in her narrow face . . . a face not unpleasing but severe, likely shaped by hard circumstances more than anything else. "Of that, I'm sure. You seemed just as surprised to see me as I was you. Imagine my astonishment when I went to retrieve some potatoes from the cellar, only to discover you carrying on your indiscretions with—" she sneered—"this man."

Cassie stiffened at his side and he smiled.

Eliza swung her scolding glare to him. "And what, pray tell, is so amusing about your shameful display?"

"There's not much shame in it if you're married." Could she see the lie that spilled far too easily? If he kept his wits about him, she would be none the wiser, and perhaps Cassie could escape her father's rage when he heard she had returned. Studying the pinched woman staring at him in shock, he was positive she would indeed tell him.

Play the part. Protect Cassie. He couldn't very well claim there was no tryst inside the cellar, although they'd only been trying to keep from freezing to death. He reached out and covered Cassie's trembling fingers with his own.

"Married?" Eliza cried as Granny burst into laughter.

"Surprised, aren't you? Imagine my delight when they showed up at my door, bursting with pride."

Bless that woman.

Eliza's gaze swung between Gabe and her grandmother as if unsure how to proceed. "And just when were you going to inform me, Granny?"

Ardie sighed in an irritated fashion. "Now how am I supposed to do that? Hop on old Barnaby and ride bareback to your place?" She shot Eliza a withering look. "You know as well as I do I can't leave here. Not anymore. I'm an old woman and can barely get up out of bed without throwing my back out of kilter." She shifted in her seat. "If you want to know something, Eliza Ann Murphy, you need to hightail it up here to see me more often."

Eliza flushed, and it was all Gabe could do to keep from laughing. Ardie was a shrewd old woman. She had shifted the blame to Eliza and left her floundering. He squeezed Cassie's slim fingers, but they stayed unmoving beneath his touch.

"Well." Eliza tightened her grip on the shawl she'd refused to relinquish when they'd entered the cabin. "This is quite a shock, but a relief, I must admit. When you abandoned Mother, I feared the worst."

Gabe heard Cassie's sharp intake of breath, and a hot anger burned in his chest. What right did Eliza have to come in and fling her accusations? Cassie was the bravest, most selfless woman he'd ever known.

Before he could spill the heated words threatening release, Ardie cast Eliza a reproving look. "Now, dear, you know your father left Cassie little choice. He was soused when he made the arrangement with Erastus, soused when he informed Cassie, and was likely soused when he realized she'd left."

Eliza lifted her chin, though her shoulders relaxed a degree. "That's true enough, but Father can't help it."

Cassie muttered, "He can. He just doesn't want to."

"Nonsense." Eliza shook her head sadly. "Ever since our brother died, he's looked for any way he can to drown his sorrow."

Cassie stiffened yet again, but her trembling increased. "At everyone else's expense." Her voice was strained and thin.

Eliza sniffed. "Not all of us are as unhappy as you claim." Her expression melted from audacity to smugness thinly veiled as pity. "Maybe you had a more difficult time of it because of your temper. You and Father never got along. Or perhaps it was because he'd so hoped you would be a boy to replace baby John. A blessing from Providence, like Job was given after his trial. But then you were born and his hopes were dashed."

Gabe saw it all in Cassie's expression. The pain. The stark rawness of rejection. The way each word sank deep inside, tearing up her worth. Just like a minié ball . . . only much more cruel.

He clenched his jaw and glared at Cassie's sister, more enraged than he'd ever been in his life. Eliza Murphy needed a thrashing.

She directed her attention toward Gabe. Amber eyes should be warm, but hers weren't. They were cold, like butterscotch drops void of sugar. "So, Mr. Avery, how did you meet my sister?"

"Our paths crossed while I was engaged with my occupation."

"And what *is* your occupation?"

He stared at her until she shifted. "I'm a photographer, Mrs. Murphy."

Her brows rose. "Odd occupation, I must say."

"A rewarding one. With the wet plate process now entrenched in the photographic world—and the precision of the Harrison lens—there is no limit to what lies ahead. And Alexander Gardner has all but perfected a new kind of capturing system so effective, the viewer feels he can almost touch the photographed person's warm skin."

Her mouth went slack. Throw out enough jargon and she would change course.

"My, you do appear well versed in the process. I've not heard of this Gardner fellow. Only a fellow named Mathew Brady. Perhaps you've read about him."

Gabe tried to keep himself civil. He felt like a cat playing with a mouse but didn't *want* to feel that way. If only this woman weren't so condescending. "Indeed. He is my employer."

Eliza offered a thin smile and turned back to Cassie. "How blessed you are, Cassandra. I'm sure your life is just one grand adventure now, isn't it?" Her smile dimmed slightly, even as her chin rose a notch. "I can't say things here have changed overly much. The boys have grown like ivy during the summer and little Clara is top speller in her studies." She arched a smug brow. "What with another child on the way, I find myself quite content."

Cassie kept her voice carefully modulated. "I'm so glad, Eliza." She offered no snide remarks, only silence. Gabe's estimation of her rose even higher, if that were possible. This time when he squeezed her hand, she responded in kind.

Eliza's mouth pinched. "Still mousy, aren't you? Never would say much, even as a child. That is, unless Father riled you, and then you mouthed plenty."

Gabe felt Cassie's muscles tighten. He patted her hand and shook his head ever so slightly. "Far from mousy, Mrs. Murphy. Still waters run deep, and all that. My Cassie is the single most clever, self-sacrificing, and kind woman I have ever known." He took a moment to gaze at her. "Beautiful, too."

Her cheeks dusted pink, and he winked at her grandmother. "Second only to Granny Ardie, of course."

Ardie beamed. "See why I like him so, Eliza? The man has sense. Good eyesight too." Cackling, she rose with a soft cracking of joints. "Would you care to dine with us, Liza? I've got a bully salmon smoked and hanging out back."

Eliza stood. "Thank you, no. I was just stopping in to check on my favorite grandmother." She turned to Gabe and Cassie. "Mr. Avery, so nice to meet you. And, Sister—" she leaned forward to brush Cassie's cheek with a peck—"don't forget about us here in Michigan when your husband is famous." She very nearly sneered. "If you can see fit to lower yourself to our humble level, that is."

With a flurry of skirts, she hastened from the cabin, no doubt intending to spread the gossip far and wide.

Gabe bolted the door behind her and scowled. "Vexing woman." He gestured toward Ardie with an apologetic cringe. "Forgive me."

Ardie waved a hand. "Eliza has always been that way. Highstrung. Always jealous of Cassie." Granny spoke to her with a twinkle. "Don't let her poison rankle you. She's unhappy."

"I know. But it does hurt. She hates me."

"She doesn't. She did give you a kiss, after all."

Cassie wrinkled her nose. "Yes, as Judas gave Jesus."

Despite the pall left behind by Eliza's sourness, Gabe chuckled.

Chapter 21

CASSIE SQUIRMED AGAINST THE SOFT BED, unable to settle her mind. Every time she neared slumber's waiting arms, the memory of Eliza's visit scattered her sleepiness away like a cyclone.

When she was little, Eliza had tolerated her. But as they'd grown older, the tolerance had turned to venom, and Cassie was helpless to know why.

Rolling to her side, she tucked the pillow under the crook of her elbow and stared out the window. A high moon shone down, bathing the cabin and woods in bright silver. Light chased away sinister shadows.

Just like Gabe defending her against her bitter sister.

Her chest tightened, her eyelids fell shut, and she remembered his warm fingers cupping hers. His praise of her abilities. Her beauty. The tangible affection that shone when he'd studied her. Heady sensations covered her like the warmth of a July sun.

But none of it was genuine. Her eyes flew open and the flicker in her chest dissipated, replaced with an empty ache.

Angry with herself for caring, she tossed to her opposite side and yanked at the covers tangled around her legs. He was dissembling. She had been too. That was the plan, after all. Act the part of the happy bride and groom if Cassie were discovered by her family.

So why did the realization sting so?

Heaving a sigh, she stood and ran her fingers through her disheveled hair. She needed the necessary. Perhaps then she could sleep.

She tiptoed down the hallway and into the kitchen, not bothering to light a lamp. She knew the path by heart.

Slipping to the row of pegs by the kitchen door, she draped a thick shawl over her shoulders and crept into the frigid night air. She clamped her teeth together to keep them from chattering as she picked her way carefully toward the outhouse. Thanks to the bright moon, the task was easy.

She'd just stepped out of the necessary and released the handle of the door when her heart slammed into her throat.

"Lo and behold, if it isn't my prodigal daughter."

That deep, slurred voice had haunted her every moment since fleeing almost seven months before. The blood leached from her face. She turned slowly, her breath erratic. She saw nothing save for a moonlit yard, the dark, looming presence of the cabin, and faceless trees lifting up their fingers to the night sky. "Wh-where are you?"

A large shadow stepped away from the back of the cabin and moved to stand in front of her. The watery light illuminated half of her father's scowling face. A beard covered his jaw. Even in the moon glow, his eyes were red-rimmed and dull, save for the flickering rage lurking in their depths.

He swayed slightly on his feet as he approached. "I can't believe you have the gall to show your face here again." The sour stench of his rancid breath assaulted her. Cringing, she took a step back. "You're a disgrace. A failure the moment you were born, and you've been a failure ever since."

The barb stung, though she knew he'd thought it often enough. He'd just never given the hateful words voice until now. The lash of his censure was quickly smothered by a fiery anger that sparked in her chest. "You're drunk."

He lumbered forward. "I have reason to be. You shamed me in front of Erastus. Humiliated me before my friends." He sneered. "Your betrayal killed your mother."

Her heartbeat skidded to a slow, dull thrum in her head. He was drunk . . . just babbling and blathering. Wasn't he?

She turned to leave, and his meaty hand curled around her arm and spun her around, yanking her to him like a rag doll. She fell against his barrel chest with a grunt of pain.

"You wretched creature!" He shook her until her teeth rattled. "You defied me and broke your mother's heart."

"No!" she whimpered against the pain of his crushing grip, but he held fast.

He was so close she could see the streaks of crimson in his eyes. His face was mottled. The veins in his neck bulged.

"What do you think happened when you ran away in your spite? Your mother went looking for you, despite rain and storms. Trudged all over kingdom come, searching, crying, praying she could find you."

Her stomach clenched as her throat and eyes burned. *No, God. Please, no.*

Shaking her until her head screamed in anguish, he shouted, "It was because of you she got sick. It's your fault. It's all your fault!"

She tried to lurch away, fumbling to free her arm. In his drunken state, he lost his grip on her flailing limb, but the escape was only temporary. Before she could flee, he backhanded her across the mouth. Pain exploded through her skull as the impact flung her to the ground. She landed on the freezing earth and groaned against the agony slicing from her hip to her head. A sob shuddered through her.

His menacing presence loomed large. She tucked her head into her hands and curled her aching legs to her middle. She knew what would happen next.

Lord, deliver me.

"If you lay another hand on her, I'll thrash you senseless."

Her chest heaved as Gabe's voice cut through the night air with all the force of a runaway horse.

Over her head, Father snapped, "Go away, boy."

"I only warn once."

Father broke into a string of slurred curses. "Maybe you need to be taught a lesson too."

The sound of flesh pounding flesh met her ears. She cringed and tried to pull herself to her feet, but as soon as she placed weight on her left ankle, it collapsed beneath her in a burning flash of pain. With a cry she fell back.

More grunts, another punch, and she blinked, watching her father's massive silhouette crumple to the ground.

In seconds, Gabe's handsome face hovered above hers, his breathing rapid. At the sight of his tender expression, she burst into tears.

He scooped her into his arms and carried her into the cabin, settling her in a kitchen chair as if she weighed little more than a kitten. A match sizzled and flared to life. He held it to the lamp's wick, and soon a bright light beamed from the glass globe, chasing away the darkness. He brought it to the table, where she sat, her arms wrapped around her middle. Her ankle throbbed. She licked her lips against the stinging sensation at their corner and tasted the metallic stickiness of blood.

He said nothing, only moved to pour water into the basin and fetch a clean rag. Carrying it to the table, he set it down and pulled up a chair for himself, settling across from her not more than three feet away. A trembling from somewhere deep inside rattled her ribs and extended to her limbs.

"Cass, look at me."

His soft voice brooked no argument. She lifted her gaze and nearly wept all over again at his tenderness.

He brushed a wayward tendril of hair from her forehead and smoothed it back as if she were a scared child. "You're safe now. He can't hurt you any longer."

Her chin trembled. She nodded as hot tears escaped and ran down her cheeks. She dropped her head and he took her in his arms, rocking her gently, murmuring words of comfort into her hair. The tremors eased and a sliver of warmth unfurled through her.

She eased back with a sniff, embarrassed at her lack of control. "Forgive me."

"You did nothing wrong. Here." He lifted her chin and gazed at her lips with an assessing eye. "The corner of your mouth is bleeding."

"I'm fine."

Ignoring her, he dipped the cloth in the water, wrung out the excess, and dabbed the torn skin with a gentleness that melted her heart. He would be a good father—and make some woman a good husband. Her thoughts scattered once more.

Unaware of her wayward reflections, he cleaned the blood from her lips. "Much better." When his fingers grazed hers, she gasped and yanked them away. His eyes gleamed with amusement. "I'm not trying to break them, you know. Only clean them."

Blinking, she looked down to see dirt and blood marring her hands. After a moment's hesitation, she held them out for his inspection. He wiped them with the cloth as well, in slow, methodical patterns. His calm manner soothed her frayed nerves.

"He told me it was my fault Mother died."

Gabe lifted his gaze to hers, holding fast, his focus unwavering. "I heard. But it's not true."

Her voice snagged on another sob. "But what if it is? What if searching for me weakened her constitution? I should have told her my plans. I should never have left."

A strange stillness passed over him. "Do you realize that if you had not left, I would have missed out on knowing you? The most wonderful person I've ever met?"

Her eyes slid shut at his praise. She didn't deserve it.

He let his thumb stroke the soft skin of her jaw. His voice was low. "Your father is drunk and angry, Cass. Nothing more. Your mother's passing is tragic, but life and death are not in your hands."

"But if I—"

"Your father hurts you because he speaks out of his own pain, from his own demons. It has nothing to do with you. Nothing."

She searched his face, leaning into the gentle fingers caressing her jaw. "It's a hard thing to believe when it's the opposite of what I've been told all my life."

His face was close. Earnest yet sad. "Just because someone hands you a blade doesn't mean you have to cut yourself with it."

A small smile broke through her sniffles. "I wish I saw myself the way you do."

"It's the way God sees you too. You're caring and kind. Intelligent and courageous." He swallowed, his gaze dropping to her lips, his voice hoarse. "You're more than just a friend, Cass."

Somehow, the distance between them disappeared. Cradling her face in his warm hands, he hovered a breath away from her lips for a moment before claiming them with a gentleness that robbed her of coherent thought. Dizzying sensations rushed through her.

Her heart took flight.

———•••———

Gabe's heart thundered a staccato rhythm as he stroked the soft skin of Cassie's lovely face. He kissed her with a heady euphoria that stole his breath. She was soft and perfect. Ecstasy.

Fearing he was hurting her bruised lips, he broke away and searched her sweet face held in his hands. She whispered his name before leaning in for more.

Her need fueled his own, and he plunged his fingers into her thick hair, pulling her to him once more. His pulse roared in his ears. He didn't want it to stop. Couldn't pull away.

"Cass . . ." He nuzzled her ear. She clung to him with a desperation that undid him. When his hands moved from her hair to stroke her back, he felt the soft fabric of her shawl under his fingers and froze. He couldn't sully her reputation. He would not.

Leaning away, he rested his forehead against hers and slipped his fingers down to clasp hers.

"What just happened?" Her voice was breathy.

He chuckled lightly and ran his thumbs over the backs of her hands. "I'm not sure, but it was enjoyable."

She blushed, and he smiled. He'd never seen her like this.

Embarrassed, unsure. The immovable soldier had melted into a feminine enchantress, unaware of the spell she had cast.

"I'm loath to tear myself away, but I fear I will lose control completely if I don't."

She nodded, looking down at their entwined fingers.

He studied the long sweep of her dark lashes. "Are you all right?"

"Yes. Yes, I am now."

He chuckled, his chest thumping when a smile curved her lips. "And physically? Your ankle?"

"My ankle is sore, but if you'll just help me to my door, I'll hop into bed and rest."

Warmth engulfed him. Heaven help him. Now that he had tasted her sweetness, he could think of little else.

He scooped her up into his arms and carried her down the hall to her bedroom door. She guided her feet to the floor and winced, releasing him to grasp the doorframe. She gazed up at him with those luminous eyes.

"Thank you."

Throat tight, he knew he couldn't trust himself. He pressed a kiss to her forehead and eased the door open with a thin squeak. She hobbled to her bed as he slipped the door closed. With a heavy breath, he rested his head against the wall and slid down to the floor to keep watch over her through the night.

Her father would not hurt her again. Gabe would see to it.

Chapter 22

CASSIE LOWERED HERSELF TO THE MILKING STOOL with a grunt, her ankle bearing testament to the previous night's struggle.

She ran her fingers over Molasses's light-brown fur, keeping her voice soothing and gentle. "There, girl. Just coming to fetch some milk for your mistress. Granny likes her coffee with cream, you know."

Molasses flicked her tail and offered a grouchy moo in response.

"I know. I'm tired this morning too."

Judging by Granny's innocent questions at breakfast, she had heard nothing of Father's fury or their tussle. Cassie said not a word to inform her, save her response when Granny asked about the faint limp she had been unable to hide.

"It's nothing. Just stepped crooked on the way back from the outhouse."

Not exactly a lie, and Granny had accepted the explanation without questioning her further. Gabe was nowhere to be found. He'd no doubt been embarrassed by Cassie's weepy neediness and her brazen behavior the night before.

Scalding mortification swamped her cheeks. How could she have acted in such a way? She was a soldier of the Union army, for mercy's sake. A sharpshooter. She had seen things that could make some men lose heart, yet one furious encounter with Father had turned her into a blubbering mess. And then into a shameless vixen.

Even now, Gabe's sweet kisses burned her lips.

Pushing away the heady sensation, she ran her fingers down to Molasses's udder and squeezed the milk out in streams, listening to the liquid as it hissed into the metal bucket. The cream foamed, frothy and rich, as she emptied the creature of her burden.

She had tiptoed outside after breakfast, wary that Father might still be lurking about, but all signs of his presence had disappeared. It was almost as if the entire thing had never happened. No, her arm was still bruised from his cruel grip, her mouth and ankle still sore, and his accusations continued to burden her heart with guilt.

I'm so sorry, Mother.

The barn door squeaked open and her muscles tightened until she saw Gabe's silhouette framed against the pale sunlight.

"Cass?"

His voice seemed gravelly this morning. Strained. As if he'd slept poorly or perhaps not at all. Had he relived what had happened in the kitchen as oft as she had? She had managed to snatch only an hour's sleep, alternating between elation and humiliation at the way she'd behaved.

Clearing her throat, she murmured, "I'm here." Molasses swatted her tail again, irritated by the interruption.

He stepped inside, blinking to adjust his eyes to the barn's shadows. The single window it boasted didn't illuminate much. He approached and she swallowed, returning her attention to the task at hand. His footfalls crunched against the straw-covered floor as he moved to stand beside her. "How did you sleep?"

"Not well."

He chuckled quietly. "Me neither." His voice sounded oddly warm and intimate.

Her pulse thudded. She must change his focus. "Where have you been?"

He grabbed an old crate, plopped it next to her, and sat down, studying her profile. "Walked a mile to the Jenkins place, per Ardie's instructions. I want to fix her porch steps before we leave in a few days, and she told me he would be the closest neighbor with fresh lumber on hand."

She kept her eyes on the rapidly filling bucket. "That's kind of you."

"Not really. I have nothing else to do except take your grandmother's photograph. She's been reminding me every hour since I first suggested it."

The comment normally would have elicited a giggle, but Cassie fell silent, her mood growing dark.

"Do you want to talk?"

The hissing streams of milk were shrinking.

"No."

Gabe sighed. "Why not?"

"Just don't."

"Pushing me away, I see."

She clenched her teeth but refused to be prodded.

"Cassie, look at me."

She released Molasses and slowly lifted her gaze to his, shame tightening within her.

"I can take a lot of things, Cass. War, flying bullets, and an angry father. But the one thing I can't bear is you pushing me out. Please don't." He reached up and skimmed her cheek with his fingers. The brick wall of her resolve crumbled into ash.

Dropping her head into her hands, she whispered, "I can't believe I acted the way I did last night."

"What do you mean? What way?"

She couldn't look at him. "Like a—a hussy."

Deep, rumbling laughter burst from his chest, and she snapped her head up, glaring. "I don't think it's funny at all."

He smiled, his green eyes darkening. "I was the one who kissed you, remember?"

"But I—I—" She didn't want to say it.

His white teeth flashed. "You enjoyed it?"

Warmth bloomed. "Yes. Far too much."

He reached for her fingers and tucked them into his own. "Is that what troubles you?"

"Partially." It felt strange confiding in him. She'd never told her deepest thoughts to anyone, save Granny. "Mostly I can't let go of Father's accusations. The thought of Mother wandering through the woods and succumbing to the chill of damp and exhaustion—" she forced down the ache in her throat—"it's tormenting me. How could I have been so selfish?"

Gabe emitted a dry laugh. "I've often wondered the same thing about myself."

"Your mother and father?"

"In the past, yes. But more recently."

She studied his downcast face. Stubble lined his angular jaw. Shadows smudged under his eyes. "Why would you feel selfish? You're the kindest person I know."

He was quiet for a long moment before locking his gaze on hers. "How did I come to be shot, Cass?"

Puzzled at the question, she frowned. "Don't you remember?

Rebels shot at you while you were getting ready to photograph our regiment crossing the Potomac."

"But why did they fire?"

Her breath thinned. He didn't need to know. She wouldn't let him know. Yet she could not force a lie past her lips.

He smiled sadly. "I know it was my fault."

Her heart churned. "But how? How did you find out?"

"There was a cheery little piece in the paper about my inadvertent signal to the Confederates camped nearby. I happened to read it on the train while you were sleeping. One of the injured soldiers told a reporter he saw a flash from my camera lens just before the firing began." Pain shuddered across his features. "After waiting half the morning for the sun to be in position, you can bet I remember how bright it finally was. Its reflection, and my foolishness, is what caused our friends to be captured. Some of them drowned." He looked away and released her hands. "And I put you in danger."

"Gabe." She reached for his arm, trying to press her words deep inside him. "It was only an accident. War is anything but predictable. Any number of things could have caused the same results. Please don't blame yourself."

"But Selby and Johnson and so many others lost everything because of me."

She frowned. "Don't you think God saw it all? Don't you believe you can trust him, despite the pain or how chaotic his way might seem at the moment?"

He stroked her cheek. "Listen to you. Couldn't the same be said of you and your mother?"

She stared at him. "So what do we do?"

"I don't know." He fingered a wayward lock of her hair. "I suppose we learn from it and keep living. Each day is a gift from God. I don't want to squander it."

"Neither do I."

He leaned in to brush her lips with a kiss, but she placed a hand on his chest, stopping him short. "Gabe—"

He watched her, the desire in his eyes palpable.

"I can't."

"Why?"

A dozen excuses flitted through her muddled mind, but they all eluded her when he looked at her with such tender longing. She latched on to the first thing she could think of. "We're not courting. It's not proper."

He kissed her forehead, murmuring against her skin, "Easy enough to rectify."

Heavens, but her body hummed to his touch like a hive of bees. She forced herself to be logical. "In the middle of war? With me dressed as Thomas Turner?"

He eased back and sighed. "That *is* a challenge." His face brightened, hopefulness replacing his weary expression. "Of course, you could just choose not to return."

A strange twinge niggled at her. "What are you saying?"

"Let Thomas Turner go."

She blinked, trying to understand what he was asking of her. "Just disappear? And do what? Make myself subject to Father's drunken tirades or whatever other lusty-eyed suitor he drags over to challenge your claim? And he will, you know."

Gabe stood and tunneled his fingers through his hair. "He thinks we're married."

"But we're not."

He looked away, a muscle ticking in his jaw.

"Have you given up your dreams, Gabe? Will you wash your hands of your photography and abandon your work?"

He frowned. "Of course not."

She held his gaze, challenging him. "Neither can I."

An uncharacteristic spark of anger lit his eyes. "Your dream is to bunk with rough, swearing men? To don a Union uniform and be shot at? To die young or be so traumatized you wish you had?"

His outburst was like a slap across the face. The sting cut deep. "What are you saying?"

He studied her, his jaw tight. "I think you know."

Dread washed over her. Yes, she knew.

"You take on a man's duty."

"Yes, and I do it well. Better than most."

His anger appeared to siphon away as he rubbed the back of his neck. His shoulders slumped. "But you only ran away to fight to avoid marriage to Leeds. To continue now, if he believes he cannot claim your hand, is ludicrous. Why put yourself through it further?"

She fought to speak calmly past the anger roiling through her. "I admit it was about that at first, but it's more than that now. Do you remember the evening the contraband soldiers sat around the fire with us, sharing how they escaped slavery only to enlist as soon as they could find the Union lines?" Her resolve hardened. "After all those years of dreaming of freedom, yearning for it, begging the Almighty for one taste, the first thing they did upon receiving it was sign up to fight." She swallowed. "They understand their purpose on earth is about more than themselves. Those men showed me the shallowness of my own motives." She looked down into the full pail. "It must be about more than hiding from Father. It has to be."

"It *has* to be? Sounds to me as if you're looking for reasons."

Tears burned as her chin rose. "If it's not, Mother may have died in vain."

"Cass—"

"This is about right and wrong. Ideals and convictions." She searched his eyes, wishing she could erase his glare. "It's my duty. I can't abandon our friends or the cause many of them have already died for. I won't."

He stared hard at the barn wall for a long moment, seemingly lost in thought. "I don't know if I can let you do that."

Let her? Did he think that exchanging kisses and affections with her entitled him to control her decisions? Her future? Panic clawed the back of her throat.

Were all men controlling like her father, demanding their own way at the risk of crushing her heart in the process?

Something within her curled in on itself. How foolish she'd been.

The thud of horse hooves clopping through dry leaves snagged her attention away from the words begging to burst past her lips. A lone man rode up to the cabin, his lumpy hat pulled low over his face. After he tethered the horse to a nearby tree, she watched his gait as he strode to the cabin's front door. Something about him seemed so familiar. . . .

The man looked from the cabin to the barn's open door and her blood froze. Erastus Leeds.

She stood on shaky legs and stepped closer to Molasses's head, hoping to hide in the shadows. Gabe must have sensed her unease, for he moved to stand like a sentinel in the frame of the barn door, his form strong and unyielding.

"May I help you?" he called across the yard, his voice jovial, though Cassie knew him well enough to realize he was as tensed as a rattler.

"The name is Leeds. I come by to verify the gossip spewing from Kendrick's mouth. Is it true his daughter has returned?"

Gabe whispered, "Let me take care of him. Stay here."

Before she could reply, Gabe walked from the barn. "It's true, all right. But his daughter won't be receiving any more marriage proposals."

As the men's voices and footfalls faded, the coil in her chest tightened. Erastus was cruel and cunning. If they came to blows . . .

She dropped her head against Molasses's, her heart sore. The cow made a guttural noise and nuzzled her neck.

She had opened her heart to a man who would surely break it. Had she learned nothing from her parents' volatile relationship? Men commanded and domineered. Women meekly obeyed and suffered in silence.

Not her. She refused to let any man control her as Father had done to Mother. She must guard her heart. Her future and happiness depended on it.

Yet she feared the damage had already been done.

———•———

"I don't know who you are, but I'd like to talk with my intended."

Gabe studied the man glaring at him. Greasy hair hung in his dark eyes. A crooked, hawkish nose jutted above a stubble-covered jaw. His form was lean but by no means weak. He looked sly and tough . . . like a hungry coyote spoiling for a fight.

"If you're speaking of Cassie, you're mistaken. She's not your intended."

Leeds spit out a curse and took a menacing step forward. "I paid what Kendrick asked. His daughter will be my wife."

Gabe planted his feet and crossed his arms. "That'll be impossible."

"Why?"

"Because she's my wife."

Leeds's jaw went slack. "What? You stole my property?" His fist swung, but Gabe ducked.

Grabbing the man by his shirt collar, Gabe slammed him

into the barn wall, letting his head bounce against it with a sickening crack. "Cassie is not your property!"

Leeds struggled against him, but Gabe tightened his push as he dug his forearm into the man's throat. The squirming reminded him of a pinned rat.

"Did you pay . . . Kendrick too?"

Gabe glared. "I've paid Cassie's father nothing."

Leeds grimaced under the pressure of Gabe's arm. His face became mottled with red as he gasped for breath. "So . . . it wasn't . . . because of his gaming debts . . . then."

Recognizing the defeat in the man's face, Gabe slackened his hold. "I have no idea why Cassie's father does what he does. What I do know is that Cassie will not be marrying you." Gabe released him with a small shove.

Leeds glared and rubbed the back of his head. "More's the pity." He smirked and Gabe's fingers curled into fists.

Leeds saw the movement and stepped toward his horse. "Kendrick will pay for this. He'll pay or I'll kill him."

And then he was gone.

Something was wrong.

Gabe watched Cassie from the corner of his eye as she observed him preparing his camera to capture Ardie's image. He could see it in her stiff shoulders, the way she averted her eyes whenever he looked toward her. Since their quarrel in the barn, she had avoided him completely. Quiet, intense . . . too much like Thomas Turner.

"You don't suppose I'll break your fancy camera box, do you?"

His focus swung back to Ardie and he smiled, watching her primp her gray curls as she sat in a patch of sunlight behind the cabin. The breeze was cool, but the sun was brilliant. The exposure would not need to be long.

"As pretty as you are, capturing your image will only improve my lens and make my work better than it normally is."

Her blue eyes danced. "Stuff and nonsense."

He chuckled as she smoothed the shawl draped over her shoulders. Ducking underneath the black curtain, he dropped the prepared plate into the camera and let his hands hover over the cap. "Here we go. On the count of three, hold very still until I tell you we're finished. One, two, three."

He removed the cap and ticked off the seconds under his breath. The image was sweet and nostalgic. Ardie sitting in a simple chair, the cabin in the background. A peaceful expression illuminated her face. He prayed he wouldn't accidentally ruin the image when he developed it. Finding a spot dark enough to finish the chemical wash would be tricky.

"All done." He stepped out from under the cover of the curtain to find he and Ardie were alone. "Where is Cassie?"

Ardie frowned. "She snuck away into the woods a moment ago. She's been acting a mite peculiar today." She speared Gabe with a sharp look. "Did you two have a tiff?"

He ran his fingers under his suddenly too-tight collar. "Something like that."

Ardie sighed. "A word of advice? Don't let any strain between you fester. My Cass is an angel, but the longer she stews about something, the bigger it seems in her mind."

He'd gathered as much already. "I'll go find her. First, let me get you inside and out of this breeze." He winked. "And thank you for letting me take your photograph. You're the prettiest thing I've captured in months."

Ardie laughed and stood carefully, placing her veined hand

in Gabe's waiting elbow. "That's not saying much when most of your work consists of photographing the dead."

He found Cassie, but she asked to be alone.

Gabe watched her retreating form as she buried herself deeper into the woods. Was it so wrong to want to protect her? To ensure her safety so they could build a happy life together?

He didn't understand her one bit. She was retreating in on herself like a turtle slinking into its shell. And he was helpless to know how to love her out of it.

They had only one more day before they must leave. One more day to listen to her silver laughter and watch her dazzling smiles. One more day for her to steal his breath with her warm looks and feminine grace. One more day to kiss her intoxicating lips. Then she would be gone, replaced by a mirage.

How could he give her up?

He stared at his curled fists. The stain of chemicals darkened the tips. Dirt from splitting firewood blackened his nails. So much like Mither's. He blinked.

So much like Mither's . . .

He'd grabbed her hand that February morning in the cold flat. Her fingers were calloused and rough from working at the textile mill day after day. Her stout figure had whittled away, and dark rings shadowed her eyes. When he'd tugged her to a stop, she had turned slowly, her face resigned, too weary to fight.

"You must not return to the mill. It's too much for you." He rubbed her frigid hands between his own and let his gaze drift to the coal bin. Empty. Again.

She smiled sadly. "I must, Gabriel. You know I must."

"It's killing you. The hours are too long. The lack of proper air, the chemicals . . ." He paused and searched her face. "Da's been gone six months. I couldn't bear to lose you too."

She tugged her shawl more tightly around her shoulders. "We're both doing all we can. Your job at the docks helps tremendously. Between that and what I make—"

He released a harsh breath and turned away. "And yet we have no money for coal. None for clothes. We barely make the rent and have stretched our food stores until we eat but two meals a day." He stared at the floor, his heart shredding. "Da would have never let this happen. I should be doing more."

"Gabriel." Mither breathed his name and rushed to him, her eyes flooding with concern. "You take on too much. You're barely out of boyhood. You can't be expected to manage as a man like your da would have, nor would anyone want you to."

He shook his head. "I tried, you know. I tried getting a better-paying job in one of the nice shops downtown. I didn't want to be working at the wharf. I applied to keep the books for shopkeepers, be a salesclerk, anything that would provide you an easy go of it." He ran a hand down his face. "No one would take me. Jobs are in short supply. If I could just find better work, all of our problems would go away. You could—"

"Gabriel." Mither cupped his cheek. "You have a beautiful heart. Everyone who meets you loves you. The way you see the world is so incredibly special, but, Son—" she shook her head slowly—"you can't take care of me alone."

And then she'd left for her shift.

His heart had twisted and bled that day.

Bitterness wrapped around him. He'd not been able to help Da, nor his mother, and now Cassie was choosing to push him away as well. He was never enough.

"The way you see the world is so incredibly special . . ."

He glanced at the camera clutched in his hands. On impulse, he'd dropped a wet plate inside after photographing Ardie that morning. He knew why now. He wanted to capture Cassie's likeness—to remember her as she truly was, not the mask she donned in battle. He wanted to cling to the warmth of her vibrant beauty, to have her entrenched in his heart. He wanted Cassie. Not Turner.

His steps quiet, he slunk through the woods, searching. He wouldn't let her see him. Leaves crunched under his feet. He drew slow breaths, his gaze roaming the gray woods . . .

There she was.

She sat on a flat rock overlooking a gentle stream wending its way through the hilly terrain. Her dark hair brushed her shoulders, curling at its tips. She leaned over the rock, a dried crimson leaf held between her fingers as she swept it over the water, watching it cut, slice, and swirl a path through the rippling creek.

Gabe held his breath. She was exquisite. Perfect.

He crept as close as he dared, lifted the camera, and removed the lens cap.

———◆———

Cassie stared glumly out the soot-streaked window, letting the speeding train lull her into a sleepy bob.

At her side, Gabe was silent. Too quiet. She ought not complain. That's what she wanted, right? To push him away so he couldn't hurt her?

She hadn't bargained for how deeply she would ache for him.

When she had entered the kitchen this morning, wearing her laundered uniform and her freshly shorn locks, his face had been filled with deep sadness . . . a sadness so intense, it had physically hurt her to see him.

Granny had shed tears as they left, but waved them away with a bright, courageous smile. Cassie had barely held back her own tears, her throat burning as they departed in the clattering wagon. Sadness mingled with relief. Seeing her grandmother had been a tonic to her spirit, but the news of Mother's death, along with the ominous shadow of Father's lurking presence, covered her like a dark blanket. Even Gabe's disapproval soured the closeness they had shared.

His presence at her side was like a hot poker, but she dared not even look his way. Unbidden, the tingling memory of his kisses, his tender touch, his strength as he held her spun through her like warm honey. How was it possible to miss someone who was sitting beside her?

It was for the best. She knew it was. They couldn't build a relationship, at least not as a man and woman, trapped in the horrors and rigor of war.

She dropped her head against the train wall, letting the rumbling vibrations rattle her skull. Perhaps the intrusive sensation would shake the memory of Gabe's touch from her mind. But it couldn't rattle the impress his love had branded on her heart.

The very thought of returning to the regiment as Thomas Turner struck her with a weariness she couldn't explain. She could just walk away. Gabe had said so. Had pleaded with her to do so. At this moment, she was surprised by how tempted she was to agree.

And that realization scared her more than anything else.

Chapter 23

"Private Turner! Did you see what the Swede brought back for us?"

Cassie turned from cleaning her rifle as Jonah raced up to her side, cheeks rosy. Why did the young never seem affected by the bitter snap of winter mornings?

Her breath fogged. "I haven't heard a thing about it."

Jonah grinned widely. "He just returned from furlough, you know. His wife is a bully good cook. Maybe that's why the Swede grew so big. I dunno. Anyhow, she packed four haversacks full of food for him, and he said he's going to share!"

"Mighty generous of him."

Jonah's eyes danced. "Especially when one of the sacks contains a ham."

Cassie's mouth watered. How long since she'd tasted a real ham? Not the fatty salt pork of their daily rations.

"Not only that. A women's relief group sent a wagon full of boxes filled to the brim with clothes, dried fruit, and new socks. And McKay is busy right now cutting down a tree for me to decorate."

"What are you going to use for decorations?"

The lad's freckled nose scrunched in thought. "Probably hardtack. Maybe some strips of dried beef." He gave a toothy smile. "I saw inside Private Hanover's tent once, and I know he has a pair of bright-red socks tucked in there. Maybe I can borrow 'em."

Cassie shook her head. Life was never dull with Jonah underfoot.

"The men are gathering in an hour to sing carols. You coming?"

"No. I volunteered to assist at Mansion House Hospital in Alexandria today. My transport will be here any minute." She had no desire to make merry with the men when her heart was so miserable. Camp was unbearable with Gabe's long looks in her direction.

Scowling, Jonah stuffed his chapped hands in his pockets. "Ain't no fair. Having to work on Christmas."

She shrugged. "I don't mind. Besides, what better way to celebrate the Savior than easing the suffering of others?"

Jonah frowned. "I reckon." He leaned in, offering a conspiratorial wink. "I'll try to save you a piece of ham."

Cassie chuckled as he scampered off. If she were ever blessed with a son, she hoped he'd be as bright and have as much gumption as Jonah Phifer.

The ride to Alexandria was cold and unadventurous in the back of the army wagon. Cassie hunkered down in her wool coat, blowing into her numb hands every few minutes.

When she entered the hospital, a burst of heat warmed her, making her face and fingers tingle. Discarding her wool coat, she tugged the kepi down over her eyes, ever mindful of the feminine graces that might give her true identity away. That had been the hardest part of returning to camp after visiting Granny: eliminating the signs of her femininity. That, and keeping Gabe at arm's length.

Stop thinking about him.

Irritated with herself, she walked toward Mrs. Grimes, the woman issuing orders with a clipped tone to the other nurses.

"Private Turner reporting for duty, ma'am."

The matron's thin lips tugged upward. "No need for military formality, Private Turner. It's Christmas." Her eyes twinkled. "And we're pleased to have your assistance today. We have the normal rounds of medicine to dispense, average duties, but we want the day to be special for our wounded men." Her face clouded as a thick cloak of sadness descended.

"You look as if you have someone on your mind, ma'am."

Blinking away the melancholy, she offered a wan smile. "Yes. My own son is in a hospital in South Carolina. You're very astute, Private Turner."

"I'm sorry you can't be with him, ma'am. Today especially."

"Thank you. All the more reason to pour my love into the brave boys here." A gentle serenity softened the lines around her eyes and mouth. "Cook is preparing dishes of plum pudding for all the patients. If you would be so kind as to distribute them upon her word, it would be appreciated."

"Yes, ma'am."

"We have a wide variety of surprises for the patients today. I'll find you when we are ready for the next round of gifts."

Nodding, Cassie walked past the largest patient room on the bottom floor, offering smiles to those she passed. With a bit of searching, she found the kitchen in the back of the hospital, as well as the harried cook attempting to dish up enough pudding for the hundreds of men inhabiting the building. A room right next to the kitchen was filled with chattering females and convalescing soldiers. Most of the women sat on the floor, their skirts billowed around them as they bent pine branches into wreaths. Pine needles and red ribbon covered the floor. The scent of cinnamon and musky pine chased away the usual sour smells of illness that inhabited the military hospital.

In the corner of the crowded room, a large stack of glass bottles filled with liquids loomed over the chaos.

"Need any help?"

Several of the volunteers looked up, offering cheery welcomes. One of them, a stout woman with her brown hair parted in a perfect line down her head, cackled loudly. "You want to bend wreaths, or did the wall of spirits catch your eye, Private?"

Cassie blinked. "Pardon?"

Another woman, slight of build with a topknot of springy gray hair, scolded her friend. "Don't tease him so, Ann." The tiny woman beamed at Cassie. "Ann believes you noticed the wall of spirits in the corner."

Cassie shrugged. "It's kind of hard to miss."

The wisp of a woman laughed. "A gift from Mary Todd Lincoln for our soldiers."

"All of that?" Cassie studied the tower of bottles, astonished at the volume of amber liquid. "Wherever did she acquire it all?"

"She gathered up all the unsolicited gifts of liquor that were brought to the White House in the past year."

Cassie spoke slowly, still in awe of the elaborate festivities the hospital had undertaken. "I spurn spirits myself, but I must say—" she chuckled—"I do believe the patients are going to have a merry Christmas indeed."

Mrs. Grimes smoothed back a wayward tendril of gray hair and dabbed a handkerchief over the sweat beading on her brow. "I can't thank you enough for your assistance, Private Turner."

Offering a tired smile, Cassie dropped the last load of wood into the stove and eased the cast-iron door shut with a twist. "My pleasure, ma'am."

Cassie straightened as Mrs. Grimes waved a hand in front of her face to cool her moist skin. "The air feels overly warm in here to me, but the men keep complaining about a draft."

"You're overheated from working so hard." Cassie tugged her kepi lower over her brow. "And the men can't do much moving. When I sprinkled lime out back, the air smelled like coming snow."

The matron sighed. "I feared as much. Well, there's nothing to be done about it." Her face brightened, though her shoulders showed the telltale sag of fatigue. "I need to get busy changing the second- and third-floor linens."

"I can help."

"Would you? I'd be so grateful."

Cassie nodded and watched her open a closet door tucked in the back of the big room, tugging down a wobbling stack of blankets and sheets.

The matron dropped them into Cassie's hands. "That should get you started. Why don't you take the second floor and I'll take the third. You can fetch more linens from this closet when you've used up this supply."

"Yes, ma'am."

Cassie climbed the hospital stairway, listening to her footsteps scrape and echo against the walls. It was well into the afternoon and she had yet to sit, but she didn't mind. Making the day nice for the patients and workers alike was far better than sitting in the cold, trying to fill the empty ache inside. At least here she was too busy to think. She had purpose.

Her back twinged as she went from room to room changing linens, encouraging the men in the occupied beds with a kind word or offering a sip of water, while ignoring the nauseating stench seeping from chamber pots that needed emptying. When she'd used up all the blankets, she stood in the hallway, wondering the best way to go back and collect the soiled linens. Perhaps there was a crate or basket in the storeroom at the end of the hall.

Hurrying forward, she pushed the door open, squinting at the sudden darkness. A thin shaft of light from the hallway spilled in behind her but did little to illuminate the small, musty room.

"May I help you?"

She gasped at the male voice coming from the darkness. "Who's there?"

A soft intake of breath. "Cass?"

Only one person knew her by that name. "Gabe? What are you doing here?"

"The hospital requested I come. I arrived yesterday. I'm to capture each soldier's photograph as a Christmas gift from the Women's Aid Committee."

She spun to flee, but his plea stopped her cold.

"No, wait. I'm almost finished developing these photographs. I can't expose them to light. I'll come to you." Scuffling sounds approached in the near darkness.

She couldn't talk with him. Couldn't be alone with him. She didn't trust herself. The pain cut too deeply.

She burst from the room, but Gabe's commanding voice forced her to stop, even as two women whisked by on errands, their boots clicking sharply against the wood floor.

"Private Turner, a word?"

She turned slowly, wishing the floor beneath her would crumble away. Nodding, she followed him into a different room, one smaller than the storage area across the hall. She entered the cramped space and swallowed when he shut the door behind her. A square window high overhead filtered watery light down into the dank space. It couldn't have been more than six feet by three feet and was lined with shelves of cleaning liquids, soaps, metal buckets, and mops. The sharp sting of ammonia and lye pinched her nose.

She was mere feet from him with no way to hide from his probing stare.

"Look at me."

Squeezing her eyes shut, she steeled her resolve and reopened them. The brittle defenses she'd built around her heart melted when she witnessed the confused sadness in his face.

"Cass, I'm sorry we quarreled. I'm sorry for suggesting you desert your post. It was wrong of me."

She looked down, watching her fingers twist and writhe until her knuckles were white. What was he doing? Father had never apologized. Ever. "I—thank you."

Long silence. He sighed. "Something else is wrong. Why won't you speak to me? Ever since we argued in your grandmother's barn, you've pushed me away."

The gentle pleading in his voice was her undoing. She whispered, "It's too risky."

His brows pinched. "Too risky for what? Are you afraid I'll let your identity slip?"

"No."

"What, then?"

The wobbly thread of her voice strained and broke. "Letting you into my heart."

He sucked in a breath and grew deathly still. "I see."

The silence stretched between them thick as taffy. Gabe looked away, but not before she witnessed the stark pain in his eyes. She hated herself for putting it there.

All the more reason to keep him at arm's length.

"I don't believe you, you know."

Her gaze swung back to his. He stepped close and skimmed his fingers over her jaw. "I think you've already let me in your heart, just as I hold you in mine."

Her chin trembled. "No, I—" She couldn't bring herself to deny it further.

"You're frightened." His eyes darkened.

Her breath thinned.

His voice was husky as he studied her. "I'm a human, Cass. I mess up. You know that well enough." The muscles in his neck shifted. "Have I done something unforgivable? Wanting to keep you safe? Tell me." His eyes flooded with longing. "Tell me how to unlock the fear around your heart. Tell me how to get back inside."

Pain squeezed her chest until she could no longer breathe.

"Private Turner? Are you up here? Private Mullins has need of your help moving one of the men." Mrs. Grimes's soft call from down the hallway nearly made her weep with relief.

"I must go."

Before he could protest, she flung the closet door open and hurried down the hallway, anxious to flee the turbulent storm he'd unleashed inside.

But no matter how hard she tried, she couldn't outrun the ache in her heart.

Chapter 24

March 14, 1862
Alexandria, Virginia

Winter melted into spring, and though the seasons changed, the Union continued to sit staunchly outside the capital. Boredom turned into its own kind of fever as the soldiers sought diversion from the endless days of drills and waiting. Always waiting.

The day Colonel Poe lined them up with the opportunity to volunteer to become regimental mail carriers, Cassie nearly jolted with excitement. Finally, change.

Never was she so thankful for change.

"Who would like the job?"

Cassie held her posture rigid as she raised her hand, keeping her eyes straight ahead, just like all the other soldiers as they stood at attention before Colonel Orlando Poe. The serious man with his stern countenance and full lips surveyed the Michigan Second with a hawk-eyed gaze. He walked with a confident stride, his left hand moving from his brass button–covered lapel to twist the ends of his wiry brown mustache. He strolled in front of Cassie and stopped, narrowing his eyes.

"Your name, Private."

She lifted her chin a notch. "Private Thomas Turner, sir."

He assessed her measure again before nodding stiffly. "Private Turner, I understand during the past winter you've been volunteering at the Alexandria hospital. Is that correct?"

"Yes, sir." She fought the urge to squirm.

"Why also volunteer to be regimental mail carrier, then?"

Why? Because they would soon be moving, and she would have no more excuses to slip away from Gabe's presence in camp. No more moments to breathe easily between locations without fearing her identity would be discovered. At camp, someone was always underfoot. Always watching.

And after the Battle of Bull Run and the disaster at Ball's Bluff, she wasn't sure she wanted to pick up arms again.

She gave none of those thoughts voice. "I—I enjoy a challenge, sir."

"As mail carrier, you have a sacred, weighty duty. If heavy mail is captured by the enemy, the results would be a calamity for your troop's safety . . . as well as the safety of all our men."

She swallowed but kept her eyes trained on the colonel, refusing to cower under his granite stare. "Yes, sir."

"I hereby relieve you of your hospital duties."

Her stomach pinched so quickly, the blood siphoned from her head in a dizzying rush. Had she been found out?

"You will be our new regimental mail carrier."

Breath filled her tight lungs in a whoosh. The relief was palpable. Her pulse pounded in her ears. "Yes, sir."

Colonel Poe studied her, his words clipped. Every fiber of the man's bearing commanded respect. "Captain Johnston believes you to be extremely competent and trustworthy. I pray his judgment is not misplaced." Colonel Poe relaxed a tad, his dark brow rising ever so slightly. "I believe you've got grit, Turner. Serve well."

"Yes, sir."

He moved past her to appoint new duties to other soldiers down the line. She heard nothing else, save the dull thrum of blood pounding her brain.

You're safe. No one knows.

A cry of surprise snagged her muddled thoughts, causing her to snap her attention down the line of blue-clad men. A soldier was thrust forward before the colonel, stumbling over his own feet. The man's smooth skin was ashen, his eyes wide. His slight body trembled like a leaf in a storm. Captain Johnston stood behind him, his neck mottled a brilliant red.

"Colonel Poe, I have just discovered Private Green is here under false pretenses."

The colonel's face showed no emotion as he studied the quivering soldier before him. "And what pretenses would those be, Captain?"

"Claiming to be a man. Private Green is actually a woman."

Audible gasps of shock rippled down the line before the entire group of men fell into stunned silence. Cassie's throat tightened until she feared she would lose all ability to breathe.

A muscle ticked near the colonel's eye. "How did you discover this deception, Captain?"

The red mottling on Captain Johnston's neck crept into his whiskered cheeks. "I would request to give you those details in private, sir."

"So be it." Colonel Poe swung his attention to Private Green. "Do you deny this charge?"

Cassie watched in horror as Green's face crumpled and she burst into hysterical shrieks. She dropped her head into her hands, answering with shrill sobs, "It's true! It's true. Please don't send me back!"

The colonel curled up his nose and waved a hand over the prostrate woman. "Take her away. I'll discuss this matter with you further, Captain."

Cassie's heart rose into her throat as they led the sobbing woman away. The contents of her stomach soured.

It could have been me. Dear Father, it could have been me.

Feeling someone's eyes on her, she turned her head to the left, startled to see Gabe watching her with an intensity that made her knees sag. He'd seen the whole thing.

Colonel Poe straightened and addressed the soldiers once more. "The reason for these new assignments comes in conjunction with a major announcement from General McClellan." The colonel reached into his jacket and pulled out a crisp note folded in perfect thirds. "After the monotony of this past winter, I'm sure you'll be relieved to hear this." He cleared his throat and read aloud.

"'The period of inaction has passed. I will bring you now face-to-face with the Rebels. Ever bear in mind that my fate is linked with yours. I am to watch over you as a parent over his children; and you know that your general loves you from the depths of his heart.'" Colonel Poe speared the regiment over the letter's rim. "Soldiers . . . men of courage, we move to crush the Rebels with a fierce determination and under the blessing of God Almighty. It's time to break camp and engage the cursed enemy."

As he rallied the men, Cassie felt faint. How had Captain Johnston discovered Green's deception? And how long before he unearthed hers?

It was strange to fear an enemy army far less than someone discovering the depths of her own lie.

When Colonel Poe finished speaking, she glanced in Gabe's direction once more. He was gone.

———◆———

Gabe longed to smash his fist into a tree. Instead, he growled and ran his fingers through his hair, the tension inside him coiled like a rattler.

He marched toward the Whatsit, troubled in mind and spirit. What was Cassie thinking? What was Colonel Poe thinking? Putting her in continual danger, having her gallivant all over kingdom come, back and forth between picket lines?

He flung open the door to his traveling darkroom and stomped inside. Glass bottles filled with chemicals clinked in their cabinets from the impact of his heavy step.

She was going to be killed. The realization swept over him, draining the strength from his legs. He groped and found a small crate he kept inside. He lowered himself to the wooden box and dropped his head in his hands, his stomach curdling. Pain constricted his chest.

He could take Cassie's ire. It was normal, considering the fear that so obviously rattled her. She was confused and scared. Even though she was doing her best to push him away, he could see through her attempts to keep her heart protected. It hurt, made him long for her even more, but this? To stand idly by and watch the vibrant life snuffed out of her beautiful eyes? To say nothing and witness her courage be struck down and silenced forever?

He wouldn't lose her. He couldn't.

Oh, God, how do I do this? How do I watch her taunt death day after day and say nothing?

In the cramped quarters of the dark wagon, he pulled tufts of his hair until needles of pain pricked his scalp. She had been in danger ever since she'd enlisted. Why did fear for her suddenly choke him now?

He loved her. That made all the difference.

The darkroom's door clattered. Light invaded and Gabe turned to the intruder with a glare.

"Hiya, Mr. Gabe! Whatcha doing in here?"

Gabe sighed and dropped his head in his hands once more. "Jonah, how many times have I told you to knock before you enter? What if I'd been in the middle of developing photographs?"

The little boy huffed in irritation. "Well, were you?"

Gabe gritted his teeth. "What do you need?"

"Did you hear we're to move out?" The lad was nearly quivering with excitement.

"I heard." Normally the news would have made him giddy. He was weary to death of the winter quarters. They'd sat for months in the monotony of drills, biting cold, and boredom. Now they were finally pressing onward, and all he could think about was Cassie.

Jonah approached his side, his voice colored with a question. "Something wrong with you? Ain't never seen you so down in the mouth."

Gabe lifted his head and shot the precocious lad a tired smile. "I am, aren't I? I'm sorry. I don't mean to take out my sour mood on you."

Jonah shrugged and swiped his nose. "You didn't hurt my feelings none. What's got you low?"

Scraping his fingers down his face, Gabe pursed his lips. "Someone is pretty riled at me, and I'm worried about them."

Jonah twisted his head to the side like a curious puppy. "It's hard to imagine anyone mad at you. You're one of the nicest fellows I know."

"Thank you."

Jonah squinted at him with a discerning look far too old for his years. "What if I'd sulked every time old Schoolmaster Howe got miffed at me?" He shook his head. "It happened so much, I'd look like a sour pickle every hour."

Gabe chuckled, though the mirth didn't reach his heart.

"What's this fellow have against you anyways?"

"I—" He broke off. "It doesn't matter. But all I want to do is keep my friend safe."

Jonah frowned. "In war? Seems like a mighty foolish goal."

The distant blast of a bugle sounded through the air. Jonah scrambled toward the door, looking back with a scowl. "Time to drill." He wrinkled his freckled nose. "You can't control war, you know."

With that abysmal thought, he scampered away, leaving Gabe alone with his cold glass plates, acrid chemicals, and tortured thoughts.

Everything was spinning from his control. Just like it had with Da. Just as it had with his mother.

"You can't control war . . ."

Everything he'd ever loved had been ripped away from him. He couldn't bear it if Cassie were too.

Chapter 25

MARCH 20, 1862
PORT RICHMOND, VIRGINIA

Cassie breathed in the perfumed scent of wild blooming jonquils, giving Abe his head as they trotted through the meadow toward a wooded area. Soft clods of dirt flew up behind the horse's hooves, occasionally striking her cheek like kisses. The sacks tied to either side of the saddle bulged with mail—much-anticipated letters from sweethearts and anxious parents, correspondence from commanders—a task that prodded her to sit a little taller in her saddle. The other sacks hung empty, ready for her day's task.

Despite Colonel Poe's stern warning that her role carried heavy responsibility, she couldn't suppress the feeling of freedom that poured through her veins like warm honey. The post was a blessed reprieve from the dreary routine of the past winter, from feeling as if she must constantly be on guard to keep her identity a secret. In addition—something tightened in her chest—the assignment allowed her to flee from seeing Gabe day in and day out.

Perhaps he was out of her sight at the moment, but he refused to leave her heart.

Pushing aside the thought, she sharpened her focus. She couldn't allow herself to become distracted. A Reb could be waiting around any tree, boulder, or bramble.

Abe trotted ahead, unaffected by her wayward emotions. At least the horse had good sense.

Since their meeting at the hospital, she and Gabe had managed a respectful relationship. When they were in their group of comrades, they spoke polite niceties and small talk, but nothing else. To his credit, he had not sought her out once. The realization should have brought a rush of relief as winter melted into spring.

Yet she'd found no reprieve from him, from herself. Instead, the desire to run to him, to be held in his arms, to give up everything so they might be together, only grew. Like a beast panting its warm breath against a window, it waited. Taunting her. Refusing to leave her be.

She was a far weaker woman than she'd feared, easily falling into the arms of a controlling man. Terrifying thought. But she would not make the same mistakes as her mother.

Cassie pulled Abe to a stop when the woods gave way, revealing a well-kept farmhouse sitting in a cleared meadow. Smoke curled from the chimney. The grass surrounding it was green. The window boxes trimmed with colorful flowers testified the place was well tended.

She clucked her tongue, urging Abe ahead in a smooth stride. No sense galloping to the front door and scaring the inhabitants away.

When the captain had insisted she procure supplies and food

for their march north, she'd nearly balked at the task. Delivering mail and riding through the country in solitude was more to her liking than knocking on strange doors, asking citizens to exchange butter, eggs, and chickens for Federal greenbacks. She kept her dismay hidden, wanting to give the captain no reason to pull her from mail duty.

As the house loomed before them, she tugged on Abe's reins, dismounted, and tethered him to a thick porch rail. The porch was painted and swept clean. As she climbed the steps, she noticed there was no give in the wood planks. Everything was pristine. Memories of Granny Ardie's sagging steps assaulted her. The steps Gabe had ripped up and replaced.

Why can't I scrub him from my mind?

Gritting her teeth, she steadied herself and knocked. Footfalls sounded beyond the door. It squeaked open slowly, revealing a tall woman draped completely in black. Her gown and shawl testified this poor soul was in deep mourning. Even the necklace resting against her bodice was polished coal. The woman smiled sweetly. "To what do I owe the pleasure of this call?"

Cassie cleared her throat, keeping her voice low. "Ma'am, I'm a soldier with the Michigan Second, sent to purchase food and supplies from anyone who might have some to spare. I've been authorized to pay for any provisions with greenbacks."

The woman's smile tightened, though her eyes stayed bright. "Of course. Do come in." Waving her arm in a gracious arc, she pushed the door open farther to allow Cassie entrance.

"Thank you, ma'am."

"I have plenty to spare." She led her through the front sitting room, her sharp heels clicking smartly against the gleaming floors. "Please take a seat while I obtain some food for you."

Something about the woman's manner put Cassie ill at ease. "I don't mind standing after riding in the saddle for so long."

She glanced about the room crammed full of delicate knick-knacks, afraid to bump any of them and start an avalanche of destruction. "I'm sorry to have interrupted you, especially since I see you're in mourning."

The woman sighed heavily as she opened cupboards in the kitchen, her voice drifting into the room with a clear cadence. "Yes, I've lost many. My father, my husband, and now two brothers."

"I'm sorry."

Cassie watched the woman through the open kitchen door. Her movements seemed aimless and scattered. Nervous even. She roamed from cabinet to cabinet, collecting nothing. Odd.

"Would you like to stay for some refreshment?"

"No thank you. I must leave soon."

More rifling through the cabinets. A pot clanged. Unease slithered up Cassie's spine. Something was wrong.

Her instincts screamed to run. She turned and burst through the front door, nearly falling down the steps as she scrambled to free Abe's reins from the porch post. A shrill shout sounded from inside.

Pulse ricocheting, Cassie mounted and kicked Abe into a run. The crack of a shotgun split the air. Something whizzed past her right ear.

"Yankee scum! You killed my men!"

The woman's deranged scream caused the hair on the back of her neck to rise. Hunkering low into Abe's mane, she urged the panting horse to make haste. Another booming blast as something white-hot sliced her upper arm.

They didn't dare slow for several miles. Her arm burned, but there was no time to stop and examine it. The lathered horse dropped into a trot, his labored breathing matched by Cassie's own.

Today, monotonous drills seemed far preferable to being regimental mail carrier.

She grimaced against the throb in her arm. Perhaps the woman's Confederate fervor had blinded her with rage. Or maybe her grief had robbed her of sense.

Something twisted in Cassie's chest. Father's heartbreak over the son he'd lost had been his undoing. They had all suffered as a result.

Her body shuddered as the horse carried her farther from the deranged woman.

What power on earth could break the chains of such grief?

———◆———

A rider burst into camp, pulling Gabe's attention away from positioning the tripod. The young boys arranged in front of the camera barely looked up, most of them deep in conversation, or engaged in a battle of aggies as they waited for him to prepare his lens and plates. Mustering the young soldiers, the buglers and drummers, hadn't been easy. Keeping their attention was proving even more challenging.

The rider barreled past, half-slumping over his saddle. Gabe glanced and froze, inhaling harshly through his teeth. Cassie.

Blood stained the blue shoulder of her coat.

Pulse tripping, he murmured to the boys, "Stay here. I'll return shortly."

A few of them moaned, but most didn't even acknowledge him as they laughed and barked out excitement over their marble competition. He ran to Cassie's side, grabbing the reins of the lathered horse in his right hand. "Easy, boy. Easy." Looking up, he saw the pain in her eyes. The tight lines marring her brow. Her skin was ashen. "What happened?"

Her voice came out low and thin. "Stopped to gather supplies. Crazy woman. She shot me."

Panic burst in his chest. Cass leaned forward to dismount but winced, nearly falling from the saddle. He grabbed her right elbow and eased her down to the ground. He had half a mind to throw her over his shoulder and ride away. This was exactly what he'd feared.

A shout bellowed from across camp. "Is that Turner? What happened?"

Cassie grabbed his arm, digging her fingernails into his flesh, and whispered harshly, "Don't let them examine me. They might find out. Please. Don't let them."

Her blue eyes flickered with such fear, such hurt, he was helpless to refuse her. He gave a curt nod. "I'll take care of it." Lifting his face, he called out to the approaching men, "Yeah, it's Turner! Just nicked a bit. I'll clean him up."

The approaching soldiers stopped. Jackson cupped his hands around his mouth and yelled, "You sure?"

Gabe raised his arm. "He's fine. I'll see to him."

The men sauntered back toward their duties. Cassie nearly slumped against him in relief. He clenched his jaw and motioned toward the Whatsit. "Let's get you inside. Don't fall against me. They might see you and come investigate."

She nodded tersely and walked toward the traveling darkroom, wrapping her right arm against the bloody sleeve of her left. It was all he could do not to sweep her up in his arms and cradle her like a wounded kitten.

He followed her into the Whatsit and shut the door behind them, fumbling to light a lantern against the slight sway of the wagon. With a hiss, the match flared to life, and he coaxed it to lick the wick of the oil lamp. He replaced the globe with a clink and blew out the match. Curls of smoke tickled his nose.

"Sit." He motioned toward the only chair he could boast and scurried to locate the medical aid box. When Mathew Brady had insisted he carry one, Gabe had nearly argued. What good could such a small thing do against an entire war? Now he saw the wisdom of such foresight.

Pulling it out from under the long shelf with a scrape, he placed it on the small worktable and flipped the metal latch open. Rolled bandages, carbolic acid, scissors, needles, thread, and a couple envelopes of pain powder filled the box. He glanced toward Cassie. Her color was pale, but she appeared to have her wits about her. Her eyes were shuttered with pain but were not listless or confused.

Not unlike that night when her father had attacked at Ardie's cabin.

His fear for her that night had been real, but it was nothing like the cold grip fisted around his heart at this moment. If the bullet had hit only a few inches to the right . . .

Bile rose up his throat and he clamped his jaw so tight, he feared his teeth would break.

He cleared his throat, desperately trying to keep the quaver from his voice. "I need to remove your coat."

She grimaced, shifting out of the bloody garment and letting it fall to the floor. Bright-red crimson stained almost the full length of her white cotton sleeve. He struggled to hold back a curse.

Forcing himself to be gentle, he knelt in front of her wounded arm. "I'm going to cut away this sleeve to see the damage."

She didn't protest, though he noticed her right hand was clenched so tightly her knuckles were white. "I have another shirt in my haversack."

He pulled out his pocketknife and cut the bloody sleeve away. She sucked in a breath as cool air struck the open wound. He winced.

The smooth skin of her slender arm had been cut through, leaving a wide, deep gash. Blood seeped from the torn muscle and flesh. He looked closely. No actual bullet hole that had cut through bone. At least, not that he could tell under the sticky crimson.

He propped a towel between her torso and her injured arm and then placed another under her elbow. "How does it feel?"

"Painful. Tingly. It alternates between sharp stabs of needles and numbness." Her lips twisted in a rueful smile. "I suppose that's a good thing, though."

He nodded and scooted the water basin closer, dunking a clean cloth into it with his free hand. "Numb is better than pain."

She swallowed. "How bad is it?"

"The bullet didn't go through the bone. Nor did it lodge in your arm. At least not that I can see."

"Just clipped, then." She expelled a sigh. "That's good."

"Yes, but it's a deep gash. Steady now. I need to wash it out." He squeezed the clean water over her wound, cringing when her whole body stiffened. She made almost no sound. Just a strangled grunt in the back of her throat. As gingerly as possible, he cleaned the gash, saying nothing.

Sweat beaded on her face. "Say it."

"Say what?"

She blew out a tight breath, her misery evident. "Say what you're thinking."

He frowned. "Time for the carbolic acid." He poured a generous amount over the angry wound, his stomach fisting when strangled, guttural cries pushed past her clenched jaw. When the worst of it had passed and her breathing returned to normal, he patted the skin around her wound dry. "And what am I thinking?"

"That I'm a foolish girl."

Pressing his lips into a line, he reached for the roll of clean bandages. "Granted."

"You think I'm addled to want to be here, risking life and limb."

A muscle ticked in his jaw, but he said nothing, knowing she was working up a full head of steam with or without his help. Instead, he wrapped the bandage around her arm, tying it off with thin strips of fabric to keep it in place.

"You think I can't manage on my own. That I need you to keep me safe."

He glared, anger churning his gut. "I do want to keep you safe, Cass. Is that so wrong?"

She thrust her chin out, radiating defiance. "I was the one who dragged you to safety at Ball's Bluff. I don't need you, or any man, telling me what to do."

He jumped to his feet, his fists clenched. "Blast it, Cass, I'm not your father. You don't have the first clue what I'm thinking."

Rising to her own feet, she faced off against him. "Then tell me. Just say it!"

"Fine! I think you're terrified."

Her eyes narrowed to slits. "I am not terrified of you or anyone else."

"Really?" He stepped so close they were a breath apart. "I think you're so afraid, you can't think straight."

Something flickered in her expression, though her steely glare remained set. "I already told you at the hospital I was scared to trust you. Scared to trust anyone."

"You're not scared of me. You're terrified of yourself."

She jolted as if she'd been slapped, her brows lowering in fury. "Myself?"

His heart raced. "You're terrified to admit you love me."

Her face suddenly paled and she stepped back, unblinking. "I—I—"

Before she could protest, he cupped her jaw and crushed her to him, robbing them both of breath, of thought, of anything other than this moment.

Gentling his hold, he deepened his kiss until she melted against him. His heart hammered like a drum inside his chest. She was honey to his lips, silky softness to his fingertips. His body hummed in response when her right hand slid around his waist.

The darkroom door slammed open and a decidedly childish voice gasped. "I don't believe it."

Alarmed, Gabe broke away from Cassie with a start, his senses reeling. A small figure stood in the light of the open doorway.

Jonah.

With a growl, Gabe lurched forward and pulled Jonah inside, slamming the door behind him. "How many times have I told you to knock?"

Cassie cupped the elbow of her injured arm and backed away, her body shaking. Jonah's gaze shifted between them, his jaw slack. Two bright splotches of red burned his cheeks. Gabe grew so warm, a bead of sweat rolled between his shoulder blades. He tugged his collar, desperate for air. "This isn't what it looks like."

Jonah stepped closer to Cassie, studying her strangely. "Take off your hat."

She hesitated, then slowly obliged. He blinked, a small smile ghosting his lips. "You're a woman."

She stood straight, didn't mumble or cower. Only nodded and licked her swollen lips. "Yes, I'm a woman."

Gabe held his breath, unsure what Jonah would do.

A thick moment of quiet. Jonah burst into raucous laughter and slapped his knee. "If that ain't the beatenest thing I ever saw! You fooled me, Turner! Got me good."

Gabe cringed, fearing Jonah's voice would carry past the walls. "Shh! Quiet! No one must know."

The boy ducked his head and reddened, though his eyes still danced. "Sorry. I can't believe it." He stared at Cassie again, his smile contagious. "Why are you pretending to be a man?"

She pinched the bridge of her nose. "It's a long story. Too long for this moment. Perhaps someday I'll tell you all of it. Just know it was safer for me to enlist than any other choices I had."

"You sure tricked me. I never saw a girl so good at acting like a man . . . excepting when you were kissing the photographer, that is."

She blushed crimson. Gabe rubbed the back of his neck, longing to wring Jonah's neck instead.

He swung his gaze to Gabe and glared. "Say, you knew Turner was a girl and never told me? I thought we were friends."

Irritation prickled his back. "I only found out myself recently."

Jonah wrinkled his freckled nose. "So the first thing you do is kiss her? Sounds like a pretty gross way to say howdy to me."

Gabe ground his jaw. "What do you need, Jonah?"

"I heard the buglers talking about a fellow that rode in bleeding, and then Myers said he saw Turner hurt and that you'd offered to bandage him up." The boy smirked wickedly.

Gabe paced, trying not to scowl at the meddling little soldier. "What now? Are you going to tell anyone?"

Jonah's eyes rounded. "Of course not! What do you take me for? A Judas?" He shook his head and grinned. "This'll be bully fun. Us three keeping a secret from everyone else?" He puffed out his chest proudly. "I can keep my lips shut." He leaned in and winked. "I always did fancy being one of them detectives like that Pinkerton fellow I've heard about."

Gabe exhaled heavily. Could Jonah keep Cassie's secret? The boy who loved to talk, who caused more mischief than Jeff Davis himself?

Jonah moved to Cassie's side. "I'm kind of surprised I took to you as fast as I did, Turner. I don't usually cotton to girls." He frowned. "Most of them are all smelly and sissified. Bossy too. But not you. You're a nice one to be around. Say, what's your real name?"

Cassie attempted a weak smile. "Just call me Turner. We don't want any slips of the tongue."

Jonah nodded seriously. "I better get back or Captain Johnston will be threatening me with cleaning out the bean pots again." With a grin, he burst from the darkroom, leaving silence in his wake.

Gabe glanced back to Cassie, dread sitting like stones on his chest. "What are you thinking?"

She slumped heavily. "I think if Jonah Phifer knows, I'm in very big trouble."

Chapter 26

Cassie kept waiting to be hauled away in irons, but nothing happened. Jonah must have been serious about keeping her secret, for three weeks had passed and her duties remained steady, even amid their ambitious trek up the river. It had been three weeks of pure misery crammed on the *Vanderbilt* steamer followed by a twenty-three-mile march through knee-high mud and squelchy marshes. The horses were exhausted, the soldiers half-starving, and the rain relentless.

She'd caught only rare glimpses of Gabe in the melee pressing forward to Richmond. She ought to be grateful. His knifing accusation had rankled her enough to steal precious sleep. Her? Scared? Yet she couldn't seem to put him from her mind. The truth was, she missed him. Desperately.

Even now, settled in front of her soggy tent on the spongy marshland, Cassie fought to keep her gaze from sifting through blue-clad men to find him. He was here somewhere.

"You are mighty quiet tonight, Turner."

She jerked her head up and offered a tight smile to Sven as he settled his muscular frame across the fire from her. "Just listening."

Sven nodded toward the dark-skinned contrabands huddled around their own fire, some of them praying, some of them lifting up their voices in song.

"'Glory to God, he watches o'er his own. . . .'"

The soothing, lilting melodies settled around the camp like a sacred christening.

"Don't let Turner fool you." On Cassie's right, Briggs puffed his pipe, cupping it between his thick, calloused fingers. "He's been quieter than normal. And that's saying something."

"Maybe you're missing someone back home, *ja*?"

More like I'm missing someone right here. How could she be so lonely when she was surrounded by people?

"Not really. Just tired." She clenched her jaw before taking another sip of the bitter coffee in her cup. She grimaced. "Once more, we're just sitting like squatters. It feels like Washington all over again."

Briggs puffed and brooded. "I agree with you on that point." He furrowed his black brows and glanced to make sure they weren't being overheard. "Little Mac hasn't done much of anything but send that aeronautic professor up and down in that hydrogen balloon of his." He exhaled a plume of white smoke from between his whiskered lips. "No one needs to watch the Rebels' position that often."

Sven frowned. "I hear the Confederates are sitting in Yorktown, crowing about the ridiculous Union with their balloon rides. One of the pickets tell me they think we are too busy playing to fight."

Irritation flared. "Why is General McClellan waiting to attack?"

Briggs tapped the pipe against the palm of his meaty hand. "If he continues to falter, he may not be our general much longer."

Sven's blue eyes rounded. "You think President Lincoln will replace him?"

"Shh!"

Briggs's hiss of warning came none too soon. A moment later, Colonel Poe approached the three of them, gaze fixed on Cassie. "Private Turner, a word?"

She rose slowly on trembling limbs and followed him to his private tent, picking her way between soldiers lounging in the calm twilight around small fires dotting the hillside. She passed Jonah on her way inside the tent. His brows rose in question, but she merely shook her head and shadowed Poe, ducking into the tent's hazy insides.

The sweet scent of cigar smoke curled around her. Several oil lamps were lit, casting a sleepy, honeyed glow over his quarters. Large maps were spread over his worktable, along with a handful of scrawled messages and fluttering letters stirred up by the evening's breeze drifting through the tent flap. She snapped her gaze to his when he turned on his heel and studied her sharply. She gritted her teeth, willing herself to remain stoic, though her insides quivered like preserves.

"Do you consider yourself a moral person, Private Turner?"

Her mouth turned to cotton and she nearly choked. Did he know? Surely he must. He was baiting her, preparing to corner her in her own deceit.

Despite her hammering heart, she managed to croak out, "I'd like to believe so, sir."

He turned to stand behind his paper-strewn table, his hands tucked behind his back. "I have an opportunity and am looking for the right man. The work requires moral courage, intelligence, and fortitude. I asked the regimental chaplain whom he would nominate for this particular work, and he recommended you above all others."

Her thoughts scattered like leaves in a storm, tumbling and circling in spinning drifts. "I—I'm flattered, sir. But I don't understand—"

Poe continued as if he hadn't heard, jutting his chin and his sharp pointed goatee forward like the thrust of a bayonet. "Have you heard of Allan Pinkerton?"

She fought the urge to frown, not comprehending the line of questioning. "Yes, sir."

"Then you know he is employed by President Lincoln. He has trained a network of spies, particularly in and around Richmond, some of whom were recently captured by the Confederacy and sentenced to death. Pinkerton and General McClellan are requesting me to send them bright, able-bodied men to assist their work."

His meaning suddenly became clear. "You mean—?"

"Yes, Turner." Poe's dark eyes snapped with a determined glint. "I'm recommending you to be a spy for Pinkerton's secret service."

Gabe stomped toward Cassie's tent, fury licking his insides like an inferno. Surely Jonah was mistaken. Cassie would never agree to anything so dangerous, so utterly foolish . . . would she?

The small fires lighting the hillside were dying, nothing more than hissing streams of blackened wood and smoke. The bugle call for sleep would sound any minute. Only a handful of soldiers lingered outside, the remaining few pulling the last drags of smoke from their cigarettes. He ignored their greetings, nearly running to Cassie's quarters. As he approached, he could make out her slender build against the faint light as she threw out the dregs of her coffee into the bushes. Brushing off Briggs's friendly hello, he marched up to Cassie and jabbed his thumb over his shoulder. "Private Turner, I must speak with you."

Briggs chuckled. "You're a mighty popular fellow tonight, Turner."

Gabe turned on his heel to march toward the Whatsit, hearing her footfalls behind him. They walked quickly toward his darkroom wagon in silence. As soon as she stepped in, he slammed the door shut and spun to face her, thrusting his nose mere inches from her own. White-hot anger flooded his veins. "Tell me it's not true."

Her eyes widened, her eyebrows high. "What's not true?"

"Jonah. Tell me he's wrong. Tell me you didn't accept Poe's invitation to be a spy."

She sucked in a harsh breath. "He heard us? He told you?"

It was true. He could see the resignation in her expression. Voice hoarse, he shook his head. "Why, Cass? Don't you realize what will happen? Don't you understand the danger you'll be in? Spying for Pinkerton . . ." Bile rose in his throat. "It's a death wish."

Her large eyes searched his. "How could I not? It's an opportunity to help. It might save lives." She gestured toward the tents beyond his door. "Lives like those contrabands out there. And Colonel Poe asked me to help. How could I say no? The need is great. Since Pinkerton's men were—" She stopped abruptly as if aware she'd shared too much.

Snatching his gaze away from hers, he leaned over the table and gripped the edges with white fingers. "What happened to them? To Pinkerton's men?"

Her voice was soft. "They were captured."

"I won't let you do it, Cass. I can't. You mean too much—"

"It's not your decision to make."

Panic tore at him. How could he make her see? "Why are you really choosing this? Are you sure you're not hiding behind it?"

She opened her mouth to reply, then clamped her lips shut, her expression cold as ice. She turned to leave but glanced over her shoulder, searing him with a piercing glare. "My physical life and my soul are in the hands of my Creator. My safety is out of your control. You are so desperate to protect me." Her expression flickered from anger to resigned sadness. "But whether I live or die is God's decision. Not yours."

Then she left, slamming the door behind her.

Gabe collapsed into his chair, digging his fingers into his scalp and twisting his hair. His chest constricted as he muttered, "You're not fooling the Almighty, and you're not fooling me either, Cassie Kendrick."

He was suddenly back in time, watching his father wobble on the edge of sanity. Seeing his mother slowly work her life away. He was helpless, unable to fix it. Unable to stop the swell of horror gaining speed and creeping toward them.

Only this time, Cassie would be swept away in the crushing tide, leaving him bereft and alone. He couldn't let her destroy herself.

He wouldn't.

———— ◆ ————

Dear Gabriel,

I write this on behalf of Jacob, who is currently in the hospital. The poor man was distraught, fearing you would think the worst of him if he did not write with haste. He tremendously enjoyed your last post and declares

he feels like a soldier fighting alongside our brave boys
after reading your descriptive reflections on life among
the ranks.

As promised, I am doing my utmost to look after Jacob,
cantankerous though he may be at times. He shoos me
away when I hover, yet his eyes betray him. He enjoys the
attention. My daughter is taking care of Sophocles while
the dear man recovers from the influenza.

He has been under the hospital's care for nearly a
fortnight and has already received a bill for services. I
continually pester him about his finances, but he refuses
to tell me if he has adequate funds to pay. I mention this
only because he has confided in you before. Does he have
sufficient funds? If he knew I were asking you such a thing,
he would consider me obnoxiously inquisitive, and rightly
so. I only desire to know if he has a need. I can contribute
to any financial necessities that may arise. It is born out of
concern on my part. Nothing more.

As soon as he is settled back at his apartment, Jacob
insists he will write. Please, tell him nothing of my
inquiry. The man is vexed enough that is he bound to bed.
We need not add his bruised pride to his list of grievances.

We are praying for your safety. May Providence bless
and keep you.

> *With kind regards,*
> *Esther Whitmore*

Gabe lowered the letter. Jacob was ill. Hospitalized and,
as Esther implied, possibly unable to pay his bills in full. All
because he'd given his funds to Gabe.

It was his fault.

Dropping the missive to the worktable, Gabe pinched the

bridge of his nose. He must find a way to care for his old friend. He would take on the bills himself. But how?

Since General McClellan had forced them to hunker down so much over the past months, Gabe had captured few photos the newspapers were willing to buy, few scenes wood engravers could easily manage to reproduce. Brady had already told him as much. His last letter had been firm. *"While in long stretches of inactivity, you must be creative. Look at your world with new eyes. Think of what the papers would want to print. Scenes from battlefields are easy enough to sell. Photographs captured during times of quiet show the grit and beauty of a world through an artist's eye. Be an artist."*

A sharp rap on the door jolted him from his troubled thoughts. A soldier's voice barked, "Ten minutes and we move, Avery!"

The rest had not been long. In mere moments, he'd be forced to climb atop the wagon and guide the plodding horses behind the mass of blue moving toward Richmond.

What could he possibly send to Brady that would garner attention? Jacob needed him. The pressure of his own failings clamped onto his soul like a hot iron. He needed money and quickly. Something must be sent today.

He riffled through the most recently developed photographs. Stern, rigid soldiers greeted him from the surfaces of the prints. They were all the same. Nameless faces holding their guns and bayonets. No action. No movement. No life.

He stilled for a moment before he yanked an altogether different image from the bottom of the stack, studying the grace and beauty of the woman who had captured his heart.

Cassie running her slender fingers through the trickling stream as she sat perched on a flat rock amid the autumn woods of her grandmother's home. Her skirts pooled around her, the curve of her full lips, perfect nose, and long lashes. A lock of dark hair brushed her shoulder. The dress she wore hugged every breathtaking curve of her body. And her face . . . an expression of haunting sadness mingled with a sweet serenity lifted the image from one of simplicity to a profound longing for peace amid war, courage through adversity, beauty within pain.

Dandelions blooming in concrete.

This was the image newspapers would clamor to print. He could title it "Beautiful Heroines of Home." Cassie's likeness encapsulated so many other women who were forging ahead to fight the good fight from their houses and farms—picking up the work abandoned by their enlisted husbands and sons. Searching for hope amid the ashes. Brave, fearless . . . this photograph shone with the angst of them all.

But would printing her likeness reveal her identity?

No. The lovely Cassie bore little resemblance to battle-worn Thomas Turner. Nobody would correlate the two. Who would draw the comparison?

Gently tracing a finger over the delicate lines of her face, he swallowed. Why was he torturing himself? She'd made it clear she wanted nothing to do with him. Had pushed him away over and over. His heart still stung at the way she had so coldly disregarded his feelings.

Repressing the niggling unease in the pit of his stomach, he grabbed an envelope and slipped the photograph inside, hastily scribbling a note to Brady.

He might not be able to protect her any longer. But he could help Jacob.

Chapter 27

APRIL 23, 1862
WASHINGTON, DC

Cassie kept careful step behind the guard escorting her through the somber office at 217 Pennsylvania Avenue. She nearly laughed at the irony of finally leaving the capital, only to find herself back once more. This time, the work would be markedly different.

They wove through a long hallway; then the guard ushered her into a room where four men turned at her approach.

"Private Thomas Turner, sir." The guard's words were clipped before he pivoted and left, abandoning Cassie to the group of staunch men, who eyed her curiously. She straightened to her full height and emptied her face of all expression.

A stocky man sporting a full dark beard, large ears, and thinning hair approached. His wide mouth quirked into a tight smile. "Allan Pinkerton, Private Turner."

She grasped his thick hand and shook it. His deep-set eyes

expressed a frankness that seemed a contradiction for someone who was a notorious spy. "An honor, sir."

Pinkerton waved toward the man standing nearest the fireplace posed in a Napoleonic stance, his hand thrust behind the row of brass buttons lining the breast of his crisp uniform. An auburn mustache framed his mouth. "May I present your esteemed commander, General McClellan."

Her mind scattered of all coherent thought. This grim, boyish-looking fellow was Little Mac? He was shorter than she'd imagined, having only ever seen him riding his horse during military parades. His broad chest was thrust forward, reminding her of a proud lion.

She saluted sharply and felt a thrill when he returned her salute with a glimmer of respect.

Pinkerton lifted a cigar from a silver case on the table. "I understand your Captain Johnston has apprised you of our current situation, as well as our need for intelligent, stout-hearted men."

"Yes, sir."

"Tell me, Turner." Pinkerton lit the thick cigar with ease and perched it between his lips. "Why would you desire to engage in so perilous an undertaking?"

She straightened her shoulders, looking Pinkerton in the eye. "It is my sacred duty, sir."

His brows rose. "Sacred, you say? In what way?"

"Slavery is morally repugnant and is against the freedom God has willed to every man."

"You speak such convictions quickly, almost as if they were memorized."

"No, sir, not memorized. A philosophy I was inundated with since my youth. Our community is filled with abolitionists and Quakers, you see. To be honest, it wasn't until I enlisted and worked side by side with the contrabands that I truly began to comprehend the depth of their suffering." She cleared her throat. "My initial motives for enlisting were not so pure, but I've grown to understand the tremendous call such a cause requires."

Pinkerton pursed his lips. "So you believe Providence is opposed to slavery, yet you feel no hesitation to deceive? To play the part of someone you are not?"

Was this not the very argument Gabe had so strongly verbalized over and over again since he'd discovered her true identity? The time since he'd first given it voice had allowed her to ruminate often over the difficult question.

"Don't the Scriptures tell us David himself acted insane to escape the wrath of Achish, king of Gath, so that he might later fight for the greater good? And what of Rahab, Joshua, and Caleb? King David employed the use of spies all through his reign, and wasn't he called a man after God's own heart?"

Suffocating silence descended. Perhaps she had overstepped. A bead of sweat rolled down her spine.

A smile tugged at Pinkerton's mouth. "Well said."

Cassie nearly sagged as she released the breath trapped in her lungs. Perhaps she was only rationalizing her own deceptive behavior.

Pinkerton turned to the other two men studying her from the corner of the room. "Forgive my manners. I need also introduce General Heintzelman and General Meagher."

She saluted each of them in turn and waited.

General Meagher stepped forward, his hands clasped behind his back as if he were a schoolmaster preparing to scold his student. His high cheekbones reminded her of a hawk, though a comical one, for despite his pomaded, meticulous hair, one long wild curl sprang forward on the right side of his head, making him appear unbalanced.

"You do understand you'll be going undercover, do you not? You will not be wearing your uniform, a uniform that garners at least a modicum of respect in war. You'll be wearing ordinary clothing. If you are caught, the Rebels will not treat you as a prisoner of war, but as a spy." He turned his head, studying her from a different angle, causing his wayward curl to bounce. "Do you know what they do to spies, Turner?"

She met his gaze coolly. "They are executed."

General Heintzelman probed, "And you are prepared to suffer the same if the worst were to happen?"

"My life is in God's hands, General. I will do my utmost for the cause of freedom and our blessed Union. And if I perish, I perish."

Passing the marksman test had been easy. But waiting in the room for the physician to give her a thorough medical exam was another matter.

Maybe it would be as inconsequential as the first exam she'd endured upon enlisting. Height, weight, and the doctor had sent her on her way.

Please, Lord, let it be of no concern.

Between her apprehension and the sharp sting of antiseptic, her stomach roiled and soured. The door opened, admitting a short, wiry man with white-gray hair that puffed out on either side of his head like clumps of cotton. He peered over the top of his spectacles. "Private Thomas Turner?"

"Yes, sir."

"I'm Dr. Smalley. I must determine if you have the God-given abilities to execute your duties."

"How is that accomplished, sir?"

He pushed the spectacles higher on the bridge of his nose, wrinkling it as he responded. "Primarily through phrenology."

She gulped. What was that?

"The shape and size of your cranium will tell me much." He plucked the spectacles from his nose and polished the lenses with a soft cloth he yanked from his pocket. "For instance, there is a marked difference in the shape of a male cranium versus a female cranium."

Her heart hammered, keeping rhythm with the blood pounding in her ears.

"A female's organs of procreation and her longing for harmony elongates the central posterior portion of the head." He hooked his spectacles back over his ears, moving toward her with outstretched hands. She resisted the urge to lunge out of reach. "Let's examine you, shall we?"

She nearly cringed when his bony fingers began massaging her scalp. Could he tell? *Please, God, don't let him find out* . . .

He grunted several times as his probing fingers traveled the length of her head. The motion would have been soothing had her nerves not been close to fraying. Several times he paused over a bump, exploring and squinting his eyes as if deep in thought. He removed his fingers and scratched several notes on a journal of some sort. Cassie tasted bile.

He reached for a measuring tape and ran it from one ear to the other before scribbling another note in the journal with the stub of his pencil. He said nothing. Spots danced before Cassie's eyes. Perspiration gathered under her shirt binding.

He pulled off his spectacles and pressed his lips tight. "Private Turner, I must say I discovered something I've rarely encountered in my profession."

Her breath seized in her rib cage.

"Your brain is remarkably developed. In particular, the organs that promote combativeness and secretive behavior are quite pronounced." His eyes glinted. "Truly a strong man's cranium."

Relief flooded her body even as she squelched the urge to laugh. Obviously the good doctor lacked much in medical knowledge—a trait that could only help her continue her work.

Forcing a solemn nod, she extended her hand. "Thank you, sir."

Dr. Smalley snapped his journal shut. "All you need complete is a renewed oath of allegiance to the United States, and your work will begin."

Three days. That was all she'd been given to smuggle her way into enemy territory. She had returned to her own regiment as they had approached the boundaries of Yorktown, waiting for General McClellan's next orders. At least she wouldn't have far to travel.

But what to do about her clothes? Cassie had mulled over the possibilities, none of them satisfactory. Anything she'd considered was likely to draw questions. The fewer people who knew of her activities, the better.

Standing outside her tent, she cast her gaze across the camp to the traveling darkroom perched under a canopy of trees.

Gabe.

He had clothes an Irish peddler would wear. But would he help?

She marched toward the Whatsit with renewed determination. The hard part would be convincing the stubborn photographer.

Chapter 28

~

"YOU WANT ME TO GIVE YOU WHAT?" Gabe's jaw went slack.

"Some clothes."

His eyes narrowed. "You all but tell me you want nothing to do with me and then waltz back here requesting I give you my clothes?" He shook his head. "I don't think so."

His words stung like a lash, but she could offer no rebuttal. They were altogether too true.

His shoulders sagged as if he was conceding. "Why do you need them?"

"I—I can't say."

A muscle ticked in his jaw. "Can't or won't?"

"Both."

"I see."

He stood staring at the walls of the darkroom, his arms folded. The way his eyes flickered back and forth between some unseen worlds told her he was wrestling over the request. When his jaw clenched, she knew he had decided to refuse her. Her heart shriveled.

She'd turned to leave when his soft voice stopped her.

"What will happen if you don't acquire them? Will it increase the likelihood you'll be caught?"

He knew it was for her spying assignment. Fearing his wrath, she was tempted to lie but pushed the temptation away. "Yes. I'll have to steal them, which will make things a tad more complicated."

"Why doesn't Pinkerton provide you the clothing you need?"

"I'm to be seen with him as little as possible. The dispatches for assignment come, and I'm expected to use what I can to fulfill the request. I could send a missive asking for the items I need, but by the time they receive it . . ."

"It will be too late."

"Yes. The generals need the information now."

With a deep breath, he moved to his bag and opened it, yanking a shirt and pair of trousers free before thrusting them toward her. "Here."

She grasped the clothes, warmth tingling up her arm when his fingers brushed hers. "Thank you."

He said nothing, only nodded and turned away. She grasped the door latch.

"Cass?"

His hoarse plea snagged her, forcing her to look back at the tight lines around his eyes.

"Be safe."

A knot lodged in her throat. "I will."

———— ◆ ————

When the latch shut with a nerve-strangling click, Gabe dropped into the chair, rubbing the palm of his hand into the socket of his eye.

Why had he given her the clothes? Was he really so smitten

that he'd hand over whatever she wanted without a complaint, no matter what it was for?

He sighed. If the garments would help her stay safe, he'd gladly give her all he had. But it was more than that. Unease gnawed at him.

The gesture had been penance on his part. If she ever learned he'd submitted her photograph to Brady without her consent, he would lose her forever.

If he hadn't already.

Every time he tried to dig himself out of the mess he made, he only sank deeper into the mire.

His carefully laid plans were unraveling faster than he could repair them.

——◆——

Cassie waited, motionless, as she watched the bugler's silhouette melt into the evening's darkness. The shrill blast signaling lights-out had just sounded, shrouding the camp in repose.

She tugged the belt tighter around her middle and slipped between the tents, darting through the rows of identical canvas shelters. She kept her step light, fearing one misplaced footfall would alert the soldiers to her departure. Although Captain Johnston knew of her mission, he'd argued she should tell no one else of her plans. The fewer men who knew, the more likely the mission would succeed.

The loamy scent of damp earth filled her nostrils as she scurried through the woods beyond the perimeter of camp. Her lumpy trouser pockets bumped against each hip. One pocket was crammed full of hard crackers; the other held her revolver. The forged papers she'd tucked into her shoes scraped the bottoms of her feet.

Her skin tingled. At least her costume was baggy and gave

her body room to breathe. Her knapsack was filled with goods she'd managed to pilfer from camp—apples, a couple oranges, sets of pasteboards, dominoes, and soap—so her disguise as an Irish peddler would be plausible. She'd even managed to swipe a flat cap from Private O'Connor, who had often bragged about the treasure he kept stowed in his knapsack. She pushed down the twinge of guilt. She would return it. That is, if she survived the ordeal.

A breeze ruffled leaves overhead, causing her to pause and listen. She was past the Union pickets. How far until she reached Confederate lines? A mile? Two?

As she pressed closer to Yorktown, her nerves grew strained, more taut than the strings of a fiddle. Every noise was a gunshot. Every sound of brush and creature stole her breath.

She mentally rehearsed all the Scriptures about fear that she could recall until her trembling eased. A sudden motion to her right snapped her senses like a whip.

A man shifted not more than fifty feet away, moving between the trees with a slow gait. The faint moonlight glinted off the rifle he rested against his shoulder. Although the silver glow made it hard to tell the exact color, this man wore a uniform and kepi.

A Confederate picket. She'd found them.

Easing behind a tree, she watched and waited. Pinkerton had assured her the troops in Yorktown were known to allow peddlers in their midst. If she could somehow manage to gain entrance, she would be able to acquire the information the Union so desperately needed. Pinkerton had been specific. They needed the numbers of Confederate troops in Yorktown, artillery strength, and how many reinforcements Lee would be sending to secure the stronghold. She'd thought, after so many months of playing Thomas Turner, taking on another role wouldn't be so nerve-racking. She was wrong. This trepidation was far worse.

She crept back the way she had come, using the trees for cover. If she'd thought herself tense before, nothing prepared her for the angst of willingly prowling around enemy territory. Once she stepped foot over the proverbial line in the morning, she would be trapped until God provided an escape.

Spying a cluster of tents in the distance, she decided to remain sheltered in the trees to wait for morning's light. She stretched out on the cold ground and listened. The sound of her breathing melted into the cadence of nature, and she gazed up at the stars scattered across the wide expanse of sky.

"He telleth the number of the stars; he calleth them all by their names."

The psalm rolled around her brain. If God knew and named every single star in creation, surely he saw her too. Saw her and knew her. Not just Thomas Turner or any other mask she might wear, but *her*.

"When I consider thy heavens, the work of thy fingers, the moon and the stars, which thou hast ordained; What is man, that thou art mindful of him?"

She exhaled slowly and squinted at the winking bodies of light. Indeed, why would the Creator be mindful of someone like her? She was nothing. Only a girl trying to escape a future of gloom and heartache. A life each of her sisters had submitted to, a future that encircled her like an ever-tightening noose.

Her throat convulsed.

Did you see, God? Did you see the way my father hurt Mother over and over again? Did you really see every time he took delight in tearing her heart to shreds? Why did you turn away when he struck me and cursed my existence? Why were you silent when he corrupted everything and everyone in his path? Why didn't you stop him?

Though a vast expanse of heaven loomed overhead, her pleas felt trapped, held captive by some unseen hand that echoed them back unheard.

She listened. Waiting. But God was silent.

It seemed to her, he grew quieter with every passing day.

Chapter 29

APRIL 26, 1862
YORKTOWN, VIRGINIA

The red-faced soldier studied her with a scowl.

"A peddler, you say?" He grinned sardonically, revealing crooked, yellow teeth. "Unless you got whiskey or rum, I doubt the boys will be interested."

Cassie smiled and let the Irish brogue spill from her lips, remembering the lilt of her brother-in-law's speech. If Peter knew she was imitating him as a way to deceive the Rebels, he'd be right proud.

Keep the accent at the front of your teeth, not the back of your throat. "Sorry I am to say I've not a drop of spirits, but I've plenty of other goods to make the heart light."

"Do you now?" His voice dripped with derision.

"Aye. Socks and apples. Playing cards and dominoes for what folks is pining for a bit o' sport." She leaned in and winked conspiratorially. "Even managed to smuggle me way into some chocolate if the price is right."

"I don't know . . ."

"Got soap too. You telling me some of you boys couldn't do with a good bath?" She grinned. "Or are ye aimin' to cut down the bloody Yanks by smell alone?"

The soldier chuckled. "You make a good point."

Cassie nodded smugly. "O' course I do. And I reckon your commanders will be happy to know I even have a few prize oranges in me pack for any soldiers sufferin' from scurvy." She shook her head and tsked. "And here ye are, refusin' to let me pass. What'll they say when they learn the dreadful news?"

The soldier laughed again. "All right, all right. You convinced me. I'll have to take you to my captain first to get his approval, but I'm sure the men will be happy to see your goods."

Cassie squeezed his hand in as manly a hold as she could manage. She could not let him detect any weakness in her grip. "Good man, ye are. I'm thankful."

"What's your name?"

She adjusted her bulging knapsack as she followed him into the Confederate camp. There was no going back now. "Barney O'Shea, at your service."

She smiled at the gray-clad Confederates who eyed her with curiosity as she walked through their camp, yet coals burned her insides at the sight of slaves being forced to shovel gravel and carry loads of rocks to repair fortifications. One of them met her eyes as she walked past. Perspiration ran down his face, and the fingers clutching his bucket were cracked and bleeding.

"Get to work on that parapet!"

The order was barked from a soldier with bulging eyes. Before the slave could move to obey, the soldier kicked the backs of his knees. He fell to the ground, scattering his load of gravel in a puff of dust.

"Darkies who are too lazy to do their share will be shot. Do you understand?"

The slave slowly rose. "Yessir."

Cassie dropped her gaze and pressed her lips shut as she walked past. *Lord, give me wisdom to focus on the task at hand.* The injustice chafed, but she would do the slaves no good if she failed in her mission.

The captain waved his approval at her arrival with a disinterested air. "Peddle your goods, but be quick about it. We don't need hawkers here all day distracting our men."

"Aye, sir. Last thing I'm wantin' is to be keepin' our brave defenders from their tasks. Just as soon as the boys are done lookin', I'll be out in two shakes of a lamb's tail."

The captain nodded and wandered off, his brows lowered. He muttered under his breath. Whether in irritation or deep in thought about some other matter, Cassie couldn't tell.

She spent the morning talking to soldier after soldier, using the glib tongue and easygoing manner of Barney O'Shea to win the favor of the Confederates. Most were friendly and curious, some suspicious. Others were downright hostile and "didn't cotton to no Irishmen." Those she gave a wide berth. No sense making enemies. Well, more so than they already were.

While plying her wares, she subtly attempted to gain information, but the soldiers were far more interested in swapping lighthearted stories and teasing each other about the need for soap. She could understand. It would be the same in her own regiment. When death constantly loomed overhead, diversion was always welcome. Still, she couldn't leave empty-handed. She would not leave unless she had something to report to Pinkerton.

By midday the sun beat down in relentless anger. Dust coated her tongue. A soldier approached, holding out a cup of water. "You look done in. Drink."

She swallowed the cool liquid so quickly, she nearly caused herself to choke. The water dribbled down her chin and ran down her heated neck. She wiped away the liquid with the back of her hand. "Much obliged."

He pointed at her deflated knapsack. "You sell all your goods?"

"Almost. Got a few things left yet."

He gestured toward some large tents in the distance. "You try peddling to some of the commanders? They can seem a bit intimidating, but if you catch them at the right moment, you might find their favor and come out with a pocketful of cash."

She chuckled, her heart leaping. Instructions to head to the commander's tent? Perfect. If she were caught lurking, she could simply blame it on the young private.

"Bully good idea. Thank ye kindly."

The young soldier adjusted his gray kepi against his straw-colored hair and nodded. "I'm thankful for the playing cards you brought. Gets mighty dull around here waiting for those cowardly Yanks to decide to do something. They're so chicken, they could be stuffed and eaten for dinner."

Cassie forced a grin. "They know how fearsome their opponent is, aye?"

"Absolutely." He punched her in the shoulder, then strolled away whistling a tune.

She narrowed her eyes and turned, her focus set on the tents in the distance.

As she approached, voices drifted through the open flaps of the large canvas tent. Cassie crept closer, running the numbers she heard over and over in her mind until they were properly committed to memory.

Fourteen twelve-pounder cannons, eight-inch columbiads, ten-inch mortars, twenty-one howitzers . . . fourteen twelve-pounder cannons, eight-inch columbiads, ten-inch mortars, twenty-one howitzers . . .

Memorizing the details must suffice until she found a private place to scratch the information on the slip of paper secreted away in her shoe. When heads turned at the arrival of the white-headed, noble General Lee, she knew the opportunity was providential. She slipped closer to the commanders' tent and hunkered behind a tree, her ears perked for anything McClellan might want to learn.

"McClellan can't keep waiting indefinitely. He's playing with us. Just like a cat toying with a mouse before it strikes. What say you, General?"

Rustle of papers. Shifting footfalls.

A deep voice drawled, "Gentlemen, the fortifications are admirably constructed, but if the information we've obtained is correct, McClellan has enough guns to blow the entire length of our parapets and barricades into dust." Lee sighed heavily, the rich timbre of his voice grim. "We cannot hold Yorktown if McClellan strikes."

A different, more nasal voice wavered through the air. "What shall be done then?"

"We must evacuate Yorktown."

A horse whinnied, causing her pulse to ricochet. She ducked low and snuck away from the tent, her mind churning over what she'd heard. She bit the inside of her cheek until she tasted blood.

McClellan and the other generals needed to know the news with all haste.

Cassie felt as if she were crawling out of her own skin.

Frustration scratched her insides. It had been four hours since she'd overheard General Lee's intentions to evacuate Yorktown, and she'd yet to find an escape. Word had drifted through the ranks about the peddler who was visiting. All were anxious to grab her dwindling supplies. If she didn't make her way out soon . . .

Pain exploded in her backside as a booted foot slammed into her posterior.

"You there!" A booming voice washed over her as she stumbled to the ground. She tasted dirt. A shadow drifted across her sprawled form, and she glanced up with gritted teeth. She recognized him—the burly fellow who had mouthed off about "cursed Irishmen."

"Come along with me, boy."

"Why would I do that?"

The grating sound of minié balls sliced the air. Cassie ducked low, but the soldier only glanced at her as if she were nothing more than a skittish cat.

"Minié balls." He jerked his thumb to some distance ahead. "Greetings from the Yankee demons."

Please, Lord . . .

"A man's life is at stake. Hurry."

Though leery, she hastened to follow him. The sun had nearly set. Dark shadows crept over the woods beyond camp. Her ankle twisted, snagging on a gnarled tree root. Cringing, she hurried to keep pace.

When they'd reached the outskirts of the Confederate camp, the soldier stopped and whirled back to her, grabbing her by the shoulder. "You're to take this wounded soldier's picket until I return."

Her eyes darted over to a man lying not twenty feet away, his leg bloody and torn apart. He said nothing but suddenly thrashed.

"Why me?"

"Because I saw you first. I've got to go find his replacement. As soon as those minié balls started up, our men had work to do."

He sneered at her. "We have *real* work, you know. Something you and your peddling kin know nothing about."

The fingers digging into her flesh tightened until she almost cried out.

"You try to wiggle out of helping and I'll hunt you down and shoot you like a rabid dog." He suddenly released his iron grip, and she nearly collapsed in relief.

He thrust a rifle into her hands and glared. "I'll be back just as soon as I get him to the medic." He hoisted the wounded man's weight and departed with a dark glower.

Cassie's legs felt like jam as she stood and waited, making sure the irate soldier was out of sight. Another minié ball shrieked overhead, landing somewhere nearby. The ground beneath her feet rumbled.

A few minutes more.

Light drizzle dampened her skin. The feathery-fine mist grew oppressive. A flash of lightning split the night sky, unleashing a torrent. Her thin clothing became heavy and sluggish with the downpour. No one would be able to hear her running.

Now.

Hot blood coursed through her veins as she pumped her legs as fast as they would carry her against her wet pants. Heart pounding, she ran like an unleashed beast. Water pelted her eyes and slapped her face. Her lungs and legs burned.

She darted between trees, splashing through watery holes and fumbling over slick tree roots. Silver fire lit up the sky. The sky boomed and growled. The rifle grew slippery and heavy in her fingers.

She was closing in, nearing the Union picket lines. She froze, gasping for air, and blinked against the lashing rain. If the Union pickets saw her running toward them, brandishing a gun, they would shoot her first and ask questions later.

Pain clutched her heart with the exertion. Dropping her hands to her wet, muddy knees, she sucked in a deep draught of air, mind spinning. A crack of thunder caused her to look up at the trees. Their tops thrashed back and forth like the ends of a broom. The ground shook. A jagged thread of white snagged the black sky.

She had no choice. It was move forward or be caught. She would have to sneak into camp just as she'd maneuvered her way into the Confederate line.

She stumbled ahead, sloshing through the mud. A sharp pain stabbed her side. The click of a hammer sounded to her right. Her pulse tripped.

"You have one second to flash the Union sign before I pump your guts full of gunpowder."

She slowly dropped her rifle to the ground, lifted her hands, and turned to the scowling soldier. Rain dripped from the brim of his kepi, but the hands he curled around his gun were steady. She flicked her fingers, contorting them into the designated sign.

With a nod of satisfaction, the soldier lowered his weapon and jerked his head toward camp. "Report to your commander."

"Yes, sir."

Heaving a sigh, she willed her heart to resume a normal pulse. She'd made it.

The urge to drop to her knees and kiss the muddy ground was overwhelming.

APRIL 29, 1862
WASHINGTON, DC

Pinkerton steepled his fingers as he sat behind his desk. Cassie kept her eyes trained on his.

"What makes you believe the Rebel forces are preparing to leave Yorktown?"

Her gaze flickered to General McClellan's grim visage not ten feet away. She straightened, swinging her focus back to the detective. "Because I heard General Lee speak the words himself."

Pinkerton's brows rose into his hairline. He leaned forward. "You saw General Lee?"

"Yes, sir. I snuck close to their tent and overheard him discussing strategies with his commanders."

Pinkerton studied her for a long moment and leaned back in his chair. The underside squeaked with his shifting weight. A smile tugged at his lips. "You know, Private Turner, it's not uncommon for new recruits in our department to misjudge information they gather. The nature of this work is often predicated on tight nerves, close encounters at being caught, and emotions that swing like a pendulum. Why, only last month, a new recruit mistakenly reported the Confederates had twenty thousand more soldiers at a Tennessee town than there actually were."

Her brows furrowed. What was he saying?

"It would be understandable if you'd misheard."

She lifted her chin, a hot fire kindled in her middle. "I heard them clearly, sir. Lee was quite adamant they could not hold Yorktown if General McClellan used the full force of our current arsenal." From her periphery, she caught the general shifting his weight from foot to foot. "He told his generals to make preparations to leave Yorktown."

Pinkerton rose and strolled to stare out the long window behind his mahogany desk, his hands clasped behind his back. "And what else did they discuss after that?"

"I'm not sure, sir. I made haste to withdraw. I was in danger of being caught."

"So you admit you did not hear the conclusion of their conversation."

She spoke slowly, clenching her teeth. "No, sir, I did not."

Pinkerton shot a look to McClellan, who ran his fingers down his mustache in a repetitive motion. "General, what say you?"

McClellan sighed and dropped his arms to his sides. "I have no doubt Private Turner performed admirably in his duty, but I cannot reconcile that General Lee would give up Yorktown so easily." The long mustache drooped. "No, it's not possible."

"But, sir, if I'm correct, you could attack Yorktown now and crush the Rebels in one fell swoop."

McClellan's eyes grew cold. "I'm well aware of the advantageous position Yorktown affords, Private."

"I heard Lee, sir. They are leaving."

McClellan's face darkened. "Thank you, Private Turner. You are dismissed."

Clamping her lips shut, she knew any further protests would fall on deaf ears and quite possibly lead to getting her court-martialed for insubordination. Pleading words burned her lips, but she saluted and left the two men instead.

What good was spying on the enemy if her own commanders refused to believe the information? She marched down the long hallway, grinding her teeth.

Her hard work had been for nothing.

Chapter 30

Dear Gabriel,

As I make preparations to depart for my own sojourn into this photographic endeavor with equal parts terror and fascination, I longed to stop and write you. This journey we have embarked upon is being marked as a successful contribution to the war efforts by General Winfield Scott. He has realized the value of photography as a kind of military topography, deeming our work invaluable. I pray other military leaders will heed his words as well. This praise is due, in no small part, to you and all the other photographers we have sent out to record this great drama.

I see you took my most recent instructions to heart. Your piece "Beautiful Heroines of Home" has been favorably received by five major newspaper publications. I suspect this is only the beginning. If other papers respond as enthusiastically as these, you shall be receiving a tidy sum for your efforts. The piece is, I think, quite intriguing. Aside from the woman's beauty, there is something quite telling in her expression. Hope, sadness, courage, uncertainty— her visage is like the multiple facets of a cut jewel. Each part just as fascinating as the last. You are to be commended.

As soon as I receive payment, I will forward you your portion posthaste, unless you have a more preferable reception point. I understand any reticence you may have in using regular parcel post. The mail delivery within regimental lines can be an arduous and uncertain endeavor, especially in light of forced marches to unknown destinations.

Rather than continuing to return to the capital to restock supplies and other necessities, I have acquired permission to use Union signal stations outside Manassas Junction and Yorktown, and at several points in between. Please avail yourself of these drop points. Glass plates, chemicals, washbasins, and a handful of small cameras have been stocked at each, as well as feed for your horses. The signalmen have been given your name and identification. You should have no trouble entering. In addition, to spare photographs from being damaged by sending them through the mail, all photographs can be stored and held at these signal stations. My esteemed assistant Alexander Gardner has been appointed the task of retrieving work stored at these depots until the war is concluded. Due diligence must be made to store your photographs together, with your name printed on the outside of the envelope or box.

Best wishes as you continue to press forward. May Providence smile on you.

Sincerely,
M. Brady

"Whatcha reading?"

Gabe crumpled the letter, keeping the information hidden from Jonah's eyes. The last thing he needed was the nosy lad learning he'd submitted a picture of a woman to the newspapers. Jonah knew far too much as it was.

"Just some correspondence." Gabe gave him a pointed look. "Nothing for you to worry yourself over." Squinting over the sun-dappled camp, he wiped away the sweat beading his forehead. The late afternoon was quiet, a rare break in the din of the siege. The scent of earth and grass perfumed the air.

Gabe nodded toward the middle of the grounds. "You finished with assignments for the day?"

Jonah kicked at a pebble near his boot—a boot that flapped open like the slobbering tongue of a panting dog. "I suppose so. Ain't much to do unless Captain Johnston sends for me. No messages for the message boy makes the day drag." His eyes brightened. "But I asked if I could be moved up to powder boy for the big cannons." His small chest puffed out like a fireplace bellows. "Captain says he'll give it a think."

Shoving Brady's letter into his pocket, Gabe walked toward the horses and released them from their bridles. "Sounds like a dangerous job to me."

Jonah sniffed. "I can handle it."

"Mm." Arguing with him would only cause the headstrong boy to dig in his heels. "I imagine so. It's understandable that you want to give up your messenger duties. After all, only a select few could bear the weight of that responsibility."

His brown brows furrowed deep. "What do you mean?"

Gabe shrugged and slapped the horses on their rumps, letting them roam unencumbered over the grassy slope beyond. They tossed their glossy heads and pranced away. "You know, carrying such privileged information is for only the most courageous soldiers. The most trustworthy." He shook his head. "I wouldn't want it. Too many people depending on me."

Jonah's mouth puckered. Gabe smothered a smile.

"Maybe you're right. My work is mighty important. Kind of like Turner's, ain't it?"

Gabe's carefree mood soured. He hadn't seen Cassie since she'd returned, but he knew she was there. Several of the soldiers had remarked on Turner's disappearance and sudden reentry.

Turning away, Gabe pinched his mouth. "Guess so."

Jonah laughed. "You guess?" He lowered his voice and darted a look side to side. "I bet she—uh, he—found out what the Rebels have planned next."

Gabe clamped his jaw.

"He can prob'ly blend right in with them." The boy grinned, revealing crooked teeth. "You got to admit, he's good at pretending."

"Yes, Turner is quite a good actor." His stomach clenched. Cassie was all too skilled at deception.

"You seem vexed. Hasn't she—he come by to see you?"

The boy's perpetual slip of Cassie's gender was disconcerting. Good thing they hadn't told him her real name. "No, not even to deliver my letter. Briggs brought it to me instead. I guess *he* has assumed postal carrier duties." Gabe looked away, wishing the precocious boy would be called away on some other errand.

Jonah pursed his lips. "I guess I don't much mind being messenger boy if I'm doing important work like Turner. Say—" his eyes rounded—"maybe President Lincoln will give me a spying job too!"

As he watched the boy race away, Gabe sighed, his heart sinking into his stomach. *No, son. No spying. I can't handle another innocent person I love wrapped in lies and danger.*

Yet was he so different? He had yet to confess he'd sent Cassie's photograph to the papers without her knowledge or permission.

He pushed the unease aside. Jacob was the one who mattered now. It was his duty to care for the man. Without Jacob, his dreams would have never left the ground.

And Cassie . . .

With a grunt, he trudged into the Whatsit. The warm temperatures and lack of ventilation made the small wagon feel like a boiler room.

If Cassie could only learn to trust him, to believe he had her best interests at heart, she would understand his desire to see her safe and protected. Then everything between them could be perfect.

Why couldn't she understand?

MAY 4, 1862
YORKTOWN, VIRGINIA

One minute they were slogging through shin-deep mud in the pouring rain. The next, the earth exploded like a geyser, shooting rock, mud, and bloody bodies through the air.

Sound ceased.

Cassie blinked away the rain flickering against her lashes. Mouths moved, shouted, but her ears registered none of it. They were numb, buzzing with a strange kind of deafness.

A shrill ringing filtered through. Another boom shook the ground, rattling her teeth in their sockets. Mud and debris rained down, pelting her face and hands.

Even after the message she had relayed to Pinkerton and General McClellan, they'd waited for two days. Why did the general refuse to move? And why now did they lurch forward to capture Yorktown, only to have pandemonium unfold before them?

Faint shouting drifted toward her. Briggs looked at her with wide eyes, his bearded face spotted with mud. "What was that? A strange new type of cannon fire?"

Cassie shook her head. "No whistle beforehand." Her voice sounded strange.

Briggs clutched his rifle with white fingers. "What, then?"

What indeed? Medics scurried to attend the men whose limbs had been ripped away and tossed into the mud like discarded clothing. It was as if a cannon had been shot from under the ground.

Under the ground . . .

She snapped to face Briggs. "Buried explosive shells."

Briggs scowled and swore.

The buzzing faded, replaced by dull sounds of life. Screaming men, the sucking squelch of mud, grunts of weary soldiers pushing forward.

They were approaching the Rebel picket lines she had crossed less than a fortnight ago. Two explosions but no gunfire. No rows of gray backs waiting for them?

A bone-breaking blast lifted her from her feet, throwing her backward. The ground erupted, flinging up large chunks of mud. The two men who had been marching in front of her were thrust into the air.

As her body slammed into the ground, pain burst all across her back. The world went eerily silent again. She tried to roll onto her side, but the quagmire made the work difficult. With a groan, she fell back and panted, staring up at the gray sky. Rain dampened her face, pinging her skin and rolling into her nose.

Briggs's face loomed over hers, his mouth moving. She couldn't hear what he was saying, but she grasped the hands he offered. She rose slowly, her uniform caked with sludge.

His mouth rounded, resembling the words *Turner, are you hurt?* His bushy black brows rose.

She shook her head, trying to gain her bearings. Noise filtered slowly through the deafening hum. The only thing she could hear well was her own pulse pounding dully in her ears. Men all around her scrambled away from the detonated shell. What good would it do? The lot of them were playing blindman's bluff with the Rebels.

Her entire frame ached.

Her fingers grew slick clutching the wet rifle. The regiment moved forward with deliberate slowness. Or did it only seem that way because sound had been sucked into another realm? When she stumbled and fell to her knees, Briggs hoisted her up, tucking his thick arm under her left limb, half-dragging her forward. Why wouldn't her body cooperate?

They pressed into the Rebel camp. White canvas tents stood erect, but no one greeted them. The entire place was deathly still. They trudged past a tent and she saw it—crude caricatures of Union soldiers painted on the canvas's broadside. Ugly curses and insults were plastered around the ridiculous drawings. A sensation both hot and cold crawled through her.

Her limbs and back tingled. She shrugged away Briggs's help. "I think I can move well enough now." Her voice was still thick, but at least she could hear it.

Rain streamed in rivulets over the abandoned camp, pooling on the ground where campfires once sat. Loose canvas flapped in the wind.

Cassie ground her teeth. The entire place had been abandoned. They were too late.

———◆———

"I'm sorry, Captain. It's too dark inside the tent, and the chemicals won't process without proper light."

Captain Johnston stroked his wiry side-whiskers. "What if

we were to carry these *letters*—" he said the word as if it were a curse—"outside? Could you photograph them then? I want President Lincoln to see what these demon Rebels left behind."

Gabe shook his head. "I'm so sorry, no. Rain is just as destructive to the wet-plate process as darkness is. And you would likely ruin the evidence. I can photograph them once weather conditions improve."

Johnston growled and thumbed through the mocking missives before tossing them to the table.

The sounds of revelry outside were a harsh contrast to the captain's sour expression. While the soldiers rejoiced that the Confederates had fled Yorktown, leaving the stronghold ripe for the plucking, Captain Johnston had found four letters waiting for them inside the largest tent. One addressed to President Lincoln, two for General McClellan, and one for "The First Yankee Who Comes."

When the captain had called for Gabe to "capture evidence the Confederates had left behind," he'd been able to read only one of the taunting messages intended for General McClellan.

You will be surprised to hear of our departure at this stage of the game, leaving you in possession of this worthless town. But the fact is, we have other engagements to attend to, and we can't wait for you to gather your courage any longer. . . .

The mocking jab at the general's pluck would not sit well.

Johnston rubbed his stumpy fingers over his balding scalp, leaving the thin strands on top in disarray. He muttered as he riffled through discarded papers left on the table, most of them, no doubt, more taunts and ridicules intended for Yankee eyes.

Johnston muttered under his breath, "Why didn't McClellan move when Turner told him they were preparing to leave?"

Gabe's breath hitched. "Turner warned him this would happen?"

Johnston's head snapped up, his eyes narrowing. "Never mind. I should not have spoken. Forget what you heard."

Feeling like he'd been punched in the gut, Gabe swallowed. "Yes, sir."

"If you are unable to take these photographs, I have nothing else at the moment, Mr. Avery." He waved his hand, shooing Gabe out the tent flap and into the infernal drizzle that refused to leave.

Gabe walked back to the Whatsit, barely noticing the thick mud covering his boots. Around him soldiers cheered and celebrated, their spirits undeterred by the damp weather. All they could see was the victory of a town abandoned.

But Gabe couldn't muster any joy. Not when he realized the depths of Cassie's work.

She'd snuck into a Confederate camp and collected military strategy from the enemy.

Rain slid under his collar, snaking down his back and dampening his shirt. He had aided her reckless plan. If something had happened to her, he would bear at least some of the responsibility.

He dropped his head against the slick walls of the wagon, letting the rain soak his clothes. Drops fell from the tips of his hair.

Forgive me, Father, for not protecting her like I should. Give me courage to do what is best for her. Something cold clamped his chest. *Even if it means I lose her.*

Chapter 31

MAY 6, 1862

Cassie sat on a fallen log at the edge of the battlefield, staring at nothing. The rain that had clung to them the past week was finally lifting, but the gloom remained like a wet cloak.

The past days had been grueling. After Yorktown had been abandoned, McClellan must have realized he'd let a golden opportunity to crush the Rebels slip through his fingers. When orders came to pursue the Confederates "until not a gray back was left," the Michigan Second, along with a host of other regiments, had attacked.

Rubbing her palms into her eyes, she tried to scrub away the images emblazoned into her mind. But nothing could wash away the horror, the disillusionment, or her own demons.

In the fiery heat of battle, she'd grabbed a litter and rushed to retrieve a fallen soldier. Cannons pounded the ground. Bullets whizzed past. Screams. Blood. She'd constantly felt covered in sticky crimson.

As she knelt to assess the soldier's condition, his eyes had sought hers and she fell backward, her heart rising into her throat. She couldn't breathe.

He was the very image of her father.

The man lifted his hand in a plea and released a strangled cry before blood bubbled from his mouth. His open blue eyes had faded into vacant orbs.

Her stomach clenched and soured. It wasn't Father. She knew it wasn't. So why did he continue to invade her dreams and snatch her sleep?

Forgive him.

Pinching her eyes shut, she heaved a thick sigh.

Time is too precious to waste in bitterness. It will steal your joy.

Time.

She reached into her pocket and brushed the cool metal of the watch Captain Johnston had gifted her.

His irritation with General McClellan's refusal to believe her report was palpable, yet instead of speaking ill of their superior, he'd thanked Thomas Turner profusely for his courageous and astute work. He'd pressed the watch into her hands, a gift for her service. The gesture had rendered her speechless.

Now she fingered the delicate carving of the encasement. The chain clinked in her fingers. Flipping the watch open, she watched the spindly hands shift ever so slowly.

Tick. Tick. Tick. Tick.

Or was that only the rhythm of her heart? It didn't matter. Both were destined to cease at some point.

She clicked the watch shut and dropped it back into her pocket. Weight settled in her chest like a brick.

When the battle had ended and both sides had declared a

truce to collect their injured comrades, she'd stood in the middle of the field watching men of blue and gray shuffling the chilled, groaning wounded into litters. Why *now* were they agreeing to cooperate after their bullets had cut each other down?

Nothing made sense. The world was a convoluted mess of rage and regrets.

She clomped through the mire, looking for signs of life among the bodies strewn throughout the slimy field. With mud coating everything, it was hard to tell whether some soldiers were Union or Confederate. In the end, it didn't really matter much.

Moans and mewling cries drifted over the quagmire. She crept close to one body that looked different from the others. Mud squelched under her boots as she approached. He was altogether odd, resting on his hands and knees. As her vision sharpened, she swallowed down the acid in her throat and turned away. His body remained but his head had been blown off.

It was too much. The carnage and death. The screams and wailing. The horror of wondering if the next moment would be her last. And the pretending. Always pretending.

Pretending to be Thomas Turner. Pretending to be a peddler. Pretending to ignore Gabe while every fiber of her being yearned for him. And worse yet, pretending her father hadn't poisoned every area of her life.

What else was to be done?

Don't think. Just do.

She trudged forward to check the breathing of the nearest prostrate man. *Don't think.*

The directive was becoming harder to follow.

"Do you think the photographer will cooperate?"

Cassie stood inside Captain Johnston's tent and fumbled

for a response. "You want Mr. Avery to sneak into Richmond with me?"

Johnston leaned back in his chair and rested his hands on the brass-buttoned rows of his uniform. "Pinkerton has readily admitted he and McClellan should have listened to you concerning Yorktown. Your information, if they had actually believed it, was invaluable. McClellan is preparing to launch an assault on Richmond but needs solid numbers. Troops, storehouses, artilleries, signal stations, anything that might help him plan the best course of action."

"I understand, but why the photographer?"

The captain pressed the bridge of his hawk-like nose between his fingers. "We want him to take photographs of the landscape. Topographical information is of utmost importance."

She frowned. "Then why would you need me?"

"You've completed several missions for us now. You have experience in spying. He doesn't. We dare not send him into such a task without an overseer. And while he captures the images we need, you can collect numbers and other valuable information."

Work side by side with Gabe? The thought both thrilled and terrified her. It would be nearly impossible to keep her emotional distance while traveling for days on end together.

"One caveat." Johnston yanked her from her tumultuous thoughts.

"Yes, sir?"

He cringed. "Pinkerton wants you to dress and act the part of a woman."

Cassie nearly choked.

"We thought it would be more prudent if you played his wife. Fewer questions. Do you think you can do it?"

She forced down the smile that threatened to form. "I'll try my best, sir."

MAY 18, 1862
NEAR RICHMOND, VIRGINIA

I've lost my mind.

He was crazy. He had to be to agree to this stunt.

He shot a sideways glance at Cassie, perched next to him on the seat of the Whatsit, her spine stiff. The swaying motion of the wagon slogging through the marshy ground of the Chickahominy swamps did little to make her relax. She looked as if she were wound tighter than a seven-day watch.

He wasn't faring much better.

Captain Johnston had conveniently omitted the fact that Turner would be playing the part of his wife, an irony that would have been laughable had it not been for the seriousness of their task. Cassie pretending to be a man who was pretending to be a woman. Who would ever believe such a thing?

The Whatsit bounced, knocking his leg against her skirt. Clearing her throat, she smoothed the dark-blue fabric and scooted away from him. If she shifted any farther, she'd be tumbling off the side. He repressed a sigh.

Johnston had promised to pay him for his part in the dangerous task. Jacob needed any financial help Gabe could provide. But if he were honest with himself, he must admit his concern for Cassie's safety had been the driving force in agreeing to this insanity. If she refused to listen to reason, he could at least accompany her.

It was either follow her and save her from herself, or reveal her identity to her superiors. Guilt gnawed his middle. If she only knew how many times he'd contemplated the latter in the past week . . .

But every time he'd convinced himself to spill the truth, images of her father's fingers wrapped around her throat assaulted him. He couldn't release her to that monster. If he hadn't been there the night her father attacked her, he had no doubt she'd be dead. The man was evil.

Crack! The wagon stalled and tilted to the left. The horses nickered and tossed their heads, straining against the harnesses. With a groan, he peered over the edge of the wagon to find the left rear wheel had broken, several of its spokes snapped in half.

"What's wrong?"

It was the only thing she'd spoken since leaving camp.

"Wheel broke. I have another one in the back, but it will take me a while to change it on this mushy ground." He jumped from the seat.

She swung her legs over the side. "I'll help you."

"No. You stay." Her blue eyes rounded. He held up a restraining hand but smiled to soften the edge of his words. "You're all dressed up and pretty. No sense spoiling your gown. Everyone will wonder what kind of husband I am to let my wife do the work."

"But you shouldn't have to do it alone."

Grasping his courage, he slid his hand over hers and squeezed warmth into her fingers. "You're not a man today, Cassie. Rest."

Her cheeks pinked just before she slid her fingers away from his and nodded.

Over an hour later, Gabe wiped the sweat from his face, praying he hadn't smeared axle grease all over his skin. Tossing the tools into the back of the Whatsit, he trudged to the front of the wagon, mopping his face with a clean cloth he'd found inside. He peered up at the driver's bench to see Cassie buffing her arms.

She attempted a smile that fell flat. "All done?"

He studied her flushed face and glassy eyes. "Yes. Are you feeling well?"

Her body trembled. "Just a little cold, is all. Did the weather change?"

Frowning, he dropped the cloth. "Not really. It feels warm and sticky to me."

"F-feels c-c-ool t-to me."

He walked around to her side of the bench and raised his arms. "Step down for a minute. I'll catch you."

Cassie blinked as if confused and grasped his forearms. He eased her down and slid his palm over her forehead. She was burning up with fever.

He lifted her into his arms, fighting back the cold alarm washing through him. She made no protest. She shivered as if she'd been dunked in an ice bath.

Her voice sounded wispy against his chest. "Wh-where are w-we going?"

"I'm tucking you into bed. You're sick, sweetheart."

"S-s-so cold."

"I know."

He carried her slight frame to the back and nudged the door open with his foot. Pulling out the bedroll, he gently laid her on it and draped a scratchy blanket over her shivering form.

"What do you think is wrong?" he asked, smoothing the dark strands of hair away from her cheek.

She clamped her jaw tight to keep her teeth from chattering. "S-seen it in th-the h-hospital. M-m-might be m-malaria."

His breath thinned as she fell into a quivering sleep.

Chapter 32

CASSIE WAS BEING SHAKEN.

Invisible hands had clamped onto her body, jolting her like cannon fire. Was it her father? She couldn't hear his curses. Time and reality were fuzzy, shifting like ripples of water. She couldn't think past the cold wrapping its icy tentacles around her. Couldn't even open her eyes.

Expressionless faces floated through her mind. The ends of rifles fired out bursts of flame. All around her, men in blue and gray ran through the mud screaming, bayonets flashing. Trees fell and shook the ground, making her knees wobble like a newborn colt's.

She looked down at her grimy boots and blinked when a deep rumbling groan rattled the earth. The ground cracked open. The yawning gap widened as man and beast fell into the abyss with bloodcurdling screams.

Gasping for air, she cringed as the shaking increased and the zigzag line separated the terrain. From across the divide, she sought and found Gabe's handsome face. His arm was out-stretched. His lips mouthed words, though at first she couldn't hear him over the terrifying roar of the earthquake.

"Jump!"

She crawled toward the edge and peered into the nothing-ness that separated them. Snapping her eyes back to his, she choked out a sob.

"Jump!"

She shook her head. It was too far. She'd never make it.

The land pushed them so far apart, she could no longer see him. Breathing erratically, she rested her palm on a splintered oak. There was no one with her on this side of the divide. No one.

A rustle of bushes. She looked up.

Her father stood before her. They were the two remaining souls.

No!

A masculine voice murmured overhead. A damp rag soothed her fevered skin. "Shh. I'm here."

The voice calmed her, chasing away the dark images and foreboding of doom.

In the hazy fog, a gentle hand stroked her brow. She grasped it and tugged it toward her, latching on to the warm flesh with urgency. Strong fingers curled around her own. Someone brushed a kiss to her forehead.

It was enough. She was safe for now.

———•———

Gabe poked at the fire, sending sparks flying upward into the dark sky, his mind whirling like a top. The fever had ravaged Cassie for two days. Two days of alternating between moving the wagon closer to Richmond and bathing her skin with cool water. He'd cradled her when her tremors had shaken her like laundry flapping on a clothesline. He'd kissed her head and murmured verses of soothing reassurance to her sleeping form. And during the hours she'd slipped into restful slumber, he'd urged the horses onward. They now sat only a mile away.

But none of it mattered if she perished.

Please, God, spare her.

He wasn't a fool. He'd seen the effects of malaria at the Alexandria hospital. Most recovered from the dreaded malady. Others did not.

The flames hissed and popped as he wrapped a cloth around the coffeepot handle and pulled it from the fire.

"Gabe?"

Cassie's soft voice caused him to jump up. She stood next to the Whatsit, her dark hair a riot. She gripped the wagon as if releasing it might cause her to crumple to the ground. Her face was pale and dark shadows smudged her eyes, but she was on her feet.

Dared he hope she was past the worst?

He took her arm and led her to the fire, supporting her slight weight as she leaned against him. He settled her on the ground, admiring the way her skirt puddled around her. Despite the effects of illness, she was lovely.

"Thank you."

He filled the two tin cups with steaming black brew. Ribbons of steam curled and rose. He passed the cup to her waiting hands. "How are you feeling?"

She smiled faintly as she gripped the cup. "Weak. Some better, though. At least the tremors have ceased. How long have I been ill?"

"Two days."

She gasped. "Two days? What about the assignment?"

"Don't fret. We're only a mile from Richmond."

She blinked. "You took care of me *and* moved us forward?" Something akin to gratitude flooded her face.

He pushed away the pleasure at her response. "The Lord has preserved us from danger or delay. And you slept deeply yesterday afternoon, which helped us travel faster." He sipped the bitter brew and grimaced. Chicory was a poor substitute for coffee.

"Did I, uh, say or do anything unseemly while I was ill?" An uncharacteristic expression of vulnerability flitted across her features.

He shook his head. "No, nothing."

Her shoulders sagged as she released a sigh laden with relief.

"Except for confessing your undying love for me."

Her cheeks blushed crimson. "I did not."

Chuckling, he took another sip. "Guess that's for me and the Almighty to know."

She bit her lip and looked into her cup.

A gunshot blasted in the warm evening air, sending reverberations through the hills. He heard Cassie's sudden intake of air. He frowned and scanned the trees surrounding them. "That was close."

A rustling sounded beyond the line of brush. Gabe set his cup on the ground and rose, reaching for the rifle not a foot away. "Stay here."

He lifted the weapon to his shoulder and moved in the direction of the noise. Cassie's soft steps fell behind his, her skirt whooshing like a whisper.

"I said to stay behind."

Her whisper was terse. "I'm a better shot than you."

Inwardly groaning, he gave up trying to convince her and crept farther into the woods. A low moan prickled the hair on the back of his neck.

Cassie clutched his elbow. "Gabe, look!"

Twenty paces ahead, a body lay on the ground.

"Stay behind me."

They crept closer, and the limp form emitted another whimper. Rifle raised, Gabe called out, "Who are you?"

The body shifted, moaning. "Shot."

He crouched and rolled the stranger over. A man with a sparse black beard looked back, his eyes pinched. The thick cords of his neck shifted as he swallowed. His hands clutched his stomach, where a circle of crimson was spreading.

"Been shot."

Cassie knelt and began ripping the hem of her petticoat.

Gabe grasped the stranger's blood-slicked hand. "What's your name? What happened?"

The man clenched his jaw and released a guttural cry from deep in his throat. "Name's Ernest Beauregard." He swallowed again, hissing through his teeth. "Shot by my no-account brother."

Cassie pressed a wad of torn fabric to the wound bubbling blood. "We heard the shot. Is he still around?"

Ernest scowled. "The coward hightailed it out of here. Good thing too, or I'd be putting a bullet through his heart."

Gabe sought Cassie's eyes. She shook her head. He turned back to the man and clutched his hand tighter. "The bleeding is bad."

Ernest coughed and winced, his chest heaving. "I ain't gonna make it, am I?"

Bowing his head, Gabe murmured, "I'm sorry."

Ernest nodded stiffly, his eyes searching the sunset-streaked sky overhead. "So be it. I wouldn't change a thing."

"Wouldn't change what?"

The dying man huffed a deep breath and grimaced. "Burning

down my brother's barn. I come home one day and found him with my wife." A deep gurgle rattled his chest. "The snake deserved it. We never did get along. He was always looking for ways to hurt me."

What could he possibly say? "I'm sorry."

Ernest fought for breath. "Ma always said I should forgive him. Never would. I guess this is the natural end, then. We fight until one of us is destroyed. I'll be going first, but I'll take my dignity with me."

Gabe heard Cassie's sharp intake of breath. He kept his eyes trained on the man's ashen face. Blood ran from the corners of his mouth. His pupils dilated, then shrank to pinpoints.

"If you see a fellow that looks like a scrawny version of myself, you shoot him for me, you hear?" With a deep wheeze, Ernest shuddered and his eyes glazed. His hand went limp as life siphoned from his body. His head rolled to the side, his mouth slack.

Gone.

Gabe released Ernest's sticky crimson hand and peered over his shoulder. Cassie sat still as a statue, her hands and cloth still pressed to the man's stomach. Her face bore a haunted look.

A single tear tracked down the smooth skin of her cheek.

Chapter 33

MAY 21, 1862
RICHMOND, VIRGINIA

Cassie forced her mind to the task at hand. Distracted thoughts while traversing through a Rebel army camp would spell disaster.

Yet try as she might, she couldn't erase the image or the words of the dying stranger from her brain.

So angry. So bitter. And what good had his choices done in the end? His thirst for revenge had not been sated, and the full potential of the length and depth of his life had been snuffed out.

Would her end be the same?

The plink of a banjo yanked her from the dark thought.

Keeping her head down, she shadowed Gabe's sure step as they followed a sergeant through the camp, weaving between the rows of squatting canvas tents. A cluster of gray backs huddled around the banjo player, tapping their feet as the cheery tune drifted through the air. She peered from under the wide brim of her bonnet, searching for anything McClellan would find useful.

She had feared entering the camp would be difficult, but when Gabe showed the Confederates a forged document—a false plea from Lieutenant Colonel Tanner requesting Mr. Smith and his wife be allowed to photograph the camp, the Rebels had made no protest. With a long look at the papers, the guard had granted them entrance.

They passed another throng of soldiers shouting and laughing as they played a crude game of baseball using a long piece of fence rail to smack a yarn-wrapped walnut.

The sergeant stopped suddenly, his stern visage showing little emotion. "Would this spot serve, Mr. Smith?"

Gabe glanced around and scratched his hair in a relaxed manner. "Reckon it'll do."

The thick-waisted sergeant nodded curtly. "I'll leave you to prepare, then." His jaundiced eye swiveled to Cassie. "Stick close to your man, ma'am. Some soldiers won't think twice of taking advantage of a pretty woman."

Cassie nearly laughed. If the man only knew she could drop any one of these Johnny Rebs with a flick of her rifle . . .

Instead, she clutched Gabe's arm and gasped. "Yes, sir."

Gabe patted her hand as if trying to console his trembling wife. "I'll keep a close eye on her, Sergeant."

The man marched away and Gabe released her, fumbling to set up the cumbersome camera and tripod. His gaze connected with hers and he murmured under his breath, "Do what you must do quickly."

With a sideways glance to make sure she was unobserved, she plucked up her skirt to free the hem from tangling around her feet and scurried from view.

Under the pretext of returning to the Whatsit for supplies,

she scanned the camp's artillery strength, keeping her ears pricked for troop placement or gossip.

Two soldiers were cleaning their guns as she passed.

"James says the Yankees are about finished with the bridges across the Chickahominy."

The other soldier spit a thick brown stream onto the ground. "Let 'em come. We got masked batteries waiting for them." He jerked his thumb over his shoulder. "Did you see that big brush heap over yonder?" He chuckled. "Yankees are gonna be blown to kingdom come when they pass it."

Keeping her head low, she hurried to the Whatsit and let the voices drift past. If Union forces were preparing to cross the Chickahominy, she and Gabe had little time. Her illness had held them back significantly.

She collided with a firm chest, the pain stealing her breath for a moment. A dark laugh washed over her, causing prickles to traverse her spine. Punishing hands curled around her upper arms.

She looked up into the sneering face of a soldier.

"You're a pretty little filly, ain't ya?" His sour breath assaulted her skin, stealing her air. "You the newest entertainment?"

She clenched her jaw and tried to pull herself free. "Unhand me."

His grip tightened, his fingers digging into her flesh. "Just one little kiss."

He leaned in, and she placed a swift kick to his middle. He bellowed, but she couldn't manage to break his ironclad grip. Squirming, she recoiled from his venomous glare, her mouth dry. "Let me go."

"You deny me?" His eyes glinted like shards of glass. "I think not."

He lurched forward, dragging her behind him, and stomped

toward a tent. As his purpose became clear, she began to claw like a maniac. Her ears buzzed, her heart racing as she cried out. "Please! Help me!"

"Unhand my wife."

Gabe's voice boomed behind them, and Cassie nearly collapsed. The foul soldier whirled. "Your wife?"

Gabe's face looked etched in stone. A fury unlike anything she'd witnessed in him darkened his face. But the brute tightened his hold on her bruised wrists.

"I don't think Sergeant Shaffer would be pleased to know you assaulted the wife of the photographer he welcomed to camp."

The odious man shifted. "Sergeant Shaffer?"

Gabe took a menacing step forward, his teeth gritted. "Release. My. Wife."

The brute shoved her forward with a growl. She fell into Gabe's arms and sucked in a deep breath, her legs quivering like jelly.

Wrapping his arm around her, Gabe glared, his voice low and unyielding. "I suggest you leave before I report your conduct to Sergeant Shaffer."

The soldier's neck turned red. Pressing his lips into a firm line, he stomped away.

"Thank you."

"Are you all right?" Gabe's eyes roved over her as if reassuring himself.

Her lungs seared as she fought to take deep, calming breaths. "Yes, I think so."

He tenderly turned over her wrists, scowling at the reddened flesh. "Have you finished acquiring what you need?"

She nodded at the double meaning. "Yes."

"Good." His tone darkened. "Because I'm not letting you out of my sight again."

As she followed him back across the enemy camp, she pressed a hand to her quaking stomach.

For all her resistance to men and their domineering ways, this time she had to confess she was thankful for the bold protection Gabe covered her in. Was she wrong about the controlling nature of men?

Or perhaps the difference between happiness and misery in marriage was the man a woman bound herself to.

———◆———

Cassie was acting strangely.

At first, Gabe thought it was merely her urgency to leave the Confederate camp with haste before the Union invaded. But even after leaving and putting miles between the Rebels and themselves, he caught Cassie staring at him at odd moments. Each time, she looked away and worried her lip when he offered a relaxed smile in return.

Perhaps the effects of the malaria continued to plague her.

He cleared his throat and snapped the reins again, urging the mares to keep their pace. "Are you anxious to reach Union lines?"

Nodding, she picked at some imaginary speck on her blue skirt. "Yes. If we delay, our boys will walk right into that hidden artillery. The news must be delivered to McClellan with speed."

He fell silent, letting the horses' reins rest easily in his hands. "Thank you."

Her husky voice snagged his attention. "For what?"

The muscles in her slender neck shifted. "For saving me from that awful soldier. I didn't—" She licked her lips. "I just—"

"I should have horsewhipped him."

She dropped her gaze back to the twisted fingers in her lap. "If you hadn't interceded when you did . . ." A shudder racked her body. "I've been thinking."

"Yes?" he prompted.

She squirmed in the wagon seat. "Perhaps I haven't been fair to you."

He stilled. What was she saying? He kept silent, knowing she would speak her mind when she was good and ready.

She stared at the woods before them and sighed. "All my life, I've looked at men through the prism of my father. I suppose in observing his relationship with Mother, with me—" she grimaced—"I might have made wrong assumptions." Her eyes sought his, and his heart hammered. "I fear I painted you with the same brush."

He dragged his eyes away to watch the road before they ended up down a ravine. "And what do you think now?"

"You're nothing like him." Her voice was little more than a hoarse whisper.

He longed to stop the wagon and pull her into his arms. Instinct told him she still wasn't ready. Instead, he slipped both reins into his left hand and sought her fingers with his right. Her touch was hesitant, but she didn't pull away when he interlaced their fingers.

For now, it was enough.

———◆———

MAY 24, 1862

Cassie erased all traces of herself, or Mrs. Smith, from her stride before returning to camp. Only a day since she and Gabe had come back, and word had drifted through the regiment. They would march toward Richmond on the morrow.

She hoisted another sackful of flour into the supply wagon. Hearing a group of boys guffawing, she sought the huddle and speared Jonah with a sharp rebuke. "What are you boys doing?"

A newspaper was stretched out between them on the ground.

Jonah looked up and grinned. "Simmons brought a new batch of papers. We're reading the opinion pieces." Jonah snorted and the other boys joined him. "There's some idiot in here spouting malarkey. Says all us Yankees are gonna be working in the fields with his slaves when the war is over."

Cassie frowned. "If the captain catches you reading the papers instead of attending to your chores, you'll pay dearly."

The boys groaned. Jonah huffed. "That stuffy old captain is no fun."

"War isn't supposed to be fun. Go on now. Get to work. The paper will be here later."

The boys mumbled their displeasure but scattered to their tasks. A breeze ruffled the edges of the open newsprint. Bending down, she retrieved the paper before the wind carried it away.

She'd just turned to stash it somewhere safe when an image caught her attention. It was a woodblock-and-ink reproduction of a photograph. This one depicted a woman running her fingers through a brook, her expression pensive.

Sharp breath seared her lungs. Her ears buzzed. It couldn't be. . . .

She was staring at herself.

A cold stone settled deep in her stomach. Gripping the oily print with white fingers, she scanned the caption.

"Beautiful Heroines of Home" was printed in bold type just beneath the image, followed by a blade that sliced her to the core. "Original photograph: Gabriel Avery, appointed by Mathew Brady."

He'd taken her photograph without her knowledge and plastered it across the newspapers. How many more was her face flaunted in? Dozens?

The gentle, timid flower of hope that had bloomed within

her since Gabe had rescued her from the Rebel soldier's clutches withered and died, leaving a hollow ache in its place.

He'd used her. Stolen her privacy and broken her trust to line his own pockets. How could he?

Something sharp twisted in her chest, causing breath-stealing spasms.

Gabe had betrayed her.

The anguish cut far deeper than she could have imagined.

Cassie stomped up to Gabe as he stood outside the Whatsit, dipping glass plates into a tub of water. Steam burned in her belly as she watched him calmly dry a dripping plate with a rag, then stack it to the side as if he didn't have a care in the world.

When he heard her approach, his face lit with a smile . . . until she pinned him with a narrow glare.

"What is this?" She shoved the newspaper into his chest with a shuddered sob. Eyes wide, he stared at the paper in his hands. He swallowed and looked away, but not before she witnessed the guilt that ghosted his expression. Icy-hot blood lashed her insides.

"How could you?" Her lips trembled, but she steeled herself against the burning tears. She would not cry. She would not.

He winced and reached for her, but she yanked her arm away.

"Don't touch me," she hissed. Anger was far safer than tears. She wouldn't give him that much power over her. Never again. Never for any man.

Gabe shot a glance to make sure no one was nearby. "It's not what you think—"

"I think you took a photograph of me without my permission and sold it to a bunch of newspapers to line your pockets."

Red streaked his neck.

"Am I wrong?"

"No! Yes!" Raking his fingers through his hair, he scraped them down his face and blew out a heavy breath. "I should have asked your permission. That's true enough. And I'm sorry. But the money wasn't for me. Remember the man I told you about in New York? Jacob? He's like my grandfather. I needed the money to pay his hospital bills." His mouth tilted into a frown. "He gave me the funds I needed to be here. I owe him, Cass."

"How magnanimous of you." A headache pounded in her skull. "Unfortunately, your gesture of goodwill might expose my identity."

He shook his head. "No one will recognize you."

"You can't promise that. You used me." A realization struck her. She sucked in a harsh breath. "Or perhaps you intended to expose me. After all, you've been against my work here since the moment you learned who I was."

Gabe's mouth went slack. "You can't really believe I would do something like that on purpose."

"What am I supposed to believe?" Her throat ached. "You've ranted often enough about independent women. Even begged me not to return." She lifted her chin. "What better way to put me in my place than exposing me for the world to see?"

His expression darkened and he took a step forward, looming over her with a glare. "If you really think I would do such an underhanded thing, you don't know me at all."

A thousand rebuttals begged for release, but giving them voice would do no good. Heart twisting, she turned on her heel, calling over her shoulder, "Good-bye, Gabe."

"Cass, please . . ." His whisper faded as she quickened her pace.

Nothing he could say would fix the damage he'd inflicted.

Chapter 34

Dear Gabriel,

Are you well? After reading the reports concerning the Battle of Front Royal, I fear the worst but trust the Almighty has kept you safe thus far. Were there truly so many Union soldiers captured as the papers reported?

My own recovery is going well, though I find it much more of a trial to recover from pneumonia at four score than it was only a few years ago. Ah, there is no denying it—I'm getting old.

Esther is smothering me, baking pastries and bread constantly, bargaining with the butcher for the cheapest meat prices. She seems to believe my health rests solely in her hands. The woman needs to be in control at all times. In many ways, she reminds me of you. Always trying to fix things so everyone is taken care of. But such perfection is not attainable this side of glory, is it? My life is in the Almighty's hands, though I would be

*hesitant to decline one of Esther's cinnamon pastries
either way.*

Write again when the opportunity affords.

Your friend,
Jacob

Gabe expelled a tight breath. Jacob had made no mention
of the funds he'd sent from the profit of Cassie's photograph.
Had they reached him? Why hadn't he reported his financial
standing with hospital? Gabe had requested information, but
Jacob remained silent on the thing he most needed to know.
Stubborn man.

Sweat rolled between Gabe's shoulder blades as he sat in the
sweltering darkroom. Working in the small, windowless confine
was like being slowly smothered. His shirt was glued to his skin.
He wiped his forehead as his mind whirled back to the past
grueling weeks. Even worse than the humiliation of Front Royal
was the bloody slaughter of the Battle of Fair Oaks Station.
The Union had claimed victory, but at a high cost. The shells
shrieked so ferociously and continually, the cannon thundered
with such force, Gabe feared the wagon would break apart. And
the aftermath . . .

Men on both sides had fallen so deeply, there was not even
enough room to walk between the bloated bodies. As he readied
the Harrison lens to capture the sickening scenes, his eyes had
landed on Cassie loading bodies as heavy and limp as sandbags
onto litters, her arms coated in blood up to her elbows.

She had straightened, her gaze burrowing into his across the
distance of the blood-soaked field, and then she glanced away.

His stomach had cinched as tight as a tourniquet.

He missed her. Desperately.

There was no one to blame but himself. He should have sought her permission before sending the photograph. He'd hoped she would come around after she'd had a few days to cool off, but it was not to be. She had studiously avoided him at all costs. Even had Briggs deliver his mail so she wouldn't be forced to see him.

He understood her hurt, but did she really believe he'd planned on having her identity exposed through a newspaper? The accusations had stung far more than he cared to admit.

He leaned back in his chair and brushed away a drop of sweat from his cheek with a shrug of his shoulder. The cotton scoured his skin and snagged on the bristle peppering his jaw. It had been days since he'd shaved. Days since he'd even cared.

Food had no taste, and his dreams were nothing but hazy nightmares.

Life without Cassie had become a gray, meaningless jumble.

And he had no idea how to fix it.

———◆———

JUNE 2, 1862
NEW BRIDGE, VIRGINIA

"Wasn't that a bully speech by Little Mac?" Jonah sat next to Cassie on a wide log, whittling a piece of wood.

She took a swig of water from her canteen and prayed for a cool breeze to cut through. The heat was suffocating. "I suppose so."

Jonah frowned. "You suppose so?" He shook his head, his kepi wobbling. "It gave me a thrill!" He lowered his voice, imitating the husky timbre of the general's. "'We are now face-to-face with the Rebels, who are held at bay in front of their capital. The final and decisive battle is at hand. Let us meet them there and crush them.'" Jonah's eyes shone. "I was ready to point a gun and start firing."

She offered a smile, but her heart wasn't in it. She was sick of it all. Sick of constantly performing. Sick of trying to be faultless in her pretense. Sick of mangled corpses. Sick of death.

"I only hope it will be finished soon." She pulled out the pocket watch Captain Johnston had given her and rubbed the engraving with the pad of her thumb.

Jonah spit into the grass and shooed away a fly buzzing near his ear. "What will you do, Turner? When the war is over?"

She swallowed. "I don't know." Truthfully, she tried not to think about it.

"Me either. Tommy wants to finish school, then go to the university." He scoffed. "Not me. I never want to step foot in another school as long as I live."

She emitted a light laugh. "Not every teacher is like School-master Howe, you know."

He looked as if he'd bitten into a pickle that turned. "I know. But reading and calculating figures . . ." He shrugged. "Seems like a waste of time."

She stared off into the distance, studying a canopy of thick trees on the outskirts of Richmond. How many would still be standing once the soldiers started firing?

"I always wanted a better education." She sighed and plucked a blade of grass near her feet. "I wish for it still. Knowledge is opportunity. It's adventure."

Jonah grunted and dropped a curl of wood near his flapping boots. "Don't see how adventure can be found between the pages of a dusty old book."

Stricken at his tainted view of life, she reached for his grubby hands and gently tugged the pocketknife and block of wood free. In their place, she dropped the pocket watch and chain.

Jonah's eyes rounded as he looked up at her. "What are you doing?"

"Giving you my watch."

His face went slack as he studied the engraved flourishes running through the shiny metal. "But it was a present for you."

"Presents are meant to be given away. Now I'm giving it to you." She closed her hands around his and squeezed. "This watch represents time. Time that is ticking away second by second. I want you to take it. Use it to remember you have only one life to live. Seek God, and a thousand adventures and dreams will pursue you."

His face lit up as she released his hands. "Thanks, Turner!" Jonah bounded to his feet and raced away, no doubt eager to tell his friends. She chuckled and glanced at the discarded wood and knife resting in the grass.

"Seek God, and a thousand adventures and dreams will pursue you. . . ."

Her mind knew the adage was true, but her heart was having trouble grasping it.

She longed for peace. For freedom to live without pretense or constantly hiding from Father's fury. She yearned for joy. For Gabe.

Perhaps her own dreams were unfulfilled because she hadn't sought God as she should have.

Perhaps.

"What are you doing?"

Gabe looked up from the camera box to judge whether the light was adequate to capture the scene before him. Confederate and Union pickets were only a meadow apart. Both of them on the cusp of Richmond, waiting in eerie silence for word. Hours had passed without any change.

Gabe glanced at Jonah's upturned face. "Getting ready to photograph the pickets."

"Ain't got nothing better to capture than a bunch of cranky old soldiers glaring at each other?"

He chuckled. "At the moment? No."

Jonah rocked back on his heels and stuffed his hands into his pockets. "Good to see you smile. Ain't seen you do much of that lately."

Gabe narrowed his eyes. "You're a mite too observant."

"Missing Turner?"

Gabe ground his teeth and busied himself with adjusting the lens. Yes, he missed her. When she wasn't away on some escapade for Pinkerton, she was delivering mail for the regiment.

"She—er, he's been busy lately, you know," Jonah said. "Running mail all over a sixty-mile stretch."

"I hadn't noticed."

Jonah finally fell silent. A mercy for which he was most grateful.

"Look what I got."

Pulling his head out from under the black curtain, Gabe glanced down at the boy's open palm. A gold pocket watch lay in the center, winking as it caught a shimmer of sunlight. He sucked in a pull of air. "Where'd you get that?"

Jonah smiled smugly. "Turner."

He frowned. "The one *he* received from Captain Johnston?"

"Yep." Jonah buffed the piece against the tattered fabric of his uniform. "Gave it to me yesterday. Said it was a reminder that each minute is a gift."

Gabe looked away. A gift indeed. Then why was Cassie so determined to squander hers?

"Turner has been almost as grumpy as you lately. You two fight or something?"

He grunted. "Don't want to talk about it."

Jonah sighed. "You fighting 'bout how stubborn you are?"

"I am not!"

"O' course you are." Jonah plopped down on the marshy ground and squinted as he examined the watch's engravings with a critical eye. "Always trying to control everything. You want everyone to be happy."

"Is there something so wrong with that?"

The boy shrugged. "No, not really. Except some people's definition of happy might not be the same as yours." Rubbing the piece against his sleeve once more, he studied it with one eye and his tongue tucked between his teeth before smiling. Satisfaction with a polishing job well done. "Just like when you take pictures with your fancy camera box." He snickered. "You get all mad when the light isn't the way you want, or if you can't get the angle just so. Say—" his face lit up—"maybe that's why you like taking your photographs. It's something you can mostly control."

Thunderstruck, Gabe stood and stared at Jonah, his frozen lips unable to form words.

"Anyway, I gotta get going. Will you show me your photographs later?"

Gabe blinked. "I—uh, yes. I should have them done tonight."

With a nod, Jonah scampered away as Gabe's mind raced.

Unbidden, Jacob's last penned words floated back to taunt him.

"Always trying to fix things so everyone is taken care of. But such perfection is not attainable this side of glory, is it?"

He wasn't the one with the stubborn pride. Cassie refused to be reasonable. Refused to see things from his point of view. It wasn't him driving the wedge between them.

Steeling his muddled tangle of emotions, Gabe clamped his jaw. He didn't have to be in control. Jonah had just misinterpreted things. He was only a kid, after all.

The lie sat cold in his chest.

Chapter 35

Sven paced back and forth, wearing the green grass thin under his feet. The Swede's perpetual motion made Gabe's head swim. Between the sticky heat and the tension lying like a blanket over their company, his nerves felt as if they were fraying.

"I could see them, Briggs. Across the valley our boys were up to their armpits in mud, screaming and fighting." Sven's blond brows dipped low. "Why won't they call us to fight?"

Briggs shot a stream of tobacco juice with a pointed arc, landing only an inch away from the Swede's massive boots. He glared, and Briggs's dark beard rose at the corners.

"We're in reserve, my friend. You know that. Be patient." Briggs rolled the snuff to the other side of his mouth, his expression somber. "We'll have our chance soon enough."

Gabe wiped a rag across the back of his sweaty neck. "Sit down. You're making me anxious."

Sven snapped, his ice-blue eyes glinting like sunlight striking glass. "And so I am. I want to be home with my Olga. We have waited far too long already. This should be done. And now Pinkerton arrives." A muscle twitched near his eye. "How much longer must we wait?"

Gabe shot Briggs a questioning look. Briggs shrugged, his shoulders hunched like a brooding gargoyle. The distant booms of cannon fire and the faint echoes of small-arms fire drifted across the valley, a present reminder that life and death were at stake mere miles away.

If only he could share a bit of encouragement with his friends. But Pinkerton had sworn him to secrecy.

When the head of Lincoln's secret service had arrived in camp, Gabe was shocked to learn the infamous detective was not searching for Thomas Turner this time. No, Pinkerton was asking for *him*. And once he'd stood before the serious gentleman, the request was too easy to consider refusing.

Pinkerton had requested Gabe make photographic copies of maps and charts that would be distributed to field and division commands. A simple task, and one that made him wonder why the secret service hadn't been utilizing photographic skill from the beginning.

In addition, Pinkerton wanted the photographs Gabe had captured in Richmond—bridges, railroad tracks, field hospitals, barracks, and terrain. He'd confessed McClellan was preparing to take the Confederate capital, and they wanted as few surprises as possible.

Gabe squinted as another echoing boom reverberated through the air. He was happy to do his part, but if he were honest, the pay he was offered solidified any concerns he had about working with Lincoln's secret service. He'd continue forwarding it to Jacob until he heard the man had paid off his bills.

"You sold it to a bunch of newspapers to line your pockets."
Cassie's haunting accusation continued to rankle.

"Has anyone seen Turner of late?" Sven's baritone intruded.

Briggs lifted the brim of his kepi, revealing a mop of sweaty, mussed brown hair. "He's running mail down the line."

Sven glowered. "Past the Chickahominy?"

Briggs yanked the kepi down over the crown of his head, his beard twitching as he chewed the thick wad of snuff. "Reckon so. Seems to me brass keeps him busier with more than just delivering mail."

"Hospital?"

Briggs narrowed his eyes. "Among other things."

Gabe squirmed. He had no intention of betraying Cassie's secrets. Still, he'd given her a hard time about joining the secret service, and here he found himself in the same situation. The irony was not lost on him.

It was different. He was a man and she was a woman. He could hold his own matched against brute strength. Cassie couldn't. If she didn't have a gun, an enemy could snap her slim form like a pencil. There was no place for women in war.

Or was there?

Cassie was the one who had dragged him to safety after he was shot at Ball's Bluff. Cassie had taken down two Confederate sharpshooters. Cassie was the one Pinkerton had turned to, and she had outperformed everyone's expectations. She had outwitted an entire regiment of soldiers with her disguise, save for one. Jonah.

But she deserved better. She should be pampered and cherished. Not eating maggot-infested hardtack among filthy, crude men.

Somehow over the past few months, though, his adamant belief in where a woman's place should be had weakened in fervor.

"You used me."

"Some people's definition of happy might not be the same as yours. . . . Maybe that's why you like taking your photographs. It's something you can mostly control."

Cassie's and Jonah's voices melded in a cacophony inside his head.

No, he wasn't controlling. He only wanted to protect her. The two were completely different . . . weren't they?

He was going to drive himself mad. He rose from the hard ground with a groan, unfolding his stiff limbs.

"Where you going?"

Gabe kneaded the back of his neck. "To write Gardner. I need him to make another trip to the drop point. I've stored a wealth of photographs there and don't want the Confederates getting their hands on them. I need more supplies, and besides—" he smiled tightly—"as long as the prints are stored, I don't get paid."

He turned to leave when Briggs called out, "Why not just go now? It'll only take a couple of days."

"Because I have a feeling we'll be moving into Richmond at any moment."

———◆———

Cassie tore open a powder cartridge with her teeth amid geysers of spraying dirt and rocks. Thunderous booms split the sky, rattling her skull and numbing her ears. Her whole body shook from the tremors.

The entire earth was ripping in two.

Inhaling a pull of acrid air, she positioned her rifle over the bulwark. She peered through the thick haze of fire bursts and pulled the trigger. The rifle kicked her shoulder, but she didn't even feel its impact anymore. Couldn't feel anything.

She dropped below the parapet, panting, and tried to swallow against the dry sawdust coating her tongue and throat. Bullets hissed. Horses screamed. Chaos had been unleashed, and she could do nothing more than load gunpowder, fire, and breathe.

She blinked away the sweat stinging her eyes and turned to see Briggs shouting to Jackson farther down the line. "Courage!"

A wild kind of panic spiraled through Jackson's eyes. "The Rebels won't stop coming! Column after column. We can't hold up much longer!"

The Zouave next to him scowled, his teeth bared and black from gunpowder. "Aye, we can and we will!"

Briggs captured her eyes and held fast. "They're mowing us down, Turner."

With a cry, she whirled and lifted the rifle once more to her shoulder. "Then we stop them!"

Trees snapped. Cannons shrieked. The hair-raising shriek of the Rebel yell grew louder. Snapping her head to the left, she watched her fellow soldiers use the fallen dead as shields as they loaded and fired, loaded and fired. The hissing thumps of bullets hitting corpses settled deep inside her eardrums, pounding to the rhythm of her heart.

Something was wrong. The Confederates were advancing with reckless abandon. Almost as if they didn't care whether they died or not. Bile rose in her throat.

A dull, rhythmic tap of thrumming snares penetrated through the chaos. *Da-dum, da-dum, dum, dum, dum . . .*

Air seared her lungs. No, it couldn't be.

Briggs's eyes grew wide. "Do you hear that?" A hail of bullets whizzing overhead forced him to duck low.

Cassie ground her teeth. "I heard it."

Jackson screamed over the din. "What is it?"

Briggs opened another pouch of gunpowder and spit out

the residue, jamming down the barrel as fast as he dared. "The drummers are signaling retreat!"

She propelled her feet forward to obey the command, but her body felt stiff. Shock turned into a fire that burned her belly.

General McClellan was giving up Richmond. The Union had just watched hundreds of their own cut down like stalks of corn. And for what?

How could they possibly win now?

———◆———

JULY 2, 1862

Dear Jacob,

You have been in my relentless prayers since I heard of your illness from Miss Esther. How are you faring? Your health is of utmost concern, second only to ensuring you are provided for.

I sent an inquiry to the hospital about your financial needs, since you did not respond to my earlier questions. I know you are a proud man and are fully capable of providing for yourself, but please, as your adopted grandson of the heart, I take on your welfare with utmost solemnity. I have not heard from the hospital in regards to your outstanding bills. Please advise and I will send them payment posthaste.

As I write this, we are leaving Richmond, stung and dismayed by the decision of General McClellan. In truth, I debated for long moments over writing the following, but knowing me as you do, you'll no doubt understand my thoughts regardless: I fear our great general has lost his fortitude. I confess feeling a righteous indignation watching the men I've grown so attached to fighting the

screeching Confederate devils, many of them cut down and
forgotten while the general was being ferried away from
the tumult on a gunboat bound for Harrison's Landing.
Our spirits are demoralized. Keep us in your prayers.

Your friend,
Gabriel

Gabe studied the written lines and sighed. He probably should not have shared his disquiet with the elderly man. Disgruntled musings like his were better suited for talk among soldiers, yet they tried to refrain as well. Among the ranks, keeping lips shut against mismanagement of troop movement and war tactics was growing increasingly difficult.

He ought to be thinking of a way to lift Jacob's spirits. His stomach churned at the thought of disheartening the kind man.

Penning the plea had brought little relief. There was only one person he wanted to talk to, and his own foolish decision had snipped their relationship to frayed ribbons.

———— ·◆· ————

Cassie dragged one foot in front of the other, her back and legs aching. The pack grew heavier with each passing hour. She blinked through the dust churned up by a thousand booted feet shuffling down the wide road. Dirt coated her teeth. Each time she bit down, she could taste the crunch of grit.

Overturned wagons, abandoned ambulances, and dead horses, interspersed with muskets and broken wheels, choked the road leading away from Richmond. It was as if God had taken this piece of earth, turned it upside down, and shaken it loose before dropping it back in place again.

Their retreat had been slowed considerably by the multitude of broken vehicles they had been forced to push out of the way.

Cut harnesses provided evidence that horses had been stolen away, leaving their owners with no choice but to abandon their wagons and walk.

The silence smothering the sluggish army was thick enough to cut with a pocketknife. Cassie forged ahead, the hot anger burning within nearly causing her limbs to shake.

Why had Little Mac given up Richmond? It didn't make any sense. Nothing did anymore. She stumbled over a discarded shoe and scowled. What would President Lincoln do? Word had filtered through the ranks that Lincoln was none too pleased with McClellan's less than stellar performance. The Rebels should have been crushed by now. Instead they gained, both ground and spirit.

A shove against her left shoulder forced her attention ahead. Sven motioned with a frown. "Look there."

Dead horses and blood-soaked blankets were mounded by the side of the road. The stench crept into her nostrils. A swarm of flies buzzed thick. She grimaced and turned away. A raspy voice drifted through the sound of shuffling boots.

"Jeff Davis is coming, oh, dear!"

Sven muttered something under his breath that Cassie couldn't understand. She squinted to see a grizzled old man sitting in a barren field beyond a broken line of fencing, its wood jutting up in haphazard confusion like a row of broken, crooked teeth. A lone tree stood guard over him, stripped of any sign of green, riddled with shot and shell.

The old man with his tobacco-stained gray beard and tattered hat was perched among discarded haversacks and abandoned items of clothing—shoes, hats, and coats. Hooking his thumbs under his suspenders, he flashed stained teeth in a leering grin as he sang.

"Jeff Davis is coming, oh, dear!
I fain would go home without shedding a tear
About Davis in taking the president's chair
But I dare not attempt it, oh, dear! Oh, dear!
I'm afraid he will hang me. Oh, dear!"

Behind her, Briggs growled, "Confederate trash."

The old man's singsong taunts only grew louder the closer they came.

"I wish I was in Dixie. Hooray! Hooray!
In Dixie Land I'll take my stand, to live and die in Dixie."

"If he wants to die in Dixie, we can accommodate." Sven spit out the threat with an uncharacteristic vehemence. They were all spent.

Cassie curled her fists and kept marching amid the man's gleeful taunts.

"While Right is strong and God has pow'r, the South shall rise
up free!"

"That's it!"

Jackson broke rank and charged toward the old man with a wild look on his face.

"Soldier, halt!" Captain Johnston barked.

Jackson whirled, his face red and eyes flashing. "I'm gonna knock the Reb out with the butt of my gun if he dares utter another word!"

The old man finally stopped singing but hummed to himself, watching the interchange as he fiddled with the straps of a haversack at his feet.

Captain Johnston sighed, his shoulders sagging. "He's lost his mind, Jackson."

"He's our enemy, sir!"

"The man is a doddering old fool, Private. Ignore him."

Before the old man could launch into more of his Confederate repertoire, the melodious timbre of one of the contraband soldiers marching with their regiment drifted through the air.

"Oh, freedom; oh, freedom; oh, freedom over me
And before I'd be a slave, I'd be buried in my grave
And go home to my Lord and be free."

The other contrabands lifted their voices and joined in, drowning out the sounds of Confederate fervor. Cassie felt her spirit unwind and lighten as she let the beauty of their song and the truth of their words wash over her.

"No more worry, no more worry, no more worry over me
And before I'd be a slave, I'd be buried in my grave
And go home to my Lord and be free."

No more worry. Was such an existence even possible? Grunting, she shifted her pack and winced. Had she ever been carefree? She reached as far back into her memories as she dared, but Father was always there. And where Father was, there was terror.

The group continued on, too weary in mind or body to think, fight, or do anything other than place one foot in front of the other. An hour passed. Then another.

A bass voice boomed behind her, starting another song. "'We marching into Canaan land . . .'"

She turned to see one of the contrabands on her left side.

The wide expanse of his arms made her feel even smaller than Jonah. His skin glistened like polished mahogany, but it was his contented air that captured her attention.

"Were you the one who led the singing?"

"Yes, sir. I's the one that started it, anyhow."

"Thank you. I needed it."

"Music is good for the soul."

They marched side by side in silence for a long moment.

Cassie swallowed. "Do you really live what you sing?"

The massive man's brows pinched as he studied her. "Sir?"

"You know: no more worry."

He lifted his face to the burning sun. "I still got worries, but I don't despair. Big difference between the two."

"No more despair because you're finally free from slavery?"

"I's been free a long time, but only physically free from my massa for a few months." He laughed big and deep. "Jesus set my spirit free long ago."

For the first time in a while, a chuckle burst from Cassie's chest. "I understand that. He set me free too."

"Then you ain't got no worries either."

Didn't she? She lived with a cloud hanging over her head every waking moment. Being caught, being discovered, being killed, being sent back home. Each prospect seemed worse than the last.

She shook her head. "But it seems different for you. You seem . . . happy."

His eyes shimmered. "Some days I am. Other days not. But I'm always joyful."

He was talking in circles. She frowned. "I don't understand."

"My massa was a mighty mean man. Some days seemed like the devil himself. I was mighty unhappy when I was with him. But joy, that's a different story. Joy comes from forgiving and being forgiven. The day I forgave him was the day I finally felt free."

"He sought your forgiveness?"

"No." The contraband's voice was wistful. "Would have made it easier perhaps. Perhaps not. Massa would likely curse my name and shoot me on sight if he saw me now, but it don't matter." He patted his chest. "I'm free in here. Ain't always been easy, though. I struggled hard with hate for that man, until one day I learned about Frederick Douglass. You hear of him?"

"Of course."

He nodded. "Douglass goes and writes a letter to his former massa, telling him that he loves him but hates slavery." His eyes glassed. "Douglass showed love to the man who used to abuse him. Love! I couldn't fathom such a thing. But God showed me he's forgiven me for a lot more."

The contraband sighed, gazing into some faraway distance as they walked. "Massa was taught to hate by his daddy, and his daddy's daddy before him. They was all miserable men, or so I's been told. Unhappy and bitter. In some ways, I think Massa was more enslaved than I ever was." He turned to her and smiled. "At least God broke my chains. Massa ain't found his freedom yet. I sure hope he does."

With that, he broke into a jaunty whistle, erasing all need for further conversation.

Cassie couldn't have spoken further if she'd tried.

Chapter 36

AUGUST 28, 1862

Grit and exhaustion burned Gabe's eyes as the horses plodded lazily along the road, the darkroom wagon bobbing behind them like a large, sleepy bear.

Less than a day's ride and he would be at Manassas Junction, happily replenished with chemicals, glass plates, and oats for the weary horses. Brady had assured him Gardner would arrive within a fortnight. None too soon. All the pictures he'd stored at the supply depot left him unsettled.

The system was necessary; he knew that. Carrying around stacks and stacks of developed photographs was reckless, and the chances of Gardner finding him among the thousands of soldiers and regiments scattered throughout the land was like looking for an ever-moving needle in a haystack. Keeping them at a fixed drop point was the logical thing to do. Still, it left an itchy feeling between Gabe's shoulder blades to know his photographs were sitting in a depot station, unguarded for weeks on end.

The wafting scent of smoke assaulted his nostrils. He frowned and stopped the horses. A yellow haze drifted over the treetops in the distance. All was calm.

He urged them forward once more, the usual clip-clop of their hooves failing to soothe him. With each step, the acrid stench grew stronger, mingled with the aroma of cooked meat.

As long as my photographs are safe, I can take care of Jacob. At least I can see to him.

Weeks, George, and Selby had been stolen away or cut down in the bloom of youth. Cassie was all but lost to him, but he still had his work. Nothing could take that away.

The thought brought him a small measure of comfort.

In half a mile, the frenzied sound of hoofbeats pounded the earth. A horse broke through the trees bearing a man hunched low, something large and round tucked under his arm.

Pulling the horses to a halt, Gabe stood on the driver's seat and waved. "Whoa, there! What's all the hullabaloo?"

The wild-eyed man with his frizzy brown hair panted and yanked on the reins of his lathered horse, attempting to fight it back into calm. "Ain't ya heard? Stonewall Jackson just tore through the Union supply depot ahead."

Gabe's stomach crawled into his throat. "When?"

"Yesterday morning. He and his cronies tore Manassas Junction apart. Burned a hundred railroad cars, and his men seized everything they could carry." The panting stranger gestured to the bundle in his arms. "There's still a couple barrels of hard bread and half a dozen hams scattered around the tracks. I'm taking this one home to the missus. I'll probably go back for more if they don't get taken."

Gabe's stomach roiled. The supplies. His photographs. Months of work . . .

"What about the nonartillery depots? Are they still there?"

The stranger shrugged. "Doesn't look to me like much is left, but take a gander if you've a mind to. Be careful, though. The place is still burning."

With that parting warning, he kicked his horse back into a run and sped away.

Gabe snapped the reins, his heart galloping faster than the horses had ever dared.

Please, God . . .

He swallowed as a faint crackling sound grew louder. Manassas Junction lay just behind that hill. Thick curls of black smoke belched up from the woods beyond. Urging the mares forward, he winced against the smoke stinging his eyes and thickening the air. He pulled the clamoring wagon to a stop at the top of the hill and jerked the wagon brake, the horses only too happy to stop.

Manassas Junction was a burning ash heap of rubble and waste.

He jumped from the driver's seat on wooden legs and walked toward the torn, disjointed tracks. Barrels lay broken open at odd angles all over the clearing. The metal shells of railroad cars smoked in crumpled heaps, some of them twisted as if wrung like laundry in the hands of God. Rifle shot peppered every conceivable tree, every railroad car, every skeletal remain of buildings and outposts.

His chest burned as he walked toward the engulfed wreckage. He winced against the blast of heat from nearby fires, barely noticing the tears that resulted from the thick smoke irritating his eyes. Coughing, he headed for the depot he and Brady used as their drop point. The place where he'd stored months of carefully cataloged photographs and prints of the most gruesome and breathtaking images of the conflict that had ripped their nation in two.

A thick knot wedged in his throat as his breath quickened. The building was gone. The sturdy logs had been reduced to a heap of disjointed sticks. Nothing more than smoking ash and rubble. A gust of wind flamed a nearby fire to life, shooting sparks into the air. A burned piece of roofing material tumbled across the clearing.

Something cold sleeted through his middle and iced his blood. His purpose. His dreams. The desire of his heart. The artistic integrity of photography had been his redemption. A way to offer restitution for the way he'd failed his parents. But it wasn't enough. He wasn't enough. Everything he'd worked so hard for had suddenly been ripped away, burned to cinders that floated away from the earth and chased the wind.

With a guttural cry, he dropped to his knees and tunneled his fingers through his sweat-soaked hair, yanking until his scalp burned. Only one thought managed to break to the surface of his drowning emotions.

Why, God? Why?

———•◦•———

Cassie gasped as artillery shrieked and exploded overhead. Leaning close to Abe's head, she clutched fistfuls of his sleek mane and kept her body low as his legs ate up the distance between the commanders' positions.

Though the sun had not yet risen, torment had broken free and rained down on the Union forces in Manassas. The situation was all too familiar. Wasn't it only a year ago that the Confederates had tried to slaughter them on the same patch of earth?

A fireball burst overhead. She yanked Abe away from the tree falling in chunks as big as fire logs. Soldiers bellowed and ran all around her. Poor Abe pawed the ground, uncertain where to place a hoof.

I must get to Colonel Emmerson.

She mustn't shirk her duties. The commanders depended on her to keep their communication open. Cringing against another shriek of ammunition followed by a thunderous boom that pelted her arms with dirt and debris, she urged Abe into a gallop, away from the skirmish. Her heart pounded in rhythm with the horse's stride.

Just a little farther.

A wide ditch loomed ahead. She leaned in to give Abe his head, but without warning, the horse's hooves left the ground. Time slowed as her body was flung into the air.

Pain exploded. A heavy pressure pinned her left side, then mercifully eased. The world dimmed.

Thump. Thump. Thump.

She blinked. Pain seared her head. The blurry image of Abe stared down at her. The horse cocked his head as if wondering why she was lying on the ground. His likeness sharpened.

Thump. Thump.

Cannon fire thudded in the distance. What happened? Her mind felt muddled.

The messages.

She tried to scramble to her feet, but white-hot pain seared down her left side. She fell back, hissing through her teeth. Her left hand felt oddly numb and tingly. Rolling onto her stomach, she managed to hook her elbows underneath her torso and used them to inch herself forward out of the grubby ditch. Rocks scraped and poked into her skin. Each movement sent ripples of pain down her side.

Crawling to the top, she gasped and cried out when she attempted to put weight on her foot. Hot, crippling fire caused it to crumple beneath her. She managed to grab on to Abe's saddle and pull herself atop the horse by sheer force of will.

As she stretched herself along his broad back, she patted his neck and urged him forward, moaning as the bouncing motion jostled her body into a new plethora of miseries.

———•———

A sea of humanity stretched out before Gabe as he surveyed the mass of wounded, moaning men smothering the land of Manassas Junction.

The faint aroma of coosh wafted through the air, but the scent of bacon grease and cornmeal soured his stomach. He couldn't eat. Not in the face of so much suffering.

With his own supplies dwindled to almost naught, he felt useless. He couldn't take any photographs. He had no water or medicine to offer the mangled, dying men begging for relief. All he could do was pray. Weak, pitiful prayers that felt like they rose no higher than his head.

He scrubbed his fingers over his stubbly jaw, wishing he could simply turn off his emotions.

"Avery!" A booming voice called to him from among the milling crowd of workers and soldiers.

Lifting a hand to shade his eyes from the sun, Gabe watched a portly man with a bushy beard pick his way slowly across the field, his gaze roving side to side, mouth agape as he drank in the sight stretched before him.

"Mr. Gardner?" Gabe stepped forward.

"Aye." Gardner stopped before him, his fingers curled around the haversack slung over his shoulder. The soft brogue was like an embrace. A reminder of home.

Gabe's throat clogged. "It's good to see you, sir."

"Likewise, Avery. When I heard about the junction, I feared for you."

"I'm fine. I arrived shortly after Jackson had burned everything up. All my work has been destroyed, though." The admission tasted bitter in his mouth.

Gardner sighed. "'Tis a shame. If I'd left Washington sooner, perhaps . . ." The Scot cleared his throat. "I'm sorry, Gabriel. General Jackson struck us all a hard blow."

His chest constricted. "I was counting on the money from those photographs, sir."

Gardner frowned. "So was Mr. Brady."

Gabe pressed his lips shut. It wasn't Gardner's fault. Who could have known the Rebels would have swung back and struck in such a way? Or that McClellan would have run such an abysmal fighting campaign?

The world was topsy-turvy. And Gabe had absolutely nothing to his name.

Gardner surveyed the field of men stretched from end to end. "What are you doing here?"

Gabe shrugged. "I'm out of supplies. The Rebs destroyed those, too. I've been walking among the dying and praying."

The ghost of a smile tugged Gardner's beard. "Come."

Interest piqued, Gabe followed on his heels. "What are we doing, sir?"

"I have a wagon full of supplies for you, Avery. Not to mention a new camera technique I want to try out. I need some assistance, though. Have you heard of stereographing?"

"No, sir."

Gardner turned his head. "Would you like to learn?"

"Yes, sir."

He nodded. "Good. We've got a war to record."

Gabe crawled onto his bedroll and slumped in exhaustion. His body was already melting under fatigue but his mind raced. He'd spent all day with Gardner, watching and learning the art of stereographing. Who could have imagined that two lenses capturing simultaneous pictures would create a three-dimensional image when seen through a viewer?

The Scotsman's innovation and quiet intelligence had been just the balm his battered spirit had needed.

He shifted onto his side and watched the sprinkling of stars overhead. The summer heat made sleeping in the Whatsit far too miserable a prospect. He would be grateful for the wagon come winter, but this night, he was thankful for the occasional stirring of air outdoors, even if it was sticky with humidity.

Footfalls and snapping twigs approached from his left.

"Avery! Have you seen Turner?"

Growling under his breath, Gabe turned over to see Briggs standing above him, a scowl marring the moonlit patch of his face. "I've been busy all day. What makes you think I've seen Turner?"

Briggs frowned. "Captain is asking, that's why. No one in the Michigan Second has seen him since the skirmish at daybreak."

Alarm skittered down Gabe's spine. Cassie was missing? Sitting up on the bedroll, he grabbed his boots. "You sure he's not among the wounded?"

"Captain checked. Twice. Turner was sent to deliver a message to Colonel Emmerson with the New York Fifth but hasn't been seen or heard from since."

Gabe's stomach knotted as he pushed to his feet. He grabbed a rifle and caught the canteen Briggs tossed his direction.

As Gabe marched away from the rows of sleeping men, Briggs called out, "Wait, I'm coming with you."

He nodded and moved into the unknown dark of night. Help or no, he wouldn't return without Cassie.

———◆———

Voices drifted overhead. Swimming in and out of her consciousness. Murky. Unlike the shards of pain that jabbed her body every time she moved.

Her tongue clung to the roof of her mouth. She tasted dirt. Darkness kept her trapped. She tried to cry out, tried to claw her way past the black net that had been cast over mind and body, but it held fast. She was too tired.

A familiar voice boomed. "It's Turner! He's here!"

Another voice. Footsteps and shuffles. Warm hands cupped her face. She longed to melt into the tenderness of the touch.

A gentle voice whispered, "Cassie. I've found you."

Strong arms lifted her, cradling her in a cocoon.

She was home.

———◆———

Gabe sat near Cassie's too-still body sleeping in her tent. His head felt heavy as he cradled it in his hands. Muffled sounds of camp life drifted through the shadowed canvas, but the noise buzzed in his ears like a swarm of flies. He was exhausted, yet he couldn't rest. Not until he knew if Cassie would be all right.

His nerves stretched taut once more. She needed to be examined, but doing so might very well reveal her secret. He felt stuck at an impasse, torn between two impossibilities, neither one satisfactory. He lifted his head and studied the soft curve of her cheek. She needed to wake up.

Everything was spinning out of control.

Who was he fooling? He had no control. It had all been a mirage.

He flexed his sore knuckles, still aching from the blows he and Briggs had exchanged when they'd arrived back at camp. The large soldier had been understandably perturbed when

Gabe had refused to let Turner be seen by the physician at the hospital corps. They had argued vehemently. Briggs seemed unconcerned with Gabe's story that Turner was deathly afraid of physicians, claiming the man was unconscious. He wouldn't know. Gabe winced remembering how he'd slammed his fist into the soldier's iron jaw.

Although he'd regretted having to resort to such measures, the punch had finally made Briggs understand the depth of Gabe's feelings on the matter. He'd returned with some morphine sulfate, tossed it to Gabe with a glare, and stalked away.

Groaning, Gabe dropped his head back in his hands. It would be so much easier if he could explain Turner's true identity to his friend. Instead, he'd slipped the morphine under Cassie's tongue and let her sleep.

She might despise him, but at least for this moment he could do his utmost to care for her and nurse her back to health. He had nothing else to offer.

Only himself.

Chapter 37

~

Cassie only half listened to Jonah's chatter as she brushed down Abe's glossy coat and winced at the aching pain in her left foot.

It had been months since Bull Run, and still her bruised body ached. She'd been thrown from her horse one moment and awakened in her darkened tent the next, her mind thick and muddled. Briggs told her he and another soldier had found her unconscious out in the woods, but whenever she asked for more information, he always pressed his lips into a line and looked away. Jonah had been a frequent visitor, keeping her entertained with silly stories and antics of camp life, but it was Gabe whose face she longed to see. He never came. Why did she think he would? She'd made it clear to him she wanted nothing further to do with him. He was only abiding by her wishes. So why the aching need for him? And why did the nagging feeling of his presence invade her memories and dreams?

Recovering from a broken foot, rib, and finger took time,

but she had far too much pluck to lie abed. Despite everyone's protests, she was back to her duties, albeit rather slowly, within several weeks.

"You ought to see Johnny Cooper spit. Never did see a fellow spit so straight or so far."

She chuckled and strapped the mailbag to Abe's saddle. "There's a talent that will take a man far in life."

"Aww." Jonah glared. "You're no fun. Can't you see the value of a good spit? What if you need to spit out some snuff but the spittoon is across the room? Or what if the only way to stop a varmint is by spitting on him?"

Cassie arched a brow. "If a varmint turns tail and runs because of some spittle, I have a feeling it wasn't much of a match to begin with."

Huffing, Jonah took an apple from his haversack and polished it on his threadbare uniform coat as Cassie pulled herself into the saddle. "You got mail to deliver?"

"Always." She smiled and tugged her kepi low.

Jonah puffed out his chest, just as he always did before he offered some manly word of advice. "I hear we're about to march within the hour. Be careful of the weather. The captain said it's fixin' to turn."

She eyed the sky, noting the swift swirl of clouds gliding past. "He's likely right. I'll catch you in a day or two."

Jonah grinned, saluting with the apple, as she kicked Abe into motion. Mile after mile. Day after day. Pretending. Always pretending.

How long could she go on this way?

Cassie shivered and hunkered lower into her coat, the wool feeling thin as paper. An oppressive cold weighted the air like an invisible cloak of iron. Odd for the middle of October.

After delivering messages to headquarters, the weather had turned, just as the captain had predicted. But the regiment had marched along a different route than previously agreed upon, and now she was aimlessly wandering through the woods of Virginia.

Something sharp pinged against her cheek. Another bounced off the brim of her kepi. Then another and another. Hail. Her breath fogged as she clamped her jaw tight, willing the tremors to cease.

Sparse leaves that had yet to fall rattled in a gust of wind. Abe seemed uneasy, anxious to continue on their way. Yet she had no idea of their destination.

Cold wind blasted her cheeks and numbed her nose, and icy rain fell in sheets. Drops clung to her lashes as the sun set, plunging the world from gray glimmers into black. She urged Abe down the only marked path, praying the poor horse would be tough enough to endure the onslaught. Their progress was slow as they slid along the muddy grit of the trail.

She could no longer feel her face, toes, or fingers. A strange knot had formed in her middle. Another hour and Abe sagged under the oppressive wind and rain. Hail had covered the path.

Peering through the blackness, Cassie spied watery spots of light dancing through the night. Lights? More than one. A village perhaps?

Abe must have sensed refuge, for his sluggish pace suddenly quickened as the outline of buildings took shape through the storm. Cassie could have cried in relief. Surely some good soul would put them up for the night.

A cluster of passing shadows on horseback caused her to pause and watch. The hairs on the back of her neck rose when the sound of shattering glass drifted through the air, breaking the whistle of wind and hissing rain. She slid from the saddle and winced when pinpricks of pain shot up her legs. She grasped his reins and moved cautiously around the side of a building, watching. One of the forms held a lantern aloft. A Southern voice cursed as another voice barked commands to take goods from a business.

She slunk into the shadows, her stomach shrinking. Confederate guerrillas. She'd heard of the vile men who plundered and murdered Union sympathizers, looting their homes and establishments for whatever purpose they deemed necessary. She couldn't stop here.

She and Abe pressed on until her entire body was soaked and chilled. What time was it? Midnight? Later? Time no longer mattered. Neither did temperature. She and her horse both seemed to be walking in a kind of numb, sleepy fog. A fog so thick, she nearly slammed into the farmhouse that appeared in her path.

Fumbling up the steps, she rapped on the door, but there was no answer. No footfalls on the other side. She could never barge her way into a stranger's house and assume residence.

However, a quick scan of the yard revealed the barn door stood open. It took only a moment to decide.

She led Abe inside, barred the door from the howling wind, and collapsed onto the hay-strewn ground, immediately falling into a dreamless sleep.

———◆———

Jackson called to Gabe over the sound of bacon sizzling on a stick above the popping fire. "Hey, Avery! You seen the latest papers?"

Gabe looked up and frowned. Next to him, Sven paused in penning a letter home to his wife. The noon break from marching was a welcome reprieve.

Jackson's breath puffed in the cold air as he loomed over them and handed a wad of inky newsprint to Gabe. "That Gardner fellow you work with? His prints are in this one. Causing quite a stir."

Gabe grasped the paper with his free hand and furrowed his brows. "Why is that?"

Jackson shrugged. "Apparently Gardner managed to talk them into printing images of the dead." The young private crossed his arms. "It's a bit of a shock."

Gabe shoved his spit of bacon to Sven, the treat all but forgotten as he riffled through the paper with shaking fingers. Sure enough. Gardner's prints covered pages two and three. Corpses lay at odd, grotesque angles. How did he manage to convince the editors to print them? Such a thing had never been done before.

He scanned the articles, the type blurring. The images had been captured at Antietam. Gardner was quoted defending the paper's decision to print the gruesome photos, saying, "Let them aid in preventing another such calamity falling upon the nation."

Gabe lowered the paper, his thoughts churning like a cyclone. Getting newspapers to buy photographs had been a selective process before. A difficult endeavor. But now . . .

Gardner might have paved the way for a multitude of photographic opportunities.

Sven looked over Gabe's shoulder and grimaced. "Do you think this will repulse the public?"

Gabe shook his head. "It will either repulse them or make them desperate for more. Sensationalism sells. Always."

Before he could ponder further, Briggs stomped up, his breath puffing from his nostrils like an enraged bull. With a hot glare, he tossed a newspaper at Gabe's feet and jabbed a thick finger in the air. "Why didn't you tell me who Turner is?"

Chapter 38

CASSIE AWOKE BEFORE DAYBREAK. Hunger gnawed at her stomach, but her body was blissfully warm, albeit stiff and sore. Abe seemed no worse for the wear, though the poor horse would need sustenance soon. At least the rain had stopped as they rode out. Even the wind had calmed.

They had traveled only a mile when she stopped in a cornfield, finding a few discarded, bird-pecked ears to feed her hungry horse. The feed would be soggy, but at least it would give his belly some fuel. As he sniffed and chomped, the sound of hoofbeats approached from the west. She hunkered low under the brown cornstalks until she recognized the flash of Union blue. Straightening, she waved to three soldiers who pulled short upon seeing her, their mounts snorting puffs of frost into the bright morning air.

"Morning, soldier." One of them tipped his kepi, his dark eyes narrowed and shrewd. "You lost?"

Cassie kept her voice low and chuckled. "In a manner of

speaking. Private Turner. I'm a courier for the Michigan Second. My regiment moved during my last delivery. I'm tracking them now." She jerked her head toward the other two soldiers. "You?"

"We've been sent to round up a band of Confederate guerrillas that's been terrorizing folks out this way. You seen or heard anything from rabble-rousers in these parts?"

She patted Abe's thick neck. "Not this morning, but I nearly ran into some Confederate guerrillas last night. Probably the same men you're looking for."

The soldier's eyes lit with interest. "How far?"

Cassie squinted. Everything last night was just a haze of cold misery. "About four or five miles east. I think, anyways. The storm made it hard to judge distance."

"Would you recognize the spot you last saw them if you were to lead us back?"

"Sure."

The soldier grinned. "You up for a Johnny Reb hunt, then?"

Cassie returned his smile with one of her own. "Why not?"

She pulled herself onto Abe's broad back and kicked him into motion, the soldiers falling into stride behind her. The cornstalks whooshed as they cut through the field.

A twitch of movement from the side of her vision caused her heart to skip a beat. The sharp clap of a rifle sounded. Then another. And another. Their echoes bouncing all around. Dull thuds as bodies hit the ground. Abe reared with a shriek and the world blurred.

Sky and wind, then an explosion of pain tore through her body. Cold mud stung her cheek. She waited for the piercing burn that would indicate a gunshot. Instead she felt nothing. Nothing but a vague achiness washing over her in waves. Nausea.

Her mind kept trying to snap shut, but she fought against the dizzying sensation. She tried to move, but her left ankle suddenly protested with a stab. Her breath seized. The barely healed break must be freshly severed once again.

She peered through slitted eyes. Abe's still form lay next to her, his chocolate eyes vacant. No breath stirred from his velvety nostrils. Reaching out, she dug her fingers into his mane and pinched her eyes closed against the tears.

Craning her neck, she saw two of the soldiers sprawled among the dripping cornstalks, their bodies coated in crimson, eyes open and limbs contorted. Dead. Where was the other one? Did it matter? They were all dead. She would be soon too. She was half-dead now.

Numbness stole over her as time slipped into nothingness. Five minutes? An hour? What did it matter? She would be gone before the sun set tonight.

Gabe's face blazed through her memory, his green eyes coaxing. *You must forgive your father.*

The thuds of approaching hoofbeats. The sound of men jumping to the ground. Southern drawl and laugh-tinged curses. The Confederate guerillas they'd been searching for had cut them all down like ducks on a pond.

And now they'd come to finish the job.

Was it only moments ago she had felt death's icy grip stealing over her body? Now her senses buzzed with life.

Her heartbeat pumped loud in her ears. She managed to push her rifle into the surrounding cornstalks, then lay still, keeping her nose half-buried in the mud so they wouldn't see her breath fogging the air.

Thwick, thwick. Boots squelching through muck. The metallic whoosh of a saber being pulled from its scabbard. The murderer sank the tip of the sword into the closest corpse and pulled it out with a grunt. Through her cracked eyes, she saw crimson drip from the end of his blade.

They were checking to make sure the dead were actually dead. She couldn't fake her way out of this.

A thump as the brute rolled the body over. Rustling as the soldiers' pockets were searched. The process was repeated for the other corpse. She was next.

God, have mercy.

A voice overhead prompted with a harsh whisper, "Come on! You're wasting time. They're dead. Just look for valuables and let's get out of here."

Hands circled her ankles and yanked. She bit down to keep from crying out. Her foot gave an odd pop followed by a pinch, then settled into a numbness. Hands groped over her clothes, turning her pockets inside out. She kept still and limp, thankful she carried nothing on her person other than some scant coinage.

The intrusive fingers disappeared and footfalls receded, followed by the faint thumps of hoofbeats. She lay still five minutes more. Then another five. When a crow landed several feet away, pecking at the ground, she peered through her lashes and sat up slowly. Her mind kept tumbling over and over.

God spared me. He spared me. Why?

Her whole body began to shake, but this time it wasn't from the cold.

———◆———

Gabe unhitched one of the mares and rode her through the mass of soldiers marching south. He was desperate for one glimpse of Cassie among the crush of blue-clad men. Briggs was livid. Gabe had to warn her. But how could he begin to find her among the thousands when they all looked the same?

The futility of his search stabbed him anew. He wanted to kick himself for capturing her likeness. How had Briggs seen the truth in the reprinted image when so many others had not?

He urged the mare into a trot and rode down the lines, searching, pleading with God for a glimpse of her. She would be on horseback most likely, fulfilling her courier duties. Time pressed down upon him like a hot iron. Briggs might even now be informing Captain Johnston of her deception.

Spying the corps of drummer boys and buglers, he rode toward them, his horse flinging up flecks of mud. Where the other boys were, Jonah would be close behind. He pulled the mare to a stop, craned his neck, and peered ahead . . . There. Just beyond the buglers.

Lurching ahead, Gabe called out from atop the horse, "Jonah Phifer!"

Jonah looked up midmarch, a wide smile splitting his freckled face. "Hiya, Gabe."

"We need to talk."

Jonah glanced around. "I can't shoot the breeze. If I'm caught, I'll be in trouble."

"I need to talk to you as messenger boy for Captain Johnston."

With a curt nod, Jonah broke formation and trotted toward him, fighting the wave of marching soldiers like a salmon in an upstream current. Gabe dismounted and faced the lad with his voice low. "I need to know something. Has Briggs come to see Captain Johnston?"

Jonah frowned, a knowing look in his eyes. "He tried, but the captain was away. He left a message with me instead."

Gabe fought the urge to swear under his breath. He rubbed the back of his neck until Jonah's giggle snagged his attention.

"I didn't say I gave the captain the message."

Gabe froze. "What do you mean?"

Jonah smirked. "Briggs stomped up, madder than a hornet, blathering that Turner was a woman and 'Be sure to give this message to the captain.' Then he stomped away."

"And?"

"I threw the message in the fire." Jonah shrugged. "I told Turner I would protect her—er, him, and I meant it."

The tight pinch in Gabe's gut unwound a fraction, but his nerves strangled nonetheless. He placed a hand on Jonah's bony shoulder. "That was a very brave thing you did, son. Do you know what would happen to you if anyone found out?"

Jonah jutted his chin forward. "I don't care. Turner is my friend. And considering he's actually a girl, I guess you could say she's like my mother."

Gabe's throat burned. He squeezed Jonah's shoulder before dropping his hand.

Jonah swiped under his nose with his arm. "So no more problem, right?"

Gabe shook his head. "I wish it were that simple. Briggs is spitting mad. Your heroics may have stalled the captain from finding out, but Briggs will hunt him down and tell him face-to-face at some point. I must find Cassie."

Jonah's eyes lit up. "So that's Turner's real name? Cassie?"

Gabe winced. There was no denying it now. "Yes."

"Cassie. It suits her," the boy mused.

Mounting the horse once again, Gabe looked down at the precocious boy and nodded. "I'm beholden to you, Private Phifer."

Jonah offered a salute in response, but his grin and the way he rocked back on his heels revealed his delight with his own part in the drama.

Stomach crawling into his throat, Gabe kicked the mare in the flanks once more, the passing faces blurring into one.

Cassie, where are you?

Chapter 39

CASSIE HAD LIMPED ALONG FOR MILES on snow-dusted roads, every muscle in her body protesting the abuse. Her stomach cramped with need. Her mind felt foggy. At least she could walk. The foot she'd feared broken had actually only been dislocated, blessedly popped back into place by a greedy Confederate guerrilla.

Her eyes and throat burned as she thought of Abe's demise. She mourned for the faithful horse who had been with her through so much. She grieved for the loss of her freedom. She missed Granny with a painful longing. She yearned for home. For Gabe. For peace.

Pebbles crunched under her feet as she shuffled along. She was alone. Utterly and completely.

You are never alone.

She lifted her face to the bright sunshine, blinking against the sharp light. *I know you are with me, Father. But why do I feel so alone?*

You must forgive your father.

She looked down.

My child, you push away all the blessings I long to give you when you refuse to forgive him. It is a weight you weren't meant to drag around. Cut him free.

Cassie pressed her fists against her temples and pinched her eyes shut, biting her lip until she tasted blood. *But he doesn't deserve it.*

The faint sound of braying drifted through the air. Her pulse tripped as she followed the noise. It grew stronger as she searched.

She stopped at the sight of a donkey thrashing its head, eyes wild with panic. It was bridled but its reins were tangled in a thicket. It brayed again, and sympathy tugged her heart.

"There, there. Easy now. Poor little fella." She reached out and stroked the soft white tuft of fur between the donkey's eyes. He calmed under her touch, his nostrils flaring even as his bucking ceased.

"Come now. How did you get in such a fix?" She dug through the brittle tangle of bramble, freeing the reins. When they finally found release, the donkey tossed his head in the air and pranced a couple of high steps.

Cassie laughed. "Going to dance a jig, are you?" She grabbed the bridle and scratched around his face as he nuzzled her hand. "Where is your owner, huh?"

She glanced around, unsure how to proceed. No buildings. Nor had she seen anything for miles. Maybe this was God's provision.

"Looks like you're mine for the time being, little fella." She gingerly pulled herself onto his bumpy back and sank down with relief. At least she wouldn't have to walk the entire distance.

A distant boom shook the air.

If that explosion meant what she thought it did, they now had a destination as well.

A wave of dizziness swept over Cassie as she rode the donkey into the valley, the boom of cannons growing louder and more ominous with each passing minute. A column of smoke billowed over the horizon. Flashes of flame, the repetitious clack of small-arms fire, and the shouts of men could barely be heard over the thunderous rumble of earth, whinnying horses, and drumming.

At her approach, she gave the Union sign to the picket, who nodded and let her pass.

Captain Johnston saw her, his intense frown melting into relief, though the somber gravity never left his eyes. "Turner. Thank God. I thought you dead."

Cassie smiled with shaky lips and saluted. "I thought so too, sir."

"I wish there was time for you to rest, but we're under attack. We need every able-bodied man out there fighting."

A wave of fatigue washed over her so hard, it nearly caused her knees to buckle. She nodded and gripped her rifle with stiff fingers. "Yes, sir."

"Go." He pointed. "Take a position behind the far parapet. I need more men on the eastern side."

The earth shook. A tree not twenty feet away cracked wide-open, sending splinters and debris flying through the air.

Bending low, she snaked her way through the hellish chaos, ignoring the acrid stench of gunpowder and the scream of horses. She limped forward but failed to look up. She didn't see the man in front of her until she collided with his strong body.

"Turner."

She stepped back quickly. Gabe. His green eyes burned like embers.

He grasped her shoulders, refusing to let go. Something was wrong. "We need to talk."

A sharp whistle rent the air. They both ducked. Seconds later, the ground behind them erupted, spraying rocks and soldiers into the air.

She captured his gaze, panting heavily. "If you haven't noticed, this isn't a great time for a chat."

"Briggs knows."

Boom. Boom. Boom.

Cannon fire nearly drowned out his voice. She yelled back, praying she'd misunderstood. "What?"

Face grim, Gabe shouted, "Briggs knows!"

Ice water thrust in her face could not have shocked her any more. The world suddenly tilted. She latched on to Gabe's eyes, seeking his strength. She winced but didn't break contact when a bullet whizzed by. "What did he say?"

Gabe hesitated only a moment. "He's furious and is planning to report you."

Nausea bubbled up to her throat. There was no hiding now. She was done for. Her pulse tripped. Breathing became difficult. "How did he find out?"

Boom. Boom. Boom. Boom.

Gabe said nothing. Not with his lips. His eyes said plenty, however. She could see the guilt in their depths.

The photograph.

A numbness stole over her. She could do nothing about it now. All she had was this moment. And in this moment, she had been given her orders. Fight.

She walked away from him, ignoring his pleas.

"Turner!"

She kept walking, though in truth, she didn't really know where. Didn't care. Didn't look for an eastern parapet. Ripping open a cartridge with her teeth, she dumped in the gunpowder and primed her gun before charging into the heat of battle.

The smoke was so thick, she could barely see. The flash of a bayonet swung near her head. She crouched, her heart pounding when its razor-sharp tip lodged in a tree. All around her were flashes of fire and screams. Blood. She didn't think. Just pulled the trigger. Over and over.

Upon reloading, she rose and came face-to-face with a gaunt Rebel with a yellow-toothed grin and a scornful laugh. He held up his rifle, bayonet pointed straight at her, and watched her like a mountain lion preparing to pounce.

Before he could thrust the weapon through her heart, she lifted her gun and fired. An explosion of crimson and smoke blurred her vision.

Trembling, she looked down and traced a path to his body. She stepped close and stopped cold.

Where the left side of his face used to be was an empty shell.

She was suddenly staring at her old doll Elizabeth, her porcelain face cracked and broken by Father's temper.

"I never wanted you, Cassie Kendrick. You're a disappointment. You always have been. Always will be."

Spots danced before her eyes.

Elizabeth's pink gown. Her missing eye. The Rebel's mocking laugh. Her father's bloodshot eyes. Mother's cries. Granny's prayers. Gabe's gentle kisses. Screams. Shouts.

Boom. Boom. Boom.

Slamming her eyes shut and dropping her rifle, she clamped her fists over her ears. She couldn't breathe. It was too much.

You must forgive your father.

As she stumbled through the smoky haze of nightmarish images, her heart beat wildly, too big for her rib cage. She tried to grope her way out of the fevered chaos, and stopped to watch a soldier turn his rifle on himself. Blood spattered as he crumpled to the ground. She dropped to her knees and retched in the grass, clutching fistfuls of churned dirt in her fingers.

Wiping her sleeve across her mouth, she rose and took shaky steps away. Why couldn't she find the way out? Panic clawed her throat. Her lungs wheezed. Her stomach cramped.

"Look at my dandelion crown, Papa. I'm a princess."

"Weeds, Cassandra. You're not a princess, and you never will be. Get those fool notions out of your head. You're playing dress up with a crown of weeds."

Her foot snagged on a fallen body and she collapsed onto the dirt with a grunt. She pushed herself to her knees, shuddering, and turned to see who it belonged to.

Her blood grew cold.

Jonah lay in the middle of the field on his side, his bright eyes vacant. A pool of crimson spread across his chest. Clutched in his right hand was the gold pocket watch she'd given him.

A scream ripped the air. It took a long moment before she realized it was her own. Salt filled her mouth. Tearing her fingers through her hair, she yanked off her kepi and cast it away, her body heaving. She gathered his little body up in her arms and rocked him, sobbing as she rested her head against his.

Jonah would have fussed over the attention in life. In death, he made no protest.

She carried Jonah's thin body away from the carnage that had descended in the Shenandoah. Away from death and disease and hate. Away from revenge. No more. She wanted no more of it.

Time slowed and ceased. How much time had passed? She didn't notice the shifting position of the sun or the moon, nor the rise or fall of temperatures as she walked. Hunger, thirst, pain, fatigue . . . all of it had vanished. Perhaps she was dead as well. She expected death to feel cold. Not like this. Not this sensation of aimless, numb wandering.

She buried him beyond the valley, behind an abandoned farmhouse, assured his body was given the respect he deserved. As she swiped away the thick blur of tears from her eyes, still more sobs burned for release. Cannons pounded in the distance, drawing closer. She couldn't think. Her empty belly cramped. Maybe the sensation meant she lived after all.

Wandering into the broken-down house, she rummaged through a dusty pantry and found several jars of canned peaches, a jar of corn, and one of applesauce. The windows rattled as artillery shook the house to its foundation. The battle was devouring the valley like the tide lapping up sand on the beach. The farmhouse would soon be swallowed. She should rejoin the Michigan Second.

Yet her feet refused to obey.

Gathering up the cans and a tattered old quilt, she slipped outside and pulled on the rusty latch of the root cellar. She stepped in, letting the damp, loamy aroma of earth soothe her frayed nerves. Sinking down to the bottom, she dropped the quilt and its contents in her lap, thankful for its warmth. With shaking hands, she strained and popped open a can, lifting it to her lips in the darkness. The sweet cinnamon taste of applesauce coated her tongue. She gulped down the contents with such speed, she feared she might cast them up moments later.

The cellar door overhead rattled as artillery roared beyond the ridge. Tiny flecks of earth rained down, pelting the skin of her face and arms. She pushed the empty jar aside, tugged the quilt up to her shoulders, and hunkered down, blinking the grit away from her eyes.

"I will say of the Lord, He is my refuge and my fortress: my God; in him will I trust."

The verse rolled through her mind, pushing away gruesome images and shrill screams that refused to quit tormenting her.

"Surely he shall deliver thee from the snare of the fowler, and from the noisome pestilence."

The ground rumbled around her. She dug her fingers into the old quilt, her breath coming in hot puffs.

"Thou shalt not be afraid for the terror by night; nor for the arrow that flieth by day."

The wail of artillery sounded overhead. Cracking trees. Whinnying horses. The sharp snap of the drummers. Pounding feet. Her stomach soured. She pinched her eyes shut.

"A thousand shall fall at thy side, and ten thousand at thy right hand; but it shall not come nigh thee."

Dirt crumbled down, tickling her face and burrowing into her hair. She rocked back and forth, head between her knees, murmuring, "Please, God, help me. I'm undone. Something is wrong. I can't do this anymore. Help me."

You must forgive your father.

Her throat burned with unshed tears.

I love you. I will sustain you.

Her heart twisted. She was weary of the burden. So tired of the pain and hurt. She couldn't walk another step under its oppressive weight. She lifted her face upward in the inky blackness of the cellar. Pinpricks of light pierced the outline of the cellar door.

"I don't know how to forgive him. The pain is so deep." Her voice cracked, breaking into shards as more artillery shrieked outside.

"For if ye forgive men their trespasses, your heavenly Father will also forgive you. . . ."

A hot tear escaped her lashes, tracing a warm path down her cheek. Yes, her father had abused her over and over again. He'd sliced her apart with his words, his fists, his negligence, and nearly every other conceivable way. Forgiving him didn't excuse him. But it would free her.

"And be ye kind one to another, tenderhearted, forgiving one another, even as God for Christ's sake hath forgiven you."

"I've lied and deceived, run away and refused to forgive. I've killed and done more in the past year than I'd ever dreamed myself capable of. And though it was in the name of war, I still have blood on my hands. Forgive me, Lord." Her breath caught, a harsh sob hitching in her chest as she choked.

I love you.

"I forgive my father!"

Cleansing sobs racked her body as she curled into a ball and fell against the cellar floor, puddled in the musty quilt. A peace long dormant washed over her in warm, tingling waves. Love and tender comfort curled like tendrils around her heart.

When she released the last heft of air, a sweet sleepiness tugged her into an embrace. For the first time in months, she fell into a deep, blissful sleep.

———— ◆ ————

Gabe scrubbed his hands through his rain-soaked hair, frustration gnawing at his middle. The battle had raged for days, shifting and moving in increments over farmland and valleys, until the Confederates had finally given up and fled, leaving only destroyed fields, bloated corpses, and exhausted Union soldiers in their wake. At last the cacophony of wailing from the dying wounded had fallen into a sacred silence.

The casualty list was still being amassed and the tally of missing soldiers continued to grow, but Thomas Turner's name was not listed. Gabe had scoured every square inch of land Cassie's boots might have touched and had uncovered nothing. He'd searched every hospital tent, every ambulance, every stretch of field, and every bloodied corpse he could find. It was as if she had vanished into thin air.

His heart still stung at the loss of young Jonah. Captain Johnston had been informed that his messenger boy was presumed dead, though his body had yet to be found. Strange. Two full days after the Confederate retreat, he should have been discovered.

Chest aching, Gabe trudged back to the Whatsit, his mind unable to rest. Cassie was alive. He could sense it. But where?

He looked up into the murky clouds and blinked against the rain sprinkling his face. *Lord, I need you. I've been a fool. Nothing else matters but following you and loving her. Help me.*

Chapter 40

CASSIE WASN'T SURE if she'd slept for hours or days. It didn't matter. Stretching her stiff, sore limbs, she let the warmth of the quilt fall away as cool air rushed in. A sense of peace enveloped her, despite the darkness of the cellar. She smiled.

Thank you, Father God. Thank you for loving me. For your patience. Transform me into the image of your Son. Continue to teach me how to forgive.

Her stomach rumbled as she groped for another of the jars she'd carried down and fumbled with the lid. It finally gave, and she lifted the jar to her lips and smiled when the sweet taste of peaches greeted her. Eating her fill, she licked the remaining syrup from her grimy fingers. All was quiet outside. Did she dare peek?

The need to use the necessary eradicated any further hesitancy. She climbed the cellar steps and pushed against the door, wincing when it creaked loudly. Bright daylight assaulted her, caused her a moment of blindness as she blinked away the black spots dancing before her. Vision sharpening, she saw cracked, split trees and patches of black earth where yellow grass once grew. Cannonball holes gaped through several outbuildings, and the main farmhouse had been riddled along its west side with bullet holes. No bodies, dead or alive, greeted her.

She eased the cellar door shut and picked her way across the yard, first to the necessary and then to the pump. She drew a bucket of water before slipping into the abandoned house. If Thomas Turner was gone, the first order of business would be new clothes and a plan. Rummaging through a trunk, she found a faded pink gown that would serve. After washing up, she brushed her shoulder-length brown curls until they shone and studied her reflection in the cracked looking glass with a critical eye.

Thomas Turner was dead. Gone and buried. She had no schedule to keep. No morning reveille or roll call to maintain. She was really and truly free.

Yet she couldn't stay here. This house had been vacated, but it wasn't hers. She smoothed the wrinkled skirt fabric. *What do you want me to do, Lord?*

She watched her blue eyes stare back at her.

Return home.

Her heart beat faster. *Go home? Back to Father? Back to the nightmare and abuse?*

Has my arm been shortened? Is my power limited?

But what of Gabe, Lord?

I have not forgotten.

Cassie squared her shoulders, releasing a shaky breath, and nodded at the woman in the glass.

She would return home. And this time, there would be no lies.

OCTOBER 29, 1862
HOWELL, MICHIGAN

She rapped on Granny's cabin door with tight knuckles, grasping her lone bag and clamping her chattering teeth together. Icy wind slithered up her skirt as she waited. No footfalls sounded on the other side. The cabin windows were dark. Cold and unwelcoming.

Shifting her weight from foot to foot, she rapped harder. She jiggled the stiff doorknob, but it held fast. Unease crawled over her. Where was Granny? The sun had only just set.

Light footsteps approached from somewhere deep in the cabin. Her trapped breath released a puff of air.

"Who's there?"

Cassie frowned. The voice didn't belong to Granny. It was far too young. "It's Cassie."

The door creaked open, revealing a drawn, weary-looking woman. Cassie blinked. "Jane?"

Her sister placed trembling fingers to her mouth. "Cassie?"

With a rush, they embraced. Cassie's throat grew thick as Jane stepped back and wiped away tears with a watery smile. "Come in. You must be freezing."

Ushered into the cabin's warmth, Cassie sighed with pleasure. The scents from her childhood wrapped her in an embrace, chasing away the demons of the past two years. For a few moments, anyway.

Red embers glowed in the fireplace. Jane leaned over and, grabbing the poker, stoked them back to life. She added a couple more logs to the fire and dusted her hands, wrapping the shawl back around her shoulders and watching Cassie as if she feared she were a phantom who might vanish.

"It's good to see you, Cass."

Cassie smiled, thankful Jane was the sister here to greet her.

Of all her siblings, they were the two who got along best. "It's good to see you too, Janie."

"When you first took off, I feared the worst."

Heat crept up her neck. "I'll tell you about that soon. But first I must see Granny. Where is she?"

Jane's gaze darted away.

"What's wrong?"

Jane sighed. "Granny is . . . not well. Last month she suffered a stroke and hasn't been the same since."

Cassie felt as if she'd been punched in the gut. "How sick is she?"

Jane's eyes filled with compassion, knowing the news was difficult to hear. "She needs constant care. Eliza, Eloise, Nellie, and I . . . we all take turns being away from our families to care for her."

It wasn't possible. Not Granny. Not the undefeatable woman she knew. "I want to see her."

Jane watched her for a long moment, then nodded, preceding her to Granny's small bedroom tucked in the back of the cabin. She placed a gentle hand on Cassie's arm just outside the door. "Prepare yourself, Cass. She won't know you."

Cassie lifted her chin. "She'll know me."

Jane said nothing as Cassie opened the door.

An oil lamp burned on the bedside table, casting honeyed light over the room and illuminating a tiny figure swallowed up by the bed. Easing to the bedside, Cassie leaned over and choked back tears.

Granny was there, staring at her, her bright-blue eyes watching, moving, yet not. Her white hair was splayed against her down pillow. She looked fragile and thin atop the soft mattress.

Gingerly resting her weight on the mattress, Cassie reached

for Granny's blue-veined hands, her heart sinking when they made no response. "Granny, it's Cassie."

Granny's eyes flickered over her face, yet no traces of recognition sparked. Cassie's heart sank low in her chest. She forced down the lump threatening to choke her. "Can she speak?"

Jane sighed. "No. Only garbled words. But I talk to her. Read to her. She can drink and eat, but only if the food is mashed up. Everything must be done for her. And with Father gone—"

"Father? Gone?"

Jane's brows rose. "Of course you wouldn't know." She straightened. "Father wed Mary Dunn months ago. They moved away almost immediately."

"How far?"

Jane shook her head. "Don't know. Joe heard they aimed to set out for Minnesota."

Cassie reached for the bedpost to steady her suddenly dizzy head. Father was gone. He could no longer hurt or threaten. And she was beginning to feel free of the bitterness that had tainted too much of her life.

Cassie looked up and caught her sister's gaze. The poor woman was exhausted. "I'm home now. You can't continue this. You have your own family to care for. I'll take care of her."

Jane's brows pinched. "But you do as well. Eliza told us about your husband, the photographer. What about him?"

Cassie sighed. "There is much I must explain. . . ."

Chapter 41

Cassie descended from the stagecoach and coughed, waving away the dust that swirled around her as the conveyance dipped and swayed. A far cry from the knee-deep mud she'd marched through during her last visit to the capital. Then again, much had changed. Not just the weather. The thought made her smile.

The clop of horses and the rattle of buggies swarmed around her, choking the busy roads of Washington.

"Here you go, miss."

Glancing upward, she smiled at the driver, who handed down her large carpetbag. "Thank you."

He nodded, eyes twinkling, yet his handlebar mustache drooped only seconds later, his concern evident. "You sure you're okay, miss? You know where you're going?"

"Perfectly sure, thank you."

"The capital is not a safe place for a lovely woman on her own."

His praise caused her cheeks to warm, yet a giggle threatened to erupt. She longed to burst out with some quip about a sharpshooter for the Union being able to defend herself but held her tongue.

"I'll be careful. Thank you."

With a tip of his hat, he clucked his tongue and the stagecoach lurched forward. She watched it go, but her mind was on the destination only blocks away. The Brady Gallery.

Her buttoned boots clicked sharply against the street as she tried to suppress the nausea rising in her stomach. She pushed her way through the throng of people crowding the street. Hawkers called out their wares. Senators and representatives smoked cigars in their black suits as they conspired in tight huddles around the government buildings. Women in feathered hats and the latest fashions strolled past the buildings, walking as fast as they dared toward the shopping district.

Granny, can you see me? I'm trying.

Granny Ardie had been gone two months, yet Cassie found herself talking to her frequently. She supposed it had become a habit while caring for the ailing woman since last fall. Only Providence knew if the stream of chatter had helped, but in her heart, Cassie felt her grandmother had clung to her words, even if her broken body could not respond in kind.

She'd talked to her about everything—shared her thoughts and feelings, told her about all her experiences during the war, read to her from the Bible as well as every scrap of news she could squeeze from the papers. She'd gobbled up every newsprint in the county, religiously following any information she could gather on the war: troop movement; the death of the Confederates' Stonewall Jackson; General McClellan being replaced by General Burnside, who was replaced by General

Hooker, who was then replaced by General Meade; the bloody battle of Gettysburg and many other battles besides.

She was relieved she was no longer dodging shot and shell as her friends were blown apart. No longer witnessing dying men wheeze out their last breaths. Yet as she lay in the darkness of her room each night, she could still hear every sound of battle: the shouts, the patterns of the drums, the timbres of each distinct voice. On particularly difficult nights, she could hear Jonah's laughter. Could see his eyes dancing with some new mischief. But it wasn't Jonah that hovered in every memory. Mostly she couldn't escape *him*.

Thoughts of Gabe filled every waking moment and sometimes her dreams as well.

After Granny had passed to glory, leaving Cassie strangely alone and aimless in the cabin, she'd been scouring the *Washington Star* when the announcement of a Brady Gallery "War View" photographic display caught her attention. It was not Brady's photographs that would be displayed, however, but those of his field photographers. Among the names listed, one leapt off the page, causing her heart to thud painfully in her chest. Gabriel Avery.

"Watch out!"

Jerking from her muddled thoughts, she looked up in time to dodge a horse that nearly ran her down, the driver uttering a slew of curses. She pressed her hand against her stomach, willing the butterflies to calm. She was likely to get herself killed if she didn't pay attention. She was almost acting as if she were afraid. But that couldn't be . . . could it?

She forced a slow, deep breath, straightened her hat and smoothed her pale-blue skirt, and took measured steps toward the gallery.

She'd run away to enlist. Had picked up a gun to fight.

Smuggled her way past Confederate pickets and had nearly lost her life on numerous occasions. Yet why did the thought of seeing Gabe wrap her nerves into a quivering mass of knots?

Before she could think further, she found herself staring at the bold lettering of the Brady Gallery, watching the crush of people blur past.

What if Gabe wasn't even here? What made her think he would be present? The announcement had only mentioned his photographs. Nothing more.

Her knees trembled. She shouldn't have come. It was a fool's errand. Just as she turned to flee, she collided with a solid chest.

"Forgive me—"

"You're not leaving, are you, miss?"

The rich baritone caused her to raise her face. When her gaze met his, her pulse ricocheted.

Gabe.

———•———

Gabe's chest constricted, joy lifting his lips and spreading throughout his entire body.

Cassie was here, looking more beautiful and feminine than he'd ever seen her. He was afraid if he reached out and touched her, she might disappear.

"Cassie . . ." He breathed her name, suddenly overcome with emotion so deep he couldn't form words.

She'd been a phantom, haunting his dreams, his days, his mind. . . . She'd consumed every part of him and had done everything but vanish. And in one jarring moment, she'd reappeared in warm flesh and blood. He couldn't think.

A pretty blush stained her cheeks. "I read about the war exhibit at the gallery and saw your name, so . . ." She let the thought trail off into an uncomfortable silence and toyed with the drawstring of her reticule. "I—that is, I know I have much I need to tell you."

A burst of light rose in his chest. He was weightless. A smile he was helpless to repress spread wide. "Later. We have all the time in the world to catch up."

She offered a tiny smile in return. He felt his own tension unwind by measures.

He extended his arm, and she slipped her hand into the crook of his elbow. "Come. Let me show you the gallery."

They strolled through the green-and-gold gallery for over an hour, studying each photograph, reliving memories of places and friends, people and battles. They fell into a comfortable camaraderie, saying nothing yet much at the same time. When the building grew so stuffy and crowded it was difficult to draw a decent breath, Gabe grasped Cassie's hand. "Follow me."

They stepped outside into the crisp October air, and he breathed deeply of the cool, refusing to relinquish Cassie's hand as they strolled toward the park.

"Your photographs are stunning."

He soaked in her praise. "Thanks to Brady's training and the kind welcome of my friends, like one Thomas Turner."

Smiling, she bit her lip and looked down as they walked.

He sobered, longing to know what had transpired during the months of silence. He led her through the park's iron gate and into the blazing-red and fiery-orange trees of autumn. "What happened, Cass? After the battle?"

She stopped walking and searched his face. "I saw him. I saw Jonah." Her chin quivered. "He'd been shot through the heart and was clutching the pocket watch I'd given him." A tear escaped.

He drew her into an embrace, tucking her head under his chin, gently rubbing her shoulders.

She pulled back and wiped her eyes. "I'm not sure what happened. Something inside me snapped. Briggs was already prepared to tell Captain Johnston about me. Then Jonah. All the noise. The screams. The deception. The pressure. I carried Jonah away from the battlefield and buried him. Then I found an abandoned farmhouse and hunkered down in a cellar until the fighting had passed. I don't know what to say other than I knew I couldn't do it a moment longer. I buried Thomas Turner with Jonah and walked away." She looked into his eyes, and his chest constricted. "I returned home only to discover my father had left town. I've spent the time ever since caring for Granny." A shadow crossed her beautiful features. "She passed away two months ago."

"I'm sorry. She was a remarkable woman. Just like her grand-daughter."

The smile she offered stole his breath. It was pure and deep and dazzling, free of any restraint. He studied her, uncertain whether he should voice his musings.

Her brows pinched. "What's wrong?"

"You. There's something different about you. A good differ-ence. What is it? You seem . . . peaceful."

"I am." Leaning in, she whispered, "I've forgiven my father. It's still hard for me on occasion. I fight bitterness toward him, but I'm learning. I've made my peace with God. Confessed my deception to my family. I'm free."

A lump wedged in his throat. *Thank you, Lord.*

"I'm so glad, Cass."

She gave him a long sideways glance. "What of you? I prayed for you every day."

He tugged her back into a walk. "There's not much to tell. I've been following the Michigan Second through their military campaign, though it hasn't been much fun without you there.

And of course, I'm sure you heard once General McClellan was replaced, Pinkerton quit, so my limited tenure with the secret service came to a quick end. It's funny you came today, seeing how I recently told Mr. Brady I could no longer record his war images."

Cassie gasped and yanked him to a stop. "You can't do that! Your talent! And what of Jacob?"

"Jacob, I'm pleased to report, is now happily married."

"What?"

Gabe laughed. "That was my reaction as well. Remember the woman who helped nurse him back to health? Miss Esther, his friend from the youth charity club? Well, they tied the knot not long after he recovered from pneumonia."

Her voice was so quiet he had to lean in to hear her question. "And the sale of my picture . . . did it, uh, help?"

He grasped her hands. "Cassie," he breathed, "how I wish I could undo that decision a thousand times over."

She shook her head, a smile teasing her lips. "I've forgiven you. It's all right."

He sighed and stroked the backs of her hands with the pads of his thumbs. "The Lord taught me a lesson about trying to do his job for him. I hurt the most wonderful person I've ever known trying to fix things my own way. Little did I know that Miss Esther is quite well-to-do. She paid the rest of his hospital bills, and they are living a comfortable life." His chest burned. "Cass, I'm so sorry."

She shook her head. "Everything happened the way it did for a reason. I'm sorry I gave you such a difficult time about it. I should have let you explain."

"I bear the entirety of the blame." He looked deeply into her eyes to gauge her reaction as he spilled his last bit of news. "I can't very well pursue the passion and acclaim of photography when my passion for a certain female soldier burns even hotter, now can I?"

He heard her soft inhale.

"Cass, I told Brady I was quitting in order to travel to Michigan, find you, and tell you I can't live one more minute without you."

Her lips parted. "That day at the hospital? You were wrong, you know."

He frowned, not understanding her train of thought. "Wrong? About what?"

She stepped close, wrapping her arms around his waist. "Remember that Christmas Day in the Alexandria hospital? You pulled me into the storage closet and asked me how to let you back into my heart?"

His mouth grew dry. "Yes."

Her voice dropped low. "I couldn't give you an answer because the truth was you were never out of my heart. You never have been and you never will be. You own it fully and completely."

Reaching up, he cupped her face and stroked her jaw with his fingertips. His gaze dropped from the sky blue of her brilliant eyes to her full lips. He lowered his head and claimed them, pulled her toward him with a sweet possessiveness. She was soft and yielding, responding to his touch in a way that stole his breath.

Heart hammering, he broke away before he forgot himself completely. He rested his head against hers, locking her in his arms.

"Now that you've found me, what will you do, Gabe? Go back to the war?"

His eyes widened at the shaky tremors racking her voice. Her face was lined with fear. She was scared. Scared she would lose him. His heart tugged. "No, darling. I'm sick of death and dying. With the newspapers asking for more of my photographs, opportunities are limitless. And not just in the war. There are a number of papers needing photographers willing to record sights of the West."

She was silent in his arms.

He leaned in and nuzzled her neck. "I thought I'd lost you." Months of anguish, of prayers and tears wiped clean in a single moment. *Thank you, Father.* "I love you, Cassie. Marry me. We can travel the world together. Or we can build a log cabin in the mountains and hide away. I don't care. As long as we're together."

Cassie laughed, causing shivers of pleasure to tease his skin. "You're really brave enough to let me loose in the Wild West?"

Chuckling, he kissed her once more. "You'll rise to any occasion, Cass. But Thomas Turner? I don't think even the Wild West is ready for that character."

Epilogue

Gabe ducked under the black curtain and adjusted the big, brass-barreled lens once more.

"All right, I think we're ready." He dropped the prepared glass plate into the slot. The stoic group of Sioux Indians sitting before him didn't move. Didn't even appear to blink in the bright sunshine. Tall grasses swayed in the warm wind around them.

"One, two, three."

Her husband removed the lens cover, and Cassie watched as he ticked off the seconds. They'd traveled through the breathtaking beauty of the Ozarks and were now picking their way through the prairie lands of Kansas. She'd watched and assisted him in his work in every conceivable circumstance. So much so, she could read his thoughts and calculate the plate exposure time. He was a brilliant photographer.

She moved to cover her still-flat stomach with her hand. She hadn't yet told him about the new life growing inside. He would likely be just as overjoyed as he'd been with their first little one. Fresh love for Gabe flooded her anew, stinging her eyes with unshed tears. She'd never seen such a loving, gentle father.

Irritated with herself, she swiped the moisture away. Love had turned her into a blubbering mess. What teasing she would endure if Granny could see her now.

"Done!"

Ducking out from under the curtain, Gabe straightened and moved to talk with the interpreter, shaking hands and thanking each one of the Indians, offering them gifts for their willingness to be photographed. When he gave a small stack of beaver pelts to the man with the most elaborate headdress, his beaming smile bathed his face in incalculable wrinkles. Gabe looked back and sought her eyes. Grinning, she shook her head. No matter who he was with, her handsome husband was a charmer.

"Momma, look! I pick dese for you."

She turned to see their son toddling toward them, his chubby legs sprinting as fast as he dared. One arm was hidden behind his back. The tall grasses and hills made an ideal playground for a curious little boy.

"And what do you have hidden behind your back, Jacob Jonah Avery?" She ruffled his brown curls as his dimpled grin widened. She tickled his tummy just before he thrust his pudgy arm forward, a wilting bouquet of dandelions held in his fist. Their downy yellow heads bobbed in the gentle breeze.

She swallowed, flooded with bittersweet memories. Gabe walked up behind their son, his lips curving gently.

"Don't like them, Mama?"

The plaintive question caused her to swing her focus back to the green-eyed boy staring at her in worry. She grasped the flowers and tugged her son into a hug, nuzzling his neck until he burst into giggles. "I love them, darling. How did you know? Dandelions happen to be my favorite."

He wrapped his little arms around her neck. "Why?"

Kissing his nose, she murmured, "Because anytime you see dandelions blooming in mortar, hope remains."

A Note from the Author

The inspiration for Cassie Kendrick came from a real woman named Emma Edmonds (also known as Emma Edmondson).

Just like Cassie, Emma enlisted to escape a doomed marriage arranged by her cruel father. She cut off her hair and assumed the name Frank Thompson. Her upbringing as a farm girl prepared her for the rigors of war, and she worked as a medical transport runner, regimental mail carrier, and eventually a spy for Allan Pinkerton. It is estimated that at least four hundred other women disguised themselves and enlisted during the Civil War.

I used some of Emma's life experiences to craft Cassie's story, yet Cassie remains completely fictitious. With the exception of a handful of historical figures like Allan Pinkerton, General George McClellan, and Mathew Brady, the characters in *Where Dandelions Bloom* have been completely spun from my imagination. And while most of the events in this book are drawn straight from history, on a few occasions I changed the timing or added a fictional battle in the interest of the story.

I encourage you to find out more about Emma and other courageous women who faced the impossible to give us the freedom we enjoy today.

TURN *the* PAGE
for a PREVIEW *of*
Engraved on the *Heart*

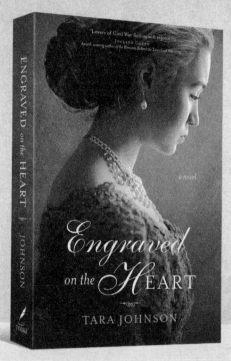

CHAPTER 1

April 12, 1861
Savannah, Georgia

Don't fail. Tonight of all nights, don't fail.

Keziah Montgomery placed her gloved fingers into the waiting hand of the man smiling at her with confident expectation.

Taking a shallow breath against the corset threatening to crush her ribs in its unyielding grip, she willed her fluttering stomach to calm and allowed Mr. Watson to lead her onto the crowded dance floor. A colorful array of bright silks and lace flurried around her in circles. The thick, sticky air carried the weight of pomade and a nauseating mixture of shaving soaps and rice powder. The din of chatter and polite laughter choked her dizzying thoughts.

From across the room, she caught Mother's penetrating stare. Elsie Montgomery had been adamant Keziah be at her best. No one must know her shameful secret. The sooner she marry, the better . . . before her future husband realized what her parents were so desperate to keep hidden.

Looking up, she smiled into the youthful face of Tate Watson as he cupped his warm hand against her waist, keeping the proper distance between them as the musicians struck up the opening strains of "The Scenes of Our Childhood." She noted the golden stubble lining his jaw, his brown eyes bright. A flush of heat crept up her neck.

She blinked away the grit filming her vision. It was late into the festivities and the night seemed to drag. Still, she maintained her pasted-on smile and allowed him to sweep her through the whirling couples and blurring faces. If only it weren't so warm.

Mr. Watson's lips moved, but it took her several moments to focus on what he was saying. "Are you enjoying the ball?"

"Yes. The Ballingers throw an exquisite party."

"Indeed, although I fear all the talk of impending war may have dampened the festivities to a degree."

She nodded demurely, though she'd never admit conversing about the possibility of war was far more interesting than being forced to make polite niceties to the elite of Savannah's upper echelon. Her mother would faint if she allowed her tongue to spill the unladylike sentiment.

"If war is declared, will you go?"

His eyes glinted, his bearing stiff as he circled her past potted palms, pulling her into the thick of the dancers. "Without hesitation. It's my sacred calling and duty to defend the freedoms Mr. Lincoln is attempting to rip from our way of life. No man worth his salt would dare flee his duty."

Keziah pressed her lips tight, unwilling to say anything further, knowing if she did, she would be unable to stop. The issues did not seem so starkly cut to her. Instead, she smiled and nodded again, praying her mother could understand the depths of her desire to please. Keziah would not mortify her. Not again.

The room suddenly dipped and twisted. Her breath thinned.

Stay upright. Focus. Blinking hard, she realized Mr. Watson was asking her something, though she didn't understand what. Alarm flooded her, followed by a frisson of something indefinable tingling up her spine.

No, God. Please, no. Not here. What will Mother think?

The prayer had hardly crossed her thoughts before she plunged into the abyss, the spinning colors collapsing into merciful blackness.

⌁

Micah Greyson scoured the crowded ballroom as he sipped the too-sweet punch. He didn't belong.

Since returning home to Savannah from medical school in Philadelphia, he felt distant, removed. He had thought to open a practice and wanted to live near Mother. He owed her much. But now? He couldn't shake the unease gnawing his middle. The feeling was odd and altogether unsettling. Not just because there were new faces, nor because old classmates and neighbors had moved away. This was something else. As if society's values were different. The perspective on human life and dignity had altered.

No, Savannah hadn't changed. It was him. Too many abolitionist rallies. He'd seen and heard far too much to leave Philadelphia unchanged and unaffected. He felt as if he'd just awakened from a long, hazy dream, suddenly aware of how different life could be, only to find himself sucked back into the foggy nightmare once more.

And what to do with the knowledge of who he was in the midst of it all? He would never belong. Could never belong again.

He took another pull of his punch, rolling the syrupy taste of cherries over his tongue, and sighed. Some men feared death;

others feared losing their loved ones. His fear was entirely different. He must not grow callous and indifferent to the plight of those suffering around him.

The raucous laughter of a man to his left grated his nerves. Placing the half-empty glass on a tray with a soft clink, he scowled. It was a mistake to have come. He'd only done so at his friend's pleading. Oliver was bursting to talk war with the other men, not to mention dance with the young debutantes. His friend could be quite convincing. But Micah was charmed by none of it. The music seemed at odds with his mood, the air too suffocating.

He had turned to make his apologies to the hostess when a muffled cry rang out from the cluster of dancers clogging the floor. A male voice shouted amid the din.

"Is there a physician here?"

He stepped forward, eyeing the crush of people who had stopped moving. They swarmed around someone who had fallen. Man or woman? He couldn't tell. There was too much commotion. Too many people.

He shouted, "I'm a physician! Make way."

The crowd parted slowly to reveal a young man leaning over an unconscious woman crumpled on the glistening waxed floor. Pushing past the mob, he frowned.

"Please, give the poor woman some air."

As he knelt down to assess her condition, he sucked in a breath at the lovely form tangled in a swirl of blue silk, observing the way her fingers twitched sporadically, the soft muscles of her throat knotting as her head thrashed. His gaze landed on her face and his heart gave an odd lurch.

He couldn't believe it. After all these years. He cradled her head gently, stroking the soft skin of her cheek, and prayed.

Kizzie Montgomery.

Micah tugged Kizzie's slight weight closer to his chest as he struggled to carry her up the stairs of the Ballinger mansion, her voluminous skirts and hoops making his progress difficult. The murmurs of shock rippling through the room faded away as he followed the hostess to a guest bedroom.

"Here. This room should serve."

Mrs. Ballinger pushed aside the heavy door and hastened to light a lamp as he laid Kizzie on the green-and-gold brocade-covered bed. He pressed his fingers to her slender neck, monitoring the thrum of her pulse. Steady.

"How can I be of help?" The concerned matron twisted her hands, looking out of place as a nursemaid in her glittering beads and filmy lavender gown. Lines deepened around her eyes.

"Could I trouble you for some clean cloths and a pitcher of cool water?"

With a nod, she breathed, "Of course. I'll send Minnie up straightaway."

"Thank you."

He smoothed Kizzie's strawberry-blonde curls away from her temples, her skin pale but warm. A slight spray of freckles on her delicate nose stood out in stark contrast to her creamy skin. She seemed to be sleeping peacefully. No more twitches or convulsions.

"Doctor, may I be so bold as to ask—" the hostess swallowed, still lingering in the room—"what malady has befallen this woman?"

Easing one of Kizzie's eyelids open, he nodded in satisfaction when the pupil in the center of her eye shrank against the light of the lamp. "I won't be sure until I've examined her more thoroughly, but I believe she's had an epileptic attack."

Mrs. Ballinger clucked her tongue. "The falling sickness."

"Yes, I believe so."

The poised woman held herself aloof as if unsure what to do. "Well, I'll fetch Minnie. She should be up shortly."

Micah barely heard himself murmur a response before leaning over Kizzie once more, admiring her long lashes, high cheekbones, and full lips. She was more beautiful than he remembered.

Beautiful and unconscious.

Troubled, he took her pulse again. Steady.

His breath froze when he saw her eyelids twitch, her lashes fluttering before her eyes opened, the walnut-and-cinnamon colors he remembered flaming to life yet filled with confusion. Her fingers roved over the silk of her bodice until he captured them between his own. He smiled and tried to keep his voice soft and calm, aware that she would be unlikely to remember this moment tomorrow.

"Kizzie, it's Micah Greyson. Do you remember me?"

She blinked and licked her lips. "Micah? From school?"

Nodding, he smiled. "From school."

Her chest rose and fell, her gaze flickering across his face. "What happened? Where am I?"

Micah squeezed her fingers, kept his voice soothing. "You're at the Ballinger house. You were dancing and collapsed."

Her eyes widened as a shadow of awareness crept over her face. "Was it . . . ?" She choked against the words forming. This had happened to her before.

"Yes. Epileptic attack."

She looked away. Her chin trembled. "Leave me, please."

"I'm a physician now. Please let me help you."

"There's nothing you can do. No one can."

"That's not true. Why, just last ye—"

She sucked in a tight breath. "No. Mother. She must have

seen it." With a groan, she squeezed her eyes shut but did not release his hand. "She'll be mortified."

Micah frowned. "You can't help what happened."

Kizzie focused on his face, a sadness flickering in her expression. "My parents believe differently."

Cruel. Ignorant. Shaming their daughter for an ailment she had no control over? He ground his teeth as she relaxed against the soft down of the bed. Her eyelids drooped.

A murmur escaped her. "So tired."

"That's normal. Rest. I'll be right here."

Eyes sliding shut, she sighed softly, causing his heart to give an odd fillip. "Thank you . . . Micah . . ."

Asleep.

A raucous shout shook the floor under his feet. The crowd downstairs yelled and whooped. The glass globe of the oil lamp rattled. What was happening?

As the tumult below settled into a humming din, he watched the gentle rise and fall of her breath beneath her limp hand. Who could have imagined he'd run into her here, his first social gathering since returning? The one girl who'd managed to capture his heart as a boy.

Not that she would ever know. He wouldn't tell her. Couldn't tell anyone. They could never be together. He'd thought by now, with distance and the passing of time, the youthful feelings would have abated, but seeing her again had caused every old memory, every one of her sweet smiles, every dream, to roar back to life with frightening speed.

The bedroom door squeaked open as a petite woman with graying blonde hair and a stricken expression crossed the threshold.

He straightened, releasing Kizzie's hand. "Dr. Micah Greyson, ma'am."

Rushing to her side, the matron leaned over Kizzie and stroked her forehead before glancing toward him as if he were little more than a nuisance.

"Elsie Montgomery. I'm Keziah's mother. It took me several minutes to escape the melee."

"I heard the shouts. What happened?"

She straightened, her face somber.

"What we've known was imminent, Dr. Greyson. Fortunately for my daughter, her . . . *illness*—" Micah noted the distaste that pinched Mrs. Montgomery's mouth—"is the least of everyone's concern now."

"Why?"

Sighing deeply, the older woman furrowed her brow into deep lines. "War, Doctor. War has begun."

Acknowledgments

WITH GRATITUDE TO . . .

Todd, Bethany, Callie, and Nate: life with you is the greatest joy. I delight in you and find no greater thrill than watching God unfurl his plans for your lives throughout each moment. I love you!

Dad and Mom, Ron and Linda, Grandma, Brian, Courtney, Brian, Kym, and all my awesome nieces and nephews: I cannot imagine my world without your smiles and laughter. Thanks for being my biggest cheering section.

Jan Stob, Danika King, Emily Bonga, Mariah Franklin, and the entire team at Tyndale: thank-you doesn't seem adequate for the love, time, and care you've put into this story. Not only have you helped it bloom into something far better than I could have conceived on my own, but you've nurtured me through a very difficult year. I see Christ in each of you.

Janet Grant, your encouragement, direction, spiritual advice, and kindness keeps me anchored when I'm overwhelmed. Thank you for walking the road of all things publication, books, and life with me.

The Books & Such family, thanks for your listening ears, sage advice, and friendships. My life is richer because of you.

Tammie Cash and Anna Magana: your friendships are rare and treasured gifts. Thank you for loving me. I pray I give far more than I receive.

Savanna Kaiser and Cara Grandle: you are far more than critique partners. You are prayer warriors, the greatest of encouragers, and shining lights that reflect the beauty of Jesus. You two are the most selfless, giving women I've ever known. Thank you for taking me into your circle of love.

ACFW Arkansas, from giggles to late-night brainstorming sessions (and consuming obscene amounts of chocolate), you ladies have shown me that the difference between a joyful journey in writing and a tedious one is the people you travel with. Thanks for making the trip a fun one!

Pilgrim Rest, your support and love mean more than I can express. You are my family.

All the amazing women I've met through speaking engagements at retreats, prisons, and conferences around the country: your courage and vulnerability are gifts that give others liberty. Thank you for entrusting me with your hearts.

Jesus, you are my Redeemer, my Treasure, my Life, and my Everything. Anything good I have is from your hand. All glory is yours alone.

About the Author

A passionate lover of stories, TARA JOHNSON uses fiction, non-fiction, song, and laughter to share her testimony of how God led her into freedom after spending years living shackled to the expectations of others. Tara is the author of two novels set during the Civil War: *Engraved on the Heart* and *Where Dandelions Bloom*. She is a member of American Christian Fiction Writers and makes her home in Arkansas with her husband and three children. Visit her online at www.tarajohnsonstories.com.

Discussion Questions

~

1. When Gabe was an impoverished child, he was inspired to pursue photography as a way to escape from—and improve upon—his difficult life. Did you have any childhood experiences that set you on the path to where you are today? What about those experiences was so formative?

2. Cassie disguised herself as a man and joined the Union Army because she felt it was her only way out of a desperate situation. Why did she come to that conclusion? Did you agree with her, or can you think of another route she might have taken?

3. Describe Gabe's view of women early in the story. What factors in society and in his own life contributed to that view? How and why does his perspective change by the end of the book?

4. Cassie is able to hide her identity, even from some of her closest friends. Would you say her ruse was acceptable, or was she wrong to pretend to be someone she wasn't? How

can a person discern when deception might be morally justified?

5. Over the course of the story, Cassie struggles to forgive her father. How does her anger toward him affect her? What causes her to finally make the decision to forgive? Is she able to find closure even though she doesn't interact with her father after she forgives him?

6. Gabe compromises Cassie's disguise when he sells her photo in order to pay Jacob's bills, but he doesn't realize that Jacob has already been provided for by someone else. Have you ever tried to take control of a situation when you should have stepped back and trusted God's provision instead? What was the outcome?

7. The Civil War was the first large-scale conflict that was documented extensively by photographers such as Brady and Gardner, whose images were printed in newspapers for the public to see. What impact do you think these photographs had on American society's view of war? When is media coverage of violence and war helpful, and in what ways can it be harmful?

8. Gabe's mother told him, "Wherever dandelions bloom in mortar, it reminds us hope is still alive." How do the characters in this story keep hope alive in the midst of war and traumatic circumstances? What are some "dandelions" that have inspired hope in your own difficult times?

9. In what ways are Gabe and Cassie able to heal from the scars of their pasts by the end of the story? How have you

seen God at work in healing your own scars or those of someone you know?

10. Why do Cassie and Gabe decide to travel to the Western frontier? What adventures await them and their family after the final pages of the novel?

TYNDALE HOUSE PUBLISHERS IS CRAZY4FICTION!

Fiction that entertains and inspires

Get to know us! Become a member of the Crazy4Fiction community. Whether you read our blog, like us on Facebook, follow us on Twitter, or receive our e-newsletter, you're sure to get the latest news on the best in Christian fiction. You might even win something along the way!

JOIN IN THE FUN TODAY.

 www.crazy4fiction.com

 Crazy4Fiction

 @Crazy4Fiction